2395
B-T
9-29-99

THE LAST DECEPTION OF
PALLISER WENTWOOD

THE LAST DECEPTION OF PALLISER WENTWOOD

Imogen de la Bere

ST. MARTIN'S PRESS
NEW YORK

Library of Congress Cataloging-in-Publication Data

De la Bere, Imogen.
    The last deception of Palliser Wentwood / Imogen de la Bere.
        p. cm.
    ISBN 0-312-20329-2
    I. Title.
PR 9639.3.D43L6   1999
823—dc21   99-27155
                                                                  CIP

First published in Great Britain by Jonathan Cape, an imprint of Random
House UK Ltd.

First U.S. Edition: August 1999

10   9   8   7   6   5   4   3   2   1

To Dolly,
himself,
the original.

I

HERE IS Salomé Wentwood, relict.

A prepossessing woman of forty-five, aspect of an archangel, hair of a gypsy, she is standing on a little stone bridge, in the middle of a swampy plain, with a shotgun in her hand. She holds this nonchalantly, as if she had picked it up by accident, mistaking it for a broom.

Which is not far from the truth, because, although it is loaded, she has no idea what to do with it. Men deal with guns. Men go out to shoot. A gentleman is generally accompanied by his gun, and Palliser Wentwood, of whom she is the relict, is a gentleman to his very core.

From which it may be deduced that Salomé Wentwood is not widowed but abandoned.

Salomé positions herself and the shotgun where the bridge ends. It's an apology for a bridge, built of left-over stones, fitted together with excessive care, far too much care for the littleness of the bridge. Left-over stones which the builder rejected. A Palliser bridge *per se*.

They are coming up the roadway towards her. Little black digits, dancing in the brilliant sunshine, could be spots in her vision rather than men. Easier to think of them like that – black spots to be blinked out, wiped out. If she shut her eyes, she could blot them out.

But they won't be blinked. They must be getting closer but she can't tell from the size of them. How many? Four.

I

Abigail said she had seen four men at the gate. Is Salomé afraid of four men? She, who has ridden to the Lygon Hunt, afraid? Of course she is. This is more than life and death; this is livelihood and honour. This concerns her home, the only belonging left to Salomé, she who was once considered an heiress. How many shots in a shotgun? A woman should know those things.

It has happened without warning. It seems to Salomé that one day she had been a girl, caught in an icicle, seventeen and lovely. Then twenty-three and handsome. So bored, so cold in the hotels of Europe. Needlework one did, and one played golf and croquet, and tennis. One drove about the place and took the waters. One wrote in one's diary and danced all night if one could manage it. And suddenly here one was, twenty-odd years later, half a world away, in a dress of very doubtful cleanness, on a crooked stone bridge clutching a shotgun with a sweaty hand.

In between, Palliser intervened.

She grows hot standing under the sun. In the southern hemisphere the sun is bare and bold; it gives no quarter, to gypsy or archangel.

Hotels were always cold, even the grand hotels. They were forced warm by small armies of servants stoking the boilers relentlessly. You knew they were cold places though, the big stairways you hurried through, drawing the fur stole over your shoulders at dinner, even though the bright fireplace filled the other end of the dining room. Was it not a better life, standing on the left-over-stone bridge, gripping the shotgun you couldn't shoot, grey skirt stained with elderberry juice, four girls in careful darns behind, four black shapes of men coming up the road?

Salomé Wentwood, whose earlier name is iced up somewhere in Europe, does not know. She does not recognise herself in the foolhardy woman on the bridge.

2

She is aware of being alive, and furiously alive since the moment that Palliser Wentwood shook her out of slumber. When she met him she was a mannequin with cunning clockwork which ran for hours and hours. He blew into her life. She had never known pleasure like the fun he made for her, and for the taste of that alone she'd have followed him running barefoot across Europe. She was used to men falling in love with her, or, more precisely, falling in love with her father's money, but she didn't care if Palliser was after her money. When Palliser fell in love, it was not like other men; it was like grand opera crossed with pantomime. He turned up on her balcony at midnight with a black cape and a big bunch of roses, except that it wasn't Salomé's balcony, but the balcony of the room next door, inhabited by a retired judge from the Indian Civil Service, with whom he made friends and got drunk, at the acme of which friendship Salomé, in her night-gown, was roused out into the night by their singing, the judge with his white moustache, perfectly curled, waving his champagne flute and addressing her with far more passion than Palliser himself.

'This is my new friend, Palliser, and he's a true gent, even if he is an Irishman. And he's in love with you.'

It has always been so funny and touching and so quintessentially Palliser. But now it has ceased to amuse; it has become conceivable that all Palliser loved was indeed her father's money, neither more nor less, for now that the money is all gone, all completely, irretrievably gone, into ditches and fences and flat green land, which itself is almost gone, Palliser himself is also gone.

It might be better if he were dead.

The four little dots are distinct now. Still little and black, and mere smudges, but clearly four of them. Four men on foot, though Josiah Butler is pushing his bicycle. Hedler usually goes about in his dirty green utility, Philip

Butterworth in his sleek black car. Four men against one woman and her daughters.

His quiverful, he called them, his bright weapons against extinction, his hostages to fortune, he called them, and gave them quaint Old Testament names. If biblical names, why not the names of the feisty women, the fighting women, Rahab, Deborah, Judith, Jael?

A Jael would be a mighty mainstay now, standing behind her on the bridge, instead of timid Jemima, so tall and yielding. Naomi is the fiercest, but she is no higher than the basket on a bicycle. What price a Jael, a tall girl, flashing fire from her eyes, slaying them with her beauty, slashing them with her tongue. And what about an Abishag, a girl who would know about guns, a crack shot maybe, with her own pistols. Instead she had Abigail, clever as a coon cat, writing her Latin and Greek on an old school slate. Curly characters, with little dashes and dots. No use against these black dashes, fast turning into men.

Perhaps, after all, Bathsheba is her best defence. A baby, you could classify her as a baby still, if you were a soft man. A woman knows of course that she is a grown girl, clear on the shortest way to get what she wants, which is to make her sisters mad and adults into her slaves.

Well, now, look at those girls! All of them wearing boots. So much for bringing up ladies (what would Mother say?). But they contrive to look proud and even stylish. How do they do that, that damned Palliser trick of looking good in everything? Jemima, now, she's wearing what you'd expect from Jemima, wellingtons, green ones, and a dress made of sacking — it looks like sacking but it's something she wove herself and is very proud of. Over the top she wears a homespun jersey; she plucked the wool, spun it, dyed it and knitted the jersey. It's long and brown and baggy like a shirt, but Jemima is so tall and graceful she makes these poor sacks chic. Abigail wears boots too, but elegant laced-up numbers which could scarcely be called boots. She made the black suit herself, long jacket, long dress sliced up the side, smart as a lawyer, but very practical, doesn't show the mud or the chalk dust much, washed and ironed every Saturday, and still black and sharp. Naomi in laced-up boots like a farm boy; dressed like a farm boy, what was to be done with the girl? The prettiest of them all, though all of them have Palliser's beautiful mouth and nose, and Salomé's brown eyes and fierce cheekbones. And her narrow waist, a much prized feature. What could such girls not do, have done in the rich resorts of Europe? Imagine them sweeping in to the Grand Hotel at Nice. No, don't imagine that; it is another hemisphere, too far to contemplate.

Bathsheba is astride Jemima's shoulders; Jemima grasps her bare legs. The little girl is beating her hands on the top of Jemima's head, calling out with excitement because she knows something's up. Luckily Jemima's hair, piled up in a big soft brown bun of sorts, takes any amount of brushing or disarranging without looking very different. Bathsheba is excited, so are the others, with varying degrees of understanding and therefore seriousness. Naomi's got the axe – the axe, for heaven's sake! What is Naomi planning to do with the axe? Much the same perhaps as Salomé is planning to do with the shotgun, put up a show of fierceness. Naomi succeeds in looking fierce. Salomé wonders what she looks like herself.

Abigail has been saying all along that you can only hope to settle matters in the courts or the bank manager's office. Shotguns and axes do no good, she says, but even so, she's striding out with the others, in her boots, to stand behind her mother on the bridge. *If you would only explain the background, Mother, I am sure we could work it out.* But how to make sense of Palliser's doings, let alone the mendacious flourishes of his commercial deals?

Explanations. Why had she never asked for explanations, but laughed and accepted what he did as the very stuff of being? Now it was come to this.

Where's Daddy? I want to show this to Daddy! I really don't understand, Mama, why you can't tell me where Papa is. You must have some idea where he went. I would like to write to him, Mother, surely you have a forwarding address? Is he dead, is he dead? Did he get murdered in a duel?

What could she say to them, four different explanations, four different fairy tales. When she didn't know herself. *Think I'll try my luck down south for a while make a few quid and set us up for good won't stay long old thing can't bear to be away from you as you very well know light of my life dearest heart don't look downcast my darling my dearest I'll be back in the twinkling of an eye my own heart plenty of money to be made down south.* Her litany, her penitential psalm. *And this shall be for music when no one else is near, the fine song for singing, the rare song to hear! That only I remember, that only you admire . . .*

How long ago was that? She knows to a detail the day and the circumstances of his leaving, but she has pretended to forget. The bitterness of that day has been overwhelmed by the bitterness of two Christmases come and gone and no word. No word except one postcard from Hong Kong, and an envelope for Naomi's last birthday. A crumpled five-pound note with a piece of English hotel writing paper. *All my love, dearest girl. Make sure you waste this properly!!!!*

So he is not dead, he has simply run away and left her to face his creditors, without a friend in the world, for every friend of Palliser's is also his creditor.

What would ye, ladies? It was ever thus. Men are unwise and curiously planned . . .

They have their dreams and do not think of us. They make the Golden Journey to Samarkand.

★   ★   ★

She can recognise them now. Of course she knows who is coming. Josiah Butler. Hedler, Marcus Hedler. Philip Butterworth and Samuel Stokes. His cronies, his drinking buddies, his pals, his racing mates, his gambling partners, his shareholders and stake-holders and IOU-holders and mortgagees. His neighbours, his lawyer, his guarantors and his dupes. And then there is his wife, desperately positioned.

If Palliser were here, matters would never have come to this pass. He would have headed them off with his talk long before. Digging deeper ditches to fall into, no doubt, but finding a way to vault out again, running rings round them with his talk and his tales, half believed but given benefit. Who could keep up in the labyrinth of his dealings – in the warren of promises, promissory notes, mortgages, letters of intent, some drawn up by his lawyer Philip and some scribbled on beer-stained envelopes in the dregs of dawn?

Where is he now, now that his melodrama has reached its climax? Why isn't he here, he who is not afraid of anything, neither shame, nor ridicule, nor poverty, nor even beauty? Why couldn't Palliser be like other men? Then he might have been afraid to build a tower in the middle of a swamp, to leave his family to fend without him, to go and seek his fortune without a penny in his pocket. He might have been afraid of God or government, of his neighbour's scorn, or of failure.

Palliser, Palliser, how could a sane man be so mad? And how could she stay sane without him, when he was her life?

Where are you, you lovely renegade, you scoundrel, tale-teller, womaniser, patriarch, clown, daddy-long-legged husk of handsomeness? In whose bed are you lavishing your seed, flaunting your highwayman's looks in whose hall? Does she recognise your misquoted poems or swoon at the melody of your voice? Is she young? Is she white and unsmirched, as I am brown and tattered? You have taken my everything, even yourself, and left me with four brave girls, a shotgun and your ditches.

Palliser's ditches.

'I have bought us a kingdom,' he said, bursting into their boarding house in the back streets of Sydney. 'In the South Island of New Zealand, no less! In a place so beautiful it ravishes the spirit. Where the mountains tickle the sky and the seas go down into darkness. Kaikoura. The place of rich pickings. A piece of heaven snipped out and dropped to earth.'

He did not tell her he had bought a swamp, land once rich and wonderful, drained and squared off into fields by energetic Victorians, but now slid into depression, the drains clogged, the fences broken, the fields squelchy with mud.

'We'll drain the swamp once again,' he said, when the truth came out. 'Drain it and lace the rich new land once more with dikes. Venice, Fenland, the Low Countries. *I will make a castle just for you and me, of green days in forest and blue days at sea. I will make my tower and you shall keep your room, Where something flows the river, and golden grows the broom.* And we'll build us a kingdom on an island in the middle, an island of green fertility surrounded by our moat. A home, a castle, but no Englishman's castle.'

He said this rolling his consonants with exaggerated Irishness. Whenever Palliser grew more Irish, she waited for trouble. His accent told you who he was playing. When she met him, Palliser had spoken with English-public-school precision, animated by the melodiousness of the Irish. If he hadn't spoken so, she would never have been allowed to speak to him. How deceptive appearances could be, how wonderfully he fooled her parents, fooled her, fooled himself and all the world that he was – sound. Well, his ditches. They were a wild fancy, at first, in keeping with his dream of a tower. A part of his medieval dream of a feudal world of which he might be lord. But it was fun, too, and good farming practice, as it turned out. The land they reclaimed, he and Marcus Hedler and Samuel Stokes, with much hard labour from Salomé and Jemima and the boys Albert and Piripi, the land turned out to be the best. Of course it flooded every year in spring and autumn, and the ditches required constant vigilance or they clogged up and fell in, but what gorgeous crops it grew – maize and beet and turnips and rich red tomatoes and strawberries for the town market, and spectacular grapes.

The ditches were pain and grief to her, day after day, Abigail playing in the mud, Jemima beside her toting buckets. The pumps furiously at work drawing off the water as they dug, trying to make progress before one of the pumps broke down and water flooded back around them. Up to their knees, sometimes up to their armpits in muddy water, tangled clumps of plants with no discernible name, waterbirds crossly displaced. And Palliser would come and work with her, wildly digging, singing non-stop, laughing and roaring with pleasure at their progress. How he enjoyed himself. And then the next day he would be somewhere else, about some scheme or other, too busy and important to dig. So Salomé dug, and Albert and Piripi dug, and Jemima toted buckets, and quite often Marcus Hedler and Samuel Stokes dug too. And when it seemed hopeless, the day when Salomé got out of bed and was violently sick and knew then that another beautiful daughter was imminent, a daughter not destined to receive a name from the Bible, or any name at all, that day, Palliser went down to the ditches, and started to work, and never stopped, morning, noon and night until they were restored.

And the land they recreated was wonderful. So rich and

fertile, with its symmetrical lines of ditches marching into the distance. Many of the ditches were dry for much of the year, but those around the homestead flowed deep and brown, a living moat around his rickety castle with its tower, necessary, he claimed in times of flood or invasion. He planted the homestead island with grass seed, to make a proper lawn. Salomé laughed at him, but even now she enjoyed the emerald of the lawn, what was left of it, after the chooks and the house sheep had taken their toll.

The ditches were deep and unpleasant if you fell into them, and deadly during times of flood. She had them fenced on the island side, so that the babies wouldn't fall in and drown their silly selves. Good fences, for which she was now doubly grateful. The ditch was her defence, strong water you wouldn't want to fall into.

Many waters cannot drown love. But maybe cold oceans can shrivel it up.

She watches the men walking towards her, along the farm road. She reckons Philip Butterworth and Samuel Stokes must have left their cars at the gate, rather than risk driving them over the potholes. The farm road is more pothole than road, really, nowadays. Hedler's old truck would cope, but it only has one seat. She has tried to keep the road mended, but some things are completely impossible. She doesn't require much from the road anyway, for she has no vehicles left, except her bicycle, which happily skirts round the holes on the rare occasions she goes into the township. Cows don't like them, but she has sold all the cows. Butler, with his mobs of cows, might need to repair the road, but Butler's cows haven't arrived yet. And never will if Salomé has her way. And her shotgun.

Perhaps Philip Butterworth suggested that approaching on foot might seem less overbearing, more neighbourly. So if they left the cars at the gate, why is Butler pushing his bicycle? Then she sees why. They aren't specks now, they are distinguishable men, and the bicycle is quite plain. They have brought the bicycle to carry the papers. She can see the basket on the front of the bicycle. And in the basket are papers poking out, some with a red ribbon around them. Legal papers; and illegal ones to boot. But why are they bringing them out here? What do they hope to achieve?

And what does she hope to achieve, standing in the bright sunlight barricading her little bridge? She doesn't know. She has run out of her resources, which, without Palliser, seem so few. She feels something is called for at this moment of confrontation, some grand, Palliser-like gesture.

The four men approach Salomé, come up to the foot of the bridge and stop. They are in their best clothes, she observes, you could have called it their Sunday best, but she is not at all sure that these men observe Sunday in any meaningful way. They have on good shoes, nicely spattered with mud. Hedler has grown too fat for his best suit, and only one button meets, and that straining. Josiah Butler by contrast is too skinny for his smart jacket – borrowed perhaps for the occasion? Philip Butterworth is impeccable as always, and even here melts into the background. You have to look at him hard to see him, but when she does, she sees his clothes are expensive, and he as neat and lovely as ever. As for Samuel Stokes – he might sometimes look like a farmer in his best suit, but he will always look like a farmer. Salomé imagines him cowering before God on the judgment seat, looking just like a farmer.

'When I was homeless, did you take me in, Samuel Stokes?'

'Lord, when were You homeless in our parts? I'd sure have given You a bed, Sir.'

'You did worse, Samuel Stokes, farmer, you threw an

II

innocent woman and her children out into the ditch. Go and look after My cows for eternity.'

'Yes Sir, yes Sir.'

The trouble was, he'd be happy looking after the celestial cows for eternity.

'Good morning, Salomé,' says Butler. Weasel words, Butler.

She draws herself up tall, assuming the bearing handed down from generation to generation by the lords of the earth.

'Mrs Wentwood to you, Mr Butler. And I won't wish you good morning. I'll wish you goodbye. I'll thank you to remove yourselves from my property. Otherwise, I shall be forced to charge you with trespass.'

'Now, Salomé . . .' says Hedler.

'Would you prefer that in writing?'

'Salomé, please,' says Philip Butterworth, very apologetic. 'There is some question now as to the rightful owner of this property.'

'Yes, Mr Butterworth, there is most certainly question, and while that question remains unanswered you have no right to come on to my husband's property. I'll thank you to remove yourselves, before I file a complaint against you.'

'Salomé, dear Salomé,' says Hedler, beaming at her from inside his folds of fat, 'we know how hard it is for you to manage without Palliser. We are here as your friends. We don't hold you responsible for his actions. Make it easy for yourself. Let us come in at least and discuss the matter. We have some papers here we think you should peruse.'

'Now, Salomé,' says Butler, 'if Palliser were contactable –'

'I'd have a word or two to say to him,' says Stokes.

'We have asked you to come in for a talk several times, Salomé,' says Philip Butterworth, 'and I know you have received my letters. We don't want to force a sale. Please let us come in and discuss matters sensibly.'

'It is not convenient,' she says.

The girls are directly behind her. They push Bathsheba forward, with what end Salomé does not know. Naomi has put down the axe, but is busy with something else. Salomé raises the shotgun. The men's faces are a picture of alarm and concern; their expressions say clearly: Has she gone mad? Is she dangerous? Can she fire that thing? *Is it really loaded*? How dare they patronise her so – daughter of grouse-hunters and a long line of colonels? And yes, it's loaded, oh yes! Naomi makes sure of that, just in case of robbers. Salomé cocks the gun as she has seen Palliser do.

'O look, a swamp hen!' she says very clearly, and fires the shotgun towards the other side of the road, through the wheels of Josiah Butler's bicycle.

The recoil and the noise take her by surprise. She steps back, and all is chaos around her.

Naomi is up on the coping of the bridge, with her catapult. Bathsheba is running forward on a mission from her sisters.

In his surprise, Josiah Butler has dropped his bicycle and the papers have spilled out of the basket into the mud. He kneels down to pick them up, hasty, discomfited. The others hesitate. Butterworth's suit is too good and Stokes and Hedler are too fat to leap to the task. It seems Butler is having some trouble picking up the papers. Small stones keep flying round his hands as he scrambles in the mud.

'Yay, a swamp hen,' Naomi yells, every time she lets off a stone. 'Another swamp hen!'

Bathsheba runs forward as if to help Butler. Hedler tries to grab her out of the way, but she wriggles too much for him. She seizes the biggest bundle of papers by its red ribbon and throws it into the ditch. Naomi yells, 'An eel, an eel!' and fires into the water.

The bundle starts to sink. Philip Butterworth gets down, suit and all, on his knees and leans into the ditch, but he can't reach the parcel. Bathsheba, squealing, has evaded the attempts of the others to grab her and scoops up almost all the other papers, and runs back across the bridge to her sisters, throwing the armful of paper and mud into the water as she goes.

Salomé waves the shotgun wildly and, scion of commanding officers, roars above the shouts and expostulation.

'Remove yourselves from my property. At once, gentlemen, *at once!*'

Jemima has lifted Bathsheba on to the coping of the bridge and is handing her big stones. She throws them into the ditch with force, and several of them land on the papers.

Butterworth scrambles up, his knees covered with mud, and starts to call for a stick or a pole. Stokes remembers himself enough to hand him a walking stick, and Butterworth kneels down all over again in the mud and tries to reach the papers, still floating gently down the ditch.

'Watch out, Mr Butterworth,' shouts Naomi, 'there's a monster eel down there,' and she lets fly with rather a big stone, right by his hand.

He pulls back in shock, loses his balance and falls into the ditch. Right up to his armpits. Salomé puts down the shotgun carefully and goes to his aid.

With Hedler's help she pulls him ashore, but when she sees him standing on the road, she starts to shake with something which might be laughter or rage.

'O Philip, how awful!' she says. 'You had better come up to the house and change your clothes.'

She leads the way across the bridge, and he walks

behind her. The other men attempt to follow, but the girls, opening ranks for Salomé and Philip, close them again immediately.

'Now look here, Salomé,' Hedler calls after her.

But Salomé will not look here. She hears Josiah Butler calling out after them, a thin voice drifting on the breeze: 'It's my land, you know. I'll have my cows on here tomorrow.'

'His cows might not care for sling-shot pellets up the bottom,' she says over her shoulder to Philip, 'and who can guarantee that the gates would stay shut?'

In this way, squelching up the flagstone path to the front door, Philip Butterworth took his first steps into a new and delightful era of his life.

He had not visited the Wentwood farm since Palliser's departure. At first he had not known that Palliser was gone; then he began to notice that his friend had not telephoned or called or stumbled upon him with a new suggestion for entertainment; next he began to hear the gossip from the valley that Palliser Wentwood had scarpered. Finally his mother told him as gospel that his worthless buddy, the bounder Wentwood, had indeed bounded, leaving debts that you, no doubt, Philip, are more aware of than anyone! As weeks turned into months, it became awkward to call on Salomé without a reason, and then less and less politic to do so. When he met her in the street he raised his hat and chatted as if nothing were changed, but he saw her in the township less and less frequently. In the meanwhile, the clamour from Butler, Hedler and Stokes that he *do* something grew ever more insistent. Salomé ignored his notes and messages; the telephone was cut off. Salomé was seen no more in the township, neither in the post office, the cinema, the garage, the stock & station agents, the drapers, the church, the fish-shop nor the bottle-store. Salomé laid low in her requisitioned castle, and Philip Butterworth did not visit.

As he pattered behind Salomé to the house, his heart gave a little skip; not a leap or a jump, just a tiny chirrup of pleasure to be back again. No matter what jaunt Palliser had dragged him on, whether a trip to the races or a round of golf, their unfruitful expedition to Dunedin to buy a taxidermist's stock, the all-night poker games of which Philip was always only a bleary observer, their round-Lyttelton-harbour-with-a-crate-of-beer yacht race, the best part of all these expeditions was tumbling back to Wentwoods' to tell Salomé an edited version of the adventure, and to sit at the kitchen table with a cup of tea and a glass of beer, and see her smile and laugh and spark and flurry and laugh again. Not all adventures could be told, alas; Philip remembered the time when he had organised Palliser into a job of carpentry work for a friend of a friend in Christchurch, and how, when Philip had dropped round to see how Pally was getting on, the place turned out to be a brothel, and the girls were suggesting they pay Palliser in kind, an arrangement which vastly amused him, and he claimed he was inclined to accept. They did not tell Salomé that story.

Now Philip noticed some differences about the place which distressed his tidy mind. Salomé's wonderful cottage garden, once as neat and pretty as a tea-tray, was higgledy-piggledy with herbs, vegetables and low-growing fruit – gooseberries, rhubarb, raspberries, lemons. The hens scuffled around, and a large black tom shot out away from Salomé's flying foot. Around the house the sheds lay empty and dilapidated. No tractor, cars or horses; hardly a cow in sight. And Salomé's hair – Salomé's hair.

It would not be true to say that Philip Butterworth adored Salomé. He was not that kind of man. But had he been asked to imagine a perfect woman, Salomé's person would have floated into his mind. He did not think of her as beautiful, any more than he thought of a racehorse as beautiful; beauty was not a practical consideration, but when she was in the room he looked at nothing else. And he was distressed by the state of her hair.

Salomé's hair was Palliser's trope. It signified magic and mystic things to him, which he could only express in song or poem, when drunk. But Salomé responded to his sacramental worship by lavishing attentions on the dressing of her hair. Sometimes it flowed out over her shoulders like silk; sometimes it was smoothed back on top of her head; sometimes it was looped into a web of plaits; sometimes it was crinkled like sand dunes after rain; sometimes it was caught up in a comb; sometimes it was coiled around her cheeks; sometimes it was laced with colours and ribbons – and always in defiance of fashion.

So when he saw her hair uncut, uncared-for, unkempt, pushed back behind her ears all anyhow, sadly in want of a comb, with strawed remnants of elderflower, he became nigglingly aware, as a tiny rupture of the cap slowly but irretrievably lets all the fizz out of a bottle, of the awfulness of Palliser's desertion.

'I really shouldn't go inside like this,' he said, standing at the door in his muddy clothes.

She looked at him and laughed. She leaned the shotgun against the door jamb.

'O you poor thing!' she said. 'Take off your shoes and socks, and we'll see to them.'

Barefoot he padded into the familiar hall. Palliser and Salomé's house, a standing joke, had not Palliser made all the jokes himself before anyone else could. Spot the right angle, he would say, waving his glass around. You can plant a marble at my front door and catch it at the back. And he would, if he were drunk enough, attempt to demonstrate.

He had built it himself on the simplest of principles
– rectangular, hall down the middle, bedrooms off each
side, kitchen and living room at the back where the sun
shone. Except for his follies – the tower and the infamous
morning room – there was little to distinguish it from
thousands of other weatherboard farmhouses all over the
country. Inside, the hallway was dark, carpeted with a strip
of cocoa-matting, harsh on pampered feet.

The sporting prints were gone. The hall had been lined
with a matched set of hand-coloured engravings showing
sportive English chaps. They must have been worth a few
quid. Palliser was fond of them; he claimed he had nicked
them from his father's library when the old man was out
for the count and replaced them with crude imitations
culled from the pages of the *Illustrated London News*. No
one believed this story.

Salomé threw open the bathroom door.

'I'll draw you a bath. There's plenty of hot water.'

Salomé started the bath and went away, leaving the door
open to signify her imminent return. Philip waited.

He looked around the bathroom and realised he was in
a house inhabited by women. No manly shaving tackle,
but lipsticks and tweezers and pink plastic combs and
powder and unidentifiable sweet smells. Nothing like this
was to be found in the spartan bathroom he shared with
his cosmetic-free mother.

Salomé returned with two big clean towels, ragged, but
burning white, and a neatly folded pile of men's clothes.
She put these on the low white bathroom chair, uplifted
a handful of cosmetics from the bathroom shelf, smiled at
Philip and shut the door behind her.

Philip Butterworth cautiously removed his suit jacket
and laid it over the end of the bath. Then he considered
that it might slip into the water, so folded it down the
middle of the back, straightened the sleeves and placed it

on the floor. It was not much muddied; a little brushing, perhaps the luxury of a visit to the dry-cleaners. But, if the trousers were beyond redemption, what use was the jacket? He unclasped the navy-blue braces from the waistband, front and back, unbuttoned the flies and stepped out of them to examine the evidence. They had assumed an awful bagginess, which was painful to Philip whose creases must be perfect. They dripped richly with swamp water, so that he felt obliged to roll them up in a tight ball over the handbasin. Greeny-brown water squeezed out on to the ceramic as he did this.

He felt uncomfortable standing in a women's bathroom in a state of undress, so leaving the rolled-up trousers in the sink, he unknotted his tie, smoothed it and placed it with the jacket. The tie was unscathed. He removed his mother-of-pearl cufflinks, put them on the sill of the frosted glass window, unbuttoned and removed his shirt. He held it up for inspection. Alas, alas, this fine American cotton shirt, special purchase, was stained swamp green with uncertain borders, like a map of the Antipodes before the voyages of Cook. Material concern conquering modesty, he experimented with the shirt tail to see how removable the stain might be.

Relieved on that score, he swiftly removed his underclothes. He was a compact man of thirty-five, pale, hairless and lean. He had no compunctions about his body, but never felt any desire to linger over it or even to glance at it in a glass. He tested the temperature of the water and lowered himself into the bath.

A bath fit for a king – Palliser had on occasion held court in his bath, sherry in one hand, loofah in the other. A tall man, Palliser required a long deep bath, and filled it with style. Philip had sat on that same white chair, while the dust of the day's expedition soaked into the warm foam of Palliser's bath and Abigail or Jemima trailed in and out at their father's behest, refilling glasses and supplying towels.

Philip at home made do with a shower, which, it was felt, had cost so much to install that it must be made to pay for itself. The pleasures of the bath, much praised by Palliser in the same breath as other pleasures of the flesh, did not leave Philip cold so much as unengaged. He enjoyed a bath when the occasion arose, and he was certainly enjoying this one, but the occasion did not often arise.

The discomfort of his ducking soaked slowly and deliciously away, leaving him only with the nagging issue of his suit. If it were ruined, would his insurance cover accidents of a watery nature? In making a claim would he have to write a full description of the circumstances, and how accurate should this be?

It was not so much the money involved, it was the untidiness that offended Philip. He was careful with money as he was careful with his possessions and actions and with himself, not because he was mean-spirited, but because tidiness was the core of his being. Palliser had represented his escape-valve, the one massively untidy area in his life; there had been many times, especially of late, when Philip Butterworth had rather regretted that he had let such mayhem into his life. But when Palliser was present, Philip's reservations lost their voices; at home with his mother, or alone with his papers in one of his three offices, they proclaimed loud and long that Palliser Wentwood was an unnecessary mess who should be mopped up at once.

Lying in Palliser's bath, in Palliser's bathroom, he was in two minds. His life was orderly now; even the puddle Palliser left behind was slowly being dried out, though no one had told Salomé this. But he missed the fun; he missed the household; and he missed Salomé. He recognised that his life had grown quite dull; his conscious mind suggested that a chap should have friends whose company he enjoyed, and a certain variety of entertainment, while his unconscious self longed for the pure exhilaration of Palliser's company, so different from the rounds of golf and whisky at the club, breakfast with Mother, encounters with clients and meetings of the board.

How pleasurable it was to lie in this bath, but how necessary it was to get out and get moving.

Palliser's clothes did not fit him in any particular. Salomé had provided a pair of bottle-green corduroy trousers, voluminous white underpants, a collarless striped shirt, black woollen socks, and a dark blue Guernsey. The trouser legs and the sleeves of the shirt were far too long for him, but by dint of shortening his braces and pulling the Guernsey down over his shirt he contrived a passable figure, although his hair stuck up rather. He put his cufflinks in his jacket breast pocket, made a neat stack of all his wet garments, rinsed the handbasin and the bath, and folded the towels. Then went to find Salomé and pay her homage.

Salomé was in the kitchen, sun streaming in through the windows and on to her hands as she worked.

'Stay to lunch,' she said.

She was transformed. She had changed into a clean white blouse and a full brown skirt, nylons and smart brown shoes with stocky heels. She had applied a little powder and little lipstick. She was wearing tiny gold earrings. Best of all she had brushed her hair and fastened it back in a tortoiseshell comb.

'Stay to lunch,' she said, and he was happy to accept.

Jemima brought Bathsheba in, washed her feet, and set her to draw with her pencils by the hearth. The papers, she said, were all accounted for. Naomi and Abigail had fished them out of the ditch with the eeling net, but they were not in specially good shape. She said this without any sort of devilment. When Naomi came in to apologise, however, she did so with a grin that belied her words.

'There *was* an eel, Mr Butterworth,' she said, 'but I am sorry you fell in.'

Philip looked sadly at the wet sack they had deposited on the linoleum before their mother told them to take it outside. It doubtless contained sole copies of agreements drafted late at night on cigarette packets, scribbled notes of promise and IOUs, worthless if illegible, as they now would be. A legal mess made messier.

Bathsheba presented Philip with a drawing, and started on the next.

'How do you write DAD?' she asked him.

The kitchen and living area, contiguous, though the latter was carpeted in dull maroon, were strikingly different from his memory, in that they were extraordinarily tidy. Gone were the piles of paper and the pyramids of empty bottles, the scattered clothes and loaded ashtrays. Gone was the varied tackle – fishing rod, life-jacket, golf clubs, tools. Gone was the pervading smell of cigarette smoke and alcohol. Gone was the prized collection of pewter mugs which had hung under the kitchen shelves.

Lunch was laid. But before serving it Salomé disappeared into the storeroom adjoining the kitchen. Knowing what it contained, Philip went after her, for a surreptitious reminder of happier days. This was her haven, this was her treasure house. The walls of the windowless room consisted of wooden racks built by Palliser, and the racks were almost full, floor to ceiling with dark brown bottles, innocent in appearance, but lying in wait. Salomé's fruit nectar – her elderberry, her blackcurrant, her apricot and pear, and her terrible parsnip.

'What shall we have, Philip, which of these little dar-lings? The '54 blackcurrant?'

She seized a bottle, dusted it on her skirt. She opened

it there in the storeroom, and sniffed it carefully, as if afraid some demon might have entered it. Philip smelt the elusive herbal wilderness. She poured a little into a glass; the colour was almost as spell-binding as the bouquet. Heraldic, velvet, ruby red, the colour of the blood of princes. He let out a sigh.

'You ought to sell this wine,' he said. 'People would pay the earth for it.'

'Salomé,' he said after lunch, 'we must be serious.'

'O Philip, I was so much hoping for some fun.'

Salomé and Philip sat sedately either side of the fireplace with their tea. Bathsheba and the specially favoured house cats sat between them. The elder girls were washing the dishes. Naomi was elsewhere.

'I believe we can renegotiate all the mortgages. It may be possible also to call in all the outstanding provable debts under one umbrella, and discharge them, leaving a single loan to be repaid over a fixed period, say twenty-five years. I mean by that, all the surviving IOUs, Palliser's so-called shares in the farm, issued, if you recall, in lieu of payment to workers, the informal chattel mortgages . . .'

Perhaps she was listening. He ploughed on, setting the truth and all the options before her. It was his duty; if he bored her, then so be it, he must be tedious.

'Philip,' she said at last. 'Do you know why I have done nothing? No, of course, you don't. You're not a married man, and so the behaviour of we women who have turned into wives is a mystery to you. I have done nothing, because none of this was ever my business. Palliser had the ideas, Palliser made the promises; I was not consulted, I simply went along for the ride – no, I was *taken* along for the ride, and I didn't mind that because, really, it was lots of fun. Then suddenly I was driving the car and it was out of control. But I never learned to drive this sort of car, if you know what I mean. I didn't know about any mortgages; I didn't know about the shares, or the loans. You can say I was a fool, but you must understand the way we are brought up. I thought it was Palliser's business to deal with land and money, as it was my business to bring up the children and put meals on the table. Not that I was bred to domestic work, but I did see it as a reasonable division of labour. I let him think for me, I suppose, and you might say that was terrible, but I dare say you might expect to think for your wife if you had one. I also trusted him, Philip, against my better judgement. My heart trusts him, though my head has begun to lose faith. My heart, I suppose, refused to let my head attend to the matter of the mortgages.'

'So what would you prefer me to do?'

'I have to make a decision? I can't remember when I was ever asked to make a decision. Except to marry Palliser, and that was not so much a decision as a foregone conclusion.' She laughed so merrily that he must smile also.

He tried to explain what she might do, repeating himself tiresomely, determined that she should understand. He wanted not to be like Palliser in any respect, except in being regarded by Salomé.

'. . . so you see, if you cede them to Hedler, and the bank is prepared to . . . we could call in . . . some of the more dubious notes . . . not stand up in court . . . probably illegible . . .'

'You are lovely, Philip,' she said.

She walked with him down to his car, carrying one of his dripping sacks. She put her arm through his, and he leaned towards her, feeling the warmth and weight of her arm on his. She had agreed with his favoured plan, she had agreed to cede certain lots to Hedler, to lease other fields to Stokes for a peppercorn, to buy off Butler with a new loan, which he had her permission to negotiate with the bank.

She stood by his car, as he settled himself in the driver's seat and prepared to light his afternoon's cigarette. She seemed to stroke the bodywork, as if she longed for his car rather more than for himself.

Nonetheless, as he drove away, new ideas were forming up in his mind, dancing little jigs among the tidy stacks. He opened the car window and breathed in sea air, and his chest filled up with promise. Dare he, dare he?

II

FROM THE TOP of Palliser's tower you could see the sea. Below lay the variegated green velvet of the fields, prettily embroidered with ribands of water, plaited together towards the sea into a delta of glistening grey mud. Between the tower and the ocean lay lumpy pates of dune, spiked along the top with mohawks of marram grass. Beyond, a strip of grey golden sand, enticingly flat and empty. And beyond that the creature of water, today as tame as a barber's cat, purring and nudging against the shore for attention and tidbits. No indication there of the pouncing fury and murderous intent which a storm might provoke. Between the arms of the huge bay, the water played at domestication.

But Abigail was not interested in the sea. The telescope, designed for gentlemanly survey of the night sky but more usually employed to spy out sails on the horizon, or storms in the hills, was trained on the main road.

There was only one road of any consistency in the valley. Most farm roads in the district, while not as perilous as the Wentwoods' – more pothole than road – tested the suspension of the average family car. The one road was maintained by the council, and ran north–south straight across the valley, parallel to the sea-shore and the rail tracks, bisecting the township. Whether you followed it north or south to escape the valley you had to wind up hills of such steepness that English immigrants referred to them as mountains, although real mountains of mythic height brooded above the valley to the west. North or south lay proper cities, harbours, plains, forests, deserts, lakes, goldmines, factories, hotels and universities: in other words, everything the great world has to offer, even a funfair or two.

Cars were only useful if a man travelled north or south regularly, or if he wished to make a statement about his wealth. The farm roads were better traversed by horse, bicycle or mud-flung truck. On a horse or bicycle you could go round the potholes; in a truck you hardly cared, with all the other bumps.

So down the main road a car had come, and slid to a halt by the Wentwoods' farm gate. The driver must therefore be no farmer, but a man who went up and down to town, in other words a man of means and sophistication. Abigail was watching for this, because Salomé had put on her war-paint, mounted her bicycle and left without explanation. This was such unusual behaviour in their mother that the other girls were filled with curiosity, and Abigail with a *frisson* of alarm. She already had her suspicions and, training the telescope carefully on the black car at the main gate, she found them to be correct.

Philip Butterworth got out of his car; he was wearing a fine grey felt hat and a navy blue suit. He looked at his watch, removed his hat, smoothed his hair with his fingers, and replaced his hat. Then he took out a cigarette, looked at his watch, lit the cigarette, and leaned against his car, half facing away from the farm and towards the sea.

He was all tidy – clean-shaven and short-haired, his jacket with every button in place, his trousers creased just so. No dandruff blemished his shoulders, no errant handkerchief bulged in his pocket. His car was unimpeachable, black, bulbous and discreet.

How was it possible that such a perfect, inoffensive man had never been married? Even Abigail knew that eligible men were generally snared into matrimony by determined women. No one had succeeded in catching Philip Butterworth; at thirty-five one had to ask why. The Wentwood family had often debated this conundrum with enthusiasm; Palliser, who had no scruples about discussing matters of human sexuality freely before his family, produced a raft of scurrilous or hilarious answers. But to Abigail, perched in the tower, spying on him, the matter seemed suddenly very serious.

Salomé wobbled up the road towards the car, trying to keep her dignity while avoiding the puddles. Philip ground out his cigarette and opened the gate for her, removing his hat at the same time. She dismounted and propped the bicycle on the farm side of the fence, and took her jacket and hat from the carrier.

Abigail watched their faces as they talked. They smiled, but looked at each other shyly. Salomé, usually so confident, was diffident, looking away into the distance, dropping her eyes whenever he caught her gaze. She put on her hat, and he adjusted it for her, smiling and chatting lightly the while. Then he handed her into the car, closed the door, got in himself and drove away, rather faster than one might expect.

Abigail watched the car race along the valley road until it was out of sight, and came to the conclusion that they were going to the races. This surmise was based on the direction (north rather than south) and the shortage of entertainments in those parts. On a Saturday morning in the valley there was nothing but the races and the pub; Philip and Salomé at the races would be cause for comment, but the pair of them entering the local pub would bring drinking to a standstill.

This was good matter for teasing, and doubtless the valley

would dissect the outing for a fortnight, but there was more to it than gossip. All kinds of implications coursed through Abigail's mind.

Philip had taken Mother to the races. Might he not have taken Abigail?

How she longed for some fun, a flutter, a ride in a nice big car. The glorious fun they used to have with Palliser – the fairground rides and the candy-floss. Shooting down the river rapids on the inner tubes of car tyres, screaming. Tobogganing on the tea trays. And the races; country races, town races. They would go in a big group, Palliser, Piripi, Albert, Josiah Butler, his son Thaddeus, Jemima, Abigail, Philip . . . but never Salomé. Abigail would clutch the hand of her father or Philip for fear of being trampled in the crowd. She remembered Philip's hand, smaller than Father's, but cool and reassuring; he never let go in the heat of the moment.

Mother had had her day. She had a magic barrel of stories of her youth: tales of balls, hunts, picnics, fancy-dress parties, weekends in the country, cruises on Lord Languid's yacht, then jaunts with Palliser, midnight swims, suicidal skiing, gypsy shows and religious processions. Why should she have the treats now, when it was Abigail who worked drilling snotty children term in term out without reward?

But there were more serious matters than the natural unfairness of nature's handouts. What if the relationship between Philip and Salomé flourished? Abigail was forced to take this possibility very seriously. Her mother had never before taken the slightest interest in any man other than Palliser, for whom her passion was palpable. *Forsaking all other, to thee only* . . . Philip Butterworth had lived the life of an unimpeachable bachelor, as far as the valley could ascertain, hosting his mother or one of her elderly friends to any social occasion requiring couples. Therefore, going out together marked a critical change in both their behaviours.

It would be regarded as flagrant adultery in every living room in the district, proof positive that Palliser Wentwood was not expected to return, and only to be countenanced if the intended destination of this stepping out was the office of the Registrar of Births, Marriages and Deaths. Philip Butterworth as stepfather now had to be considered.

Philip sharing Mother's bed, Philip appearing at breakfast, unshaven, his shirt open, Philip and Mother cosy together, touching each other affectionately, and Palliser's name never heard in the house. Abigail shrank from the prospect. Once she had had a crush on Philip; but then she was fourteen and undiscerning. Now the thought of Philip as an object of love seemed slightly distasteful.

She would not imagine them at the races, Mother leaning on his arm, him bending his ear towards her mouth so that her lips almost touched his skin. They were shouting, Mother cheering on her horse, screaming with abandon, then they were laughing, throwing their betting slips in the air, peeling away from the track, into the bar, sitting opposite each other at a little table slimy with other people's beer, their elbows sliding together, their eyes meeting.

Abigail contemplating nice Mr Butterworth felt like Hamlet regarding Claudius. What a clownish imitation, what an apology for a lover, what an appendix of a man!

But everyone, most feelingly the pair sneaking away on their guilty outing, everyone knew that Palliser wasn't dead and, knowing Palliser, as they all did, there was nothing to say he wouldn't reappear up the road on the next bus. He derived huge pleasure from surprising people; he often said that he never knew himself what he was going to do next. If he came back now, while they were at the races, popped his head over the horizon, Robin Goodfellow doubling as Oberon, would Salomé keep hold of Philip's arm? No, of course not, she would forget all about sweet

Mr Butterworth and rush into her rightful husband's arms. No one could shrug off Palliser present. But should Palliser delay his return, a month, a year longer – we must try and be realistic – he might come home, find Philip with his feet under the table, have a laugh and drink with them all and bugger off again.

He was her father, faults, manifold faults, and all, for ever and ever, and she did not want him replaced.

On the other hand . . .

Abigail was an intrepid girl, endowed with her father's vision and her mother's practicality, and rather more common sense than either of them had. Shock was expressed in the valley at her lack of feeling, balanced by admiration for her pragmatism. *How different you are from your dad!* She had become by default the father of her family, and was now the breadwinner. For early in her schooldays she worked out that the fastest way to earn a living in a small rural community was to become a pupil-teacher and then a junior teacher, thus acquiring training and a small income while educating oneself. She had no great desire to impart knowledge or particular fondness for the young, but she saw teaching as an honourable career, and one in which women could rise smoothly to the top.

To this end, she made sure to be first or second in the class at every subject – no challenge in a district which prized the ability of children to catch fish above their ability to form letters. She achieved this without appearing bookish or uppity, and also took care to press her gym-slip, shine her shoes, clean her teeth, and smile when spoken to. Her advancement was fast. At fourteen she was unpaid school monitor. At fifteen she was tutor to the junior school, paid a pittance per pupil. At sixteen she was officially pupil-teacher, on five pounds a term, and dux of the school. At seventeen she was on the staff, two pounds a week, and learning Latin and Greek laboriously from a lexicon and texts in translation in the top of the tower.

Eighteen beckoned; she must leave the valley and go to university, or she would self-destruct. She desired this with every fibre of her body and every centimetre of her brain. But she was trapped. Her salary, such as it was, was the family's sole income, the farm was mortgaged, the chattels sold, and at the door bayed the wolves, Josiah Butler, Marcus Hedler and Samuel Stokes – and yes, even Philip Butterworth.

In the tower, the black dot of car shooting into the distance, Abigail felt a sudden weariness. Earning the family bread, fighting for survival, coming up time and time again, smooth and well turned out and never discountenanced, here she was eighteen, more adult than the adults around her, and drawn by adult exhaustion of spirit.

For her reason declared that, however she felt about it, Philip Butterworth as Mother's friend and admirer was useful. First, he was a partner in the syndicate which claimed to hold title to Wentwood Farm. Second, he was a lawyer, and they were in sore need of the unpaid counsels of a lawyer. Third, and most importantly, he was known to be comfortable, co-owner with his mother, uncle and cousins of three fat department stores, a man of solid worth.

If Palliser came back – when Palliser came back – he would have no money, or so little that it would soon evaporate. His ideas for spending money were as amusing as his ways of getting it. Palliser's return, however much longed for, would spell even more poverty, even less chance of escape for Abigail. She used to think that once he came home, everything would be all right again: the cows back in the paddock, a tractor in the shed. But she understood now that it would not be so. Abigail might win a scholarship to see herself through university, but that would not keep shoes on her sisters' feet and pay the rates.

If Philip were only an ally, restricted to outings and visits, kept at a distance by the gossip of the village and the chilliness within the Wentwood household, Palliser's return would see the retreat of him and all his lovely professionalism and more lovely wealth. The only way to be sure of Philip Butterworth and his essential assets was make him fall in love with and marry Salomé, and as soon as possible. His money must be inextricably mixed in with them, and none of it Palliser's. This was the only escape Abigail had; there was no one else with money, no one eligible in the whole valley, which might as well be the world, for all that Salomé would stir out of it. Salomé had to marry him, because there was no other way out of the valley. If Salomé wanted the treats and the outings, then she'd have to take the consequences and marry the man. As a father, Philip wasn't much of a substitute for Palliser, but as a benefactor he had the road to himself. Abigail determined to make sure of him. Surely this was not selfishness on Abigail's part? The whole valley attested how hard she worked for her family; so charming and obliging too.

Salomé returned that evening, her cheeks flushed, her hat askew. The laughter in her eyes made Abigail first curl and shrink inside, then smile approvingly.

Bathsheba raided her pockets and found a shower of betting slips. Naomi seized upon her race book and took it away to gloat over by the fire.

'Mother,' said Abigail, 'I'm sure you brought us up to disapprove of gambling.'

'I did no such thing, Abby. Don't tease. Your father was a great gambler.'

'I've no doubt Father is still a great gambler.'

Salomé sat at the table and Jemima brought her a cup of tea.

'We had supper, Mum, Sheba was hungry.'

'This is so wonderful, Mum,' said Naomi, lost in the intricacies of form.

Bathsheba, washed and in her night-clothes, smoothed out the betting slips in rows.

'We came out ahead,' said Salomé. 'So I bought you some chocolates.'

Abigail took a chocolate, although she didn't like them much, and refrained from mentioning the unpaid doctor's bill or the state of Naomi's shoes.

'It was such fun, I never *knew* the races could be such fun.'

'Didn't you ever go to the races with Dad?' said Jemima.

'When we were young, in Ireland, and France, before the war. But latterly I got so nervous when he placed bets that I couldn't enjoy myself.'

'And Mr Butterworth is more moderate?'

'Moderate, and also rather better off than we.'

Abigail remembered walking with her father among the impossibly long legs of racehorses, clutching his hand because of the terrifying hooves and the equally terrifying eyes, so large and deranged. Palliser gesticulating with his free hand, fondling the horses, kissing them on the nose, talking in a loud continuous stream to the pinched men in caps. Then the ring of sawdust, like the circus, only horses, and the man with a hammer. Palliser always seemed as if he were about to buy a horse, and she'd get very excited and scared about taking home this beauty or that, and what would Mother say, and will we learn to ride him? But somehow they always went home without the horse.

On Monday, after school, Abigail left her marking stacked up for the next morning; in the second week of term, who would dare to complain if she delayed a little? There was a price tag on being punctilious: everyone expected perfection. She whipped round the classroom, picking pencil shavings and ink pellets from the desks, putting away Jake Hedler's work book, and sighing at the four brown apple cores and wads of chewing gum in his desk. She cleaned the blackboard properly, even though the monitors had theoretically relieved her of that chore, and set out the geometric paper, pencils and compasses for tomorrow morning's maths test. That would give her time to mark today's work. Then she thought better, and put the compasses back in the cupboard. Better not put temptation in their vicious little paths. *Blessed be he*, Palliser would say, *who putteth a stumbling block, even in the form of a single glass of champers, in his brother's way.*

Thought of Palliser made her frown and move more swiftly through the classroom. The nature table could stay untended tonight. She had plans afoot.

She hastened out of school, an old stone building squatting in the middle of a field, with an uninterrupted view of the sea and the hills. The first settlers had built it, laboriously placing stone on stone, in the hope of a great educational future. Abigail did her best, but Jake Hedler and his crew were not destined for the heights of academe. Reading the beef schedule was about their mark. On the other hand, Jemima's Thaddeus had cut a swath through that very school four years before Abigail, and was now far away, studying for a doctor.

She kept a bone-shaking bike at the school which took her to and from the railway yards, whence she generally rode home on the freight train. Today she headed for the township, but instead of the yards, rattled down Main Street to the post office.

The interior of the post office was utilitarian, pale linoleum which did not invite you to linger, counter tops with peeling varnish like tobacco juice inscribed with the names of generations of waiting children; posters faded to the colour of the floor, announcing long-archived stamp issues. Abigail did not mind, because the place was workmanlike and intended for nothing else.

Mr Kennet, the postmaster beamed from within his cardigan.

'Hel-lo Ab-i-gail,' he pushed out a series of rich Welsh syllables. 'Writing more letters, are we?'

'No, I want some of my money.' She knew how to smile enchantingly.

She presented her battered brown Post Office Savings Bank book. Her escape fund, her lifeline, preciously hoarded against the day . . . Now she was withdrawing half of it, a gamble on the future.

He was dying to know why; Abigail knew that if she told him, the Methodist Circle and the Golden Bowls Association and the Gardening Group would be clacking. That was all to the good.

'Running away to sea, are you?'

'No, I'm going to pay the butcher's bill.'

The butcher's shop was three doors down, its window full of cheerful cardboard animals and their fleshy dismembered limbs. Tim the butcher was an expansive young man, tall and free, with a big white smile, the sort of man she might like to go to the races with.

'I want to pay the bill.'

'Good on you, Abigail. Jeez, though, that's going back a bit. Hang on, I'll have a geezer.'

He found his account book and turned over the blood-thumbed pages with his big fingers. Lots of crossed-out entries in biro with PAID written over them in writing as big and generous as his frame.

'It's mainly that pig you butchered for Father.'

'That's a ways back.'

'It certainly is. We lived off that pig for ages.' Pickled pork, salt pork, ham and bacon.

'Your dad liked his ham. Tell you what, Abigail, make it fifteen pounds and we're square.'

'It's got to be more than that.'

'Well, yes, probably, hey, that's OK. Tell you what, Abigail, I've got to go to this church social. Saturday week. It's a sort of fancy dress thing – you know pirates and that. Could you give us a hand with the costume? Then she'll be jake.'

'You're not inviting me to the social are you, Tim?'

'Well, kind of.'

'Thank you. I will come and I will help you with your costume. And here's fifteen pounds.'

He wrote PAID over the Wentwood entries.

Abigail smiled at him lovingly and handed over the money, carefully wrapping the remaining notes inside the book. Then she cast a longing eye at the window.

'I'd like a leg of lamb too. But I don't think I've got enough money left. Can you charge it?'

He selected a beauty from the window, pale pink flesh, thin coating of white fat, and wrapped it up in white greaseproof paper, then brown paper, then string.

'Special occasion, is it? Someone coming home, fatted calf and all that?'

She leaned towards him and said in a whisper designed to echo round the whole valley: 'Mr Butterworth is coming to dinner!'

'I've never been so mortified in my life,' said Salomé. 'How could you walk in there and invite him? And pretend the invitation came from me!'

'Well, Mother, I'm afraid it is too late to un-invite him. You just have to make sure he has the best evening of his life.'

The day was rainy and grew depressing. Naomi ran all the way to the gate and back in the rain, spreading muddy footprints on the linoleum of the kitchen floor just after Jemima had washed it. To add misery to nuisance, Naomi brought the mail – no letter from Thaddeus, but a nasty-looking official letter addressed to Mrs Palliser Wentwood.

Salomé became very quiet when she read the letter, and handed it to Abigail without comment. It was an eviction order, drawn up at Philip Butterworth's legal office, but signed by his partner. It stated that under the terms of the loan agreement signed between Palliser Wentwood and the partnership of Marcus Hedler, Josiah Butler, Philip Butterworth and Samuel Stokes, since repayment of the debt had not been made by the agreed date, the lands and farmhouse, stock, appurtenances, improvements, vehicles and machinery were forfeit to the said partnership.

'It's not enforceable,' said Abigail bravely. 'The mortgage wasn't legal in the first place.'

'The bailiffs won't care about that.'

'They can't get the bailiffs in without a court order, and they can't get a court order without a hearing, and they can't get a hearing without a legal document. And the only copy of the agreement is so water-damaged that it can't be used in evidence.'

'Hmm,' said Salomé. 'They wouldn't try this if Palliser were here.' Then she added, 'I must say I am rather glad Philip is coming to dinner tonight.'

Abigail and Naomi were allotted the task of making the morning room guest-ready, no mean task, for damp was layered over the room like blankets on a fever victim. The morning room was Palliser's afterthought, *my coup de grâce, darlings, the stroke of civilisation that makes the house a mansion.* Taller by two feet than the rest of the house, its handsome windows looked south, exactly away from the morning sun, with an unparalleled view across the marshy wastes – *Thou coveredst the earth with the deep like as with a garment:*

the waters stand in the hills. The floor was by no means level and the piles extremely suspect.

Its purpose, naturally — surely you don't need to be told? — was to house the morning-room suite, seven pieces of what Palliser claimed was the finest Queen Anne furniture: a chaise-longue, a grandfather chair, a grandmother chair, and four straight-backed visitors' chairs — *don't ever in your wildest dreams inflict them on our guests!* Palliser had bought these for what he called a song — *well perhaps an aria* — from a fine family who had emigrated, taken one look at the marshes and the mountains, and packed up for Home. Having acquired them, he felt the need to accommodate them suitably, and so applied himself to adding on the morning room. Salomé laughed at him, but when the room was finished she had her cousin in France send out wallpaper, maroon and gold stripes, and applied it herself. Consequently, though stark, the morning room was extremely elegant.

The north wall was dominated by a massive Victorian fireplace which Palliser had salvaged after the great earthquake. It was rather cracked and chipped here and there, but naked marble cherubs were discernible. Here Naomi laid a fire after breakfast and stoked it religiously all day. They opened the big sash windows to let the air circulate, and the room grew slowly less oppressive.

Salomé sacrificed a pile of dry towels with which the girls wiped down the walls and dried the marble and the windows. Abigail carefully dabbed at the solitary painting — *The Triumph of Boadicea* — which hung over the mantel. Mighty of arm, and improbably helmeted, Boadicea rose above a sea of Roman bodies. Time and travels had darkened her surroundings, so that she seemed to be conducting her battle in twilight.

The two girls swept the polished boards of the floor punctiliously and spread mats over them. The mats, a motley collection from all over the house, had to be disposed so as to cover the gaps in the floorboards, through which the wind would shortly whistle.

'Poo, this chair smells!' said Naomi, jumping from the grandfather chair.

'Cat or mildew?'

'Both, probably.'

'We must contrive that Mr Butterworth doesn't sit in it. Can't think how.'

'Mum can sit on the chaise-longue and he will sit next to her.'

'Naomi, don't be vulgar.'

They sprinkled the chair with rosewater, which gave it an interesting herbal smell, not easily identifiable as unpleasant. In a cubby-hole in the bottom of the tower, which Palliser called his study, they found an occasional table made of mahogany, buried under a decade of paper. Covered with a lace-edged cloth, it nicely filled the void in the middle of the morning room. They found four sets of triple-branched brass candlesticks, somehow liberated from a Roman Catholic church — *did you never hear the tale of the Bishop's Candlesticks, and the Miserable Jean Valjean? Well these I won from the Cardinal Archbishop of Manila himself in similar circumstances. Yes, Father, yes we're sure you did.* Two they placed on the mantlepiece, two on the hearth. Twelve candles would be too great a challenge, so they compromised on eight.

'Once they're lit it'll be too dark to see the gaps,' said Naomi.

'Flowers,' Abigail decreed.

Naomi got happily rained on, picking daisies and chrysanthemums, late roses and early camellias.

'We're going to use the best things,' Abigail told Salomé. 'We must remind him who we were.'

Salomé said in slightly acid tones that a man who needed that pointing out to him was not worthy to be reminded of it, but nonetheless she unearthed the best lace tablecloth and a few crystal glasses that had miraculously survived earthquake and moving house. Jemima had starched five linen table napkins and proceeded to iron them crisp. The three women had decided to dine in the kitchen, since dining in the morning room meant negotiating too many corners with the table. In the original plan for the house there had been a dining room, but Palliser never quite built it, and made a virtue of this shortcoming by declaring that the best meals in his life had all been eaten in kitchens, so why break the pattern of a lifetime?

They tidied the living area within an inch of its life, which Salomé said was a jolly good thing anyway.

He was invited for six o'clock. At five-thirty Abigail retired to the room she shared with Jemima, to change her clothes.

She looked in the mirror over which she and Jemima jostled of a morning. Like her mother and her father, who treated their handsomeness as so much coin, she had no illusions about her attractions, their limitations and their usefulness. She looked frankly at the girl in the mirror, noted without vanity, that her looks should do to gain her most ends, but noted also with some asperity that the lovely lips she had from her father had yet to be kissed.

She took off her workaday clothes, blue jersey, black skirt and white blouse, and let them fall to the floor. She stood in her satin petticoat and looked at the reflected person in the modest square of mirror. If fashion magazines were to be trusted, then what she saw was fashionably shaped. But she didn't care, for the girl in oyster satin was a stranger to her, an unknown quantity, too like Palliser to be trusted, too unformed and suggestive to be cool and clever Abigail. She looked at the strange girl in dishabille and wondered what it would be like to be her dressing for an intimate dinner with an admirer.

She imagined the heart beating and stomach turning over; she imagined the meticulous choosing of clothes, jewellery and makeup to enhance what was lovely and disguise what was not. And being a modern girl, well educated by her salacious-tongued father, she imagined putting on clothes with a view to having them removed.

She did not think that next Saturday's church social with Tim the butcher would lead to anything as dangerous as a kiss, let alone the removal of any clothing, for she had her sights on loftier targets than a fumble behind the parish hall. When she took off her clothes for a man, if she ever did, it would be a solemn observance, for the sacrifice of Abigail's privacy must not be effected without a suitable price.

Still, she wished for a moment that it was she who was dressing for dinner with Philip, dinner not in the rickety farmhouse but in a silver service restaurant with a spectacular view of mountains, and a menu without prices.

She surveyed her clothes, in what passed for a wardrobe – two tiers of tea chests with a pole suspended between them. Jemima's clothes were jumbled on hangers on one end of the pole, and stuffed into the tea chests, but Abigail's hung precisely, one garment to a hanger. She sighed, for it must be the tiresome old tartan with the blue blouse, nothing redolent of the schoolmarm and nothing sexy. Then she picked up her clothes from the floor and hung each one carefully in its place.

At ten past six, Naomi, in gumboots and a hacked-down army greatcoat over her dress, came charging into the kitchen, saying that Philip's car was crawling along the road, bumping on every pothole. She dashed into her room and shed the coat and gumboots, and came out resplendent in a white lace dress that Jemima and Abigail had both doted upon, and worn about twelve times between them.

Bathsheba, already bathed and in her nightie, and indignant about it, cried out in deepest sibling envy. Jemima, in mourning over Thaddeus's failure to write a letter, was wearing her browns, and Salomé struck a matronly note in maroon crêpe. Abigail was unhappy with this choice, but could not persuade her mother to change; luckily for her amorous intent even maroon crêpe could not disguise Salomé's wonderfully unmatronly figure.

Philip's car crept up to the bridge. Salomé, her old opera-going black coat over head and shoulders, went out into the rain to greet him. Abigail opened two bottles of fruit nectar: apricot and elderberry.

It was such a jolly evening. Philip patently loved the company of the whole family – always had been an *habitué* of the household, before the trouble started, though they had not really noticed him much in those days.

They played Snap, and Strip Jack Naked and Black Bitch. And Palliser's fiendish version of the numbers drinking game, which for some reason he called Toddy and Tallow because it was played with Roman numerals.

Abigail studied her mother and Philip across the table to see how close they had grown. Salomé shone with good humour and attention. She laughed at Philip's jokes, but she did not flirt. As for him, his eyes were round with happiness, but he looked at them all. His attention seemed no more directed to Salomé than to Jemima, or Abigail, or Naomi. *He's in love with us all. Well, that's not good enough.*

They ate and drank well, and the fire burnt merrily.

'The chicken soup,' said Jemima, 'used to be called Hermione.'

'That's most unfair,' said Philip. 'How can I consume her now?'

'I think she'd be happy to know she was useful in death as in life,' said Salomé. 'She was a dutiful fowl.'

44

'Everything you see before you is our own work,' Salomé said. 'Except that my grandmother made the table-cloth, and Abigail bought the lamb with her savings. And we did have a little help in chopping the firewood.'

'I do most of it,' said Naomi, 'but Albert splits the big logs.'

Bathsheba was supposed to be in bed, but kept finding excuses to get up. On one of her excursions she stopped by Philip and asked him, 'Are you our daddy now?'

The women laughed, but Philip answered her solemnly, 'You only have one daddy, and he's my good friend Palliser.'

After Bathsheba had been sent to bed, *this is absolutely the last time*, Philip told a Palliser story . . .

. . . about the time that Palliser conceived an interest in a racehorse whose record inspired no one but himself . . . He related Palliser's herculean efforts to involve others in its career, culminating in an all-night session when Palliser, Philip and others held a vigil in the horse's stall, rubbing it with brandy and feeding it and the jockey concoctions of obscure Irish origin. The acme of the story was that Palliser & Co., and the jockey, all fell fast asleep and missed their race . . .

And another narrative, this one about fishing, and Palliser's notion that trout would respond to music . . .

Philip told stories well; he made them laugh.

But Palliser stories were not going to do the trick at all. Abigail checked the fire in the morning room and shepherded Salomé and Philip in. She replenished the coffee pot and filled Philip's glass with apricot nectar.

'Out,' she said to her sisters, and shut the door behind her.

Delaying just a moment, she heard the scraping of a chair betokening movement. Then quite distinctly she heard him say, 'Salomé, I've been thinking. I have a proposition for you . . .'

The largest space in the world is a double bed with one person; the coldest a double bed long abandoned. She'd thought this many times, lying in it, remembering how it should be. Palliser's long cool body, thin as a drink of water. Refreshing as a drink of water, enlivening – no, more like a good beakerful of fruit nectar, fragrant, full of promise.

How did Palliser smell? She couldn't remember, nor how his voice sounded, nor the feel of his hands. There was no trace of him, not a hair in his hairbrush, not a whisker under his razor. A wardrobe of empty clothes, which might have been a dead man's. She no longer kept his place vacant in the bed, but slept right in the middle of it, spreading out comfortably and sleeping like a baby – yes, exactly like a baby, sleep as sound as death, or, as at present, hours of fretful crying.

If he were dead, would she have mourned as long? Wouldn't she have cleared his clothes out of the house, sold his hairbrushes and his telescope and got on with living? Wouldn't she be a respectable, even desirable widow, her love for Palliser preserved, like a parable in stained glass, glowing with captured colours, fixed, admirable, and unable to interfere. Instead, it was a reproach, an ulcer, something to be hidden and not referred to, though no one was fooled. A woman in love, abandoned: pathetic, embarrassing. And a woman no longer young. She knew what they said in the village: . . . *left her for something younger, I'll be bound. Always had a roving eye. And more than an eye. Did I ever tell you . . . poor woman, that damp, useless place, those great big girls, getting out of hand . . . silly woman, I say, a bit of a snob, always thought she was better than us. That voice, that la-de-da manner. Well, who's better*

*now? Got an eviction order. Mortgagee sale, I heard . . . never
see him again. Couldn't show his face here after all that. Owes
hundreds. Mrs Stokes told me . . . Nancy Hedler told me . . .
I heard . . .*

In Palliser's make-believe, life was more real than real, a
fairy tale in brilliant colours. Everything not included in
the tale was grey and insubstantial, could be laughed off.
Palliser would have laughed off the eviction notice. She had
hung it on the wall and given it mocking glances, trying to
see it as he would see it, a scrap of paper. They could not be
serious, Samuel Stokes and Marc Hedler and Josiah Butler.
They were too ridiculous to be serious. Men so minuscule,
he would say, little Lilliput men, could not throw giantess
Salomé out of her house. It was an oversight, a bureaucratic
jumble, a piece of farce.

She loved him because he made the tiresome funny, he
made the bullies risible, he made the cold exhilarating and
the heat luxurious. That was the second-worst thing about
his absence: life had been so gloriously unreal for so long
that reality, faced alone, seemed intolerably dull and dreary.
The worst thing was that he had left her to fend for herself
without a self to fend.

Tears, idle tears, I know not what they mean.

One of Pally's poems. He had one for every occasion;
some of them were appropriate, some of them were absurd.
I know very well what these tears mean. They mean I am
angry and lonely and afraid. And you have left me, and
therefore it seems that you love me no more, and without
you and your infernal love I am nothing.

Nothing, nothing. You made me who I am – created
me a Salomé in your own image – fascinating, desirable,
splendid. You made me laugh and you made me love
myself because I was the object of your love. So without you, with the creator suddenly withdrawn from the

project, what happens to Salomé? She danced her dance for you, just as you taught her, veil after veil, and now you look the other way, now she is no longer young.

Before Palliser she was in stasis – Sleeping Beauty, he had called her, clambering on to her balcony and gesturing to the invisible wall of thorns. She hadn't been offended – how could she be offended by one so charming? And it was true; she had been in something resembling sleep. Going through the motions – dancing, riding, flirting, reading, walking, always walking, to and fro, to and fro along the terraces of the hotels of Europe, looking out beyond the jewelled gardens, looking out towards the invisible sea, up and down, up and down, to burn off the undeclared energy. Evening after evening, spring dusk turning into autumn chill, year folding into year, and still nothing. The horizon blank, the parade cycling round and round before her, dull, dull, dull.

And then Palliser.

She never had any illusions about him, magician though he was. He must marry money. He was clearly in some disgrace, for his immediate family was wealthy and he had nothing but debts. There were deep questions hanging over Palliser, from the very beginning. Salomé declined to ask them; her parents knew too little to ask, and when they did, it was too late. Salomé was a cause lost to reason.

Unreason ruled in their life together. Reason stated that he would pursue a woman endowed with money, youth and beauty; unreason decreed that he should also love her. She had never doubted that he loved her, for Palliser, curiously for such a tale-teller, seemed, as far as one could make out, to tell the truth about his heart. Reason stated that a young woman sentenced to a life of repetitious propriety should fall for a handsome adventurer; unreason dictated that she should love him with fiery determination when his crimes and deceptions began to be uncovered, and should follow him to the ends of the earth, laughing and growing in love with him more and more.

Then he was gone. Unreasonably.

Oh surely he must love her still? How was it possible even for such a performer as Palliser to counterfeit such love? If he were here, anywhere near, wouldn't his love spring up for her, as strong as ever, just as desire springs up in the presence of the beloved? And as for her, if she saw his shape at the end of the valley she'd run all the way, as he turned his cartwheels down dirt tracks, the silly darling fool.

But he is not anywhere near. Wherever he is, it's too far away for my love to reach. He can't hear me crying, though he must know that I do. No letter, no word. Thoughts don't reach that far; feelings don't stretch over years and miles of silence.

Even Salomé's love wasn't – wasn't . . . wasn't enough. She'd said it now. Not enough to cancel out her abandonment. She had thought her devotion to Palliser was a fire that would never go out. She had thought that, whatever he did, she would not cease to love him. But she had thought wrong. She did not know that anger and loneliness would be stronger than love. The poets, like Palliser, talked nothing but fine nonsense. She tossed and turned in a cold bed. Without the conviction of her love, what did she have left to warm her? Palliser, and Palliser only, had taken away the chill of her early life. He set her alight, and now she was huddled over the dying fire.

That was her choice. Renounce the best and warmest thing in the world, or huddle down, pretending. Either way she would grow cold.

My heart in the midst of my body is even like melting wax.

I shall commence to die without my life, my love.

I have commenced to die already. Slow cold is creeping into my heart.

If he lives, if he loves me, he would make some sign. Even

Palliser, the motley man himself, must live by that rule. If he be not subject to the simple rule of love, then all the world is topsy-turvy, without rhyme or reason. A man who kills a woman might claim he loved her; but love's rules say he did not. By definition. A man who abandons his wife to poverty might claim he loved her, but humanity says that he does not.

And even the rules of unreason must draw their line to hold out madness.

I will not let my love become a madness. I will not love in the face of reason.

And yet, I do, I do.

He swung up the hotel balcony, his favourite trick, and was sitting on the balustrade smoking a cigar. She was stamping up and down her bedroom, in her white silk night-dress, brushing her hair, angry strokes, down, down, down, because he had ignored her all evening. Dancing with the dowagers, winning smiles and pats from them, sizing up their bosoms and their fortunes. Oh she'd have hated him if she hadn't loved him then. She smelt the cigar smoke and there he was, comfortable as a cat on a cushion, his thin frame balanced on the stone.

Why did you treat me like that? she stormed. She hadn't known how to be so angry. Even anger around him was a pleasure. And he smiled and told her a tale. Did she believe his reasons?

Fiction was as good as fact, it was indistinguishable from fact, from his lips. The lips she wanted to kiss so much that she stopped hearing the honey words that dripped from them. He didn't offer to kiss her, or move from his perch, just drew her with his beautiful honey mouth until she moved towards him, night-dress, hairbrush and all. Oh the kisses, oh the promises.

One word, that's all it will take, one stupid word on a scrap of paper, one message handed from person to person, Palliser sends his love, Palliser says he'll be back when he's –

– when he's what? Extracted himself from his new love, told her enough tales to sneak away for a week or month? been discharged from prison, thrown out of the army, jumped ship, been washed up on the shore and rowed to home? what will it take now to bring him home . . .

Love that cannot breathe a word surely will not draw a man home again.

Why do you treat me like this? When one tremor of your voice, one echo of your voice over the mountains would set me trembling and bind me to you for another span of years. So little a gesture for so long enduring.

No more. I'm tired of this, and so is Salomé. We've had enough of lovesick girlishness. Be a woman, Salomé.

Take what you can get. File for divorce, take nice Mr Butterworth, since he's the best going, and forget the romance of your girlhood. It's all over, woman, like a trip to the funfair, riot and colour but eventually the money runs out and you're left with sticky fingers and a crumple of tickets. Outside under the streetlights, the young daredevil is quite dull, and the walk home awfully long.

The young daredevil – his derring-do was harmless when he told it, and bitter, dangerous, sordid in the mouth of his enemies. The same facts, such different stories. Look at the Palliser stories from a different perspective. Take the story about Mrs Kingston's daughter . . .

So many shadows had hung over Palliser as a young man that she'd given up trying to cast light on him. She found out why his family disinherited him – or one of the reasons; then why he was thrown out of medical school – or one of the reasons; then why his godfather cut him off without a shilling – or one of the reasons. Such a catalogue of seduction, drunkenness and vandalism, so lightly borne.

Don't tell me any more tales! she shouted at him on their honeymoon.

So she never found out why he had been refused a commission, or why he had fled Ireland as if the dogs were at his heels. If she had to imagine all the abandoned women with their dresses torn at the bosom, she might find herself in their number. She must believe that there was some qualitative difference in her story or she could not allow herself to love him.

In the cold the stories came back to her; ghosts that had lurked in her memory waiting for this moment. Stories he had told her himself, whose truth she had no reason to doubt. Mrs Kingston's daughter, for instance.

Mrs Kingston and her daughter. Mrs Kingston, blowsy, busty, endowed with some money and rather more appetite, who devoured young Palliser for breakfast and lunch, and then with him connived to serve up her sixteen-year-old daughter as aperitif. The daughter must be initiated into the mysteries of womanhood, and who better to do it than the insatiable, light-fingered young Mr W.?

But what about the girl, what about the young body and the young heart? What did you tear that afternoon between lunch and dinner, that you could not mend?

How could such a tale be amusing? But he told the story and made it amusing, made himself a madcap hero of the boudoir. Exploitation and depravity, funny.

Not any more; neither that escapade – *escapade* – nor the forcing of the Provost's daughter's window, nor the insults in Latin painted on the Dean's doorstep beside a neat pile of turds, nor any other of the hilarious and disgusting stories; none of them had the power to amuse. Palliser's enemies were right after all: he did deserve punishment – disinheritance, banishment. He was a man to be shunned. He was despicable.

Mr Butterworth may well be dull, by your count, he

may be a good butt for your jokes, a straight man for your comedy turn, but he's no rapist; he's no vandal, no drunken hooligan, spreading his turds and his semen about and laughing at others' discomfort. He would not force himself into a woman's bedroom and call it gallantry. He is civilised, gentle, agreeable, well-mannered and educated. And comfortable. All the best things in the world, things you are not.

You won't getter better, not here, not today, you won't getter better, Palliser often said, down at the saleyards when he was auctioning cattle. Well, that's perfectly all right, I may take him or I may not. And then, thank you, maybe I don't need one at all. Sleep, sleep, without dream, the sleep of a good woman who has worked hard and lived honestly, whose only fault is that she is a good woman. Sleep in the release from the bondage of romance, the subjugation called love by poets. Sleep in the freedom of being Salomé without Palliser.

Early Monday morning the law came thumping on the door, having bumped up the farm road in an old truck.

On the front doorstep Samuel Stokes and, stationed at his side, Finian, the policeman from the next village, long and lugubrious, and twitching for his breakfast cuppa. Samuel Stokes, genuinely unmoved; just something that had to be done. That's why they sent him; put on his best suit, though. A sense of occasion, if not a sense of honour. He handed Salomé a paper.

Salomé had risen at dawn, as always, so that no one, seen or unseen, might ever reproach her. Only Bathsheba was with her, bathing her dolls in front of the kitchen fire; the other girls, having no concept of reproach, preferred sleep.

'You can't evict us,' she said spitting fire at him, poor blob of lard, not worthy of combustion. 'The mortgage is *sub judice*, and Mr Butterworth himself has agreed to a stay of proceedings. I have a letter —'

'It's not the eviction, Missus,' said Finian the policeman into his moustache. 'I suggest you peruse this paper.'

She perused it, too proud to go for her glasses, but it was writ large, in careful copyhand, probably by Mrs Stokes herself.

Debtor to Stokes Family Grocers and Drapers

To groceries items:
   3mths: £45 3s.
   6mths: £28 10s.

To draperies items (cloth, thread, strip leather, hot water bottle, corks for wine bottles, trimming lace):
   3 mths: £18 2s. 6d.

'Do you dispute any of the items?' asked Samuel Stokes carefully, rehearsing a prepared lesson. *Eight twelves are ninety-six.*

Salomé laughed.

'I dispute that corks are an item of drapery.'

'So you dispute the bill?'

'Not at all. I'm sure Mrs Stokes's arithmetic is impeccable. But I am not in a position to pay it, as you know very well, Mr Stokes.'

'Then you leave me no alternatives.' *Eleven twelves are one hundred and thirty-two.*

'I have no alternatives either, Mr Stokes, but I intend to pay your bill as soon as I am able. I am, of course, a woman of my word.'

This wasn't in Mr Stokes's script. Finian, impassioned by his desire for his wife's kitchen, took over.

'I'm sorry m', the law states I am empowered to seize goods to the valyer of one hundred pounds.'

'The bill only amounts to ninety-one pounds fifteen shillings and sixpence,' said Salomé.

Bathsheba trailed to the door, and held her dolls up for Mr Stokes to approve.

'Look at the lacy dresses I made them. Jemima helped.'

Mr Stokes did not register the shamefully inessential lace trimmings formed into little dresses – dresses of the kind Salomé sincerely hoped no daughter of hers would ever wear.

'Administerating costs,' said Finian.

Stokes ventured over the doorstep and stood on the cocoa-matting in the hallway, looking about for items of value.

'I don't think I have goods to the value of ninety-one or a hundred pounds. You may remove my husband's clothes if you wish, but I doubt that they will fetch twenty.'

'No personal effects.'

'Then, gentlemen, I must send you away empty-handed.' *You are not having his telescope. I am entitled to my memories.*

'Not so fast,' said Stokes. Salomé tried not to smile, for neither man seemed capable of any speed. 'What's in here?'

He pointed to the morning-room door, tight shut to discourage its particular brand of dampness from spreading through the house. Had Mr Stokes ever crossed the portal of the morning room? Whether he had or no, he would know the legend of the morning-room furniture. Must it not be valuable, for a man to build a room to contain it?

Mrs Stokes wanted a selection of this furniture for herself. She wanted to be queen of the valley, and tell the tale of its provenance. She would not tell her visitors, perched on the woeful straight-back chairs, that the furniture was seized. She would imply it had been paid for fair and square.

Salomé laughed. Let her have the triumph, if that was the extent of her battlefield.

She flung open the morning-room door to reveal Palliser's pride and joy. All seven pieces disposed stiffly around the dead fireplace, a family too well brought up to move or to complain.

Who wants Palliser's horrible Irish youth relived twelve thousand miles away, in the middle of a swamp? Who cares about the drawing rooms of syphilitic old Europe? Not me, not Salomé. Not any more.

'Take it, gentlemen, if it settles your debt. Take it all.'

'But Mrs Wentwood — Salomé —' cried Stokes, floundering, 'all this is worth —'

'There will be other debts, no doubt.'

'Not sure,' said Finian.

'Mr Stokes,' said Salomé, favouring him with her most queenly smile, 'this furniture is valuable as a set. It has been together since it was made in the days of Queen Anne. Each piece alone will fetch a fraction of its worth as part of the whole. Take it all or take none of it.'

'But I don't want —'

'Mr Stokes, I am a very busy woman. I have four daughters to care for and a farm to run. I am sure you are equally busy, and Mr Finian is clearly on a tight timetable. Do not waste my time or your own. Remove this furniture, give me a receipt and be gone.'

She drew herself up by the morning-room fireplace, centuries of command coming to her aid. Thus we spoke to the tradesmen who bothered us with bills; thus we spoke to the tenant farmers who demanded maintenance; thus we spoke to the vulgar reformers who would alienate our ancient rights. Thus we affect poverty and make it honourable; thus we take the advantage when we should by rights be the loser.

Mr Stokes and Finian, lost for words, looking like

lumpen schoolboys in the courts of Byzantium, began to carry out the morning-room furniture and load it on the truck. Salomé urged them to swaddle it in sacks and take extreme care. Four journeys to the truck it took them, the first carrying the chaise-longue between them. The truck was not designed for such large and awkward loads. The sight of exquisite cabriolet legs poking up from the tray more commonly used for taking pigs to market filled her with glee. She was transported by the thought of telling Palliser what had happened to his wonderful grandfather chair, swathed in Stokes's flour sacks and stacked up in the corner among trampled straw and split lentils.

But she kept her face straight as she watched the procession from the house to the truck, standing vigilantly by her gate to prevent accidental damage to the garden.

Naomi climbed out of her bedroom window in ragged trousers, red spotted scarf and one of her father's patched shirts, and was preparing to leap on the plunderers.

'No pirating, Naomi. Not today.'

'Dang!' said Naomi and climbed on to the roof, where she contented herself with pulling clods out of the gutter and throwing them down.

'Not on the furniture, Naomi.'

'Course not, Cap'n,' she said and dropped a handful of rotted moss neatly on to Mr Stokes's shoulder.

Clutching her receipt, Salomé saw them off the property, and then allowed herself to laugh. Her laughter rang across the damp acres of her farm; she felt it would reach the mountains and echo about, rolling up into a great wave of sound, up and over the world until it reached Palliser — he'd hear the mockery and triumph and wince with pain, not knowing who was laughing at him or why. One day he'd walk into an auction room, in Salisbury or La Paz, and there it would be, all seven lovely displaced pieces of it, just like himself, elegant and useless, costing lots of money and absurdly out of date.

III

To HIS REGRET, Palliser was in a very prosaic place, a small market town in Hertfordshire, England. From there he could not hear Salomé's laughter ringing through the world towards him, although he often heard its echo in his head, as he thought he remembered it.

I have been faithful to thee, Cynara! in my fashion.

No one knew what Palliser would do next, not even Palliser himself. In his life he had had good ideas, cornucopias of good ideas, packed down, running over, pouring out of his dreams into his lap.

Now he had run out of ideas. He had one left, and it was a long, long shot, and humiliating into the bargain.

It was a law of nature that a man of Palliser's stamp should have wealth. First, he looked like a gentleman. Second, he had so many excellent ways of disposing of it. Third, when enmoneyed, he was a bigger thing altogether, he was as nature intended.

Nature had clearly intended him to be a man of means, but society had slipped up in the execution of nature's plan. Palliser did not rail at either – railing was not his style – for he considered that nature had dealt him quite a pretty hand, and society had granted him ample opportunities to play it out in congenial circumstances. And though he had had more than his measure of success in the existential card game, somehow the pool was never quite sufficient to his needs.

The question now was: how to maximise those advantages he had left, from nature and society, in order to perfect nature's plan, fulfil biological destiny, and make Palliser a rich man, and his family minions of fortune?

Thus he stood in an upper bedroom of the White Hart Hotel, in the early hours of a Home Counties dawn, taking stock of himself, and peering into the small square of speckled glass furnished grudgingly by the hotel management as if it was their duty to guard against vanity.

Jesus, you'd think we were in a convent.

Are there rags and tatters of handsomeness to trade on? Teeth – crooked, and not complete, but white, and all my own. Something engaging, I think, about slightly imperfect, but essentially fine teeth. Creating a splendid smile, which is hard to resist. The lips – who am I to judge them? But evidence leads me to the conclusion that they are tasty.

Well, and the eyes – arctic blue, perilously exciting, fit to tear open a woman's heart and cause her to cast caution to the winds. It is scarcely my fault if nature gave me such eyes.

A manly stubble on the chin, but the brow smooth and noble, betokening nobility; the nose ditto, most aristocratic. But the hair now, distinctly in retreat, with too much silver for a pauper.

What else have we to offer? Six foot two in his socks, with his shoes (Guardsman's shine) parked tidily under your bed, and a long lean, highly serviceable body therein. Honey tongue, good company, fit for any circumstance from the high table to the pub. Many minor talents – the ability to dance any step, to vault a horse and swing from the parallel bars, the capacity to doctor a cow and conduct a fluent auction, to sing loudly the tenor part of most Welsh hymns. To drain a swamp and grow the most splendid vegetables.

(O Salomé, Salomé.)

Now with these manifest talents, what can a man do?

As a young man, the line was clear: marry a rich woman, that was the ticket. Fortune had been kind, and put in his path Salomé – delightful, steely enough to follow him to the end of the earth, and copiously endowed with wealth. Nature and society had smiled upon him then. Surely they must do so again? As a young man it had been necessary to put himself about to find Salomé, and once found, work had been required to win her. Once again it was necessary to put himself about, but the course was now more cluttered. With wife, daughters, mortgages and grey hair.

He paced away from his scrap of mirror and stood at the window. It was a square sash with furry deposits in the corners, and scatterings of mould on the base of the glass. The paint peeled along the frame in runnels; and he knew from jolting experience that the upper frame would not stay up unassisted.

He lifted it nonetheless, and swung his orang-utan body out to sit on the sill, jamming the window open with the curve of his back. In the street below the street-cleaner was inching its way along, roaring with subdued displeasure at the garbage in the gutters.

To be late to bed is to be up betimes!

He had not been to bed, he remembered, but no consequence, by Corydon! A man of Palliser's stamp worked best without sleep. As long as he could shave himself without cuts. A shaving cut would do his cause no good.

The song of the street-sweeper threatened to turn into a lullaby, and he leaned back against the window, seeing the sun rise over the dull wet roofs, turning them to gingerbread.

The brushes whirred up and back, like gigantic dental machinery, and the pavements, clean and wet for a moment, might have been fairy-tale gold-paved.

The streets of London (and possibly of the towns surrounding her) are paved with gold.

And why not? Why should our ordinary tales not have fairy-tale endings?

I'll come back a rich man, in a black limousine. You'll come out to meet me, dancing and singing, beating your tambourines and clanking with gold chains.

He could not go home without money, not now that he had been gone so long. If he were penniless, he could no more dismount from a bus and walk up the long muddy stretch between his gate and his doorstep than he could fly to the moon.

The wider the gap stretched between him and his home, the longer the silence grew, the more imperative it was that he return rich.

The first year or so he had been content with adventuring. He had been drunk on freedom and possibility. There were so many places on the map, so many countries, and he had been too long stuck in the bottom corner of the world. He jumped on and off trains and ferries, rarely with a ticket, relying on his stature and his best suit to disentangle him from trouble. He worked his passage on a liner between Manila and Hong Kong; then carried a highly suspect battered brown suitcase from Hong Kong to Valletta. At Valletta he was relieved of the suitcase by another containing enough English pound notes to keep him in style for six months. He declined to make the return journey, by simply disappearing.

Many waters cannot entirely drown a chap's sense of honour.

Eventually he washed up in England, more or less where he had started from twenty-five years before, with a pair of hand–made shoes, a suit that should see him to the grave, a silk dressing gown and a five–pound note. He found he was tired of adventuring; bars in exotic locations were bars, and cafés remarkably unchanging. Ports and women smelt much the same. The necessity to make his fortune, or his living, did not change.

This morning, as the street–sweeper inched its way along, spraying and swirling, Palliser once more rehearsed the articles of his profession. Last night's vomit and crumpled tickets disappeared into the machine's maw. Palliser's ideas spilled out in abundance – at m' best after a night's drinking, drink clears away the litter of living, makes a man creative and prophetic. A drunk man sees the truth, and shouts it from the rooftops.

> *I cried for madder music, and for stronger wine,*
> *Flung roses, roses riotously with the throng*

He had one last scheme. It had been in his head for some time, but it seemed the last resort, and he had rejected it more than once. Carrying the battered suitcase from Hong Kong to Valletta had not seemed as dishonourable as the scheme he had in mind. He could no longer tot up the different jobs, of varying degrees of meniality, that he had done, but he had always drawn the line.

Curious, he thought, stretching his long arms over his head to greet the dawn, about that line. He could hear his mother's voice, echoing across the vastness of the bleak drawing room, ever so refined her voice, working over the traces of Irish but never rubbing them out. Poor woman, she never recovered from the knowledge that she was a lesser being than the Wentwoods, knowledge her mother–in–law, the fearsome Grandmamma, laboured over many years to inculcate. Poor woman, Palliser thought, though she was as distant to him as Ireland itself, poor woman, she dedicated her life to preserving what she perceived as the class values of the Wentwoods.

One mustn't, one didn't, we have never, it's our duty to, it's our custom to. How Irish you sound, Palliser.

Such a fog all that, the drawing room, the bone china (which broke so exquisitely – *Another teacup! One is reduced to such appalling help nowadays – if one reprimands them for clumsiness they simply up and leave for the next place. I'd stop it out of her wages, but she always denies breaking them*).

Palliser chuckled to himself. *Like many of the upper class, he liked the sound of breaking glass.*

Amazing how his mother's voice was still so clear through all that fog!

One doesn't. We have never. It is so far beneath the line that we do not even need to mention it.

But the same class values of his upbringing dictated that a gentleman must have means; a gentleman may marry for money, but a gentleman does not divorce an honourable wife, nor does a gentleman commit bigamy. A gentleman may be temporarily embarrassed, and may engage in a suitable occupation. But a gentleman never, never, under any circumstances, no matter how reduced, goes into service.

Alas, Mother, there is no other way to get near money but to serve it.

And Joseph was brought down to Egypt; and Potiphar, an officer, an Egyptian, bought him of the hands of the Ishmaelites, and the Lord was with Joseph, and he, that is Potiphar, was a prosperous man.

He had selected the White Hart Hotel for its capacious baths and its extreme cheapness. He also liked its location, which allowed him to sit in his window and look down at the haunts of the wealthy. He studied them as they slipped from their silent cars into the tea-shops, banks and department stores below. In the twenty years that he had been labouring in the countryside he had lost touch with the urban rich, and needed to remind himself of their ways.

His study so far had led him to the conclusion that they had not changed. They were much as he remembered them from his youth, when he had rubbed shoulders with varieties of the rich and landed in hotels and ballrooms, round gambling and dinner tables: they remained as ever obsessed with status and paranoid about being overcharged. The meanness of the rich never ceased to amaze him, nor their passion for appearances. This cut both ways, he remembered: if one looked the part, they would accept one into their number. Looking the part was all he had left.

Seated in the window, he fumbled with the laces of his shoes, his beloved shoes, crafted, he liked to explain, by gnarled peasants who lived only to make shoes, from leather softened between the thighs of Spanish virgins. Succeeding in untying them, he swung back into the room and let them slide neatly on to the floor. He loosened his tie, and found it already loose, his black French silk tie, which had witnessed things no self-respecting tie should mention. He leaned against the window frame and closed his eyes. If he fell asleep in his good suit, he would wake rumpled, which would cost him effort to undo. Take the trouble now, Pally, it will repay you. He removed his suit languorously piece by piece, wishing, as he always did, that a woman was doing this for him. He laid it lovingly on the single chair; it still had the power to please. Folded his socks and shirt and put them on the floor; he would wash them later. Lay down in his undershirt and underpants and fell at once asleep.

When he awoke several hours later, like a giant refreshed with wine, he sat straight up and recited the Lord's Prayer, as was his custom, with the sweet Irish lilt of his nanny.

Then he leapt from the bed and performed his routine of gymnastic exercises, reciting throughout, for reasons lost in the mists of time, lines by Miss Christina Rossetti:

> *Raise me a dais of silk and down*
> *Hang it with vair and purple dyes.*
> *Carve it with doves and pomegranates*
> *And peacocks with a hundred eyes . . .*
>
> *Because the birthday of my life*
> *Is come, my love is come to me.*

He saw Salomé preparing a soft bed for him, taking down her luscious hair, turning towards him and smiling, loosening her dressing gown – then Salomé's charms tumbled up with those of numerous other women, more recent but less distinct.

Exercise over, he threw on his silk dressing gown, apparel fit for a prince of the realm, and went down to take his bath, an unfailingly pleasant experience, and wash his clothes, an unfailingly unpleasant experience. He had one good suit and two of everything else, and had to wash and iron one set every day, otherwise he would slip and present an inappropriate image. One of his shirts was beginning to show wear around the cuffs, and must be immediately mended and soon replaced. But how, but how? He cleaned his shoes, brushed his suit, dressed and descended, most glorious, in pursuit of a breakfast.

Mrs Winifred Hogg managed the White Hart Hotel, a brisk, glossy woman, over whom no one had ever put one. Palliser, sensing no contest, had never attempted to put one of any kind over. She always made him a fresh pot of tea. Her liking did not stretch to breakfast. He had various ruses for that, but first he made the most of his tea.

'Well, Winifred,' he said, 'what chance of breakfast?'

Across the kitchen table, like an old married couple, a brown teapot as glossy as Mrs Hogg between them. It was Mrs Hogg's elevenses. Mrs Hogg had possession of the newspaper and kept her bread bin as firmly closed as her knees.

'You know the score, Mr Wentwood. Five guineas a week excluding meals. You owe me ten guineas at present.'

Mrs Hogg smoothed the paper and read him a tidbit about Princess Margaret.

'As luck would have it, I have ten pounds on my person. A run of luck.'

'Guineas, Mr Wentwood. And I suppose you were playing poker in my back parlour all night. I shall lose my licence. And I dare say you have a wide sleeve in that suit of yours.'

Palliser bestowed upon her his most irresistible smile. He counted out ten pounds and ten shillings.

'May one have breakfast?'

'On tick? No. Half a crown.'

Palliser sighed theatrically and counted out five sixpenny pieces.

'Chap I was talking to last night,' said Palliser, 'was telling me tall tales of a family hereabouts called Lovelace.'

'Not so tall,' said Mrs Hogg, busy with breakfast, 'I'll be bound. They're the bigwigs round here for sure and certain. Not that they do a darned thing about it. You never catch them heading a committee or holding a coffee morning. Never darken the doors of a church, not a regular parish church anyrate. Own everything from Brent Bottom to Childers Green. It's all leased out. The grandfather made his money in diamonds in South Africa. Then there's the grand house over Thule, off the London Road, great cold tomb of a place. No one gets asked up there. Not that you'd care to go – very strange people, those Lovelaces. Something not quite right in that family. You can tell by looking at them. Bad blood, I should say, or a touch of the tarbrush. My friend Mrs Gray used to do for them up there, in the old days, when Mrs Lovelace was alive, not that she was there ever, always on the Riveera, then after she died, the two of them were still at school.'

'Indeed,' said Palliser, leaning forward and opening wide his eyes.

'And mean,' said Mrs Hogg, warming to her tale, 'like all rich folk, only more so. A pound sticks to the pocket, but with them it's like a religion. Rich enough to put lights in every window of that great big pile and a fire in every room, but you never see it lit, not even at Christmas. My friend Mrs Gray gave it up then, after Mrs Lovelace died. She said it was too gloomy rattling round there when it was empty, and worse when they were home from school – the two of them, such a strange, spooky pair. Like fairground freaks, she used to say, aristocracy or not.

'Now they've got some live-in help, a foreign woman. Comes in here for a port on market days, ever so refeened, but no better than she should be by all accounts, and I believe them. And the son!'

Palliser replenished their teacups, and moved his chair into intimate proximity.

'The foreign woman – calls herself Mrs, but I don't know. And that boy, looks more like a girl, long blond hair flopping all over his eyes. Never been to school; she brings him in here, schooldays or not, you know, carrying the shopping. Oh yes, she has to take the bus, though there's a perfectly good car sitting in the stables. You see that Mr Hubert drive it sometimes. Rolls-Royce. Shocking waste. The place has gone to rack and ruin – they can't get help of course – too mean and too proud, I'll be bound . . .

'Well I've got work to do, Mr W., even if you haven't.'

She swept up, leaving him breakfast and her *Daily Mail*. He relaxed into the paper, long legs under the table. He read with fascination about a medical pamphlet called *Is Chastity Outmoded?*, which got him worrying about the virtue of his girls. He took out his pen, a sheet of the White Hart's writing paper and began:

> *Dearest heart, I cannot describe how miserably I miss you. I have been in this polite but dull town for three dreary months, picking up a living as best I can, as auctioneer and occasional tenor lay clerk in the Abbey choir.*

How could he explain to Salomé that he was breakfasting on toast, eggs, bacon as pink as an infant's tongue, frilly and crisp, with a tomato lightly grilled for ballast? Four pieces of toast, handsome slabs of butter, the kitchen's very own jar of Oxford Bitter Thick-Cut Marmalade, and a big pot of tea, when she was probably, at this very moment, making the porridge for five come out even, and poking yesterday's bread for sponginess? How could he explain why, since he left home, he had never found it necessary to make himself a pot of tea? It was Salomé's pattern of life to swill the teapot with hot water, carefully measure out the black leaf, wait patiently while the kettle reached peak performance, lay out the tea-strainer, the clean china cups . . . He did not think himself above such things; could he be blamed if his lot fell out that way?

Mrs Hogg banged her head around the door, like a disgruntled comedian peering round a curtain. 'You're not going to believe this,' she declared, 'but Blanche Lovelace just sailed into Hampton's.'

Palliser was suddenly a rush of energy. On his feet, pulling on his jacket, brushing his shoulders, he glanced in the hall mirror (much larger than that in his bedroom) and was out the door. Opposite, the big glass doors of

Hampton's department store were closing behind Miss Blanche Lovelace, the doorman resuming his statutory position. Palliser sprinted across the street, dodging a delivery van and two bicycles and eliciting several toots. He did not wait for the doorman, but pushed into the store, becoming nonchalant the instant he was inside the hallowed halls.

Nothing in Mrs Hogg's potted biography had prepared him for Miss Lovelace in the flesh. She was, in the most flattering of metaphors, a galleon of a woman, and much younger than he'd expected, about twenty-two or twenty-three. Huge, fleshy, and very tall, she sailed across the floor tightly braced into a coat of crimson camel-hair, tacking determinedly towards the home furnishings counter. It was early in the day, and although a kind summer's morning, neither Easter nor Christmas nor Mother's Day nor Valentine's Day approached or receded. Custom was quiet in the great emporium. Behind the counters of Ladies' Wear, Hosiery, Haberdashery, Gentlemen's Outfitting, Millinery, gentlewomen in black dresses and straitened circumstances held themselves erect, neither smiling nor exactly grim. Tidying their stock, they waited, as women do the world over, for something to happen.

Miss Lovelace, by contrast, was making things happen in Home Furnishings. Several attendant gentlemen, slightly bowed, were rallying around her, as she flung open on the counter her parcels. Even from a distance her complaint was clear. *These fabrics do not match these cushions!*

As a young man, Palliser Wentwood had been famous, first at St Edwards, then in drawing rooms in Dublin, then in the Aldershot and District Players, and in other places besides, as an actor. He specialised in elegant heroes and upper-class villains. Typecasting, said the envious; a natural, said his many fans. He made a great mark in the plays of Pinero and Wilde, Shaw, Ibsen, Chekhov, Barrie and Galsworthy, and in farces, French or Aldwych.

It was said that when Mr Palliser Wentwood strolled on to the stage one was instantly transported from a stage to a drawing room.

Subsequently, forgoing amateur theatricals, he had used his theatrical talents to other ends. And he did so today.

He sauntered towards Home Furnishings for all the world as if he were a good-natured chap who had been pressed into company, and was waiting for his fair companion to finish her business. He positioned himself by a rack of cushions, twelve different styles, each in its cubbyhole, and a sheaf of materials running down beside them, so one could choose the fabric and consider the cushion, along with varieties of piping and frill. Palliser browsed as if he might conceivably be interested in cushions some time in the future.

A sales attendant approached him, politely inclined.

'No, no, just, you know . . .' Palliser said in his best silly-ass voice and waved his hand towards Miss Lovelace.

He assumed the posture of a man waiting for a beloved but exasperating woman, out of her line of sight but in clear view of the attendants. It was not the first time he had done this trick, though never, of course, in Hampton's.

He set to study his prey. Above all subjects of study, Palliser revelled in and excelled at the study of women, and now was the time to put into practice all his observance. But the scrutiny of Miss Lovelace almost defeated him. He found it difficult to see her. For one thing, crimson was not her colour, and there was such a quantity of crimson cladding her frame. For another, there was so much of Miss Lovelace. She was as tall as Palliser himself, something he had always fantasised about, but which, encountered, made him uncomfortable. She wore no makeup or adornment of any kind, and her hair was cruelly confined into tight waves by venerable tortoiseshell clips. All that was visible of her person, above and below the acreage of crimson, was in such contrast as to suggest a person made up in a children's game of head-body-feet. Her face was in proportion to the body, substantial as a ship's figurehead, great big white cheeks and rolls of fat under the chin, a brow as wide as Pegwell Bay, eyes half hidden in the plenitude of padding. But the mouth, ah, thought Palliser, the mouth – tiny and sweet, perfect, cowering away from the world, afraid to be found out. And the skin of her cheeks and neck (such of the neck as could be seen above the gingery fur of the coat collar), what peerless soft whiteness, and what that softness implied about the body. He thought fleetingly of the body, the munificence of untouched whiteness, a drowning in flesh . . . He gulped and concentrated on the feet.

The feet, far too dainty, were strapped into splendid but ancient crocodile-skin shoes, rescued from some long-gone shoe cupboard and pressed into service. Absurdly, they had short stubby heels, which raised Miss Lovelace another, completely unnecessary inch.

But oh, how terrifying was the cumulative effect!

The curtain fabric did not match the cushions, she announced in a voice as deep and uninviting as the late queen empress, *and both were guaranteed to be from the same bolt! And now they were cut out, it was such a tremendous waste!*

Like Palliser, the senior salesman had difficulty seeing the discrepancy in the fabrics, and had to be marched to the front door to see for himself in daylight. Palliser lounged against the counter and yawned.

'Miss Lovelace has a few things on her mind,' he said to the junior salesmen.

'Yes, we understand that, sir.'

'Can't see it with the curtains m'self, but women, you know . . .'

'Is sir perhaps interested in something in the furnishing line?'

'Well I generally leave all that stuff to Blanche, you

know, but I must say I find it pretty interesting myself. I'm quite intrigued by this –'

– and he wove them into his web.

Miss Lovelace returned to the counter and gave her instructions, including the address to which the goods were to be delivered.

She moved on without giving Palliser a second glance; he uttered a hasty *I say!* and dashed after her.

Fortunately for his deception, she turned a sharp corner and descended to the tea rooms. Palliser bounced down parallel with her, as a gentleman might, and turned briskly away at the bottom of the stairs.

He spent a few minutes perusing the hairbrushes, then walked into the tea rooms with a mighty air, and strode across the concourse, where the ladies sat in cosy pairs, bending over their gossip. The heads were raised, in a wave of blue and silver. Miss Lovelace's head also lifted for a moment. Palliser knew she had seen him. He spoke sternly to a young waitress, cast a patriarchal scrutiny around the tea rooms and stalked out again.

So far, so good. He had successfully established two personae now, each to his purpose.

He went back to the home furnishings counter.

'Ah, Mr . . .'

'Wentwood. Palliser Wentwood.' *At ease.* 'Miss Lovelace's curtains – have you started?'

'Well, not quite, sir, just a minor hitch –'

'Well, between you and me, well, actually,' the silly-ass voice was such an asset, 'I couldn't see any difference.'

'No, sir, nor could we.'

'Well, it did occur to me, that if, well, if, one were to, as it were, not replace the goods –'

'I'm not quite sure, sir . . .'

'I think – it may not be necessary – lot of fuss – extra

expense – probably embarrassin' explanations in order – why not just pack up the curtains?'

The salesman looked aghast and then delighted.

'Certainly, sir. Will sir – or shall we deliver –'

'No, no, I'll take 'em, save trouble.'

The offending curtains were packaged up with crisp new paper and loops of thick brown string. Palliser took possession of the parcel and departed in the direction of the tea rooms. He then made his escape in a dignified manner through the Gentlemen's.

Outside, the street was suddenly cheerful and colourful where it had been dull and grey. He took big euphoric strides along the pavement in any old direction, singing to himself inside his head.

Palliser enjoyed his games of ruse and deception, but he never intended them to be the stuff of his life. He had noticed, however, that it had become his habit over the last twenty years to spin yarns and assume characters. Other people made it painfully easy for him, by enjoying the tales and readily believing his fictions. He had begun to feel that nature had made him amusing and others gullible, and it was therefore his allotted task to fool them. Besides, it made wonderful stories to tell in the pub. He sometimes imagined a life in which there was no reason to tell a tale, and no tales to be told, and it seemed dull dull dull. If society continued to throw sweet innocents in his path, and refused to offer him an honest way to make his living, what was he to do?

. . . my darling, I am filled with confidence that I may soon be back in the bosom of my family, or more precisely your bosom, my darling girl. I have a scheme afoot.

Many letters had started themselves, but had somehow remained unfinished. The flaw was always in the possibility that never quite turned into the reality. Somehow schemes had a habit of not living up to expectation, and even as he described them to Salomé, he had doubts. So the letters never found their way into an envelope. And was this scheme also doomed to disappoint?

He dreamed of Salomé and his girls. He longed for the house he had built, with all its flaws, for the smoky kitchen and the slant-floored bedroom. You took off your slippers in one corner and picked them up next morning in the opposite. He longed for the smell of Salomé's stock-pot, endlessly recycled soup of no identifiable source, piping hot and potent as a witch's brew. He would expire if he conjured up the first whiff of her blackcurrant, the first sip of her apricot wine. Than which none better – *But might I of Jove's nectar sup, I would not change for thine.* Salomé's hair, undulating past the mirror as she brushed it. Black, black, slivers of silver you'd miss if you blinked, magic silver; Salomé's brown eyes like a wild animal, inadequately tamed. Her spirit like a waterspout: you had to stand on the edge, enjoy the spectacle, lean towards the thrust, but if you leaned too far you might be swept away.

Palliser, for all his ruses and deceptive appearance, thought of himself as an honest man. When challenged with a failure he was happy to plead guilty, and to turn his failures heroic and funny in the telling of them. He recognised the folly of his ways before others had a chance to point it out to him; but he also brought things off when others scoffed. He had drained the swamp and built his stone bridge; he had built a tower with his bare hands, and set up his gymnastic equipment and his father's telescope in the topmost room; he had married for love, a rich and beautiful woman. When he was successful, he enjoyed his triumph to the maximum, and when he failed he did not need to be told. But what he found most difficult was to figure out, in advance, which schemes were top-hole and which schemes were tom-fool.

Now, was the assault on the Lovelace household going to be top-hole or tom-fool?

He sat in the snug of the White Hart with a lunch of cheese, ham and pickles, washed down, as it must be, by a glass or two of beer, and worked on the letter home. His eye fell on a forgotten copy of yesterday's *Times*, left by another patron. The crossword was half finished.

A God is said to be our supporter.

By the time he finished the crossword – *Of course, Bacchus!* – and his lunch, it was time to launch his attack on Miss Lovelace. He pushed his plate forward and his chair back, stretched every limb, and contemplated his scheme.

He was committed to action now, by the brown paper parcel lurking beneath his chair. If his courage failed him he must still dispose of the parcel, and there seemed nothing to be gained by not delivering it in person. It was a long shot, he admitted, but worthy of his talents. He would succeed if fate intended this – his ultimate humiliation, his ultimate triumph.

The path to blessedness lay through the lowest place . . . *my righteous servant shall see the travail of his soul and be satisfied. He was oppressed, he was afflicted, yet he opened not his mouth. Therefore I will divide him a portion with the great . . .*

This was his last chance; if he failed now, he would have to crawl home, if he could. If he succeeded, he promised he would take his gains quickly and leave the gaming table quickly.

It was only after he was settled on the bus that he remembered he had left the letter to Salomé inside the discarded copy of yesterday's *Times*.

The bus-driver's directions for Thule were simple, if a trifle depressing. *Off at Brent Bottom, turn right at the Fortune of War, up the hill, can't miss it. A bit muddy underfoot.*

At Brent Bottom, a village of outstanding somnolence, Palliser alighted, found a signpost for Thule and set to trudge, worried at every step about the shine on his shoes. He was not a man affected by long distances or strange circumstances, but he found the walk up to Thule strangely depressing.

For one thing, there was the silence. A rich hush hung over the treetops, unbroken by cheerful agriculture. Even the birds and squirrels were subdued. For another, there was the long overgrown lane leading up the hill towards the house, disappearing into dark nothingness beyond. And for a third, there was the wall. An old brick wall, on Palliser's left as he climbed the hill, a sombre, funerary brick; underneath the blackness a lovely mellow ochre that seemed its natural colour, deliberately suppressed. The coping, once a proud limestone, well over Palliser's head, had crumbled and fallen away, and now the top of the wall was a fine garden for every wall-growing lime-loving species. The wall went on for yard after yard, without break or ornament.

He found himself filled with unusual gloom; he was a forlorn, see-through trickster, a worn-out Lothario, a runaway, twelve thousand miles away from home in a dark lane with mud underfoot.

But the moment passed.

The wall curved away to the left, and the tunnel abruptly ended. Palliser emerged, carrying the brown paper parcel before him and thinking himself into the role of Palliser Wentwood, assistant manager of Hampton's department store.

Before him stood one of the dwellings of the rich. Old land, lovely old land, crossed with lovely new money, designed by nature to be judiciously shared.

He walked up an uneven stone path into a battleground

of climbing roses, once trained over arches but now guarding the approach to the house in a more effective but less disciplined manner. On either side, behind the arches, were lawns, more or less kept, on which geese grazed. Low stone walls defined the boundaries of the garden; what chaos lay beyond one could only wonder. Flowerbeds marched in line towards the broad front steps and terrace of the house, but their layout was the only mark of precision that remained. Nonetheless, a great many flowers struggled out of the rout of a once glorious garden.

Up ahead reared a huge brick house, three storeys high, some Elizabethan Lord High Treasurer's dream of immortality, born of embezzlement and ending in disgrace. Forests of absurd twisted chimneypots sprouted from its roofs, fancy brickwork pricked out the initials of the panjandrum who built it. Mythical beasts mounted over the porch, thrusting some forgotten family's coat of arms forward, in your face, peasant.

It reminded Palliser of a jigsaw he had completed six or seven times while recuperating from tonsillitis in the school San.

> *I know a little garden-close*
> *Set thick with lily and red rose,*
> *Where I would wander if I might*
> *From dewy dawn to dewy night,*
> *And have one with me wandering.*

Palliser came of a class that was neither impressed by antiquity nor overwhelmed by decay. He approached the front door and vigorously pulled the bell. He heard it sounding, far far away in the depths of the scullery, and knew he would have to wait. As the front door was ajar, he knocked politely and, stooping slightly as became the gentleman-manager of a genteel store, let himself in.

The entrance hall was exactly as he expected, graceless and dark. The only light came from a large mullioned window by the front door. The room had been formed by some Victorian person arbitrarily placing a wall part-way down a much larger hall, so that the height of the roof was completely out of proportion to the floor. Three walls were panelled in dark Jacobean linenfold, and the fourth, the newer wall, in a nineteenth-century version of the same. An ungainly wooden staircase, dimly perceived, led up from the back into Piranesian heights. Palliser was sure it would be carved with crude lions and men in breeches holding garden implements.

There was a fireplace on the right-hand wall, in which a neglected pile of logs sat for decoration rather than use. Above the fireplace on the mantelshelf stood two bronze Mercuries, fig leaves clamped to their genitals, holding gas lamps. On the walls half a dozen big but otherwise quite unremarkable paintings – portraits (school of Lely, studio of Lawrence), scenes of various kinds, about which neither the painter nor the viewer cared a toss. And inevitably, the antlers of a dozen long-rotten stags.

Palliser sat down on a piece of furniture infelicitously called a settle. He studied the dark floorboards, unpolished, not even a strip of cocoa-matting to relieve them. The cold of centuries trickled through the cracks in the floor and down from the galleries. He wished he had worn his overcoat, shabby or not. At last a door in the back panelling opened and light streamed out. A woman stood framed there. Palliser leapt to his feet.

'Yos?'

The foreign woman, patently. Palliser exercised his connoisseur's eye on the silhouette, and was impressed. A middle-aged woman wearing a floral apron over a plain black dress, but with a figure that would grace any stage. As he approached he saw that her plentiful dusty blonde hair was caught up all anyhow into a species of bun, with a multitude of pins, but only to keep the stuff out of the way. She was striking, a worn, tragic battered beauty, her face pulled down by troughs and ridges of sorrow, but all the more extraordinary for that. Her eyes, Palliser noted, were black, and rimmed by unfashionable but striking black liner, and her hands long, flourishing with rings and red nails. How impractical for a housekeeper, but how dramatic!

He approached, humbly as befitted his role, but the housekeeper's face was filled with fear.

'Wentwood, Palliser Wentwood – from Hampton's. About curtains for Miss Lovelace.'

The woman's accent was almost stagily European; she said she would find her mistress, and fled up the stairs. Palliser was consumed by curiosity, but stayed in role, though his natural impulse was to run after her and startle her into some sort of outburst.

After another long wait, Miss Lovelace appeared at the top of the stairs. Very slowly she moved downwards, pausing at the middle landing, her hand resting on the banister.

Palliser took a deep breath, overcome by the glory before him. Without her coat, she was laid bare to his eye, though poured into a brown suit of indeterminate fashion, most inexpertly altered to swathe the great body. She wore the same crocodile shoes, with the nastiest of brown stockings. Between waist and neck bellied a white lisle blouse. She seemed reluctant to descend any further. Palliser longed to feast his eyes on her, and more fervently to feast her with his eyes.

The tongue of the just is as choice silver.

'Wentwood, Palliser Wentwood, from Hampton's.'

Her expression registered that she had seen him in the store that morning, and she accepted his credentials. He held the parcel in front of him like a peace offering. She would have to descend to take it from him.

'We heard of your difficulties with our furnishings departments. We felt that it was incumbent on us to ensure that you were satisfied.' He used his most caressing voice, his kind-father-story-time voice, rich with Irish colour but just a little dark and dangerous, a suggestion of the Black Knight from the Western Isles, a man on the side of good – but by no means nice.

It was amazing what one could do with an ordinary sentence.

'That really wasn't necessary.' Her voice was innocent of artifice, as was her person. She did not know what an instrument she wielded. She sounded like a little girl speaking through a megaphone.

'I would greatly appreciate it, Miss Lovelace, if you would examine the goods now, so we can be assured that they are correct this time.'

That'd get her down the stairs. *Just let me get a bit nearer, get her into my orbit; just let me get a proper look at her.* He couldn't help enjoying himself. What a great story it would make if she fell for this. Even if the rest of his stratagem failed, there would be one good joke out the end of it.

He held out the parcel and backed away towards what he hoped was the drawing room.

'Perhaps we should examine them in the light – in their proper place?'

Without a word she came down, took the parcel from him and proceeded into the room to the left of the doorway.

It was a handsome room, and attempts had been made to humanise it. The floor was bare and echoing, but several fine Oriental rugs were disposed across it. Light streamed in from a window the height of the room, which looked out on to the garden. Two straight-back Queen Anne chairs

— *geniune Queen Anne chairs!* — stood by the fireplace, which showed signs of recent use. Above the mantel hung a Burne-Jones maiden — possibly Leda or St Agnes — in a perfect plain frame. Palliser estimated that it was an original. A great bowl of flowers sat on a table in the middle, and two occasional tables, eighteenth century, very fine, stood handy to the chairs. Otherwise the room was bare.

Miss Lovelace walked across to the window seat, already covered in new maroon velvet. She sat down and began to open the package. Palliser slid into the seat beside her.

Second base.

'Allow me to open it?'

He laid the paper back ceremoniously and revealed the contents, birds and leaves, indigo and strawberry. A completed cushion cover lay on top, neatly folded, and beneath it, in perfect slacks, lengths of curtain material. She took out the fabric, with Palliser's careful assistance, and held it up. He estimated how close he could lean while evaluation proceeded; fractionally inside the zone of politeness. Did she move away?

On close observation her white blouse seemed a sadder thing than ever; he was aware of the inadequacy of her corsetry, the great bosom struggling to free itself from whalebone which neither supported, shaped nor concealed the wonders beneath. He was transported by the thought of such copiousness, and thrilled equally by the discovery that her stomach and hips, while broader than an armchair, were in proportion to the grandeur of her frame. Miss Lovelace, meanwhile, mercifully unaware of his catalogue of her parts, frowned over the material. She did not move away from his charmed circle.

Still on second base, and holding!

'I'm not completely sure,' he said frowning, his voice dropping half an octave. He stood up, holding a length of material, and then a second, to all intents and purposes identical. 'I'm not absolutely convinced.'

He knew he was closer than politeness dictated; he willed her to look him in the face, but saw how that was almost impossible for her. To give her credit, she did look at it all critically, and he saw that she was doubtful. He saw that she saw what she had seen before, when she brought it back to complain. But something else flittered across her face, which he watched as a fisherman watches the sky. He saw the amazonian effort it had cost her to complain in the first place; she blushed merely at the thought of complaining again, bit her lip and turned over the material. Palliser sensed distress. But he was also aware that she wanted to be agreeable to him.

Starting running for third base, Pally.

The blush ran down her cheeks and inside her blouse. She summoned up her courage to complain again, but could not do so.

'I really am not sure,' Palliser repeated, as if he were singing a Schubert *Lied*. With a dash of crimson across the lips, he thought, and the eyebrows plucked and arched, framed by hair washed in soft water and allowed free, her face would shine like a Venus by Titian.

She gave up the unequal battle against him.

'It will do very well. Thank you very much, Mr –'

'Wentwood, Palliser Wentwood. A most original choice of fabric, if I may be so bold –'

'My brother, Hubert –'

She didn't move away. Perhaps she didn't know how to disengage herself; perhaps she enjoyed his proximity. But it seemed far more likely that she was transfixed by shyness. He engaged her in conversation about soft furnishings for some minutes, contriving to make it feel like an exchange of intimacies. Her voice did not lose its indecision, but her brow lost some of its corrugations.

Even Palliser could not chat about curtains for ever.

The conversation fell away. She did not know how to end it. He took pity on her and rose to his feet. It was a delicate business to balance her social discomfort with the need to acquaint her better with his charms. He felt she might have liked to show him around the gardens, leaning on his arm, and had he been a man of means he would have suggested it. But that was not his scheme.

'Goodbye, Mr Wentwood. Thank you for your trouble.'

Look at me, girl, just once, look at me, damn you.

Just behind her, stepping out into the hall, he said, 'I say, Miss Lovelace, there's something I'd like to ask.'

She turned and for a second met his eyes. *Hazel. Lovely, and copper highlights in her dark hair. Emerald green, I think. Or scarlet. Scarlet taffeta. With a scooped back and a nipped-in waist. Full length.* A second was sometimes long enough for Palliser's eyes to have their effect.

'It's frightfully impertinent.' He struggled a little against her embarrassed silence. 'I don't know quite how to put this . . .'

She moved fractionally back into the drawing room. Was it about money, she's thinking, an extra charge? Her eyes flitted to the stairs, as if help might be summoned.

'May I speak frankly?' How, he marvelled, could someone so substantial be so tentative? She blushed furiously, but he saw no course but onwards. 'I could pretend it was for a friend of mine, but in fact I am speaking for myself.'

They were perhaps an inch further into the drawing room.

'A word of explanation – just a word. I won't detain you with stories. In a word, I have been a long time out of this country, in the colonies, and I find England greatly changed. Openings in my profession are much rarer than I had expected.'

Now I've confused her.

'It has passed through my mind, Miss Lovelace, that your family might be aware of a position – being so well-connected in the county.'

'A position?'

O dear Mother, do not turn in your grave now. If I were not at the end of my luck, would I be doing this? I have my pride, Mother, I have my pride.

'Before I went to New Zealand, Miss Lovelace, I was seventeen years butler for two great houses, and proud to be such. But since I washed up on these shores again, I've been unable to find a position.'

'But – Hampton's?'

'Is a very fine store, but do you know, Miss Lovelace, *it's not the same!*'

Lightning strike thee, thou bare-faced liar! And yet they say, Tush, the Lord shall not see: neither shall the God of Jacob regard it.

The heavens were strangely quiet.

'I'm not sure I –'

'I was a butler. I am looking for a butler's position. I am not concerned whether city or country. I was born to the service and I hope to die in it.'

The words slid out of him as if Galsworthy had written them and he had run through them a dozen times at rehearsal. So easy to lie, so easy.

'Why did you leave – they call New Zealand the Promised Land –'

He looked away from her, out of the window, fixing his gaze on far distant shores.

'In New Zealand, I farmed a few acres of swamp, drained it all, built a farmhouse, grew very fine vegetables. But last winter, the floods came – my wife –' He allowed something like a tear to spring into his eye as he gazed tragically out into the jungle of Thule, seeing his household swept away by these convenient floods, Salomé's hair fanning out on the brown waters.

Punish me, Lord, but not yet.

'Oh.'

He let the silence ride. She must find her own way out of this abashment, and the only way was his way.

'I don't know. I can ask Hubert.'

Third base.

He reached into his pocket and extracted a sheet of writing paper from the White Hart Hotel.

'Lowly,' he said, 'but very convenient to the shop.'

She took it, folded it, and folding it to and fro, to and fro in her fingers, preceded him into the hall, then, remembering the drill, she rang for the housekeeper.

'Mrs Nagy, please show Mr Wentwood out.'

Mrs Nagy, now without her apron, Tosca, Lady Macbeth, Medea, escorted him to the door. He bowed low and ceremonious, his best Hungarian bow.

On his way back through the garden, he laughed out loud and plucked a rose for his buttonhole.

IV

THREE DAYS LATER, Palliser, full of virtue at having done
an honest morning's work, was seated in the snug of the
White Hart, drinking a midday pint. He had conducted
an auction, which always gives a man a thirst even in
courteous Hertfordshire; thus it was perfectly reasonable
to have a drink or two in the middle of the day. In New
Zealand drinking during the day is frowned upon, though
men make up for this at night. In the dear old country
matters are otherwise. As Palliser stretched out his legs
under the table, he could not help some wry amusement at
the contrast between the cattle auctions through which he
hectored his way in Otautahi, and the discreet apportioning
of household goods he had just performed.

Thoughts of New Zealand cattle yards filled him with
uneasy nostalgia; the constant complaining of cattle and
badgering of dogs, hay and manure smells, the cold hard
beer at the end of a hot day, so long awaited, bumping
home in the dark in a cattle truck with real money in his
pocket to throw at Salomé's feet.

Into the yard of the White Hart slid a Rolls-Royce, 1929
Phantom, proceeding as delicately as a maiden aunt in a
bath chair. Palliser, catapulted back from the Antipodes,
licked his lips, and watched it park, ever so gently, back
and forward, back and forward until it was just so. Out
of the passenger door came the housekeeper of Thule

Hall, Mrs Nagy, in a full-length mink coat that had a tale to tell. Her hair was newly flung up, and her nails, clutching a large black handbag, were resplendent. Her handsome shoes, Palliser surmised, came from the same supply that Miss Lovelace favoured — the shoe cupboard of the late Mrs L., he guessed. Behind Mrs Nagy was the boy, slender creature in tight black trousers and a black leather jacket, long blond hair over his eyes, wearing the unreasonable beauty hinted at in his mother's face.

The boy poked the ground with his narrow pointed shoes, trying to be elsewhere, while his mother engaged in a heated discussion with a large man in black, presumably Hubert Lovelace. He was slightly obscured from Palliser's vision, so it was not until the three came through the hotel doorway and into the public bar that he saw Lovelace properly.

No mistaking the resemblance to his younger sister; Hubert Lovelace was solid from six feet two down to the ground, but all the more striking because of the black cloak he wore over a black cassock, with a cerise cummerbund. Though not yet thirty, the young man's height and fleshiness gave him a spurious authority. Palliser rapidly readjusted his expectations of Mr Hubert to Father Hubert, and pondered the implications.

Meanwhile Hubert was buying drinks from Mrs Hogg, leaning over the bar and addressing her confidentially. Palliser shrank back into the corner, sensing his person was in question.

The three sat down at a table in Palliser's earshot but out of sight. Mrs Nagy immediately resumed the debate from outside, which was conducted in French at a very low volume, but high intensity. Fr Hubert rejoined in French of suspect grammar but considerable fluency, perhaps weathered by such exchanges. The boy kicked the rails of his chair with his pointy shoes and sipped a lemon shandy. Palliser was consumed with curiosity but could not catch enough of the conversation to make sense of it.

Mrs Nagy managed to sip her sizeable port and deliver a stream of words simultaneously, but she broke off when a small man in a corduroy jacket came into the bar. Palliser recognised him as the owner of a secondhand book stall in the market. He made directly for Mrs Nagy's table, hardly seeing anyone else. Hubert sent the boy to buy more drinks, but Mrs Nagy seemed anxious to be gone. She left with the boy and the small man in her wake. As she went out a man in a brown bowler hat wished her a fervent good day, and seemed half inclined to follow her. Hubert Lovelace, left alone at his table, polished off his gin, levered himself up and made for the bar. Palliser saw he was to be further discussed, and that Mrs Hogg was busy and distracted, so he slipped out of the back door of the bar, took his hat and coat from their accustomed hook, and made his way round to the front of the White Hart and in by the front door, for all the world like the assistant manager of Hampton's on his dinner hour.

'Well speak of the devil,' said Mrs Hogg in a carrying voice. 'You can find out for yourself. Mr Wentwood, this gentleman would like a word.'

Palliser shook Hubert's large soft hand and, suffering himself to be bought a drink, chose a gin and tonic. They sat down together, for what Palliser supposed was his employment interview. He was delighted it should take this form, for he knew from experience that the clergy in general were terrible judges of character, determinedly seeing the best in everyone and eternally hopeful of a moral reform, and therefore inclined to ignore or dismiss anything suspicious or reserved in a testimonial. That very morning he had had Mrs Hogg dispatch for him two telegrams, one to the Hon. Andrew Charlton, of Porturet House, in Gloucestershire, and the other to Sir Roderick Lonsdale, of

Belmont in Maryborough, Co. Laoghis; both read simply: *Play the game, old boy. Pally.* It now seemed that such precautions were unnecessary.

Statuesque build notwithstanding, the details of Fr. Hubert's person were in striking contrast to his sister. He was lugubrious in aspect and florid of countenance. Even his voice differed. It had all the worst characteristics of the clerical voice: the nasal Oxford overtones that lent the flavour of wit to everything he said, however ordinary, an incipient W for R, and a little lisp. Palliser wondered if he had worked at this accent or simply acquired it. He found it hard to believe that anyone could speak like that without clericalism aforethought. Fr. Hubert's manner was a mixture of middle-aged bishop and ancient eccentric aunt. Here was a soulmate, thought Palliser, another man using his physical presence to assist an artifice. Though quite who Hubert was trying to be or trying to impress he could not deduce.

Their conversation turned first on that English staple, the weather, but Hubert soon turned to the current state of England, the colonies, and New Zealand in particular, not a subject that Hubert was normally much engaged with. But he was avid for conversation and curious about Palliser's past, though unwilling to betray either interest. Concurrently, Palliser was concerned to preserve his fictions while keeping actual untruths to a minimum. It was, therefore, a delicate conversation.

After a dullish opening phase, the talk turned to anecdotes, probably intended by Hubert as a device to elicit the true nature of his incipient employee, but channelled by Palliser into one for entertaining his prospective employer. Palliser knew a few good tales about the High Church clergy, some of them requiring to be told in a lowered voice. Hubert's face grew happy; he laughed, his eyes spelled eagerness. A scrap of youth showed beneath the hem of his cassock. Palliser was sent off with a pound note for more drinks;

he returned with no change, a stiff gin for Father, and a tonic for himself. He told a lubricious story about sheep.

At ten to one he glanced at the clock and said he was expected back.

'Oh but you can't go *yet*,' cried Hubert. 'We've scarcely begun our chat.'

'Father Lovelace,' said Palliser, treating him to the full glory of the Wentwood gaze, 'alas, I am still elsewhere employed, albeit unwillingly. If I were to return even five minutes late to my post at Hampton's, and compound my crime with a whiff of gin, I should lose my position. I simply cannot take that risk, loath though I am to commit *dialectus interruptus*.'

Hubert threw back his head and laughed.

'Look here, Wentwood, there's no need to leave just yet. You're about to hand in your notice.'

'Am I?'

'For God's sake, man, what are you playing at? Of course you are.'

'Father Lovelace, neither you nor your sister has made me any sort of offer.'

'Well, I shall. Here and now. For God's sake, sit down. No, buy us another drink, first.'

Another pound.

Palliser went to the bar.

'Dearest Winifred, will you make as to send a message across to Hampton's for me? And two more of the same.'

'No gin in yours, then?'

'No, but it makes no odds to him. It is our duty to help the rich dispose of their wealth.'

Mrs Hogg chuckled darkly into her bosom, poured the drinks, took the money and went out of the bar to deliver his message.

'Let us trust they are not unduly distressed,' he said smiling enchantingly at Hubert. 'I would not as a normal practice abandon ship so peremptorily. Mercifully, it is not a busy season in retailing – though a whole ritual surrounds the need always to appear busy.'

Later that afternoon, when Mrs Nagy and her son returned from the market, caparisoned with string bags of shopping, Hubert and Palliser were well away. Hubert was as happy as the fat boy befriended by the super new boy. Palliser had elicited the following promises, and got Hubert to sign them, viz.:

1. Palliser Wentwood to be employed by Hubert and Blanche Lovelace of Thule Hall as household manager from Monday, 24 August 1959.
2. Initial period of employ to be three months, after which date, salary and conditions shall be subject to review.
3. Duties to be those consistent with the management of a gentleman's house: supervision of staff, provisioning, upkeep of the grounds, and assistance with entertainment.
4. Full board and clothing and other accoutrements suitable to the position shall be provided by the employers during the term of employment; such clothing and accoutrements to remain the property of Palliser Wentwood.
5. Hours of duty shall normally be daylight hours, six days a week; duties performed in the evening shall be negotiated as required.
6. Initial emolument shall be £40 a month.

Forty pounds a month and full board was daylight robbery, but Hubert was happy to be ignorant of such matters, and accept Palliser's word on the going rate. The salary was the least of Palliser's concerns, and in his current state he'd have settled for his keep alone. Another drink, this time a tonic with gin lurking beneath, and a round of anecdotes, more respectable ones, sealed the bargain.

Dearest Salomé,

You see from the address above that I have fallen at last on some good fortune. How can I write to you, my own dear heart? How can I pen any kind of justification or apology, or beg for hope or kindness? I love you as much now as ever I did when you were a delectable young thing with the fire flaring in your eyes at me across the ballroom. But how can I convince you of that now, after all that I have done? Could I hope for forgiveness . . .

He paused, pen in hand; a crony came into the private bar, and bought him a drink.

So Palliser began his assault on the household at Thule.

'Edward the Confessor. Good example of why not to have a saint as a head of state. Not that we're likely to . . .'

'Noticed you did him today,' says Palliser. 'Saw you scrabbling about in the Not Virgins, Not Martyrs section of the book.'

Hubert laughed.

'Another of these eggs would slide down, old chap.'

Palliser and Hubert are sitting at breakfast, in the breakfast room as befits gentlemen. Sun pours on to the table, but Palliser has arranged for a cracking little fire as well. There is no virtue, he tells Hubert, in unnecessary discomfort. In Lent perhaps one might choose to suffer, but if one suffers all year, routinely, one becomes a pinched person and Lent has no meaning. Might as well go the whole hog, says Palliser, and join a monastery if you're going to deny yourself a fire in September.

Hubert is immune to cold, his frame entirely upholstered in buttoned black serge, but Palliser, long and thin, is motivated by the provision of warmth. He has already secured the household of Thule a winter's supply of logs and coal at very good prices, and does not intend to be cold.

Breakfast is dishabille, by Hubert's decree. 'It's not necessary to dress like a gigolo at this hour.' He removes his cummerbund; Palliser attends in cords and cravat, and has yet to shave. God, he told Hubert, doesn't require him to shave before partaking, so neither should His servant. Although Palliser attends mass daily without partaking, this minor detail has not been allowed to affect the argument.

The table in the breakfast room is spread with a white linen cloth; in its centre a small arrangement of late daisies. Spread around are plates and newspapers. So far they have consumed five cups of tea, two cups of coffee (heaven knows where she gets this coffee from), with cream from a local cow, nine rashers of bacon, three fried eggs, four kidneys and four pieces of fried bread. All of this is prepared by Palliser, the newly fledged chef, on a little gas chauffer, so that Mrs Nagy is not obliged to trek in and out of the room, causing draughts and disruptions, each time the gentlemen require another round of breakfast.

'Got to teach Peter to find the places properly,' says Hubert. 'When I was an altar boy I'd have swooned if any of the Fathers so much as looked at me, let alone glared. He seems immune to hints, veiled or otherwise.'

Palliser is obliged to concentrate when frying an egg, faithfully recalling his monosyllabic lessons from Mrs Nagy and summoning up memories of Salomé's adroit wrist.

Hubert continues:

'I have tried to talk to him – during the day, of course, because he gives such a good impression of sleepwalking during mass. But she regards any attempt at engaging him in conversation as a breach of her contract. I don't know why she lets him out of her sight to serve mass.'

'That's a conundrum. Your egg, Father.'

Palliser puts a muffin on the end of the toasting fork for himself.

'I've had all manner of men up here to persuade her

to send him to school. And women. Every time it came to the sticking point, on the day he was to start school, I'd get up in the morning and find her cases standing in the hall, and a taxicab ordered. Now he's past the age of compulsory schooling, so the tempest has abated. I fear for us when he reaches the age for National Service.'

'She'll find a loophole. She has the cunning of the oppressed.'

'He's not ignorant — I've seen to that. He does his lessons; she's taught him several languages — French, German, Hungarian. To her own standard of course, so the German is likely to be as execrable as the French and English. One can only hope she speaks Hungarian rather better. They use that to converse in, so one can't overhear. I expect you've noticed.'

'Indeed I have,' says Palliser, buttering his muffin.

'I say, that does look fine. Shall you toast one for me?'

Palliser spreads marmalade on his muffin, closes its jaws and takes one heavenly bite, before turning back to the toasting fork.

'I want to send him to Oxford, to my old place. Then the Foreign Office, something like that. Or the BBC. He's clever, you know, very talented.'

'I think he could go far. In the right field.'

A pause.

'Here's a clue for you — *A thorny as well as a horny problem*. Seven letters.'

Palliser considers.

'She'll only be able to keep him tied to her apron for another year or two,' says Hubert. 'The thing that bothers me most is that when he turns his back on her, he'll turn his back on all of us.'

'Your muffin, Father.'

'*Benedictus benedicat.*' Hubert makes the sign of the cross. He holds the muffin up and makes circular motions with it, intoning in a squeaky queen's voice, 'Father Polly at the eleven o'clock.'

Into this nest of breakfast breaks Blanche, never normally seen before eleven. Clad in her virgin armour of sensible brown, she looks from one to other, taking in the butter dripping from Hubert's fingers, Palliser's unshaven cheek, the debris of newspapers. She could scarcely look more shocked had she found them in bed together.

Hubert seizes a napkin and wipes the butter from his fingers. Palliser takes his feet off the fender.

Blanche holds a piece of paper, and her hands are shaking.

Trouble ahead.

'Hubert I need to speak to you.'

'Fire ahead, Blanchy, my dear, but do sit down first. Breakfast is well and truly served. Allow Palliser to toast you a muffin or fry you a kidney or two.'

'No. No thank you. I mean alone.'

Palliser is on his feet and towards the door, faster than you could say thief. But he slips across the room like a ballet dancer, willing her to watch him. He passes just close enough to see what is in her hand.

As he guessed, she has just received the bill from Hampton's for his new butler's wardrobe.

Palliser is polishing silver, in the manner prescribed by his drinking mate, Jacob, the verger of St Cyriac's, Childers Green, who ought to know. He wears a proper butler's apron, black weskit and trousers, and white shirt, but his sleeves are rolled manfully to the elbow. He is perfectly shaven, and sings 'Guide me, O Thou Great Jehovah,' as delicately as if it were a love song.

Mrs Nagy, neck to ankle in black, is positioned at the Aga, doing something mystical with garlic and spice. Above her head stands a row of glass jars filled with pickled vegetables, bottled sauces and drunken fruits, in every autumn colour from chrysanthemum gold to deep soil red. Bay leaves, green peppers and cloves float in their depths, like fragments of an ancient world. Around her head hangs a garrison of salami, keeping her close guard, but not quite touching. On the bench is the lump of dough about to be transformed into white bread for the master's table; on the kitchen table is a warm loaf of dark brown bread.

Peter Nagy eats this bread, slice by slice. His hand reaches out; he does not look up to see whether a slice is ready for him. His mother turns from her work and cuts them, two or three at once, before he can feel the need. Beside the bread is a bottle of black ink, an exercise book and a copy of Durrell's *Algebra for Upper Forms*. He dips his pen into the ink, conveys it to the page, writes out the problem and the solution in one movement, never spilling a drop. Palliser tries to do the algebra, upside down and in his head. Instead he is mesmerised by the threat of black ink to the white tablecloth, the care of which has become dear to his heart.

Hubert said: 'Send out the laundry, by all means, old chap, but try to keep the costs down.'

Mrs Nagy said: 'Make sure it is the same exactly every month. She doesn't know how much it should cost, but if it is different, be wary!'

Palliser sings because he cannot talk. Peter will simply fail to hear him if he tries to chat. Mrs Nagy does hear him, but regards everything, even his pleasantries, with deepest suspicion.

A loud knocking on the outer kitchen door, some layers away. The kitchens at Thule are a rabbit warren, largely uninhabited, even by vermin. Mrs Nagy stiffens, looks about her for the source of the intrusion, her hand firm on the bread knife. Palliser removes his apron, and goes to answer it, for Mrs Nagy will wait for the second or even the third flurry of knocking before venturing out.

A man in a cloth cap and leather gaiters stands at the kitchen door. He is not known to Palliser. He has a yellow dog at his heels and holds out a pair of pheasants.

'For Mrs Nagy?' says Palliser. 'Come in, I am sure she will be delighted.'

The man stuffs his cap in his pocket, commands his dog to stay, and follows Palliser through his kingdom, past the room once used for hanging game, past the room once used for hanging pork carcasses, the room with huge mortars fixed in the bench for grinding things, the room entirely filled by a stew-pot, under which a fire burned for the entire seventeenth century.

'For you, ma'am.'

Mrs Nagy is standing upright by the table, waiting. When she recognises her visitor she does not smile, but removes her apron.

'A nice cup of coffee,' she pronounces, and pours one from the pot she keeps by her on the Aga, as a watercolourist keeps to hand his glass of water.

The man sits down and consents to chat with Palliser, watching with rapt attention as Mrs Nagy kneads bread. He calls her Doris.

Peter looks up briefly and slices the visitor in small pieces with a flick-knife, then resumes his algebra. Palliser is glad not to be a contender for Mrs Nagy's favours.

The man makes his farewells, leaving the pheasants lying on the table. Palliser worries about bloodstains and whips them into a chill outlying region of the kitchens. He resumes polishing silver, singing 'Roses Are Blooming in Picardy.' Soon Blanche will come to discuss lunch with Mrs Nagy. Will it be ham and boiled potatoes, corned beef and mashed potatoes, or shepherd's pie? Brussels sprouts, carrots, and perhaps a field mushroom, for that exotic touch. Palliser remembers breakfast and is glad. He lusts after the garlic concoctions of Mrs Nagy, but dare not share them; at any moment he might be required to draw near to Blanche, and a whiff of garlic is too dangerous an anaphrodisiac.

Another knocking at the door. Once again Mrs Nagy goes through her anxious pantomime. Palliser sighs, removes his apron, and makes his way through the maze of kitchens.

'Something else for Mrs Nagy?'

A man in a brown grocer's coat has brought a big wooden crate up to the kitchen door on a sack barrow. It's a lovely crate made of new white wood, with curling fronds of yellow wood shaving escaping from the slats, just like Mrs Nagy's hair.

''Ere you are mate. Sign 'ere.'

'Why don't you take it to her yourself?'

'Nar, I'm not an admirer. I'm a delivery man.'

'Well take it inside, will you, there's a good chap. I'm not carryin' it.'

He does, however, take charge of the delivery note. *Information, rather than knowledge, is power.*

The box is trundled through the stone corridors, right into the main kitchen, where Mrs Nagy stands waiting. The delivery man escapes as if he had ventured on to the stage by accident.

'Oh, look Peter, it is here again.'

Palliser tries to read Mrs Nagy's expression on receipt of this largesse. *Resignation? Exasperation? Delight?*

'Oh goody, more salamis to hang with the others.'

'But you love salami.'

'Yes, to eat, not to hang up and admire as works of art.'

Palliser is keen to open the box. It's firmly nailed down, so he has to prise off the lid with the claws of a hammer. By happy timing, just as he's engaged in this masculine, but quite servile task, Blanche enters the kitchen.

'I see it's arrived again, Mrs Nagy.'

Mrs Nagy fetches an operatic sigh. '*Oui, hélas, hélas.*'

Palliser pulls off the lid and finds, snuggling among the wood shaving, not only salamis but jars of sweet red peppers, tins of American coffee, a square tin of black olives, and a cake of pumpernickel wrapped in silver paper.

'Where am I to put this?' cries Mrs Nagy. There are tears in her eyes.

Peter gets up from the table and takes the pumpernickel back with him. He starts to eat it, as if he were a creature specifically designed to devour.

In the bottom of the box is a white envelope addressed to Mrs Nagy in a continental hand. Mrs Nagy takes this and consigns it to the flames of the Aga without opening it.

'We could send it back,' says Palliser.

Both women turn on him. Blanche tries to retort, but blushes instead. Mrs Nagy cries, '*Impossible!*' in French, and weeps.

Palliser unpacks the box, carrying the peppers and olives to the pantry. The latest delivery of salami needs a place to hang. He takes one of the nails from the crate and hammers it into the wall. Blanche watches him, as she is supposed to do.

Mrs Nagy and Blanche engage in some ritual haggling over the tins of American coffee.

'You will buy this?'

'I suppose we might. How much?'

'I know it is eleven shillings and sixpence in Harrods because I have seen it. So I will sell it to you for ten.'

'Ten shillings is far too much for a tin of coffee.'

'Mr Hubert very much he likes this coffee. But he can drink ground-up acorns with the chicory if he wants.'

'I think six shillings would be fair. Harrods' prices are notoriously inflated.'

Palliser takes the delivery note out of his pocket. 'I could give the suppliers a bell, and find out what they charge for it.'

Blanche glances at him as if he has just broken down a door and saved her from a gang of bandits. 'That is a good idea, Mr Wentwood.'

The tins of coffee are lined up in the pantry with the other ten tins of coffee. Palliser thinks he might go up to town some time and visit Levi and Sons, Purveyors of Fine Food, Putney Bridge.

Palliser is shocked by the dullness of Blanche's life. He has always moved among lively folk, in his youth at spas and resorts, at places of devotion for gamblers, horse-racers, bon vivants, for the rich and beautiful, and their parasites. Always so much activity, so many novel ways to fill the hours. Then in the second phase of his life, he was surrounded by people so hard-working and vigorous that to merely recount their deeds made the hearer flag. He himself, regarded as prodigiously energetic in the old country, passed for nothing in the new. Dig, plough, saw, chop, shear and hammer, all day under the sun or in the rain, and then drink and tell yarns into the night and up again before dawn. And hospitality everywhere: tea and supper and drinks all round. Come in for a scone, you must stay for a jar, no trouble, mate, just sit yourself down there. Salomé dug in the garden, sewed, cooked, cleaned, bumped into town to gossip at the store, chopped up kindling, fed the hens, sold the eggs, preserved and boiled and brewed, and entertained and partied. There was never enough time to fit in everything that might be done. There was always a hunting trip that had to be declined, an outing to the races that could not be made, a stand of late green tomatoes that didn't quite make it to chutney.

What a sad waste, he thinks, standing with Miss Lovelace in the small front drawing room, the room by the front door. She is still worried about her curtains. After six weeks she has finished one set, sewing them herself laboriously on a hand-driven Singer sewing machine. Palliser has never seen her at this activity, for she performs it behind closed doors, in a room he is not permitted to enter. He has heard the machine from the corridor, stop start, stop start, and imagined her frowning and struggling over her work. She has no one to learn from. Palliser thinks of his girls sewing by the fire, Jemima darning her father's socks, Abigail treddling away at a jacket on their venerable Singer, their mother barking correction, or crying out in admiration at a lovely darn. Bathsheba, little blob by the fire, with a big blunt tapestry needle and a piece of red wool, is making great big stitches in a bit of sacking. It is sew well or fall apart, in Salomé's world.

But Miss Lovelace does not need to make her own curtains, nor is swift, straight sewing a skill that was imparted to her at the academy for young ladies. The curtains show evidence of rework, crooked seams, bumbled thread. And they have taken her a long time. Palliser is not aware of any other activities.

Every day he observes Blanche's behaviour minutely, looking for advantage. He still cannot believe what he sees, and fantasises that she has another life, a lover she creeps away to visit in the wood, because how otherwise could a human being survive a life of such stultifying nothingness?

Every morning she bathes and dresses, breakfasts in her room, and reads the *Daily Telegraph*. In theory, she has all the mail delivered to her room, even mail addressed to her brother. As it is Palliser's job to take up the mail, he has set up an arrangement with Hubert over certain items which are to be diverted. These are of two kinds: envelopes hand-addressed in black italic from two of his friends in London, and items in larger brown envelopes with typewritten labels and no provenance. Everything else for Hubert – catalogues, bills, letters from the country, requests for money, invitations to Anglo-Catholic events – goes up with Blanche's post. Mrs Nagy receives occasional letters in official envelopes which she burns unopened.

At eleven each day Blanche descends and gives Hubert his post and the bills to be paid, and tells him sternly of queries that have to be made. There are frequent faults to be followed up, but Blanche will not use the telephone or write the letters of complaint. She then goes into the kitchen to order lunch. Before lunch, while Hubert tinkers with his harpsichord, she walks about the garden with a pair of secateurs in her pocket and returns with an armful of flowers and greenery.

Palliser surmises that arranging flowers was one of the ladylike arts she has been taught. She certainly seems happy when she comes back into the scullery, her face buried in foliage. Palliser has watched her, and sees the expectation in her face, day after day, when she takes apart some previous arrangement, discards the moribund, lays out today's flowers and starts to build something lovely. Then, day after day, he has seen the expectation die and the tears rise as she finds she is in Mrs Nagy's way, and that she has once again run out of time before lunch. She pushes the remaining flowers into the vase all anyhow, and takes it into another room.

He wishes he could suggest a different approach – she has all afternoon to spend on this work if she pleases – but with Blanche he bides his time.

After lunch she goes into the garden, regardless of the weather. She will state she is going to talk to the gardener, but Palliser thinks she speaks to him as briefly as possible, about once a week. It's hard to follow her movements, because he has few excuses to go into the great overgrown garden himself. Discussions about the supply of vegetables and weeding the terrace do not consume much of his time; the gardener is a monosyllabic man whom no threat or inducement will hurry.

Beyond the garden is the park, occupied by a local farmer's benign cattle. Once from an upstairs window Palliser saw her far in the distance, striding along a footpath.

After she has walked about the garden and the park, she returns to the house and occupies herself usefully, most recently on the curtains.

She has no callers, makes no visits, has no invitations to tea, dinner, supper, cards or outings. She receives very occasional letters in girlish hands. She attends no parish functions, no church committee meetings, belongs to no amateur societies or local interest groups. She does not attend fairs or go to the market. She has no family except Hubert.

Therefore, in the evening, she sits with Hubert and listens to the wireless, occupying her hands with some piece of limp embroidery. Once or twice a month Hubert goes out of an evening, and twice a month he hosts the Thule Early Music Group to sherry and Dowland in the Music Room. On these occasions, Blanche retires to her room and listens to the wireless there. She does not have a fire in her room, though it is possible she has a gas heater.

And her glorious self, fit to warm the world.

The pattern of Blanche's week is broken only on Sundays when she goes to church, and on the days when she goes into the market town. Perhaps because braving the town is an ordeal, she rises early and departs early, cutting off Hubert's breakfast in its prime. Palliser is happy to sacrifice his breakfast since he gets to drive the car and sashay around the town, visiting his old haunts; he has to wear a cap to perform this duty, but he has contrived a way to make it look jaunty while driving. He removes it once he is out of Miss Lovelace's sight.

Following this pattern of life, she has achieved one set of curtains, and it is Palliser's duty to hang them, and somehow make them look appropriate. It is his earnest desire to disguise their imperfections and give her cause to approve of herself.

Salomé, Salomé, now I need your help.

The irony of this wish does not escape him. He stands on the top of a stepladder, looking down at Blanche and imagining the spectacular view he would have if she were wearing an evening gown. He doubts she possesses an evening gown, and a passion takes hold of him to make her acquire one, and to provide an occasion for her to wear it.

From above she is diminished a little, not so overwhelming. He feels less tentative towards her; curiously, it seems that she is less alarmed by him at a safe distance.

He asks her to pass up the first curtain. Their hands touch. For a tiny needle hole of time she looks at him. He gives her his best warm smile – Father Christmas crossed with Robin Goodfellow – not the Black Knight for the moment; she's terrified of him. But this smile makes her blush beautifully. Palliser looks down upon her with more tenderness than he knew was in him, and sees with leaping heart the incipience of infatuation.

Poor girl, she has no defences, not even the knowledge that she is under attack. How is she to know he's a bounder and a fortune hunter, when Hubert trusts him – trusts him to the extent of letting him spend money almost at will. Hubert is the one who knows about people; Hubert's been out in the world and mingled with the wicked. Hubert knows a scoundrel when he meets one. Her acquaintance with men is limited to a couple of Hubert's friends, whom she has met perhaps twice, a dancing master at her school, and the men who call on Mrs Nagy. She has never had a conversation with a man or looked a man in the eye.

Palliser does not know this; he still clings to his theory of the lover in the parkland because he cannot imagine such poverty. But he can imagine her falling in love with him. As he stands on the ladder, smiling down, he feels a great wash of familiarity. She will fall in love with him, and instead of money he will come into trouble. He will enjoy her, and then have to disentangle himself. There will be tears and anger, desperate pleas, promises, dark hints of pregnancy, letters and pressed flowers and telegrams.

Well what else did you expect, you silly old fool?

It is now too late. Even if the lover in the park did exist, he wouldn't stand a chance. Even if Palliser does nothing more to win her, she is lost. His charm is so powerful that once a woman has let down her defences, it must have its effect.

> *Let the doors be all bolted and the windows all pinned,*
> *And leave not a hole for a mouse to creep in.*
> *The doors were all bolted and the windows all pinned,*
> *Except one little window where Long Lankin crept in.*

He hooks up the curtain and slips down the ladder, seizing an armful of the material, and bellies it back towards the window.

'Now all you need, is a tie-back, like this – pull them back and let them bulge over the top a little. Then put one of your little cushions in the window-seat like so, and another one like so, and there – perfect.'

She stands back to admire his arrangement of her work. And indeed, it pleases her. He stands holding the curtain artfully in place, and watches her smile. He hopes she will not insist on his drawing the curtain fully. Tonight he will take the curtain down and persuade Mrs Nagy to straighten the hem and turn back the edges of the linings properly. He does not know how he will persuade Mrs Nagy to do this, but his mind works on the problem. In the meantime he must distract Blanche.

He holds a cushion up against the bunched-up curtain.

'You know I am still not perfectly convinced of the match of these fabrics . . .'

Her misery is palpable; he rushes to her rescue.

'It must be a natural variation in the fabric. A little fading, and nothing will be visible.'

A north-facing window? she wonders.

'I've known it even from Liberty's. Shall we tie this back and view the effect? Have you a strip of the fabric over?'

> *Will you come into my parlour*
> *says the spider to the fly*

They go into the garden to admire the effect of the new curtain looped up. He offers his arm, and shoulder to shoulder they walk down the steps into the front garden. They pick their way through the goose-droppings to the middle of the lawn and look back at the house.

'Shall we take a turn about the garden?' he says.

The gardens of Thule are as manifold as the rooms of the house. Palliser has not yet explored them, but here is a golden opportunity. She shows him the French garden – an overgrown parterre – the knot garden, the sunken garden with its trees pruned to unnatural shapes, and strange statues of monsters and slaves, eaten away by time. Finally the rose bower, encircled by its warm brick wall. Here they linger, still arm in arm, as she examines the late roses.

It is too early in his campaign for the rose garden, Palliser thinks. A visit to the rose garden should be at night, a warm gentle night, when matters are progressing satisfactorily, but need to be tipped into the next stage . . .

The rose garden has been haphazardly pruned. Some hybrid teas, yellow and strident scarlet, are trim and glossy, but the ramblers, climbers and bush roses, white, soft pink and crimson, and faded churchy purple, have been ignored. They run riot around the standard roses, like children in the playground, avoiding and taunting the goody-goodies.

'A great rose lover lived here?'

'Generations of them. My grandfather wrote a book, a little pamphlet, after he came back from South Africa. The first published work on old-fashioned roses. But my mother hated them. She didn't dare pull them out, though.'

'And you?'

'I love them. I love almost everything that grows, except maybe nettles – but even nettles make good soup, and they'll grow where nothing else will, and flower in dark places.'

She blushes bright pink, a lovely colour. Palliser presses her arm, like the favourite uncle during the sad bit in the film, when the dog dies.

'You'd need an army of gardeners to do justice to this place.'

'Help is so hard to find. The current man – he – well, he – he's very good on vegetables, and he prunes awfully well . . .' She founders.

'But he doesn't like to do what you want him to do? You could employ another one.'

'But then I'd have two of them to deal with.' He senses tears at the very thought of the struggle.

'I could deal with them for you.'

'O would you?' she cries, and turns to him. Then she realises what she has done. She feels her limbs sticking fast on the silk of his web. Her voice grows chilly and she draws away. 'I think perhaps not –'

Dangerous caution is creeping about like a snake in the grass. Scotch it, scotch it. Palliser lets go her arm, turns away and breaks off a rose. It is a white blowsy bloom, almost flopping apart, close to its demise, but its petals are velvet and its scent divine. He takes her hand and presses the flower into it, folds his hands over hers, and thereby forces her to look at him. He stands far too close, and lowers his voice to Orphean softness.

> *'Oh come with old Khayyám and leave the Wise*
> *To talk; one thing is certain, that Life flies;*
> *One thing is certain, and the Rest is Lies;*
> *The Flower that once has blown for ever dies.'*

Then he takes the flower from her, kisses it and puts it in his lapel.

They walk in silence for a while. They go into the house and Mrs Nagy makes them a cup of tea in the kitchen. Her eyes rest on the white rose in Palliser's buttonhole. She sniffs, but says nothing.

V

TINY STEP BY tiny step, Blanche ventured into his web. She hesitated a fraction on the stair when he came into the hall. She suffered him to drive her to church and share a hymn-book. She raised her head from her embroidery when he came in at night, singing, from the Fortune of War.

But the regime of the household was not allowed to vary. She clung to this as to a life-raft in uncertain waters. Every day she descended, papers in hand and brow furrowed. Every morning she flurried over her flower-arranging; every afternoon she disappeared into the parkland, and returned to preside over the echoing dining-table. Every evening she sat by the wireless playing Happy Families with her restless brother. Those among us who observe Palliser minutely, and who follow the manoeuvres of his mind, may detect the onset of boredom at such infinitesimal progress. It must be borne in mind, dear reader, that regular meals and good fires are a powerful inducement to content, dull though they might be to read or write about. But happily for us all, Hubert initiated changes in the routine.

'It's a great good fortune you're here,' he said early one evening, 'because I'm on my way up to town. And Blanchy does so hate it when I go up to town. Could you keep her company tonight? And bring the car round for me, would you, dear fellow?'

He wore his black going-out suit under a priestly cloak, and held a black shovel hat in his hands; Palliser hoped he would not actually don it if he had any care for style: *would look like a pimple on a pumpkin.*

'I'm away up to town, my dear,' he said to Blanche. 'Pally said he'd look after you, did you not, old chap?'

'When will you be back, Hubert?'

'That depends upon a great many factors, my dear. I shall be at my altar betimes in the morning, have no fear. *Pax tecum, soror; pax tecum, amice.*'

'*Et cum spiritu tuo, Pater,*' said Palliser.

The car purred off down the lane, and both of them listened to it above the dance music on the wireless.

Palliser stood in front of the fire as he had stood habitually by his own hearth, heels on fender, hands in back pockets. *A man should warm his arse by his own fireside.*

Blanche stitched at her embroidery. A rustic scene, roses around the door of a cottage, dog in the foreground. It was almost complete. Palliser lit a cigarette.

She had to speak first. What she said would tell him where he was placed. The radio wittered through their silence. *Fine Goings On,* the comedy was called. Hubert's brandy winked at him from the sideboard. He eyed it back, willing it into his hand.

'Hubert always has a drink about now. Would you like one, Mr Wentwood?'

Ah blessed angel, I am thine, wilt thou be mine?

'Will you join me?'

She opened her mouth to protest; clearly Hubert never thought to offer. It was very expensive brandy, Palliser knew, for he was charged with buying it, but so far, alas, not a drop had touched his lips.

He grinned at her, teasing. 'O go on, Miss Lovelace, a little brandy to keep out the autumn.'

'Do you know, I think I will!' And she giggled, though in her register it sounded more like a chuckle.

'Good on you, as we say in New Zealand!'

He poured them both a very stiff brandy.

'Tell me about New Zealand, Mr Wentwood.'

Well, he was away now. All he had to do was to talk, and as long as he avoided mention of Salomé, he'd be right as rain. So he told her about mountains as high as heaven and seas as deep as death, of dolphins and whales that came up curious when you sailed offshore a little, of seals which roared at you and rushed at you if you cut them off from their young, of the rich fishing, the sacks full of crayfish bodies, their tails ripped off and sent to Japan. He told her about the soggy acres of his farm, the endless digging of ditches, the shoring up of muddy banks, the rain scouring potholes in the long road that led to his gate. And the little bridge lovingly constructed of left-over stones.

He heard his voice ringing through the drawing room, then dying away into a choke. On the wireless, an announcer started to introduce the evening's play, a light comedy about the Women's Institute and the Confusion that Ensues when a Prize Marrow Goes Missing. Blanche rose from her chair and switched it off.

'Have another brandy, Mr Wentwood.'

He filled her glass also, standing closer than he should have done. He looked longingly at her bosom, firmly contained within cream crêpe de Chine; he wished he could bury his head against it. Perhaps she longed to comfort him thus.

Palliser steered the conversation to safer topics. They talked about the war. Blanche's father, a shadowy, but presumably extremely large, figure, had been killed very early on, and her mother had fled to America as soon as was decent, leaving the children to a shaky network of nannies, housekeepers and poor relations. Blanche remembered little, except the Christmas when she was seven.

'There was nowhere for me to go. Mother was still in America, and we were to join her, but something went wrong with the arrangements. So in the end, Hubert went to his friend's and I stayed on at school. On Christmas Day I went to the school chapel, and there was only me and the head and her companion and the chaplain's wife and the cook. The deputy matron who was supposed to look after me was chapel. And then I had Christmas dinner with the head, and they tried to be kind, but no one had thought to buy me a present, and after that what was I to do?'

Seeing the tears in her eyes, Palliser could not stop himself patting her shoulder, while producing a perfect handkerchief at the same time, like a conjuring trick.

'It's over now. You never need spend Christmas alone again.'

'Oh it's easy for you to say that.'

Palliser wondered how his girls would spend this coming Christmas. Would they miss him, talk about him round the tree? He determined to send a great parcel of Christmas presents for them all to exclaim over.

'What did you do during the war, Mr Wentwood?'

'I farmed.' He grimaced at the image of himself, the farmer. He wondered how best to represent his war, how to tell the smallest number of lies. 'Farming was a protected occupation for most of the war, and when they changed their bureaucratic mind about that, I was too old, heaven be praised.'

He pushed down the memories of the complicated battles he had fought with the authorities to stay on the land and out of the army. The monster lies he had told and then had somehow to substantiate. He remembered sending tiny little Abigail to lose a letter from the recruitment officer in a ditch. He remembered bribing the doctor with eggs in case questions were asked regarding Salomé's supposed neurasthenia. At first it had been fun, fighting the paper war, then it grew desperate, as the Japanese crept closer and the war was no longer a distant jape, but a present threat. He remembered scanning the sweep of the bay and calculating how many people were left to defend it, per foot of coastline.

None of this he told Blanche.

'I hate it when Hubert goes to London,' she said suddenly.

Palliser left an encouraging pause.

'He never tells me where he's going,' she said. 'I'm afraid that if he doesn't come back in the morning, I won't know what to tell the police.'

Palliser nodded kindly; his silence forced her to go on.

'I don't even know the names of his friends,' she said. 'I don't know if they're men or women. Why does he need to keep parts of his life secret?'

Two glasses of brandy encouraged Palliser to take a chance.

'Well, maybe he likes to feel exciting to himself. They're probably just priests like himself, all sitting about sippin' gin and being scandalous about other priests.'

'Do you think so? Do you really think so?'

'I don't know why that should make you so happy, Miss Lovelace. Sounds dreary to me, though I'm sure they enjoy themselves no end.'

'I — it's just that — it does sound so silly, but . . .'

'You fear he has a lady friend, and that one day he'll announce he's getting married and leavin' you.'

She was aghast.

'And how did I figure that out? I am an old man, Miss Lovelace.'

For some reason this caused her to blush and look away.

'Have no fear, my dear,' he continued, well into his stride now, 'Hubert is not a marrying man.'

'How do you know that?'

'In this world, Miss Lovelace, there are marrying men, who do, and not-marrying men who will never. Your brother is one of the latter kind.'

'I suppose that should make me happy.'

Palliser opened his cigarette case – family silver, someone's – and offered her a cigarette. She declined, but was confused. He suspected no one had offered her a smoke before, poor girl. He lit up himself, and resumed his position by the fire, his nostalgia evaporating in a haze of brandy and nicotine.

'Well, yes and no. It should make you happy in the short term, in that your safe happy life with your brother at your side can continue indefinitely. But it should grieve you in the longer term, in that your brother marrying, bringing a whole new person into your lives, and children and in-laws, and all the strife and tumble and energy – that will not happen.'

She was very quiet. Palliser knew that no one had ever talked to her in this way before, or made her think about such things. He knew that he was risking his whole enterprise. His curiosity got the better of his cunning.

'Tell me, Miss Lovelace, how did you get on when your brother was at university, and at theological college?'

'Oh but he wasn't – I mean he was – but you see he was only at Oxford for a year. Oxford didn't suit him – he was much happier here.'

Palliser refilled his glass; hers sadly could not be construed as empty.

'But theological college – ordination and all that? I mean, he is in holy orders and what not?'

'The patriarch made an exception.'

Palliser, never at a loss, was at a loss.

'The patriarch.'

'I think so.'

Palliser wanted to laugh out loud, to explode at the absurdity of where he found himself. He was consumed with the desire to tell this tale to Salomé, this Gothic nonsense he was living in – but by God he was living it! He could not laugh at poor Blanche.

Poor Blanche – he had called her so in his head. This was the girl he was setting about to ruin, to make money out of, seduce and abandon. If he thought of her as poor Blanche, he'd have to go home right now with his tale between his legs.

He went on living out the farce, acting his part.

'So Hubert is not Church of England?'

'I know I am. I know Father and Mother were. Hubert says he's in communion with the Church of England.'

'Mother really wanted it, you see,' she said. 'Mother wanted Hubert to be a clergyman. It was somehow to do with her father and his father. Not that she went to church herself. She made him promise.'

'And what did she make you promise?'

Blanche pulled a final thread of brown wool through the embroidered dog's tail, and broke it off with her teeth.

'I don't remember.'

Palliser wondered whose fault it was that women never had plans. His mother, taking tea in the drawing room with her cohorts, as she called them, while the Pater was elsewhere, about his business. His dear nanny, always in the nursery with his tea ready, waiting for him to come in from play. Salomé, when he met her, just promenading around Europe, waiting for someone to happen. She had so much native wit, and, as it transpired, enormous amounts of energy and courage, but she had never thought, or no one had ever allowed her to think, that she should do anything. His own eldest girl, lovely Jemima, always waiting on someone else's activity, fitting in, being attentive and patient. Little Abigail, his young sprig, squirrelling away learning, without a thought of how to spend it. And this sweet Blanche, amply possessed of every attribute that a person needs for advancement – youth, wealth, energy and moral fortitude – imprisoned in a cardboard cut-out model of womanly activity waiting for some man to come along and take advantage of her. How could women allow themselves to be like that? Lucky for Palliser that they were so, but it made no sense. Mostly women were cleverer than he was, most were more sensible, talented and better organised. But he had always done things, made things happen, not very successfully he granted, but at least he'd never sat still. What was so different about Blanche, that while Hubert went out and got himself some sort of orders from some sort of Church, she was content to sit at home and embroider?

If he were to ask her, would she ever speak to him again? The risk was too great; he supposed that nature had moulded women as wives and mothers, and therefore in their minds such questions did not arise. He supposed it was nature's beneficence, in fact, that Blanche was prepared to sit at home and wait. Some day a man would come along and scoop up all her bounty, and nature would run its course. Palliser naturally wanted to be part of that process, so who was he to question what nature had decreed?

Salomé, he thought, Salomé, thank God, and the girls, will wait at home for me. It is in their very natures. Heaven is merciful to us men. I shall take them home a prize worthy of their patience.

Hubert, as he promised, did make it to his altar next morning, but not without difficulty. At five to seven Palliser was sitting along a pew in the chapel, his arms folded, legs stretched out in front of him and eyes closed.

He was dressed, but not impeccably; he had not shaved, but at least he had brushed his hair, which was more than could be said for the boy Peter, whose blond coif stuck up like a very poorly adjusted halo. The boy came out into the gloom in his cassock to light the candles. Palliser heard him swearing as the healthy breeze that aired the chapel extinguished matches one after another.

'He's not here,' said the boy.

Palliser half opened an eye. Visions of Hubert mangled in a ditch or face down in a gutter came to him. He dismissed them.

'We'll wait.'

The boy sat down in a pew across from Palliser. The house chapel was collegial, with tall dark box pews facing one another. It had no natural light; the only windows were filled to the edges with brightly coloured stained glass. Scenes from the Old and New Testaments, balanced so that one commented on the other. Many were unfamiliar to Palliser, and the captions in Latin defeated him, so the complex typological parallel between Jonah in the Whale and the Raising of Lazarus was lost on him. But he picked out Abraham sacrificing Isaac, with a tidy ram peering out of the thicket, just asking to be cut up instead of the little boy, and he supposed that the damsel in flimsies before an army of chaps with banners was the ill-fated daughter of Jephthah, for whom no ewe was forthcoming. Daniel in the lions' den he recognised, and the supernatural handwriting on the wall: mene, mene, tekel, upharsin. *The Moving Finger writes; and having writ, moves on; nor all your Piety nor Wit shall lure it back nor all your Tears wash out a Word of it.* He warmed to the Prodigal Son, rooting with the pigs in one corner, while his father, resplendent in the cerulean robes of a Jacobean burgher, ran towards him with open arms.

Below the windows, the brightly coloured theme was

taken up by Hubert's altar, correctly decked in the frontal of the season. To either side, Hubert had placed two plaster statues of fairground hue, refugees from some Roman Catholic disposal. The Blessed Virgin with her hand cupped modestly over her sacred heart, as if she was proud and embarrassed to show off so private an organ. The other, a boy Jesus with blond curls not unlike Peter's, topped by a fetching circlet of thorns, held a bird in his hands and looking intently upwards. To one side, in a murky corner, Palliser noticed for the first time an icon of Middle Eastern style on a kind of easel, with a tray of lights before it. A nod to the sponsoring body, he supposed.

'Did you know he wasn't Church of England?'

The boy grinned.

'It's all the same to me. Silly fat fool.'

'Then why do it, every morning?'

'Why do you then?'

Palliser had asked himself this question more than once. It was not from any religious motive.

'It goes with the job,' he said, not entirely convinced that this was so.

Peter yawned and slumped in his pew.

'Go back to bed,' Palliser said, 'I'll do the business for you.'

'Would ya? You're a champion.'

He did not wait for a reconsideration.

Palliser sat on in the chapel for a minute or two, but growing uncomfortable in the holy silence he went outside for a smoke. In the corridor he collided with Hubert, dressed as the night before, unshaven, harassed and smelling strongly of brandy.

'Well, you're safe and well. Glory be to God.'

'Safe, but not well, Pally, not well at all. O Jesus, Mary. Where's Peter?'

Palliser followed Hubert as he hastened into the chapel towards the little vestry. 'I sent him back to bed.'

Hubert stopped in his tracks, turned away from the vestry door and sat down heavily in a pew. He thrust his head in his hands and bent over as near double as his proportions allowed.

'O why, why today?' he said. He burst into tears.

Palliser stood, unlit cigarette in hand, and considered his employer.

'I wanted to see him, today more than ever. It's the high point of my day to see Peter, just see him, alone without that woman. Just to look at him, to have him to myself, for a moment. By my side.'

He fetched a great sob. 'Today of all days, when I'm at my lowest ebb.'

Palliser sat down in the adjacent pew; he lit a cigarette and, touching Hubert lightly on the hand, gave it to him. Then he lit another for himself.

'I don't expect him to understand why I feel so unhappy. I don't expect anyone to understand. But just looking at him brings light into my day, makes my miserable life worthwhile.'

Palliser thought it was terrible to see so large a man shudder and weep, and his hands tremble. The cigarette was consumed almost at once. Hubert felt for his own cigars.

'Do you want to tell me, old chap?' said Palliser as kindly as he knew how.

'Where can I start? I know I shall sound like a perfect fool whatever I say. How could I expect you to understand?'

'I'll do my best.'

Sometimes people were moved to confide in Palliser, not because he played the confidant, but because he was in company so much it was hard to avoid the role entirely. There was a certain class of woman from whom he encouraged the pouring-out of woe, but here was a new situation. He was duty bound to listen to Hubert's trouble, but he heartily wished not to be told anything that might later be regretted.

Hubert's suit was crumpled and his face red. His hair stood up from his forehead. He tried to light his cigar. Palliser struck a match and lit it for him.

'Shouldn't smoke in here, should we? Oh dear. I should get ready.'

'I don't think you should say mass this morning.'

Hubert sat back and closed his eyes, cigar poised daintily against his knee. 'They threw me out, you know,' he said, eyes closed, 'rejected me. Declined to accept my application. After all this time. My friends, so I thought. Jocelyn and Father Linchin, and Francis. It's that Alban from All Saints' put them up to it. He always hated me. Jealous, I suppose. Working-class background, Halifax churches, that kind of thing.

'I've been an associate for ages. SSC – Society of the Sacred Cross – I always go up to the meetings, they're my friends, have been for years. I don't know,' he said with a great boy's sob, 'I don't know how to get through the month otherwise. How can I go back now?'

'What happened?'

'Someone, I think it was that Alban, suggested I should apply for full membership. I've been an associate ever since I was a student, but everyone else has moved on to full, and there aren't any associates now. No young ones at all. Must be the war, I suppose, new age dawning, that kind of thing. Not that we're old, I'm the youngest I suppose, but several of them are round my age. Father Burton took me along; I suppose I was his protégé. But he went to the colonies in '54, got married. I'd have been all right if he stayed, I'd have done everything properly. He'd have made sure of that. He would have protected me, stood up for me. None of my so-called friends said a word in the meeting, not even Jocelyn. How can I go back now?

'They read out the committee's ruling. Restricted to priests of the Anglican Communion. Unfortunately, *Father*, said that Alban – called me Father – your orders are not compatible. Not compatible – we're in communion, I'm episcopally ordained, according to the Apostolic Succession. It's nothing personal, says he, we have to be so precise in these liberal days, who knows *who* might apply to join. There was this little snigger, because someone had made a joke earlier about the woman in Hong Kong who got a bishop to lay hands on her.'

'Where have you been since?'

'Jocelyn took me back to his place, Holy Cross. And Francis came, and I'm afraid I had a bit to drink. In the end they threw me out, ever so politely – well, Jocelyn said he had to get up early to say mass, and Francis sort of walked me out with him. I just wandered around a bit. Ever been round London at night, Pally, really late?'

'Matter of fact, I have.' *Many times, me old mate, but enough of that.*

'Gets to you, don't it? Surreal, is that the word? Nothing seems like itself. Makes you question everything. Awful place Jocelyn works in. So I walked right down to the Embankment, and along the river. Terrible and lovely, isn't it? Like a book by Blake. But there wasn't any sign of God or even the Archangel Michael. I just walked. Then I saw the dawn coming up, and I thought of Peter. And hurried back. And he's not here.'

'I'm sorry. I'm truly sorry. Come and I'll make you breakfast.'

Hubert shambled behind him down the corridor.

'First day I haven't said mass since I was ordained. I was so chuffed, you know, when they accepted me, the Syrians. I swore I'd say mass every day. Now I've failed.'

'You have not failed. You are distressed and unwell.'

'What shall I do, Pally?'

'About Peter, or about your friends or about the Society?'

'All three.'

'Well, in general my motto is: keep moving, but never turn down the possibility of pleasure. So right now my advice to you as an old world-weary man to a younger is to have a damned good breakfast, and then I shall draw you a bath, and then you should go to bed.'

'You're a good man, Pally.'

Palliser reckoned he had never been so severely misjudged.

Rat-tat-tat at the door. It's mid-morning and a sense of purpose is abroad. Palliser is in the Great Scullery and his shirt sleeves, fixing a tap.

Dammit, another damn follower of Mrs Nagy. She can damn well get the door herself.

He allows water to gush loudly as a cover. He's been on best behaviour for a while now and the benign effect of enough food and warmth is beginning to take effect. He forgets to play the butler. Especially now he's the custodian of fears.

I could stay here for ever. This is a placing for life.

It suits him. No one demands or expects – or what they expect he can easily deliver. They think him kind; they love his company. They are rich and lonely; he is entertaining and handy. He is fixing a tap. Shortly he will take the car down to the mechanic in Great Boreham, and come back via two buses and the pub. No one will cross-question him on how long his errand took, and where he went. They will be happy because he has done the job that they would find almost impossible. Soon their dependence on him will be such that he will name his price. And what will he ask?

The hammering on the door continues. Palliser feels contrary.

What do I want? Ah, now there's an existential question. How does one know what one wants until one's gotten it and found it to be wanting? There's the flaw in your plan too, old man. Not clear on the desired outcome.

Enough money to get home? Money to take home? Money to send home? Lucrative situation for life? A permanent income? Expensive presents? Rich wife? Wealthy friends?

Jesus, Mary and Joseph, said the voice of his nanny, *who's like a dog at a fair? One toffee at a time, Palliser, that's how you enjoy life.*

Yes, but which toffee? All of them would do very nicely.

Bang bang bang. The chap at the door isn't going away. Would that woman never give in?

Life had frequently appeared to Palliser very much as a bag of toffees that you could stuff in your pocket and dip into, over and over again, pushing them into your mouth and throwing away the papers with abandon. But then came the moment when your hand met paper at the bottom of the pocket, when you scrabbled round frantically to find the last toffee, and brought up with it the empty bag. That also would get screwed up and thrown away.

If there was moral justice in this world, or any sort of useful God, my choices would be clear. Good that way, bad the other. What would Hubert say?

He laughs out loud at the prospect of himself going to Hubert with his moral problem. He is still laughing when Mrs Nagy propels herself into the corridor. 'Wentwood, Wentwood!' she screams.

Palliser turns the tap more forcefully and says, 'Yes, Mrs Nagy?'

She bursts into the scullery in full flight and copious tears.

'Answer the door, answer the door. Tell him to go away, whoever it is. I don't like this banging.'

'You could send Peter,' says Palliser amicably. 'I'm in a state of undress. And engaged.'

'No, no, Peter must never answer the door. Never.'

'Well, Peter is going to find adult life quite a challenge. Who could be at the door, Mrs Nagy, that poses you such difficulty?'

Mrs Nagy sobs and opens the floodgates in Hungarian. Reasoned conversation becomes difficult, but the visitor has not gone away. He starts to knock at the side door, very loudly.

At this point, Blanche sails into view. She stands at the doorway to the scullery looking as if she wishes to speak. Palliser is tidying up and rolling down his sleeves. Mrs Nagy switches to French, but Palliser can't catch her meaning.

'Palliser, get the door.'

Palliser goes without hesitation. It is only when he is opening the side door to the delivery boy in the brown coat from Levi and Sons that he takes note that she used his first name. Is this a good sign?

He signs the delivery note for a box, presumably of continental delicacies, reminding himself that he has done nothing yet to track down the sender. He has not been up to London for weeks. This thought alarms him.

'Who sends this?'

'Search me, guv. I just do the deliveries. Secret admirer, eh? She's got plenty.'

'Can't see it myself,' says Palliser.

'Nor me, but then she's more like me mum's age, ent she?'

Palliser takes the box of delights into the big kitchen and locates his hammer, or rather the hammer he has purchased for his use with Hubert's funds. Scrupulous, he is, in spending their money. He is preparing to open the box, delaying the moment of manliness until Blanche should appear. Which she does on cue, escorting Mrs Nagy, whom she seems to have pacified.

On seeing the delivery, Mrs Nagy launches into a different speech, still in French, or possibly French mixed with Hungarian, this time spitting fury.

'Who sends these boxes?' asks Palliser.

'She doesn't like to talk about him. Or not in English anyway.' A tiny smile. 'A box has come every month almost since she's been here. Every month. There's always a letter or card, and she burns them unopened.'

'He must be one of her more persistent admirers.'

'I think it's rather horrid,' says Blanche.

Peter, whom they have failed to notice, looks up from his book, *Commercial Practice for Upper Forms*.

'You could ask her directly, Miss Lovelace. It's not a particularly difficult question to construct. Mother, tell Miss Lovelace who sends the box every month.'

Mrs Nagy lets out a wail like Andromache over the body of Astyanax, flings her apron over her head and flees from the room. They hear her feet battering on the stairs of the servants' staircase.

'Peter could tell us,' says Palliser.

'But he won't,' says Peter.

Miss Lovelace sets out on her morning flower-gathering expedition. This time of the year it takes her longer, as the flowers shrivel with the expectation of winter. Happily, Dick, the cheerful under-gardener whom Palliser has now employed, often brings down a bucket of flowers from his other employers, the Eltons at the Manor. They like things ever so tidy at the Manor, Dick says, horrible. Not like here, so wild and lovely.

Palliser cleans up the Great Scullery and then disposes Mrs Nagy's tribute once more in the pantry and kitchen. Some tins of coffee are put away in a safe place. He samples the least garlic-ridden of the salami, and opens a tin of olives.

'Unobtainable on my side of the world,' he says, sharing the olives with Peter.

He picks up the white envelope from the bottom of the box and sniffs it. Peter watches him, daring him to open it.

'You'd better look after this for your mother.'

Peter gets up and pokes the envelope into the fire. Man and boy stand watching the paper curl and die, taking its message to the grave.

When Blanche returns from the garden, defenceless behind a great mass of fern, Palliser is lying in wait for her. He has everything prepared. In the Great Scullery he has placed her vases, netting frames, sharp scissors, and the bucket of flowers from the Manor.

'I thought,' he says, confronting her at the door of the kitchen, 'you might find it easier in here.'

He takes her arm and steers her into the Great Scullery.

'The beauty of it is, Mrs Nagy won't get in your way. And if you ain't finished before luncheon, well you just leave everything here. It's purpose-built for flowers. Clever chaps, those Tudors.'

And indeed the room is perfect. Although half sunk beneath the ground, it has a large window facing south on to the Broad Terrace. Under the window is a big working surface of wood, and on the next wall a capacious sink with a long marble bench. There are high shelves and cubby-holes, hooks and a drying rack suspended from the roof. There is even a small coal-fired stove tucked into a recess, with a hot plate on which a kettle may be boiled.

Palliser cannot tear himself away. He wants to see her happiness and he wants to see her gratitude. He observes her exterior carefully, but all he sees is the portcullis. She is trying to understand why he has done this for her. To delay his departure he offers to light the fire.

'Oh no, no, it's far too warm. If you are cold, Mr Wentwood, you should go for a walk.'

'I like company when walking, Miss Lovelace.'

She is unable to deal with this invitation, but deposits the flowers on the bench and starts to sort them. She begins to feel the space and liberty he has given her, and her movements grow less tentative. A foretaste of the woman she might become seeps into Palliser's mouth. But as she grows into his gift, he feels he is no longer present.

'Shall I fetch you the vase from the library?'

'Thank you,' she says sweetly, but without looking at him.

When he returns, carrying last week's arrangement from the library before him like someone else's embarrassing trophy, she is so happily at work that she hardly seems aware of his presence.

Palliser doesn't know whether this pleases him or not.

It seems that Hubert's friend Jocelyn is possessed of a tender conscience. After the night of his fall from grace, Palliser persuaded Hubert to write good long letters to his friends, and in return he received an invitation from Jocelyn to stay for the weekend, and to preach at benediction. Hubert is elated; the Syrians, he says, do not appreciate his gifts as a preacher.

The sound of the harpsichord is heard in the halls.

Palliser drove Hubert to the station; he was to be left in charge of the car, and instructed to take Blanche out. Hubert opened his wallet and took out a quantity of notes. These he folded carefully and poked over into the front of the car.

'Make sure she has a nice time.'

He hesitated, with more to say. Palliser turned to look at him.

'You know, Palliser, you've done a great deal for me, but when I took you on it was for Blanchy's sake. She doesn't know any men, you see. I thought she would benefit from a little male company. Broaden her horizons.'

'Should I take her to coffee bar, or a beat club?'

Hubert saw this was a joke, and laughed obediently.

'There's an autumn festival at the Abbey. Flowers and things. I think that's more her style.'

Driving back from the station, Palliser wound down the window and encouraged the light breeze to tousle his hair. He felt young again; well, a good deal younger. It was a gorgeous day, considering that it was English autumn. Gentle sunlight patted the baroque golds and red of the distant trees, and dappled the brooks and puddles. A soft haziness crept in from the corners, like a gentleman painter taking his time. It was a comforting scene, familiar from ten thousand faded calendars celebrating the Beauties of England, pinned to back doors in all corners of the Empire.

And yet it was foreign to his eye, which was accustomed to the sharpness of a different light. The very nature of the light unsettled him, made him long for home, and the mountains violent against the sky.

What am I doing here, wasting away? When I might fly to the ends of the earth, and remain in the uttermost parts of the sea . . .

On the plus side, he was spinning down the lanes in the dear old Roller, for all the world as if he were a man of means.

What would he do if he had free choice? He could drive somewhere really lovely, like Cookham, maybe, and sit by the river in a pub, pick up a long-haired art student, and take her for a spin and back to his hotel for a slap-up dinner, and whatever. Or he could do his duty and escort Miss Blanche Lovelace to the flower festival at the Abbey.

'Get your hat, my dear, we're going out.'

For once, in taking a young woman out for the day, he had no shortage of money, no shortage of time, and no immediate prospect of sexual conquest. All normal causes of anxiety were therefore removed. The drawbacks were that she was so appallingly dressed, and so haltingly short of conversation. Today Palliser did not feel the need to wear the chauffeur's cap.

Since it was too early for lunch, he suggested a detour via the public library. He claimed he needed a reference from the London Yellow Pages, but in truth he felt that borrowing books from a library was a simple pleasure that had been denied to Blanche. The library with its utilitarian floors and forbidding notices was alien territory for her; she had never entered such a place before. She thought libraries, except school libraries and the British Library, were for the indigent. She would not have got past the reading room, with its scattering of tramps and retired City gents, passing their hours of useless time by scanning the newspapers. Many an hour Palliser had spent in their company. These persons found Blanche's entrance of great interest; some of them recognised Palliser, but made no sign. Palliser had to propel her through a minefield of strangers, past Recent Acquisitions and New Fiction to the safe body of the library, where almost no one came to disturb the peace. He knew the place well, having spent many hours in its comforting arms, keeping warm and writing down addresses. He guided her to Home Crafts, and said he would return.

He calculated the amount of time needed to hook his fish correctly then made his way back from the Reference Section, and caught sight of her between the stacks. She was holding four books in her arm and frowning over another with the single-mindedness of a six-year-old. When he appeared around the end of the stack, she looked up suddenly and smiled at him, happy that he had come back for her, happy at her new discovery.

'Can one really borrow all these books?'

He had to guide her through the bureaucratic terrors of the membership desk, and deal with the potential embarrassment of borrowing five books, when a temporary ticket only allowed one to take out two. He did not want her disappointed at this stage. He polished up his accent and his smile and explained to the young woman on Issues that Miss Lovelace had an urgent need for these books, as she was opening Thule Hall for a society wedding, and that Membership had given them special leave. The girl on Issues, who had pert breasts under her librarian's smock and pretty brown eyes, smiled at Palliser. He wondered fleetingly if she might care for a coffee some evening.

He took the library books, and offered Blanche his arm down the library steps.

'Mr Wentwood, that wasn't true.'

'Sometimes, it's necessary to enhance the facts, if systems get in the way.'

'I don't know very much, but I do know it is wrong to lie, whatever the circumstances.'

O Jesus Mary Joseph, here's a swamp and a half to cross! How am I going to talk my way out of this?

'The difficulty is, Miss Lovelace, what is a lie? Now consider this. We are about to go into the White Hart for luncheon. But if instead we were to go into the Angel, the chatelaine of that worthy establishment would assume that I am a gentleman taking his young lady out for the day, with my own money. Whereas Mrs Hogg at the White Hart will know that I am your employee, and squiring you at your brother's request and with your brother's money. I would not have told any lies at the Angel, but a falsity would have been committed. Would I be obliged to explain to the landlady of the Angel that I am not your beau, but simply your butler? If I go up to London and stay in the Ritz, and give my address as Thule Hall, the persons at the front desk will all believe that I am the master of Thule Hall, and a man of means. Now I have not told a lie, but an untruth has been perpetrated.'

'Do you do that often?'

He chose to interpret this as light-heartedly as possible.

'Not of latter years, but as a young man I might often be found frequenting those hallowed halls.'

'On a butler's salary?'

Arrival at the entrance to the White Hart saved Palliser's skin, for the time being.

You will not make up any stories. You will not improve on the truth. Don't do it, Pally, don't. She don't like it. Watch your tongue, old man, not to mention your hands.

They strolled down the hill to where the Abbey stood, squat and defiant in its age. *So you don't think I'm beautiful?* it said. *When you're as old as I am, worm, you don't need to be beautiful.*

They went in by the west door, gaunt Gothic beautified by some rich Victorian. On entrance, Palliser passed over a silver coin for the festival programme, and handed it to Blanche with a flourish, but she was hardly aware of him.

'Oh lovely,' she cried.

The nave was crawling with vegetation; all the grumpy Norman pillars were bedecked with greenery as high as a ladder might reach. At the base of each pillar, where a monk's altar used to stand, was a shrine to Ceres, each a showpiece of ingenuity with flower, branch, berry, dried frond and found object. And behind each display, one of

133

its creators, trying to look uninvolved while surveying the passers-by surreptitiously for admiration.

Blanche was transported by delight, so Palliser set her carefully adrift. He had a mission of his own at this event. He had decided that these good ladies were Blanche's natural allies, and this festival her habitat. He must help her bond, good shepherd that he was trying to be.

He sauntered around the stands, looking not at the flowers but the women beside them, always his hobby, today his task. He knew the one he wanted, not for himself, but for Blanche. She must be slightly older than Blanche, married, kind and outgoing. And the right class and level of income, otherwise discomfort would breed.

He walked right around the nave, sizing up twin-sets and tweed skirts, and lamenting the sexless lives of the English middle classes. He looked at thick brown stockings and sensible shoes, and handbags the size of hutches, gloves and hats bowing down in imitation of the Queen Mum. He brightened at a young woman in a white dress blotched with huge pale blue flowers, narrow waist, huge flared skirt, shapely legs, bright red lips, hooped earrings. She would not do for Blanche, though she would suit Palliser rather well. He sighed.

He hesitated by an elegant young woman in light beige cashmere, beautifully made up, with pale pink lips, manicured nails, black high-heeled shoes, and a most agreeably shaped bottom. She did not seem to be very interested in flowers, however, judging by the bored remarks she exchanged with Palliser, though she clearly was interested in him. He sighed.

Out of curiosity he engaged in chat a handsome lady who must have been the wife of one of the senior clergy, since she referred to the Abbey as 'ours'. She recognised him, presumably from the days when he earned a few shillings deputising in the choir, but seemed to think he was a clergyman in mufti; if Palliser had not been on his best behaviour he might have had no end of fun with this mistake, but he made a little bow and passed on.

Up around the saint's shrine, in a dark unfrequented passage, were some late entries, with disconsolate ladies chatting one to another, and then beyond, a cluster of enthusiasm around a small chapel. The chapel itself had been decorated; ivy had been persuaded to climb around behind the altar; orchids clambered up the stonework, and where saints used to nestle, lilies and roses hung. It was exuberant and extravagant, and fun. And there she was.

About twenty-five, he thought, inclining to stoutness, but fit, and most agreeable, a nice woman's body, standard fittings all in good shape. More importantly, bright brown eyes and a big mouth, smiling and talking madly to all comers. Outdoorsy complexion, wedding ring, nice brogues, decent tweed suit, well cut and well fitted. Expensive pearls, thrown on for the event. Italian silk scarf in pocket of coat.

Yes, said Palliser, she's the one.

It took him some time to ingratiate himself; she was merrily in conversation with an elderly couple, great orchid people. He didn't pretend to any knowledge of orchids, or flowers at all, but confined himself to honest admiration of her handiwork.

'Oh it's not mine,' she said. 'I'm just taking the credit. Isn't it awful? Well I did grow the things, but as soon as I try to arrange them, they just go all wonky. I can see you're a flower man?' She indicated the books in his arm.

They were away; after ten minutes they were old acquaintances, even flirting a tiny bit. Blanche appeared round the feretory, saw him and for a second her face registered unhappiness. Quick as a breath he brought her forward.

'You must meet Blanche,' he exclaimed to his new discovery. 'Blanche, do come and meet –'

'Clarissa,' she said, 'Clarissa Elton. No relation to Mrs E – Jane Austen – never mind.'

'Blanche Lovelace, and I am Palliser Wentwood.'

Palliser gave a little bow. Blanche and Clarissa shook hands.

'Lovelace,' she said. 'From Thule Hall? Oh gosh, I know all about you! One of my gardeners, Dick, he's always talking about Thule.'

Blanche blushed deeply.

'Oh not like that, good heavens no! He loves it; he's always going on about the garden and the house. He thinks we're far too tidy at the Manor, but he doesn't reckon with the military mind. I'd have a place just like yours, in fact you should see my greenhouses! But Roland was in charge of the greens at Sandhurst and he just can't stand a flower out of place. Oh I've heard so much about you!'

It was evident to Palliser that she knew exactly who he was.

'Well, it is a stroke of luck meeting you, Blanche – may I call you Blanche? It does seem rude when we've only just met, but these days it's awfully hard to know how formal one should be. It's such a stroke of luck, because I really have been meaning to write you a little note. I'm frightfully interested in your garden, you see, I write these little monographs, well sort of pamphlets really, with photographs, colour cover, they're very nicely done, Pitkins. I do them on gardens, houses and gardens, but the emphasis on the garden, and I thought yours would be wonderful – so fascinating and so much history.'

Oh ye heavens how you look upon your servant to pour blessings on his head!

At that moment the prebendary went by, and seeing sometime choirman Palliser, he stopped to chat about the latest developments in the choir. Palliser turned away slightly from the two women, but heard a steady burble of conversation behind him. Clarissa's commanding tones, but enough of Blanche's rumble to indicate dialogue. When the prebendary swished on, patting Palliser's arm and hoping to see him back with them soon, Palliser rejoined the women, his churchy connections established, and found himself slightly *de trop*. They were talking flowers so devotedly that the conversation was entirely appropriate to its surroundings.

He stood at Blanche's elbow, amusing himself by undressing her slowly and making love to her against the stone pier behind them.

Delicious thing about a tall woman . . .

He wanted to keep Clarissa talking to Blanche as long as possible. He wandered about a bit and chatted some more to the woman in beige cashmere until caution decreed he move on. He bought a picture postcard of the Abbey, borrowed a pen from Mrs Canon Perkins of St Cyriac's, and wrote on the card;

Dearest Naomi, thought you might like to see where I am living – not actually in the Abbey, but nearby, in a house called Thule. Abigail will be able to tell you about the real Thule. I am doing well, at last, and hope to be home for next Christmas. Smoke me a nice fat eel, all ready. Yr loving father.

'Tell me, Mr Wentwood, I ought to be able to work out where you come from . . .'

'Palliser.'

'Oh righty, Palliser. What an absolutely splendid name – Oh I know, Trollope.'

'I think he borrowed it from us. We certainly predate him and his naughty thieving novels. Not that we had any pretensions to politics, you understand. My provenance, to answer your question, Clarissa, is complicated.'

'Palliser,' said Blanche, using his name as if it were a piece of bone china, 'has recently returned from New Zealand.'

She closed the subject, as if she wanted no opportunity to arise for Clarissa to investigate or for Palliser to tell any tales. Clarissa, unperturbed, talked merrily about New Zealand lamb, butter, rationing and her Cook, and made Blanche laugh.

Then Palliser overheard the words for which he had hoped.

'Why don't you come to tea? Come on Monday – would that be all right? Then I can show you round. Palliser will drop you over, won't you? I can show you my greenhouses. Oh, it will be fun! I am so glad we met!'

Driving home, Blanche was feverish with new excitements. She grew bold.

'You'll want to stop in the village, and post your card.'

So Palliser was constrained to post his card, and he too felt the flurry of unfamiliar emotion.

Thus Blanche Lovelace, at the prompting of Palliser Wentwood, supposed butler and potential lover, made her first friend. It was a joy to observe; on the day when her friend was expected to tea, her step was light and fast. When she was invited to the Manor, she spent the morning in happy turmoil. Palliser taught her how to use the telephone, how to make small talk with the Elton children, aged three and five.

It was the most benign of autumns. All through the golden days, Blanche and Clarissa pottered together about their gardens, Clarissa talking and Blanche smiling at her every word. Clarissa put her on the flower rota at St Cyriac's, and made her help out at the Harvest Festival bring and buy. Clarissa lent her books to read, thrillers and light novels, thus feeding her now weekly visits to the library with new purpose. One library day she plumped back into the back seat of the car with two romantic novels in her haul. Palliser cocked an eyebrow and smiled to himself.

His role of drawing Blanche out into the world was to some extent taken over by Clarissa, but he did not resent this. It allowed him to concentrate on his main aim, with which Clarissa helped indirectly by her determination to be modern, combined with an good old-fashioned streak of bawdiness. She lent Blanche a novel with brown paper covers, and a sex guide. Palliser knew of these books only by inference, sensing in Blanche a slight difference in the way she looked at him.

She looks at him when she thinks it safe, when he's busy. Here he is chopping wood, his sleeves rolled up, taking his time about it, but making nice long strokes with a nice sharp axe. She is supposed to watch this performance, and she does, pretending to be busy with her flowers. He has positioned himself in good view of the window where she works, not the most obvious place to chop wood, but who's to quiz him about it? Up goes the axe, Palliser's muscles flex, and down it comes, neatly splitting a log for the fire. He's got more than enough for this week, but she's still at the window. He pauses, takes a red spotted kerchief out of his pocket to wipe his brow, like a Thomas Hardy labourer. He's suitably dressed for the occasion – cords and a collarless shirt several buttons open. He reckons he could pass for Lady Chatterley's gamekeeper in middle age. But does she think like that?

It's all very well to soften her up so far – now she calls him Palliser, sometimes addresses remarks directly to him. He dines with her, sits in front of the fire with her every night. She shows him her library books and shares his hymn-book in church. But there is still a long distance to her bed and the sort of money he needs to set him up for life. Clarissa measures him up with her eyes every time she sees them together. Her measuring says: watch your step, I've got my eye on you. Mrs Nagy watches him, seeing what he does, saying nothing. Peter Nagy watches him, grins.

They're watching him. The question is, how long can his cover hold? He's too comfortable by half, that's part of the difficulty – breakfast, lunch, dinner, clothes, fire and ten pounds a week. He could sink back into comfort, forget what he came for, do nothing more. It's tempting. It's less reprehensible than seducing a sweet girl who's done him no harm.

But am I not doing her good? Am I not sent to make women happy? Doesn't she love to watch me work, see the sweat on the brow and the muscles work? How much more is she going to enjoy me as a lover, a role I was born to fulfil.

Palliser, according to his own assessment, makes sex the pleasure it is meant to be; therefore it will hold no fears for her.

But how to get there, when they're all watching? Watching and waiting. I make a false move, scare her and get repulsed, and they'll be in for the kill. Even Hubert will turn against me. Sex always gets the wind up men like Hubert. The move has to come from her, but she doesn't have a shit show of making it. Sure, I've taught her how to borrow a library book, but that's not much of a preparation for a sexual advance. I'll never get home at this rate, neither this Christmas, nor next. We'll get comfy like an old married couple of three, without the best bits.

What he hasn't worked out, the great big flaw in the Palliser plan, is how he is going to make the transition from lover – assuming he gets that far – to pensioned-off lover, back home in the bosom of his family. His plan is flawed, as usual. Will Hubert pay him off? Will Blanche give him a big present, after which he can behave like a cad and flee the country? Pocketing a present and running away requires the sort of cold-bloodedness that he thinks he lacks.

How do you judge Palliser Wentwood now? If you judge him on his deeds as herein described, rather than his motives, as also herein described, how much wrong has he done? Setting aside the initial desertion of his wife, which we must deal with separately, does the fruit of his labours so far taste bitter?

Now, gentle reader, I am not defending Palliser's deceptions simply because his inexhaustible charm also works on me, a woman of a certain age. I was brought up by the rulebook which stated that to do a good deed for an evil reason weighs very light in the moral balances, almost as damning as to do an evil deed for good ends.

But, observing Palliser as I do, I cannot bring myself to condemn him, perhaps because good and evil are not lump sums in the spiritual account book, but like the commercial transactions of a lifetime, thousands and thousands of small entries, which taken together make up a whole. Palliser is still in mid-session trading.

He has stopped chopping wood, and leans on his axe. Unhappiness washes all over him – you observe, he is not a man without conscience. He forgets where he is, sees himself in his backyard, at the wood block, cursing over the hardness of the blue gum. Salomé comes down the flags towards him, lifting her skirts out of the mud, hens scattering before her. She's got a glass in her hand, the last crystal rummer. The liquid is magenta, a thick, magical brew. She comes towards him, holding it before her, an offering, a sacrament. She's smiling, her whole person smiles, smiling shoots out the ends of her electric hair. Taste it, she says, it's the new batch, the best ever.

A tiny taste of heaven, she says. He puts down the axe, leans it on the chopping block, puts his arm right around her fabulously narrow waist and drinks the wine in teaspoonfuls, closing his eyes with each sip. Then he puts the glass down with infinite care and embraces his wife, kissing her with all the passion her wonderful wine and great person summon up.

Suddenly he recalls himself and, looking about, sees that Blanche is standing in the doorway, watching him. She is carrying a creation of bright berries and late autumn gold for his approval. She says nothing. Her watching him says everything that is necessary. He feels moved to make some gesture to express the sadness and beauty that are in his heart.

He puts down the axe, leans it on the chopping block, and goes towards her. He runs his hand down her cheek, slowly, slowly, so that his fingers brush the skin as carefully as if he were dusting the gold leaf on a book of hours.

'You are so beautiful,' he says.

She shakes her head, very slightly, a breeze, a murmur of disbelief.

'Oh, but you are, and not knowing it makes you more beautiful still.'

He leans towards her through the thicket of berberis and sloe and kisses her.

Palliser's bedroom, the largest of the servants' rooms, is on the fourth level of the house, counting upwards from the sculleries, with a gentleman's view to the south of the park. Furnished in the plainest manner, to which he has added nothing, being but a bird of passage, it contains an iron bed barely long enough for him. Its narrowness, so far, had caused him no inconvenience. He has contrived to exchange the original, geographically interesting, mattress for a duller one from the floor below. On the wall a holy picture, Our Lady of Perpetual Succour, with rosy cheeks overlaid on her flat gold skin, her uncompromising Eastern gaze softened by some Western softness about the mouth. Palliser does not like it; he feels that the Virgin should be either soft and yielding or worshipfully strong. But he knows he is sometimes unrealistic about women.

The morning after the kiss, a Sunday, Palliser stands at his window, testing the floorboards with his bare feet and thinking about the slippers lined with possum fur that Jemima made him for his fortieth birthday. Lovely soft fluffy fur, from such a nasty little animal. Fur that reminds him of nothing so much as –

Sunday is officially his day off and, there being no breakfast provided in this strictly fasting household, he has nothing to detain him. More than once he has given up his Sunday morning to take Blanche to the parish church for the advantage that is to be gained from sitting close by her side through the longueurs of the sermon. Sermons always provoke thoughts of the flesh in his mind, and he prays that they might in hers. But today he feels moved to go out into the autumn and find a bit of skirt. In his pocket is a month's salary, in crunchy pound notes. In his limbs is energy and in his loins fire. The sun is shining, and there is life in the old dog yet.

VI

'SHALL I MAKE myself plain? I do not approve, Mrs Wentwood. I do not approve of your association with my son.'

Mrs Butterworth's mouth, a perfect upturned U, snaps shut as if it was crafted that way. She sits, Salomé stands, but Mrs B. commands her room.

So it's come to this, has it? Salomé's last stand. Arraigned before the fireplace in the parlour like a promiscuous housemaid. Better this than the whispering behind hands in the post office, the covert glances at the pub. You can't help admiring the old bag for having it out decently.

'You invited me up for tea, Mrs Butterworth.'

'I didn't think you'd take tea when you heard what I have to say.'

'I walked a distance.'

Mrs Butterworth levers herself to her feet and makes for the kitchen. Salomé has taken the high ground already, and both know it.

Mrs Butterworth trudges into the back part of the house; she looks like Mr Toad disguised as the washerwoman. Over her shoulder she flings:

'I expect my son to marry a decent girl quite soon. I don't want his chances ruined by any stories.'

'Philip's ruin is the last thing either of us wants.'

'Don't you bandy words with me, young woman.'

Young woman indeed, there's a great laugh. Palliser, why aren't you here to share the joke?

Into the dark cavern of the kitchen; the only thing moving is the flypaper by the window. *Electric Zip water heater, I'd like one of those. You turn a tap, up she fills – gallons if necessary, enough for a mountain of dishes, or just enough for a pot of tea – then you pull the cord and wait for the whistle – like a ship's whistle, only friendly, not sad. Why can't I have those things? Simple things that make life easier. She's got a refrigerator too, and a dishwasher. Just her and Philip and he leaves his plate as clean as a nun.*

'I insist that you terminate the relationship.'

'Mrs Butterworth, I think we had better be clear.'

'Oh I'm very clear, my girl, very clear!' The skin of her cheeks wobbles in agitation. Salomé wants to laugh. But she sucks her cheeks in and tries to look like a matron. *I am a matron, heaven help me! Four girls and forty-five years to prove it.* To prove it further, she busies herself with the tea tray. Mrs Butterworth reaches up to a high cupboard and brings down a biscuit tin with a picture of the young Queen on it. She puts four Anzac biscuits on a plate, and carries it back into the living room.

Salomé sits down in the chair opposite Mrs Butterworth's throne. *I bet no one has sat here since the late Mr B. died in it. Philip likes to sit upright on a straight chair. He only relaxes when he sits in the driving seat of his car.*

On the mantelpiece are photographs – wouldn't you have guessed it? The dimmer the lives, the more photographs. Salomé has none, not outside of old shoe boxes anyway. She can't even recall the shape of Palliser's nose. The Butterworth photos are mostly of Philip in various stages of development, but always recognisably the same sweet solemn person, with his oval face and round wondering eyes. *If I were in love with him, I'd be transfixed by these.* Mr & Mrs B. on their wedding day, glory be, a short skirt. Mrs B.'s legs weren't much better then. Mr B. in uniform. Mrs B. opening Butterworth's store in Timaru. Mr & Mrs B. at the reception for the Queen, big one that.

Salomé takes her tea as graciously as possible, because she was properly brought up, and anyway she's thirsty. She feels confident.

'Now Mrs Butterworth, let us get some things straight –'

Mrs B. is going to interrupt her every sentence of the way, you can tell, she likes to hold the floor. Mr B. was probably as meek as Philip; she's never known what it's like to hear out a paragraph, except in church. Probably pops up and interrupts the preacher. *Now listen here young man, I remember my catechism.*

Just talk on over the top, in a loud voice, with plenty of repetition. Like talking to Bathsheba about baths.

'Philip is my lawyer, in fact he is my husband's lawyer also. He has been our lawyer for several years. Recently your son Philip, our lawyer, has been working very hard on our behalf renegotiating our mortgage. He has however taken a fee for this work, a fairly substantial fee, at my insistence. Your son Philip, our lawyer, has done this out of kindness and out of duty, and as a result, as a result of his efforts, I am no longer in the embarrassing financial position in which I found myself previously. Your son is a good man and a professional man, and I am sure you are proud of him.'

'But –'

Salomé takes a slurp of tea. *Better let her have her head before she bursts.*

'But I am not referring, as you well know, to your professional dealing with my son. Though I think it highly improper that he should get involved at all, when he was one of the mortgagees, and should have stood by the others.'

'In evicting an innocent woman from her home? Indeed, none of those gentlemen could quite bring themselves to do that. You would not do such a thing either, Mrs Butterworth.'

'Nonsense, don't dramatise your situation! If the place is over-mortgaged, simply sell up and cut your losses. In your situation you cannot afford such sentimentality!'

'My situation, as you call it, is this: thanks to Philip's professionalism and skill, my children and I have a safe roof over our heads.'

Mrs B. is gripping her cup in fury. It's the cheap china, just as well. Rejects from the store, maybe the line the Railways rejected as too plain.

'But there's so much more, isn't there, Mrs Wentwood? You, a married woman –'

'Well, indeed, I hadn't finished.' The old cut-glass accent comes back. Goodness, how useful it is at times. Never thought to employ it like this. Tones of Great-Aunt Rupertia thrilling through the salon. 'I am a married woman, Mrs Butterworth, an unimpeachable fact. I am not divorced from my husband. I have nothing to reproach myself with.'

'Nothing? Then why is it, Mrs Wentwood, that my son visits your farm practically every evening, returning too late for his tea? And almost every Saturday he is unavailable to me? And all of this most recently – certainly since your husband disappeared.'

Salomé leapt to the attack.

'If I were having an affair with your son, *which I am not*, do you think he would come home to *this* house in the evenings? Philip is a free man; he's also an adult. He can come and go as he pleases. He visits my farm and my family because he wishes to. Besides, we are in business together.'

Maybe it wasn't so clever to tell her that, but she'd have found out one day. It will make her angry, but it's hard to raise any moral indignation about a business venture. Well, maybe not, but it's a different sort of moral indignation.

Mrs Butterworth splutters, or would if she knew how. A certain colour has invaded her cheeks; she looks like an actress hauled out of retirement for the pantomime and allowed to apply her own rouge.

'Business! What business?'

Rage has reduced her eloquence to explosions. Best to tell her and get it done.

'We are business partners. Has he not told you? It's all legally set up. Even if I did refuse his visits, we would still be obliged to meet.' *I'm stringing her along, making her wait. What does she think I've inveigled him into? Lingerie? Side-shows?*

'Doing what?'

Poor Mrs B. cannot imagine, and she is shocked. This is worse than an affair – she could understand that.

'Wine. I make fruit wines. You may have tasted some at your own table.'

You can see that she has. She has a memory like a pincushion, she can even see the bottle it's been poured from, and Philip's hand pouring it. *You'll like this, Mother.*

'Ridiculous. How much money has he frittered away on this?'

'We have a business plan. We have capital; we have accounts; I am sure Philip will show them to you. He has invested his own money as he has every right to do, and he has limited his liability with the care you would expect. He does the bookwork, I supply the goods.'

The truth is, it's pure pleasure to say these things. *And it's all true, I can hardly believe it myself when I hear it.*

'Of course, the business may not succeed.'

'Extremely likely, given your track record.'

'That's a remarkably offensive remark, Mrs Butterworth. But I understand why you might feel moved to make it. However, you must begin to distinguish between my husband and myself.'

She feels moved to pour herself a second cup of tea. She does not see that she need tell Mrs Butterworth of the pact, cast in concrete between herself and Philip, that Palliser shall never, ever, under any circumstances whatsoever, have an interest, a say, a hand or a foot in the business that bears his name. This was Philip's first condition, and one for which Salomé thanked him.

'This husband of yours, what's he up to?'

Now here's the test – Palliser would tell a tale, totally convincing at the time, but leaving a strange sound in the ear. But the truth, it's too awful and too unlikely. Tell it anyway.

'I don't know.'

The tea is thick and brown this time, it's been sitting stewing a while. *I will not cry. I will not show any weakness. I am myself. I shall drink my tea.*

'Have you tried to find him?'

'I haven't set the police on him, if that's what you mean.'

'You should know your own husband's habits and likely whereabouts by now.'

I'm sure you knew where Mr B. was, to within a whisker, every hour of every day.

'Have you the pleasure of my husband's acquaintance? I think not, for if you had, you would know that he is not a predictable man.'

'I think the law nowadays allows you to sue for divorce after desertion – seven years. How long has he been absent?'

If there is a God, I hope he's stirring you up right now, Palliser, with dreams of me. Vivid, painful dreams, that cut your heart in half. I hope you're racked with guilt, so that you can't lie easy in your bed.

'I have no intention of divorcing him. After twenty-five years of marriage, I think I should give him the benefit of the doubt.'

'Ridiculous.'

You could see she approved though, because something crept underneath the disapproval. A trickle of admiration? You could sense spring water under the glacier.

Mrs Butterworth did not ask the hard questions. Her interrogation was an expression of feeling, and once she had flipped the safety catch on the pressure cooker in her heart and let out a great jet of steam, the interview was over. She did not require a rigorous intellectual or moral defence from Salomé, she wanted nothing more than to burst out with the anger she felt at being deserted. She knew she had already lost the battle but her spirit required a final gesture of defiance.

It is we who must ask Salomé the hard questions.

Does she really believe that if Palliser turned up on the doorstep she could welcome him as if nothing had happened? *The benefit of the doubt*: what does she mean by that? Can there *be* any doubt about his actions? He has spent his wife's fortune, mortgaged his farm illegally, borrowed from his friends, cheated on his mates, then, when even the very Palliser could no longer talk his way out of the ditches he had dug, he has upped and gone away and left his family to fend for themselves. He has added insult to injury by not so much as a letter. How can there be any doubt?

A storyteller can tell Palliser's tale this way or that, can shed light on his motives, indulge in special pleading on his behalf, but there is only one way to see what he has done. Is there not? So let us look at what he has done, see it without making allowances, and let us not be afraid to say what we see. Why should we be afraid to make moral judgements? It is impossible to wipe away his act of cowardice and cruelty. There is no grace in the world that can do it.

Only a ridiculous romantic or a credulous fool would make allowances for Palliser now. Surely Salomé is neither of these things?

You are perhaps afraid, dear reader, that Salomé will prove a romantic or a fool, and will forget to see Palliser's deeds clearly when he comes whining and fawning to the door. You are afraid that she will do as women have always done: pretend that what is, is not, for the sake of safety or for the sake of love.

For love's sake – what a little word to bear the weight of so much tyranny. It is too late now for love, for that kind of love. We have suffered too much indignity in the name of love.

It seems that Salomé has two choices – turn him away or pretend to folly in the name of love. Mrs Butterworth might have put it to her like that.

But what if there were another possibility – to give him the benefit of the doubt, not for the sake of tyrannous, myopic romantic love, but for another sake? For whose sake? For what cause? I want another word to name what she should do, without the overtones of ancient bondage and musty obligation. The word is in my mind but not in the language, and so I cannot tell you. You must wait and watch and see what she will do, and maybe the word will come to us both.

The Butterworth house was built – and is built, for it still stands – with a commanding view of the area: not difficult, because it was built on an artificial hillock, the only bump between sea and mountain. From the steps of the Butterworth family mansion, all two storeys and twelve rooms of it, you can see all the way to Antarctica.

Salomé stands on the step, putting on her gloves. She gets out her compact and views the angle of her hat. It's a new hat, a dashing number, Philip bought it at staff rates in Butterworth's spring sale, and she owes him two pounds for it.

She looks out to the sea which is almost too bright to behold. The sky and the sea are fighting it out for brilliance – such extravagance of light. It's a perfect spring afternoon, not meant for taking tea indoors, but for running up hillsides in bare feet. Small chance of that . . .

Where are you now, you demon lover, you? Sunning yourself on someone's doorstep, paused in the middle of someone else's paddock? Slaving away in the cold hell of a freezing works, longing for the whistle and escape into the sun? Bronzed on an Australian gold dredge, pale in a Canadian mine? While I am trapped here, unable to leave this valley, blinded by this one sun and dazzled by this one sea. I'd be trapped happy if you were here, twenty years I was happy here. Crazy times, never a moment to reflect – and that's how it should be. Friends would write, in the early days, and say aren't you bored, poor dear, shut in your idyllic corner, would you like to come over for the season, see some bright lights and a little bit of fun. But action and fun we had, a damned roller-coaster.

I suppose I might grow peaceful now, enjoy order and calm. Spring is time to let nature take her course, time to start growing straight and staying still. A new life stretches out, not a road, not a track, but a garden.

Philip's big black car draws up. He's wearing a blue suit with the creases sharp, even at four o'clock.

'Hello! What are you doing here? I must say you do look nice!'

'Your mother invited me to tea.'

'Oh gosh! Was she – was it all right?'

'She's impressive, your mama.'

Salomé walks away from the house.

'Can I take you home?' he says.

'Your mother thinks you spend too much time at the farm.'

'Oh dear, do I?'

He opens the passenger door for her.

'No, of course not. You're always welcome. But if I were your mother, I might worry too.'

He settles himself in the driver's seat.

'Might you? I think I'm a bit out of my depth. I've got a surprise for you; two surprises actually. One nice, and the other I'm not sure about.'

'Show me, please. Nice one first.'

He reaches past her, into the back seat of the car and brings out a flattened cardboard box. He places it between them and pats it until it is a nice rectangular shape. On all four sides is printed in solid black Gothic lettering:

Wentwood's fruit Nectar
1 dozen

then a space for the variety, and at the bottom

P.O. Box 53
Kaikoura
New Zealand

'It's a sample, but I got a jolly good price for a gross.'

'Philip, it's splendid, just right – but a gross? How are we are going to produce that much wine? I don't have enough fruit.'

'Come the summer, we'll buy it. Quality control, that's

the new word. You control the quality, not produce all the raw materials.'

'And the money?'

'Dear Salomé, how many times have I told you? It's capital investment, and this year it's all tax write-off, and next year too, because we'll be buying so much plant. We don't want to show a profit at all if we can help it until the year after next, and then only a tiddly one to keep the Revenue happy. We sink all the profits into equipment – new bottling plant, new company truck, pay the girls a salary, so on. Advertising. The *Weekly News*, the *Listener*. And then across the Tasman; sales trip; give ourselves an Australian holiday and write it off as well.'

'Your mother will have apoplexy.'

'O gosh, yes, it won't look too good, will it? Do you care? That reminds me. Surprise number two.'

Out of his breast pocket, a trainee conjurer, he produces a card.

'When I picked up the box at the post office, they gave me this. I'm afraid the whole valley has read it first.'

I don't want it, I don't want to know where you are, be reminded that you're real. See your handwriting, that hand that should be touching mine. I don't want to think of the real you, now you've become a legend. I want my quiet life.

'Amazing where he lands up,' says Philip. 'Full of surprises, Palliser.'

He starts up the car and heads towards Wentwood Farm.

Dearest Naomi, thought you might like to see where I am living – not actually in the Abbey, but nearby, in a house called Thule. Abigail will be able to tell you about the real Thule. I am doing well, at last, and hope to be home for next Christmas. Smoke me a nice fat eel, all ready. Yr loving father.

I will not weep. I will not tear the card into a dozen angry pieces. I will laugh at his folly and his waywardness. I will, I will.

'Are you all right, Salomé?'

'No, Philip, I am not. Perhaps if you drove out to Seal Point first, before going home.'

A long silent drive. Philip's not there. She's alone in the car, in the vast space around, with the old rocks, the old seals like rocks turned silken, the waves that keep breaking, breaking. How to contain such sadness, and turn it into peace? *This to happen just when I was over it, over him, when he had passed over into legend, all his deeds and nonsense, over, over. Like the waves over and over and never ceasing.*

I will not weep, I will not be angry. I will not hate him or long for him. I am myself. I am Salomé, and I have my life now.

But I'm not rid of you, am I? One twitch of your damned fingers, one postcard tossed off after a year of nothing, and I'm destroyed. I will be rid of you. I will pull you out of my heart, piece by piece, till you're hanging on by those fingers, and I'll prise them off the edge, till you fall, down, down out of my life. You think you made me, and I am your creature, but you arrogant God-usurper, you were incidental, any man would have done to take me out of the ice age I was born into. You filled up my head and my heart with yourself, so I couldn't see the world, but it's a big place the world, I can do well in it. It's better without you, quiet in the garden I'm making, without the spins and bends of your way. I was a fool not looking past you, but I won't make that mistake again.

We swallow the bait, stupid women, the bait poisons the brain, and on the end is a dirty big hook that lodges in the gut and because of the poison we can't feel the hook, but we feel the line. We can't see the line, so we think we have chosen to stay close, but really we're on a line, like a goat in a paddock, round and round the same point. I shall rip your hook out of my body. I shall feel my longing for you as lust, lust that men feel, lust that can be ignored, not love that's holy and must be preserved. I shall scour you out of my head, that you filled with your stories, stories of yourself—and who was there to interpret them for me, but yourself? I was reeled in so far that I have become you, as I was bidden by the Bible: the two shall become one, he shall cleave unto her. The two shall be one flesh. Rather the two shall become one mind—one mind shall eat the other, until there is only one mind left, but the bodies can be parted at a whim. So my flesh is suddenly no longer your flesh, but you have broken my heart and taken my mind.

I claim it back from you. I shall grow it again from the stump, like an old elderberry tree, chop it down as much as you might, with your strong arms and your sharp axe; it springs back up when your back's turned and flowers its truculent flowers and squirts out its blood-red berries.

I am Salomé. I am.

On the drive home, she straightens her hat and says, 'I don't think we are ready for the Australian market yet, Philip.'

Show Day approached — the Canterbury Royal Agricultural and Pastoral Show, when the whole of that agricultural province came together to revere the twin gods of the thresher and the new improved animal weighing machine. The Wentworths were thrown into a fury of activity, for Philip had booked a stall at the show. He had shamelessly called up an old school chum on the organising committee, and contrived a first-rate site, with an awning, just at the point where the crowds, coming out of the animal exhibition shed and overwhelmed by the glories of the pig and extra-woolly breeds of sheep, would hesitate before making their way to the ring to engage in the gladiatorial rigours of the dressage. At Wentwood's stall they might linger for a quiet moment and sample the wine: complexities of the licensing laws prevented its sale but the passers-by might try discreet sips in proper wineglasses. And be handed information pamphlets. And place orders. Bottle or case. 7s. 6d. a bottle, four guineas a dozen.

On the Friday night, two weeks before Show Day, Philip presented himself at the farm, fresh as the man in the shaving cream ad, even though he had just driven two hours from the city, bumped along the dirt track, and walked from the bridge.

He knocked and waited to be let in.

'Is it convenient?' he said, as always.

Salomé clucked her tongue at his silliness, took his hat and coat and gave him a peck on the cheek.

Once inside the kitchen she pressed a glass of black-currant into his hand. He sat down on the edge of his usual chair, knees spread, back straight, at ease, but apart.

Bathsheba came and balanced on his knee. 'I've got a new apron,' she said, 'with Wentwood Wine on it. Like Jemima's.'

'We have been very busy today,' said Salomé, poking the potatoes simmering in their pan. 'Naomi, a lettuce. Now. And cut the stem off *before* you bring it in.'

'You are very busy every day.'

'But some days we achieve something,' said Abigail, laying the table around him. 'Other days we are just busy staying alive.'

Philip sipped his wine over Bathsheba's head.

'Well, we have all achieved a great deal recently,' he said. 'Last night the council decided to form the road up to here, and take it through to Goat Valley. If you agree, of course. They'll pay you compensation for the land use, and you get the road right to the door.'

'How did you pull that off, Philip? You can't have been at school with the whole council.'

'Abigail! I would apologise for my daughter, Philip, but she does it quite deliberately.'

He was merely amused. 'I asked to speak to the meeting; actually they rather want me on the council, not having a lawyer or any business people. In my address I talked about diversifying into new business areas, meaning of course mainly Wentwood's Wines, and also about opening up Goat Valley for recreation and tourism, thus injecting outside money into the local economy. I told them we had plans next summer to put up signs on the main road directing visitors to Wentwood's Wines, so we'd like the road to the gate done before then.'

'And they agreed.'

'Well, yes.'

Salomé felt as if all the world was laid out flat before her, and she could walk in it at her ease.

'You are clever,' she said and gave him another kiss on the cheek.

'No, no, not at all. It's all good business sense. I'm just a shopkeeper really.'

'I don't like the idea of outsiders driving down our road,' said Jemima. She was chopping up mint for the sauce.

'We'll station Naomi under the bridge with a slingshot and exact a toll,' said Abigail, 'like little Billy Goat Gruff.'

'It was the troll,' cried Bathsheba. 'Philip, tell her it was the troll.'

'It was the troll, Abigail.'

'I'm a troll, fol de rol rol,' sang Naomi coming through the back door.

'Naomi, *boots!*' shrieked her mother.

Cold leg of lamb, mint sauce, new potatoes straight out of the ground, and *still screaming*, as Abigail said in imitation of her father. Philip, when he first heard this

159

saying, was a little confused. Naomi explained to him that vegetables had feelings too, but they ate them all the same. With puddles of butter. Lettuce, carrots, runner beans and beetroot. Salomé's wonderful bottled beetroot, sweet and sharp and spicy.

'What's for pudding, Jem?'

'I thought you were on puds today.'

'I've spent all afternoon in the school hall laying out this damned banner for the show —'

'*Abigail!*'

'And then a spotty child in Standard 4 ran into it and I had to start all over again.'

'I was joking about the pud. It's lemon meringue pie.'

'O yummy yummy yummy,' cried the young girls.

'Actually Naomi, you could learn how to make it. It's not hard,' said Salomé.

'Well I like that!'

'There are pies and pies,' said Philip. 'And Jemima's lemon meringue pie is really special.'

'You should taste Mother's.'

'No, he shouldn't,' said Abigail.

After dinner that evening Naomi and Bathsheba cleared the table and Abigail washed the dishes, while Philip and Salomé dried them. Jemima took the younger girls away to supervise their baths. Bathsheba came back in her nightie and held her face up to be kissed by everyone, then ambled off to bed with Naomi in her wake, carrying *The Wind in the Willows*.

'Some bits are too dull for her, so I skip them,' was her verdict.

Jemima made tea and they sat down once again to plan for the show.

'I managed to get the tablecloths,' said Jemima. 'Actually, Mrs Butterworth lent them to me in the end. I have to return them blindingly white, she said, or she'll roast me alive.'

'That's Mother,' said Philip.

Salomé poured him a glass of her apricot liqueur.

'I talked to the chap at Caxton Press today,' he said. 'Now I do know *him* from school, Abigail. He stuck to his price though. But I talked him down in the end. Had to promise him next year's Butterworth's Christmas brochure to get him to budge a penny.'

'That sounds unethical,' said Salomé.

'Oh do you think so? I hadn't really thought so. I don't think so. The board had decided to take it away from the other crowd because of the poor quality of this year's. And the price. He's expensive, but he is the best.'

'Hmm.'

'Mother, you are so upright, you just don't belong in the twentieth century,' said Abigail.

'I admit I do often wish I was an eighteenth-century lady explorer,' said Salomé, 'but I don't think they were particularly upright, except in posture.'

'Well, I'm glad you were born in this century,' said Philip, emboldened by apricot liqueur.

Abigail and Jemima made noises in the territory between groan, hoot and yodel. Philip and Salomé ignored them, although Philip might have been observed to turn a little pink.

'I'm increasingly reluctant to take the little girls,' said Salomé. 'They will get bored and hot and dusty. I remember losing Abigail at the show once.'

'I remember getting lost. It was all Father's fault. He promised me we'd go back to the horses, and then he didn't. Typical.'

'Putting that aside, we can't afford time chasing after Naomi and entertaining Sheba. We have to look absolutely professional.'

Oh for a grandmother or aunt, or any female relative of a certain age, starved of occupation, on whom one could impose. In the past Salomé had sometimes railed at being plucked from the bosom of her family and losing the benefits of statutory baby-sitters, until Palliser would remind her that neither her mother, sister, aunts, cousin nor any woman that was hers, would have a child in the drawing room, let alone to stay.

'Now *my* family –' he would begin, then pause extravagantly with a big gesture '– are exactly the same.' And she would laugh, and let it pass, and the children would go with them to whatever entertainment was in hand. Or Palliser would go alone.

'They could stay with Mother,' said Philip.

All three women stared at him.

'Why not?' he said, widening his baby eyes back at them. 'Mother likes children, and she's got plenty of room. Naomi and she have a lot in common. I shall ask her.'

'Philip, have you *any* idea what your mother said to me?'

'I'm afraid she's said some of it to me too. I felt quite wicked.'

'That must have been a novel sensation,' said Abigail.

'She was very kind to me over the tablecloths,' said Jemima. 'I'd never have dared to ask her, but Mrs Hird, her next-door neighbour, said hers had too many holes, and why not ask Fleur – isn't that a lovely name? You think of her differently knowing her name is Fleur.'

'I don't,' said Salomé.

'Mrs Hird took me over and asked for me, otherwise I really wouldn't have dared. Your house is so *big*, Philip, with that proper front door.'

Into Salomé's mind flashed a picture of the probable size of Thule Hall, Herts, and she pressed down hard on the bitter amusement of it.

★　　★　　★

Good as his word, Philip did ask his mother if the two younger Wentwood girls could stay with her for two days and a night while the rest of the family, and Philip himself (though this was not exactly mentioned), manned their stall at the show, and to the astonishment of everyone, including Mrs Butterworth, she agreed. Opinion in the valley was divided: some said Mrs Butterworth was a charitable woman always doing good; others that she wanted to compete with her neighbour Mrs Hird in the grandchildren stakes; others that she wanted to snatch the innocent children from the wicked influence of their mother; others that as Philip and Salomé were secretly engaged, Mrs B. had swallowed the pill and accepted she must love these children. All of these versions contain a nut of truth, as is frequently the case with gossip, but none took into account Philip's observation that his mother, in common with many reputedly fierce women, genuinely liked children.

So, on the Thursday of Show Week, clutching her schoolbag stuffed with clean clothes and the postcard from her father, a highly suspicious Naomi was deposited on the Butterworth front step at six in the morning. Salomé carried the sleeping Bathsheba inside and tucked her up on the horsehair sofa, on which no one had reclined in half a century.

'Now Naomi,' said Mrs Butterworth, 'if you take that scowl off your face I might just be able to find the key to the attic. Do you know what's up there?'

Slight shaking of the head.

'All of Philip's toys, including his model railway.'

'Yes,' said Philip, 'it's mostly set up and it still runs. I tried it out.'

'And this afternoon possibly we could watch *Lassie* on the television.'

163

Bathsheba was suddenly awake.

Salomé kissed them both profusely. She thanked Mrs Butterworth, who evinced a sort of smile. Then she climbed into her newly purchased truck, a heroically battered vehicle, survivor from the war, and marked still with the insignia and graffiti of the Long Range Desert Corps. The door had to be banged several times to make it shut. Philip, with Abigail and Jemima as his passengers, followed her in his car, and off they went in convoy to take the city by storm.

At four o'clock on the Friday, last day of the show, they were preparing to pack up. There was only one bottle of wine left, which they were saving for supper. They had a sheaf of orders adding up to £147 10s. 6d., and a banker's bag heavy with threepences from the sale of muffins and biscuits. Their total outlay had been £21 14s. 6d. including the printing of a year's supply of brochures.

An eager man in glasses and a brown check jacket approached them.

'Hello Mr Butterworth! Gee, Gee from the *Press*.'

'Of course! How are you, Mr Gee?'

Philip took him out of the concourse of weary show-goers, and started to tell him the story of Wentwood's Wines.

'Salomé, we have a sample for Mr Gee, haven't we?'

'Absolutely, Philip.'

She opened the last bottle, ignoring Abigail's passionate *Mother!* and poured Mr Gee a hot-Friday-afternoon-sized sample.

'And we have two biscuits left, just for you.'

Salomé knew that when gracious, she was irresistible. Mr Gee enjoyed his wine and was persuaded to a refill.

Philip talked in his measured, agreeable tones about the rural economy and the need for horticulture to underpin the pastoral sector, and Mr Gee wrote it all down in shorthand, while Salomé, Jemima and Abigail disassembled the stall and loaded the truck.

So of course he must have a photograph.

They were just re-erecting their brave banner for the photo-opportunity, when Jemima's Thaddeus turned up, scuffed and out of place, in his Fair Isle jersey with leather patches. He walked slightly stooped over, as though his heavy black-rimmed glasses were weighing him down. Salomé thought him a most agreeable person.

'Can I help, Mrs Wentwood?'

'Absolutely. See those boxes of empty bottles, and that truck? Good lad.'

Mr Gee was disposing them to his liking.

'Just stand a bit closer would you, Mr Butterworth, so I can get you all in. Pr'aps if you two young ladies sat down, on the stools there – that's it, in front, and Mr Butterworth and Mrs Wentwood behind. Why don't we have the young man in the picture too, even things up a bit, if you know what I mean? Like to stand at the back there, son, next to Mrs Wentwood. Can we take those glasses off, just for the picture. No? All right, all right, suit yourself, son, but here's a comb you can borrow. Thanks, wonderful, bonzer! Now, could you two gentleman stand in a bit closer to Mrs Wentwood, a bit more family. That's it! A real beaut.'

And so the fateful photograph was taken.

After they had taken everything down again and loaded the truck, Salomé drove delicately out of the showgrounds, and on to the main road leading into town. Abigail was her navigator. Jemima and Thaddeus were with Philip, and they were all going to Fail's fish restaurant for tea. Nothing was said on this score, lest Philip be discomfited, but it was remembered that eating in this quotidian café, with plastic-covered menus and bottles of ketchup in the shape of a jovial tomato on every table, was a favourite jape of Palliser's.

'I wouldn't have believed there were so many cars in the world,' said Salomé, jammed in a sea of Vivas and Valiants and Ford Prefects.

'And you lived in London for how long?'

'I only remember taxis. I was rich then,' she laughed.

'You're rich now,' said Abigail, shaking the bag of threepences. 'Go, Mother, go. It's only amber.'

It's an expungable nightmare, driving a large vehicle through unfamiliar streets packed with traffic, but still a nightmare. Salomé gripped the wheel and gritted her teeth, and reminded herself of the desert rat who had gripped this wheel before her, and her officer uncles, dying like flies on the Western Front. Such memories neatly put trivial unpleasantness like heavy traffic into its place. She made it to the rendezvous point outside Philip's cousin's house on Park Terrace. Her vehicle was not inconspicuous in such a neighbourhood, so she parked it in a side street out of sight, before going inside to freshen up.

Buoyant and showered, with powder and lipstick freshly applied and a new pair of nylons, Salomé stepped down the stairs to meet the men. Jemima wore her new dress – pink and red poppies on a white background, flared skirt, tight waist, pink belt and, thrillingly, pink lipstick.

'Gosh,' said Thaddeus in the hallway, twisting his fingers.

Abigail wore her black suit with a white blouse, but she didn't care.

Philip drove them all into town, and somehow made inconsequential the big old Chevrolets with their insolent cargo of Brylcreemed youths. He slid without deviation into the car park behind his club, whence it was, naturally, but a short walk to the restaurant.

He offered Salomé one arm, and the other to Abigail,

who declined and walked aloof, but alongside her mother. Jemima and Thaddeus trailed further and further behind, reaching the door of Fail's when the others were already scanning the menu, looking up only to comment and tease.

In silent memory of Palliser, his family ordered orgiastic quantities of fish and chips, there not being, as Salomé remarked, much in the line of *coq au vin*. The three young people giggled as they swung in and out on the revolving metal chairs, just as they had done as children.

A glass of wine would have gone down very nicely, Philip remarked, and it was a pity he couldn't take them all into the club.

'The licensing laws in this country are positively barbaric —' Salomé began, but stopped, hearing the echo of another voice.

Abigail explained that they were going to the pictures anyway, and did Philip and Salomé want to come with them?

'I can't remember when I last saw a film,' said Salomé. 'Your father had a passion for Greta Garbo.'

'I expect he still does.'

The young decided to go and see *Some Like it Hot*.

'That sounds remarkably risqué. Perhaps we should join them, after all, Philip? We could sit in another part of the cinema, so as not to embarrass you.'

But Philip demurred, so, after he had paid the bill, he and Salomé parted company with the young, reassuring themselves that they had all the requisite information about pass-keys. Thaddeus would see the girls home and walk back to his university hostel.

Philip and Salomé walked slowly back towards the car, and by some harmonious confusion found themselves making a detour along the river bank in the balmy darkness. Philip put his arm around Salomé's waist. His head was just above the level of her shoulder. Her hat with its wonderful brim sheltered them both as she inclined her head towards him.

They walked in silence around the curve of the river. This bank was almost deserted, but on the other side they could see the crowds flowing along the streets, into the picture theatres and shops. Here the only sound was the current washing the willow branches, and changing its tenor as it met a little island in midstream.

They stopped opposite the island; it was dominated by big rhododendrons which blanked out the people and traffic on the other bank.

'When I was a little boy, I always wanted to explore that island. It seemed so far away. Now it's just a step away; it hardly seems worth getting wet for.'

'That's the sad thing about growing up. Nothing really seems worth the nuisance of getting it.'

But she could see Palliser rolling up his trouser legs and striding into the water: one leap of his long legs and he'd be across. He'd halloo like a pirate in a pantomime. *Come on over, the water's fine.*

They tarried by the island, then made their way down the bank, and sat on a wooden bench made of stout slats of wood, rather wide apart, curved into a fat S shape. Not a structure designed for the comfort of benighted tramps or courting couples.

Salomé took off her gloves and hat. She was tired of playing ladies. Philip put his arm around her shoulders, and she leaned against him. His leg pressed so hard against her thigh that she was sure he'd take the impression of a suspender away with him.

'Philip.'

'Mmmmm.'

'I want to ask you for something.'

'Of course.'

'I'd really rather not ask you for anything more.'

'I'd do anything for you, Salomé.'

Let's not put that to the test.

'You have been so generous to me, to all of us. I think you are a truly good man. So I don't want to take advantage of your kindness.'

'I don't think you could. I can't tell you how happy you have made me. Helping you makes me happy.'

'I know you think we'll be solvent next year, but I have to be cautious – you do understand? I've been practically bankrupt for so long . . . It becomes habit not to commit oneself. Not to make plans. Not to make promises. But now, right now, I want to make a promise. But I can't unless you help me.'

'I love to help you,' he said, and his hand tightened around her upper arm. She took his other hand in hers. It seemed only fair.

'I want Abigail to go to university. I want her to go next year, and to be assured she can finish at least a Bachelor's degree. I can't give her that assurance without your backing.'

'Nothing would make me happier.'

Nothing?

'Three years is a long time to promise. Anything might happen.'

'I would promise you a lifetime.'

If she said nothing to this declaration it was not from lack of interest, but because, now the long-awaited moment had come, she doubted how she felt. Strange; she should be ready, since she, and the whole valley, had expected for months now that he would make some sort of proposal.

So ambivalent a statement could be met with silence. She squeezed his hand a little harder, turned towards him, and they kissed.

Salomé tried not to remember what kissing might be. Philip was a boy, eager, awkward – that was the way to

169

think of him. What he lacked in finesse, he might make up for in enthusiasm.

He was not a boy, but a grown man, with years of well-developed self-control flowing in every vein.

'Let's walk some more,' he said.

The path along the river led past the gentlemen's club, where the car lay, and on through the Gothic grounds of the Council Chambers. They took this route, although it would mean doubling back later.

The gates were open, although the gardens were plunged in darkness. Only lovers came here; even the tramps found more illuminated shelter. Philip and Salomé walked along the Tennysonian length of the river, and lingered in the dark shadow of the Gothic pile. There they kissed again, this time with more purpose and less constraint.

It was an exhilarating darkness, without any charge of terror or accumulated sadness. The place in which they embraced was rich and hopeful. The spring wind skimmed across the water and through the bushes, disappearing purposefully into the stone courtyards behind them. The stones and the trees and the water took in the vigour and bounced it back again. Salomé could have unpinned her hair and thrown off her shoes and stockings and run through the dark trees and buildings playing catch as catch can with the wind, the shadows, the man, any man. She felt the surge in the body that drives the young, but which the older body pretends to have tamed.

Vigour and exhilaration notwithstanding, it was a decorous embrace. Salomé held on to her gloves and hat in one hand, and never felt the need to drop them. No undress was committed. No part of the uncovered body made contact with naked flesh. No hand strayed on to any part of the body which might be classified as private. His kisses were moist, exploratory, indicative. They had as much in common with Palliser's ravishing, breath-denying, minor masterpieces of copulation performed with the mouth, as the kitchen tap has with the waterfall.

When he decided the amorous episode was ended, Philip took out his handkerchief and wiped any traces of lipstick off his mouth. They walked back arm in arm, and talked about their business.

Later that night, in the second guest bedroom of Philip's cousin's house in Park Terrace, Salomé stood regarding her reflection in a full-length mirror. Such luxuries were denied her in the cramped quarters of her farmhouse bedroom, but she did not think she was the worse for the deprivation. She had thrown down the hat and jacket on entering the room – such externals irritated her now, when once they had been the stuff of life. In the mirror she saw a person she did not feel entirely sure about: the woman bore some resemblance to the elegant Salomé who had once decked herself out religiously for the evenings, but the resemblance was complicated and tired. She felt, against the judgement of her eye, that this Salomé, though undeniably middle-aged and work-worn, was more agreeable to look upon.

The woman in the mirror had the shape of the long-gone Salomé, which might once have been cause for surreptitious pride, but now seemed irrelevant. It was the manner that intrigued her – she looked for all the world like a white witch in mufti. An undercover agent for natural magic, a crone in waiting.

She turned off the light and removed her dress and the silly things under it – slip, brassière, nylons, suspender belt, knickers. One by one, on to the floor. How meaningfully they used to slide off, even on ordinary nights, item by item, while he watched. Even if he were bushed and it was dark, he'd watch. She realised, as she let them fall to the floor now without any kind of implication, that she had grown to hate the falsity of that performance, that she had been prevented from undressing as a normal person might, just as she had been unable to brush her hair without significance, or leave it unwashed without causing grief. Such nonsense – no, worse – such dishonesty it was, to force meanings into little things too plain to bear them, and deny them to the big, difficult things. So that Palliser invested her undressing or her brushing of her hair with the significance of poetry, but overlooked the magnitude of the sacrifices she had made for him.

What I made for him was what I am – marriage, the farm, the children, the garden, the cows, the pigs, the soup, the wine. But I was Woman Undressing, Woman Brushing her Hair.

Not any more.

She did not bother to look in the mirror at the naked body. It was an object of no interest to her now, and surely less and less to anyone else. It seemed to her that a man who loved her now must love her for something other than the form she took. She wished it had always been so.

In her night-gown, she opened the window as wide as it would go; the warm evening poured in with the light from the streetlamps. From the window she could see the same secretive little river by which she and Philip had kissed, and beyond it massive trees – sycamores and chestnuts and oaks, giant versions of their English counterparts – and beyond the trees an expanse of shadowy parkland, with lakes and walkways and dells and grottoes, all begging to be explored. It was no good imagining what Palliser would do. Palliser was like one's secret dreams, you could imagine him doing all the things you wanted a person to do, all the things you wanted to do yourself, but were constrained from by cowardice or conditioning. He was a universal fantasy. It would be so easy to imagine him now, if he were in Philip's place, climbing out of his window and round the guttering to her open window, and tempting her down in her night-gown into the outer darkness. Not necessarily to make love, just for the thrill of it, running around the park in one's night-gown.

It would be easy to imagine, but she would not. Instead she thought about money and orders and meeting demand without overproduction, and streamlining her operation, and finding time to learn new techniques. Now she knew they could sell every drop she produced, and although customers agreed their commodity was expensive no one had thought it overpriced. Philip had been right to price it high, even though it was not expensive to make. She was selling technique, he told her, nothing to be ashamed of. Supply and demand. Price what the market will bear.

Curious how these matters seemed more engrossing than the problem of whether to marry Philip. I suppose this is how men's lives are, she thought. Romance takes up a small part of the thinking, occasionally insistent, when the sap rises, but easily subdued. Business is more rewarding: it fills up the mind and engages the enthusiasm and makes one feel gainfully employed even when thinking. You never have to sit and wait in business, you can always be doing something to improve your lot. You can go and make things happen, not hang around hoping *he* might turn up. You are never the victim of feelings you can't understand, which make you do stupid and embarrassing things. Like hover by the telephone all day, just in case.

How novel and peculiar to have what is, in effect, a declaration; but in the event, it's just like being given a certificate at the prize-giving, agreeable, but forgettable. You frame it, hang it up, and it plays no further part in things. I might marry him, I might not. It will really depend on how the business goes. How appallingly unromantic, and yet how powerful it makes me feel.

And yet she remembered love – how the body sang, how every square of skin became beautiful, how glory ran through the veins. She remembered how it made one touch heaven and savour earth. And then the sweetness

173

of half waking in the night and feeling him safely asleep, and curling up against the promise of that body. And in the morning, tousled hair, and unshaven cheeks, and smell of man in the sheets, the playful warmth, the half-awake banter, the nestling and teasing that might prove serious.

Would it be that way with Philip? Or would it be a pale shadow of heaven, fraught with inadequacy and ill-expressed emotions? Would the act of love require allowances to be made? Would the waking beside him always hold echoes of different awakenings? Better not to ask the question. Better not to raise the ghost of the demon lover.

It's just as well that the need for physical love diminishes with time, she thought; like truffles and champagne, one learns to do very well without.

She slept and dreamed that she was walking along a cliff edge. The scenery was spectacular, but the drop down to the sea was too scary to look at. She was carrying a life-belt, a circular tyre, like a Polo mint, but striped like a barber's pole. Down below in the turbulent sea was a tiny figure, gesturing like mad. She knew that if she threw the life-belt over the cliff to the tiny little person in the sea, she could lose her balance and fall in also. She was terrified.

Poor Philip also tossed and turned, consumed more with indecision than frustrated love. He had never been happier, not even at school. His practice was ticking over, the family stores were well managed and effortlessly profitable; now the little venture with Salomé, which had started as a practical way of helping her, seemed like a business right out of the textbook, and such fun with it. More fun than the stores, which ran themselves with the oversight of the stuffy old board and the dreary old department managers. More fun than the practice, which was repetitive conveyancing and wills. Business was like a model train set: once you got it running smoothly, you just had to keep extending and improving, otherwise there was no point in doing it at all.

Business was good, but domestic life was lovely too. He had never expected to be part of a family, and now he was right in the middle of one, and it was pure satisfaction. He loved the noise and flurry, the warmth and jokes and the outbursts of anger and tears. He loved the food and the firelight, and the beauty of the women, and the hints of wildness and danger. He loved Salomé's stories of grand old Europe before the war. He loved the endless adventures of Naomi, usually involving mud.

And when it all got too much he slid into the car and went home to the ordered calm of his mother's.

But could it continue thus? Tonight, perhaps rashly, he had made some kind of declaration of love. It had not been as definite as a proposal, nor had she treated it that way. She had not answered the question he had not asked, but she had given him a sort of answer to a different question. He knew that he, Philip Butterworth, was acceptable as a lover. Otherwise, surely she would not have allowed him to kiss her *in that way*. For to Philip, such kisses were a symbol and a seal of serious passion. He had wanted to kiss her terribly, just as he always wanted to put his arm around her, and it had seemed wrong to take advantage without saying something. Though quite how one might take advantage of Salomé he didn't know.

Declaration or not, he didn't want anything to change; he wanted life to go on exactly as it was. But he was afraid that if he did nothing, if he didn't position himself fair and square as the Man in Salomé's life, someone else would come along and take over. Then he would be shoved to one side, and no longer enjoy the comfort of the hearth at Wentwood's Farm in the same way. To be cast out into the cold again was not to be contemplated.

To be the man in Salomé's life, to Philip, inevitably

implied marriage. But if Salomé did agree to get a divorce and marry him, he would have to leave his mother in her big house, resentful and alone. The guilt of leaving her would niggle away at him. How bad would that be? Some men, like Palliser, seemed to manage to live cheerfully with guilt, but Philip, as he was often reminded, was a very different man. Would the happiness of waking up beside Salomé each morning wash away the coldness of his mother's voice? He felt protective of his mother, long widowed and short of occupation. She had always provided a home for him; should he not provide one for her?

Marriage would naturally require him, also, to give up the calm of his bachelor life, his every need attended to, his reading never disturbed, his papers exactly where he left them. No complaints were made if he stayed over at the club, if he had a whisky or two; his mother never demanded a share of the newspaper in the morning. She did not expect him to talk to her in the evening.

Life with Salomé, life in the shadow of Palliser, would certainly be other than calm.

Of all his uncertainties, his severest concerned sex, for him a great unknown. He was not technically a virgin, for in his youth, while the mayhem of war scattered convention to the wind, he had several times availed himself of what was on offer. Being a pretty youth and well-off, there had been little need to go searching. But the act had not seemed much to sing about, a messy, unsatisfactory process, never fulfilling the hopes one had of it, hedged about with misunderstandings, awkwardness and unspoken obligations. Latterly he had managed perfectly well without. He had always assumed that when one fell in love with the right woman, all those sexual feelings got turned on to appropriate levels, and one enjoyed physical love because it was undertaken with the beloved. He also assumed that the special benefits of that sort of love then compensated one for having one's papers disturbed. A sort of natural orderliness, a series of locks in the canal of life.

But what if that wasn't the case? The older he got, the more married people he saw, the less probable it seemed. Married people did not seem as contented as he was. Married people came to him for divorces. They complained long and hard about each other. His married friends, in the city, who were manifold, spent a lot of time at the club and made disparaging jokes about their wives.

For years Salomé and Palliser had been his ideal of a married couple. They had seemed to match perfectly, and clearly adored one another. When he thought of marriage, and that mysterious element that made sex more than a conjunction of organs, he thought of them. He had always expected when he married that he would fit next to his wife as Palliser fitted next to Salomé, that between him and this nebulous wife would exist the psychic connectors, the dovetailed joints of matrimony that he detected between those two.

But now his ideal of married love was shattered. He had kissed Salomé, the perfect wife, under the willows. How could he, Philip, ever be more husband to her than Palliser? He was sure that his emotion towards Salomé was as close to love as he would ever know. He felt comfortable saying to himself *I love Salomé and shall do so for ever*. But his ardour seemed so tame compared to the stuff he had read about in books, where the young hero is prepared to die for his beloved. He wouldn't die for Salomé, he wouldn't die if he were parted from her. He'd be awfully unhappy, but he would carry on with life much as before. He didn't see how his version of love, the best he could do, could suffice when Palliser had failed.

Dare he take the risk of finding out? Was it possible to leave things in stasis?

He slept, and dreamed that he was in the accounts

office at Butterworth's and the papers were piling up round him, like straw around the heroine in the story of Rumpelstiltskin, and a funny little man with a beard, but a nose like Palliser's, popped up, and said, 'I can show you,' then leapt out of the window.

What a success the expedition to the Royal Agricultural and Pastoral Show turned out to be! Mid-afternoon on Saturday, Philip rolled up at the farm, smiling all over his face, with Naomi, Bathsheba and the biggest edition the *Christchurch Press* had published all year.

'Look! Look at us in the paper!' cried Naomi.

There, plumb in the middle of the Home page, a photograph of the Wentwood family, and accompanying article. A big article with a solid headline: FAMILY WINE BUSINESS SPELLS VARIETY. There were remarkably few mistakes in the copy.

'My cousin Simon rang earlier,' said Philip. 'He's the buyer for Malings – you know, the wine and spirits merchants.'

'Actually, he owns most of it,' said Abigail, not looking up from her study of Thaddeus's copy of the University Calendar.

'Well, yes, that's true, but he's also the buyer. He'd seen the paper, and he's very interested in our lines.'

'We'll have to try him on the broom flower. It's all we can rustle up in a hurry,' cried Salomé, and laughed, shaking her hair out of its pins and throwing back her head, rejoicing.

Happiest of all was Bathsheba. She came home from Mrs Butterworth's glowing with ecstasy. Everyone had to gather round the kitchen table to see. She opened the biscuit tin, and took them out one by one, placing them on the table.

'This is a hippo, and this is an elephant, and this is a red horse, and a blue horse. And a lion. And this is another hippo. And a seal . . . And Mrs Butterworth's said I can keep them all, and she's going to give me every single one she gets. Aren't they beautiful?'

And everyone agreed, that yes, the little plastic creatures from the Kornies were indeed beautiful.

VII

MERELY BEING BLANCHE took up much of Blanche's attention, not because she was a vain or selfish girl, but because conveying her person through the world, and disposing it correctly, required serious care. Simple things which ordinary people took for granted to her were obstacles to be surmounted – she could not run on the stairs, lest the house shake. She could not buy underwear or corsets, let alone nylons. Even a watch strap posed a problem.

But lying in bed the morning after Palliser's kiss, she felt transfigured. Her body floated in the sheets, when generally it was firmly grounded on the mattress. She felt like an angel in one of Hubert's Burne-Joneses, hovering fractionally above the ground. Her body, instead of a lump of flesh she must drag after her, was made of some substance lighter than air – something like the wonderful ices the Italian man sold outside the British Museum, which, insubstantial as you bit into them, dissolved into something more vital than any normal ice-cream. Blanche had only tasted the Italian ices once, but she didn't forget.

She would never forget that Palliser had stroked her face. 'You are so beautiful,' he had said. She had shaken her head in disbelief. 'Oh, but you are, and not knowing it makes you more beautiful still.' And then he kissed her.

All night she had felt his hand on her cheek, and tasted

that kiss. No one had ever told Blanche she was beautiful; no man had ever kissed her. She was in heaven.

It was inevitable that she should fall in love with him. It had been so from the hour he slid into the house and said a kind word. Blanche had known this, and had fought against it, willing herself to be less silly than a girl who falls for the first handsome man who is kind to her. But there was no hope for her now.

Even had her friends despised him – and they did not, for Hubert depended on him, and Clarissa, only last week, had said that some might regard him as a very eligible widower – it would have made not an ounce of difference. She was not in control of the gigantic emotion inside her, a passion for love which she had stamped down resolutely for as long as she remembered. It had always been absurd, the thought of anyone loving Blanche, she was too big to hug, too big to sit on a knee, too big to be chosen as a dancing partner, too gauche for her affection to be anything but embarrassing.

'You are beautiful,' he said and kissed her.

He had said it, the wonderful dashing man of the world, the man who was so perfectly designed for her dreams that she hardly dared believe in him – handsome, assured, funny, daring, practical, masculine, and even sorrowful. In a way, she wished nothing more would ever happen to her, so she could hug this glorious night to herself for ever and keep it so. If only she had a friend to whom she could whisper this precious secret.

She wiggled her toes under the bedclothes – beautiful toes, for she knew her feet were pretty, even in the normal world. The dancing master had told her: you have very pretty feet, perfect for dancing. Observe Miss Lovelace, girls, she has the footwork just so. The girls had giggled, but she had adored the dancing master for quite a long time afterwards. He was the only man she had felt anything for, before now.

She wished she could jump out of bed like Anne of Green Gables and throw up her arms to greet the morning. Instead she swung her legs over the side of the bed and delicately stepped on to the floorboards. In her big white night-dress, a great deflating balloon of cotton, she tripped to the window. Her windows faced in the same direction as Palliser's — a fact of which she was vaguely aware — but were much broader and had more gracious an aspect. She looked across the near lawn and the French garden, and out into the parkland where the morning fog was rolling off the ground as if the sunlight was in hot pursuit along the grass. On the terrace she saw Hubert, smoking and taking the air before mass; Peter too, smoking and sitting on an urn with his back to Hubert. In the further distance, Gerald the gamekeeper, Mrs Nagy's adherent, came out of the thicket with his dog and touched his cap to Jacob, the verger from St Cyriac's on his way to church. Little black squiggles on her vision. She saw them, but did not see them, any more than they saw her, the blessed damozel leaning out of heaven. But Palliser could see her as she was inside, and he thought she was beautiful. She hugged herself in anticipation of the bright new day.

At eight years old Blanche had claimed this bedroom for herself, and now it was her refuge, the place where she was comfortable being herself. She liked the room because it was dark and odd, the walls carved in panels of deep brown, each representing an obscure mythological scene, and between the panels a strange creature, each one different, each one a sport of nature. An eagle with a woman's face and breasts, a snake with a tiger's head and a man's face, a faun with a dragon's tail, a mermaid with two tails. The creatures stared at Blanche without emotion, neutral observers of human folly. They had become Blanche's companions, but not her friends.

She had mitigated their influence with a row of teddy

bears and dolls on the window-seat – toys she had found in the attic trunks and taken to her heart. There was, however, one teddy bear, stark and still clean after many years, which had been sent from America by Mother. Now Blanche was grown up she had added a flower stand on which she displayed her latest floral creation, so that each evening when she went to bed she could look at it, and each morning as she woke up she could think about what to try next. She had placed this in front of the black fireplace, insensitively hacked into the panels by some Victorian comfort-seeker. The chimney was blocked by a sheet of hardboard painted with pansies. The furnishings were simple: a carved bed of the same workmanship as the wall panels but adorned only with curls and grooves; a standard lamp with a pink shade, and a cable trailing out of the door to the nearest electric power point; her sewing machine by the window; nearby a sea-chest full of materials and sewing notions, tidily arranged, below which in neat stacks was her collection of books and games, playing cards, puzzles and old Christmas cards. On a table by the bed, a pile of books: Great-Grandfather's *Pilgrim's Progress* and *Holy Living & Holy Dying* and her library books; a radio whose electric cable ran out of the room and whose aerial splayed the other way, across the heads of the monsters and out of the window.

In the adjacent dressing room were a full-length looking-glass on a stand, a tiny collection of brushes and cosmetics on a shelf by the window, a washbasin and towel rack, two wardrobes stuffed with Mother's gowns, and one in which Blanche's few garments hung. A small chest of drawers held her other clothes, such as they were.

Blanche's getting dressed was not a matter of putting on clothes. It had to be taken slowly; her garments required consideration and forethought. All her undergarments she had made or altered herself, with variously unhappy results.

Suitable materials and patterns were hard to come by, and Blanche was no seamstress, with no one to guide her faltering efforts. As she took a pair of knickers out of the drawer – parachute silk, but unsatisfactorily turned around the crotch – she reflected that it was time for a review of all her lingerie. These knickers simply would not do.

For, even in her innocence, she was aware that there was a connection between falling in love with Palliser and the state of her undergarments. She knew that somewhere, some time, the end result of love between woman and man was nakedness. The prospect of standing naked before any other human being terrified her, but she accepted it might be necessary. She had not leapt straight from one kiss to an expectation of marriage, for she was too humbly adoring and too sensible to expect him to love her in return, let alone to propose marriage, but it seemed to her that if she were to accept that she was in love with him, she must also build into her picture the possible implications of that love. She had read *Madame Bovary* and *Manon Lescaut*; she had read Clarissa's copy of *Lady Chatterley's Lover* purchased in Paris by her husband Roland. She knew that love did not simply result in the happy couple driving away in a barouche-landau.

She could not dare to contemplate what might happen to her now, but she did think that her knickers would not do.

She wondered how to get nicer ones. Could one buy them? There were shops in London with patronising names like Generous Proportions and Rubens Modes. She knew about them because kind people sometimes gave her an address on a slip of paper, absent-mindedly, like handing a pound note to an indigent curate. But she could no more go up to London and visit such a shop than she could fly to the moon. Perhaps Clarissa – Clarissa declared she was a frightful needlewoman, but she had this scrumptious nanny who was a whiz with the sewing machine and did all the children's clothes, up to and including a party frock with wide silk sash, and you couldn't possibly tell it had been cut from Clarissa's mother's pre-war evening dress. Blanche thought it would be lovely to have someone who could whip up a petticoat just like that. She thought she might ask; Clarissa was always wanting to do things for her: Why don't we get you a new hat? and Why don't I take you to the hairdresser's, Blanche?

With the gift of the new black dress Clarissa had scored a success, finding it in a forgotten corner of Debenhams, possibly, Blanche suspected, a maternity item which had washed up there. Someone, presumably the nanny, had altered it cleverly with inserts of black velvet so that it fitted across Blanche's mighty shoulders and reached to mid-calf. It was, perforce, not an elegant garment, with a scooped neck, square cut bodice, eschewing a waistline or any kind of flare in the skirt, but the delight that it gave her was extraordinary. Clarissa was able to hint that a few dresses made to measure might do much to lift the spirits. Blanche, looking in the glass, agreed.

The black dress must be worn today, as nothing else would do for the first encounter with the beloved. Blanche began to long for a new dress, something which fitted, something which proclaimed her body was the shape that it was, something fresh and full. Perhaps now, emboldened by a kiss, she might find the courage to visit a dressmaker.

A knock on the bedroom door indicated that Peter had left her breakfast tray outside. She could hardly wait to get up and catch her first glimpse of Palliser, but custom, which she had herself laid down, dictated that she must breakfast in a stately manner while reading the *Sunday Mail*, and descend in time for church. Would she see him in the hall, outlined against the doorway, a Heathcliff figure, or sitting at the wheel of the Phantom, leaning nonchalantly out the car window with a cigarette, like Lord Peter Wimsey?

But there was no sign of Palliser all day. Blanche listened for his step at every moment. She haunted the kitchen quarters, finding excuses to move between the Great Scullery, kitchen, hall, dining room, and butler's strongroom. She circuited the grounds, watching the lane that led to the village.

Sunday was Palliser's day off, so Blanche had no excuse to ask after him. Of course he was entitled to take himself off for the day, nothing would be more natural; Blanche told herself this over and over again during the long dull afternoon, while Hubert's harpsichord chimed in the distance. She felt she must go out for her walk and afterwards dare to take in early evensong in the village. Perhaps she would meet him in the lane under the canopy of trees . . . what would he say? what would he do?

The imagined encounter with Palliser was played out down the lane to the village, all through evensong, and all the way back to the house, under the dark guard of trees. But it did not take place. Blanche dallied in the kitchen while Mrs Nagy made the tea. She troubled Hubert smoking in the study. She went hither and thither in the garden until it was too dark for comfort. Still he did not come.

In the evening, Hubert went out to the Abbey, and Blanche, distracted beyond her own understanding, gathered together the shreds of her courage and went into the kitchen. She asked Mrs Nagy if she knew where Palliser might be.

Mrs Nagy was sitting in an easy chair by the Aga listening to her wireless and knitting. When she heard Blanche's question, she put down her knitting and rose to her feet. 'So that's how it is, eh?' she said.

Blanche was taken aback and did not answer.

'A man, is it? Always must be a man, and what do you know about men? I will tell you about men. They are all the same, that's the first thing about them. They are monsters, not one can you trust, not one. The mothers bring them up to be good, but as soon as they want to be men they want to be like all the other men, liars, cheats. They learn from the other men how to do it, they teach one another, you see them in their bars and places, drinking, always drinking and telling each other about women. And if they don't do like the others, they get told, he is a sissy, the men don't want to know him, so they all learn, quickly, it becomes the way they are and then they cheat from women and lie, and hurt and take away what is ours, and throw us to the ground, and tramp on us.'

'Oh Mrs Nagy, I never realised you felt so strongly –'

'And when we fight back, what happens? I tell you what happens, we get beaten and laughed at and told we are whores and killed sometimes, yes killed. And no money for shoes, while he spends it all on drink with the other men. And if she tries to leave her husband, everyone will tell her she is a bad person, a wife must accept these things. Even if he rape or kill her, it is sacred. The men have taught the priests to say this, and the women learn it from the priests, who are men too. They are all in the plot together, the nice ones, they are the worst. The ones like that Wentwood. Oh he is very charming now, very kind. They are all charming and kind in the first, they are like the spider in the middle of the web.'

'But Palliser –'

'That Wentwood, where are his children? Do you ask that? His little girls, that he sheds a tear on – who is putting food in their mouth? Not that man, no he is too busy here having breakfast and dinner and brandies. Do you think his children have breakfasts and dinners? Do they have shoes of leather? He sits and drinks, because all men must sit and drink, that is the first thing, then the money goes to the whores, then maybe shoes for the children. Do not shake your head at me, Miss Blanche, I know.'

Mrs Nagy's voice was alarmingly loud. Blanche looked for a retreat, but Mrs Nagy was not letting go.

'Out in the world, everyone smiles at them and says what a nice man, what a kind man, look he gives his wife flowers, every day he takes her flowers from the market, even if he is drunk, he is a drunk man with flowers in his arms. That is all a man has to do to be a good man – he has to look like a good man, even though he is a bad bad man to all his family, and in his heart.'

It seemed to Blanche that more was at issue here than Palliser's honour. 'Did things like this happen to you?' she asked.

Mrs Nagy let out something like a wail, started to weep and broke into a language Blanche did not recognise. She guessed the subject was perhaps a certain Mr Nagy, of whom nothing had ever been said before. Though used to Mrs Nagy raging, Blanche had seen nothing quite like this before, and felt more than ordinarily helpless. The tears were terrible, real tears, not the historionic kind she sometimes produced. Confronted with genuine grief, Blanche felt like a sheep before a tiger, paralysed into inaction. A part of her wanted to put her arms around Mrs Nagy and comfort her, but she couldn't make herself cross the kitchen to perform this extraordinary act. Part of her wanted to run in search of a man to restore calm. But instead she said, 'What happened, Mrs Nagy?'

Mrs Nagy sank down in her chair and threw her hands over her face. Blanche watched as the tears oozed through her fingers and along her wrists, then sat down herself precariously on one of the kitchen chairs and touched Mrs Nagy on the shoulder.

'Can I help you?'

'No, no, there is nothing you can do, nothing anyone can do except bring me the news of that man's death. He deserves to die, over and over he deserves it. So many times I was afraid for my life and for Peter. On our wedding night he hit me and said I was a whore because my cousin kissed me. And after everyone said what beautiful couple we were, so happy to look at. Everyone loved him, all the men, all the wives, my brothers, my father thought him a hero because of the partisans, you know. He told stories and sang songs and drank with them. I wish I was born a man. A thousand times I wish it, so I could hit back, and hurt him, and have him crawl on the floor. I had a knife in my mattress but he found it. I thought he would kill me then. I lost a baby.'

'You ran away?'

'I tried to run away and he found me. Twice, three times. Every time he beat me so I had to stay home, not visit my family. They all loved him so, so charming, so good. But then he said he would lock me up and take Peter away, and I could not bear that. He said he would beat Peter and make him a man. I do not want Peter to be like them. I would rather he died than grew like them. They are all the same. Because they are stronger than us they have made us slaves, but they want us to love them also. With the flowers and the soft words.'

Blanche, who had never encountered sorrow other than her own, moved her chair and put her arm around Mrs Nagy. She did not know how she found the courage to do this. It seemed very odd and embarrassing, but Mrs Nagy turned her face and wept into Blanche's shoulder. She felt Mrs Nagy's grief in her own body and realised that she could no longer regard this woman as an embarrassing side-show. God had delivered her a charge.

'I am so sorry, Mrs Nagy, I am so sorry. I didn't

know. We really didn't understand. Can I make you a cup of tea?'

'You do not know how,' said Mrs Nagy, not entirely accurately. 'I would like a brandy.'

Blanche got up at once and went to the small drawing room, which was dark and cold, without Palliser to set the fire. She found the brandy on the sideboard and poured a big glassful then, hesitating, poured a second smaller, for herself. She was negotiating her way back to the kitchen in the dark when the front door banged behind Palliser.

He didn't expect her there in the darkened hall so late, certainly not carrying two glasses of brandy. He was taken off guard, and something registered in his face that she didn't understand. She saw something in his face before he had time to adjust it: a smallness, a tiredness, something less than beautiful, which she saw but could not name, but which she hoarded in the bottom of the chest with all her other impressions of Palliser. There was also something else about him – a smell? an air? – which she didn't recognise, was it perhaps that he was drunk, or was it just the new sheepskin jacket he wore, not brand new, but new in Palliser's possession?

Her heart had almost stopped beating when she saw him. He didn't immediately smile, but as soon as she spoke, his manner changed, he became solicitous.

'What is amiss? One day out of the house and everything's at sixes and sevens?'

'Oh no, nothing, nothing really. I am so glad you are home.'

'The brandy?' he said, and smiled naughtily.

'I must go back to Mrs Nagy. She's rather upset.'

He followed her into the kitchen. She was half inclined to discourage him, suspecting that the last thing Mrs Nagy wanted was sympathy from Palliser, but she was unable to frame the correct words.

Mrs Nagy was sitting with her hands loosely joined, staring ahead of her at the dark window. She looked at Palliser, sniffed, took the brandy, while Blanche hovered over her, a very corporeal guardian angel.

'It is Nagy,' said Mrs Nagy. 'It is Nagy who sends the boxes. I know it is him. When we came to London he had no English to speak, so he was lost. But I had some English from schooling which was better than his. I took some money and my jewels and Peter and got on the train and got off the train here, and look for a job. A cleaning job I asked, live in. It takes three days to find.'

'I remember how grateful I was.'

'But I wrote to my family in Budapest, to tell them the address, so they can be sure I am safe. And my cousin escaped out of Hungary and found Nagy and so he gets my address. And he writes. I was so afraid he would come, then he sends the boxes, with letters in them, saying I am getting rich, soon I shall come for you. Soon Peter can come and live with me. Now the boxes come. I do not want to run away again, but if Nagy comes for me, what shall I do?'

'You shall refuse to go with him,' said Blanche, 'and if he is troublesome we shall call the police.'

Mrs Nagy shook her head sadly as if to imply that the local policeman was no conceivable match for the violence of her husband.

Palliser, uncharacteristically silent, helped himself to coffee from the stove. Blanche watched his hands as they lifted the coffee pot, raised the cup to his mouth, watched his lips as the coffee passed them.

'Where is Peter?' asked Palliser.

'In his room of course with the pop records.'

'Ah,' said Palliser, sitting down wearily at the kitchen table. He hunched a little and lit a cigarette. Blanche watched his hands as if he were a conjuror at a children's party that she was determined to catch out.

'A new coat,' Mrs Nagy said to Blanche. 'He has a new coat, you see.'

Blanche was well aware, for she thought he looked so handsome in it that he should be in films. She thought it was almost unfair that anyone should look so good, just by acquiring a new coat. She sat next to Mrs Nagy and sipped brandy.

'And the children, do they have new coats?'

Palliser's aspect became so miserable that Blanche wanted to protect him from this onslaught.

'Oh Doris,' he said, 'if only it were that simple.'

Mrs Nagy turned up the volume on the radio, to discourage conversation. Blanche sat on, for it was pleasant in the kitchen, warm by the stove, companionable among the festoons of salami and the lovely shelves of pickles. She could no more have torn herself away from the room Palliser hallowed than dive into the Grand Union Canal. At last Mrs Nagy removed herself to bed, but not before delivering her parting volley.

'You remember, Miss Blanche, what I said. I know about these things because I have suffered. You are too good for them, for any of them. Especially for that one with the children far away.' She flowed into Hungarian as she banged the kitchen door.

Silence settled slowly on the kitchen.

'Did you have a pleasant day?' asked Blanche.

His eyes slid on to her face and away as he considered his answer.

'Yes, and no. I saw lovely scenery, but I was so lonely.'

She could not know, nor would ever discover that, quite to the contrary, he had spent the day at a funfair near Luton, trying to persuade a youngish woman in a pink dress and fluffy cardigan to have sex with him, that he had bought her chocolates and a stuffed pink teddy bear, taken her up a Ferris wheel and down to a pub, plying her with gin until she consented to remove her knickers in the copse beside the rifle range, that she had refused to believe in his vasectomy and insisted on a French letter, which once produced from his back pocket proved recalcitrant and ill-lubricated, thus ensuring that neither derived any pleasure from the 360-second conjunction. Blanche neither knew nor guessed any of this, and it is an open question whether, had she known it, it would have shaken her out of her passion.

The front door banged loudly, and Hubert's tread resounded through the hall.

'Someone is with him,' said Blanche.

'Peter, no doubt.' Palliser flicked ash into the sink. 'He often slips out about now for a cigarette in the garden. Poor Doris, but you can't blame the boy for being a boy. It's in our blood, the passion to be free.'

'Blanche,' he said, 'do you think I might be so bold as to join you in a brandy?'

He made them an impromptu supper to soak up the brandy, shamelessly raiding Mrs Nagy's supplies.

'Did you have no supper?'

'I was a trifle melancholic,' he said.

'So was I,' she said and smiled with her whole being, because she was no longer melancholy.

When she could delay the moment of retiring no longer, she rose slowly to her feet, brushed the crumbs from her lap and with every vibrating chord in her body willed him to give her some sign.

It was as if he knew his cue, and he did not disappoint.

'I wish you could have been with me today. We could have viewed the autumn colours at Kew. You would like that.' He also rose to go and came with her to the door. 'Goodnight, sweet chuck,' he said. He took her hand between his and stroked it. 'And flights of angels wing thee to thy rest.' He turned her hand over and kissed the palm. She climbed to bed on a cloud of blessedness, barely noticing that Palliser went back to the kitchen and the brandy.

One evening in early December Palliser, sitting with Hubert and Blanche before the Lovelaces' fire, brandy, cigar and *New Yorker* in hand, realised that he was in serious danger of becoming bored.

Now that the spectres of hunger and cold had retreated and he found himself more comfortable than he had been since he was summarily ejected from his mother's house, he found himself face to face with his oldest enemy.

Palliser:

There you are again, you old snake you, coming to distract me from my purpose. How many grand schemes of mine have you ruined? Just for the sake of a little fun, as you call it, along the way to ease the tedium. And sometimes we wrestled and I've beaten you – I did finish building the tower, as near as dammit, I did get the ditches dug even though it was pain and grief to me, day after stinking sodden hot day in the mud with you whisperin' in my ear the while. But you never lie down and die: here you are again. When will you ever leave me in peace? I'm not a young man any more, I don't find your funfairs and drunkenness and fast cars and japes have any savour now. Yes, so I'm getting old, I'm gettin' boring too, well pax, let me be dull, and comfortable for a bit.

The demon Palliser:

But you aren't old yet, are you? You're scarcely middle-aged. Why play at old man when there's years of that enforced ahead? You're as vigorous as ever, just as likely to jump in the fountain and climb to the top, and the women still fall for you, silly fools. And there are so many women in the world, more all the time, just think about them, tiny women like boys with tits, black women with haunches that shine like a racehorse, Oriental women with mystic arts, crazy teenaged girls with self-destructive energy and bouncy hair, faded European aristocrats with jewels and memories of kings and princes who were their lovers. And there are cars to drive over mountain passes in the snow, and follies to picnic under in the moonlight, and gracious lawns to turn cartwheels upon, and Sicilian seaports luring a man with the stink of fish and the smell of garlic. And what are you doing here?

Palliser:

I know exactly what I'm doing here, and it's all going exactly to plan, and you are not going to subvert it. I'm sitting here with my kind hosts and employers, who happen to be one of the richer families in the county, a moderate portion of whose yearly income would set me up for life. I've got this gorgeous monument to womankind eating out of my hand, and I'll be damned if I don't take her to bed. And take her virginity. And make her a happy woman with a past to dream on. I won't be distracted, I tell you, this is my last chance: if I throw it away, I'll be an old man with stained clothes dancing in fountains while the passers-by lob pennies.

The demon Palliser:

Well, well, very well, I can see you're determined to sink into middle age, but why not create a bit of entertainment, just a soupçon of excitement, to speed things up a bit, and keep me from desperate measures?

196

At that moment in the debate, the relief squadron arrived in the form of a medley of Viennese Waltzes on the Light Programme. Palliser threw down his magazine, abandoned cigar and glass to their fate, and leapt to his feet. He made a deep and courtly bow.

'Madam, may I have the pleasure.' And he whirled Blanche off without waiting, her embroidery dropping to the floor in the confusion.

It became quickly apparent that Blanche loved to dance and danced extremely well; Palliser was rather rusty, but had been a swooningly fine dancer in his day. Together they found their feet and swept around the drawing room, and around again, while Hubert gazed in amazement. Then out into the hall, right around its echoing bareness, fast and precise, pressed together. Into the Great Hall, the music fading to a distant trilling, the moonlight marking lanes on the floor, round and round the huge table in the hall's centre, under the uninterpretable stares of a dozen dead Lovelaces.

They were almost exactly the same height, although Palliser's right arm reached only a short distance around Blanche's back. He thought how deliciously different she was to any dancing partner he had enjoyed before, how she enfolded him innocently, by being herself. He dimly recalled other bodies he had pressed himself against, but nothing compared to Blanche Lovelace. He imagined all that lovely white young flesh consumed with pleasure, absorbing him into herself, as was the natural and proper end of the male of the species.

Pressed against her body, Palliser discovered a palpable erection, and considered whether he might die of ill-contained desire. She was in no way provocative: modestly dressed, she was seriously intent on guiding her feet in the darkness. But her hugeness and warmth and willingness to be clasped close engendered in him more lust than he had felt since Salomé let down her hair on the balcony. As on that occasion, he was possessed by a lust of the mind, as well as the body: *I must have this wonderful creature, I must consume her loveliness and be consumed by it, or I shall perish.*

His body pounded with it, but worse, his mind was bursting. Tumescent, that was how to describe it, if it needed a word, the passion in his head.

So damn you, he said to his demon, *I'll not throw this away for anything. I'll be bored for her sake. Bored stiff, if you like. I'll dance in the moonlight to the radio and find it fun. I'll make it a tale to tell my grandchildren!*

They steered their way around the hall again and back towards the light, readjusted themselves to the music and made another circuit. Hubert came out of the drawing room with his cigar to watch. Blanche, used to leading, guided him back towards the darkness, either by design or instinct, searching for something more.

Palliser dared not kiss her in the hall, knowing where he would go from there. Hubert was too much in evidence; not disapproving, but simply present. The next moves, regardless of what his body loudly suggested, required the utmost delicacy. They came to earth in the drawing room, a little out of breath, and in Palliser's case discomfited.

'We'll put on a dance,' he cried, 'a Christmas dance! What do you say, Hubert, a party for the neighbourhood? With a band of fiddles and a few songs, and lots of punch and dancing? What do you say, what do you say?'

'Splendid!' cried Hubert. 'Absolutely splendid! Hasn't been a party here since Grandfather's time.'

'But we don't know anyone,' said Blanche.

'Ah, but you will! If you invite them, they'll come. In their droves. Especially if you invite parents and children; children can't get enough parties. Speak to Clarissa and Roland, they know everyone.'

'Oh, yes!' cried Blanche, now that the social weight

was shifted on to Clarissa's shoulders. 'Shall I ring her up?'

'In the morning, perhaps. Hubert, old chap, you could organise a little concert, a few songs, a little ensemble, some carols for everyone to join in.'

'And Father Christmas! Why don't you be Father Christmas, Hubert! And give out presents to all the children!'

Hubert positively beamed.

There you are – sometimes it is possible to have one's cake and eat it. You know how much I love to give a party. We'll have some fun, and at the end of the party, we'll do or die. And then I'm off – agreed?

Agreed.

So Palliser found himself seated opposite Blanche in the first-class compartment of the train. Outside the darkness suggested that the muddy skirts of London were a lovely spangled gown, and Palliser felt he was living in a Cinderella world. Today he had seen the streets of London wet with recent rain glinting in the afternoon sun, and discreetly suggesting that they were, after all, paved with gold. Perhaps fairy tales do intersect with life; now and then Palliser's fantasies took on form – a tower rose out of the swamp, and the ice maiden caught fire. Today he had achieved another dream: he had escorted Blanche to London to buy a dress. He had steered her into a gown shop in Covent Garden used to bedizening opera singers, and helped her choose a style and a spectacular shade of red taffeta. He had left her for a full hour in the hands of a discreet corsetière, to be petted and measured.

Then after a cosy lunch tête-à-tête, on to the shopping!

Palliser loved shopping – preferably with other people's money – and Blanche was a child to whom every single thing was new. Palliser found himself restraining her from purchases.

'But Clarissa says we must have slightly more than enough presents! In case absolutely everybody accepts,' cried Blanche at the model soldiers.

'But Clarissa said I must buy two hundred *yards* of tinsel. She really did, Palliser. Two hundred *yards*. And at least a hundred fairy lights. There are only seventy-two in that box.'

Clarissa had taken to the organisation of the party with almost as much enthusiasm as Palliser, though it is to be hoped from more innocent motives. And given the way Clarissa watches Palliser, day in, day out, it is likely that she suspects his motives, while enjoying his energetic practice. Clarissa, Palliser thinks, and perhaps for once he is right in this, cannot decide whether she distrusts him more than she enjoys him. She and Palliser, left to their own devices, would have had the most spiffing time arranging the party, but both, in their different ways, are conscious of Blanche and Hubert's sensitivities.

Hubert has invited his friend Jocelyn, an excellent performer on the treble recorder, to perform at the concert. Hubert now rehearses the Thule Early Music Group three times a week. He is a man with a mission. Hubert has suggested that Peter, like Palliser, be hired evening dress.

Blanche attends. She listens to the debates about supper, and the jokes about the Watford Palm Court Orchestra. She calms Mrs Nagy when rage at the inequity of the workload overwhelms her. She nods and smiles as Roland Elton explains about running a cable all the way to the front lawn, and the likely effect on the mains. O brave new world that has such details in it.

Blanche, sitting on the train from London, was now exhausted; the manic excitement which had propelled her up Hamley's toyshop stair by stair was all spent. At her feet were bags and boxes containing the spoils of their raid – the most elegant Christmas decorations London afforded, and a present for every child attending the party.

'What a wonderful place,' she sighed. 'I never dreamed.'

London, or the toyshop? Or Harrods? Or Covent Garden? Or little old Oxford Street, cheerfully lit up and electric with commerce? Blanche had exclaimed over everything. It had finally dawned upon Palliser that she had been up to London but once or twice before, so that the train trip, the jolting Underground, the jammed streets and impossible traffic, the dirt, and even the beggars, were exciting.

But in spite of so much wonder, she took notice of small things.

'Did you buy anything for your girls?' she asked.

'It's hard to know,' improvised Palliser. 'They are so grown up now. What does one buy young women nowadays? You will have to help me.'

Blanche smiled, and fell silent. Even the endlessly fascinating topic of the party arrangements did not tempt her to talk.

Palliser loved to tempt her so – to drop the word 'catering' and hear her grow voluble about Mrs Nagy, or Doris as she was sometimes called these days, and how wonderful a cook and how energetic, and how kind of her to offer to do everything – but how impossible she was! And Peter, so clever and clear with his lists, but how – Palliser remembered the carefully rationed utterances of the Blanche he had first met, and he smiled at the transformation he had effected.

Palliser regarded her as she fell gently asleep. Most people asleep on the train take on the aspect of a caricature by Du Maurier or Tenniel, grey lines dragging down their cheeks, mouths unnaturally wide, heads in clownish posture. Not so Blanche. She remained solidly upright, her head turned sideways with her cheek resting on the upholstery as sweetly as on a down pillow. That her eyes were closed seemed almost accidental. Her face was pretty in repose, the purity of her skin all the more apparent, the gentle outlines of her nose and cheek as lovely as any rose of Rubens. The face of a child lodged in the body of an empress.

Palliser felt the terrifying onset of protectiveness. Here was a child who had been delivered into his hands – how could he do anything to harm her? He was the one to protect her from the heartless seducer.

He thought of the girls who were legitimately his charge: Jemima, Abigail, Naomi, Bathsheba – what ringing names they had, what pride each one had chalked up in his heart. Each pretty bundle that he carried on his hip while ranging through the fields had grown into a slim little body busily trotting behind him as he went about his business, doggedly following, an instant audience for the great performer. How did they look now? Bathsheba – how old was she? Surely she was not at school yet? He was appalled by not knowing. Jemima and Abigail – were they tall and lovely? Of course they were. Jemima, so graceful and soft-hearted, always trying to mediate when tempers flared, she might be married already – how could the young men resist such beauty and sweet temper, and such domestic skills? Abigail, wily, subtle, questioning him, challenging him, defying him: did he love her best of all? But Naomi, brave and funny, always fishing and trapping and banging about, never a word when she fell into the ditch, up she came, covered in mud, spluttering a bit and then grinning. He loved them all best of all, as he loved their mother who was already himself.

He must go home, he could not delay, his heart hurt and stomach yearned, and yet his path to those lovely girls and their mother, on whom but to gaze was heaven, lay through the girl before him. How could he be so cruel? How could he, who thought of himself as essentially a kind man, behave in so abominable a manner?

But there was no way back. He had committed himself to this task at Thule and he must bring it to some conclusion. For one thing, to desert now would throw away all his hard work for no reward; for another, he would hurt Blanche so deeply that no version of the story he might concoct in later life could disguise the pain. He switched his mind away from this dilemma, lest he start to hate himself.

And then Palliser received information about his family.

The morning after he had escorted Blanche to London, he dozed piously through mass as usual then collected the mail from the postman and took it to Hubert in the breakfast room. Hubert had personally written out the invitations in his lovely cursive script. Replies were arriving thick and fast; as Clarissa predicted, the majority of those invited had accepted. Christmas cards, a rare item in the Lovelace household, were also arriving *en masse*, as though the Lovelaces had recently returned from a prolonged absence overseas. Hubert now openly went through the post each morning, took out the replies and any letters or pamphlets of interest to himself, and sent the cards, bills and miscellaneous items up to Blanche's little accounts room.

'I say, Pally, here's one for you! A Christmas card from New Zealand.'

Palliser's hand shook as he took the card. He scanned the envelope as if it were a conscription order. A New Zealand Christmas stamp, an anodyne angel blowing a trumpet, franked in Kaikoura. Handwriting he did not recognise, certainly not Salomé's, too mature a hand for any of the girls, a bold hand from an era when penmanship was firmly practised.

Palliser Wentwood Esq.,
Thule Hall
Nr St Albans
England

'It's a miracle that card made it here,' said Hubert. 'Go on, man, open it. Why, Palliser, you're as white as a sheet.'

Palliser's heart beat terrifyingly fast, as at the last twenty seconds of a horserace on which £100 had been staked, but his emotion was fear rather than excitement. He took the letter-opener from Hubert as if it were a sacrificial knife and he Abraham poised above Isaac. No ram appeared in the thicket. He slit open the envelope.

Inside was a card of utmost cheerfulness and vulgarity. A Father Christmas with a brilliant red face, with two robins whose breasts were of the same cheery hue. Snow lay all around, snow on snow, the like of which none of his girls had ever seen. The handwriting was a child's – printed for the most part, with some letters joined up to show it could be done. It must be Naomi, since Bathsheba could not possibly be of an age to write – could she?

The writing on the card spread all over the inside and back. A folded cutting from the newspaper fell to the floor as he opened it, but Palliser did not immediately examine this.

The card read:

Dear Daddy,

I hope you are well. Mrs Butterworth said I should write to you, because you have been away to long and we miss you. I am very well. I got top in mental arithmetic and got a one and three twos on my report. I will show it to you. I caught two Trevvali (sp.??) off the wharf. Mum is very well. She has a shop selling wine in the tower and we get tourists. Next year I shall

be in Standard Five and Bathy will be in Primer One.
I got Anne of Green Gables for a prize which is really
good. She is like me, only redhead. Mum bought a
big truck. It used to be in the desert with the army.
I am aloud to play with Phillips trainset all the time,
it is really bonzer. Love and kisses from Naomi.
P.S. Mrs B said to send you this. They didn't take
me. Not fair!!!
P.P.S. Jemma and Aby are very well and send love.

With a row of crosses for kisses and circles for hugs.
Palliser tried to brush the tears out of his eyes, but could
not prevent Hubert from noticing.

'They are all well,' he said. 'I was so afraid.'

'Thank God! You miss them very deeply.'

Palliser reached for his handkerchief and unfolded the
cutting, and his heart, already in uncertain motion, turned
a cartwheel.

The cutting included a little ribbon of paper running
up to the date at the top of the page of newspaper.
Saturday, 14 November 1959. Under their brave banner
they posed, so good-humoured and well pleased with
themselves, two lovely girls in matching white aprons,
Abigail's legs elegantly poised, Jemima less self-conscious,
holding her hands in her lap with saintlike grace. And
behind them a youth in spectacles whom Palliser did
not recognise, although the caption proclaimed him to
be Thaddeus Butler. Philip Butterworth. And between
them Salomé Wentwood, bare-headed, her hair pulled
into a matronly bun, soberly dressed, shining out of the
picture like a Madonna enthroned between four saints.
Palliser sat down at the breakfast table and covered his
face with his hand. At the same time he had the foresight
to keep the picture well out of Hubert's view.

He wanted to crumple it into a ball; he wanted to

frame it in gold. He saw how close she stood to Philip Butterworth, how her body swayed towards him. He saw the proprietorial expression on Butterworth's face, the cat consuming the cream in front of the whole province. Mrs Salomé Wentwood, the caption said, *Mrs* — but he could not see whether she still wore a wedding ring.

Hubert prised himself out of his chair and poured Palliser a cup of coffee. Palliser folded the cutting inside the card and lit a cigarette, though he could hardly make the lighter and cigarette connect.

'Do you want to talk about it?'

Palliser shook his head. His hands would not stop shaking; he could not stop tears from welling up in his eyes. He came of the old school, in which men did not weep in front of other men; his misery was mixed with embarrassment. He had not known he felt this way; he had not known he would cry when he saw a picture of his family. This was not the Palliser he knew.

When had he wept? Each time a child was born, a clean swaddled bundle delivered into his arms, everything clean and fresh after the smoke-filled irritation of the fathers' waiting room. Each time he had taken the baby and breathed her name on to her forehead and tears had spilt on to her face; always joy, never a moment's disappointment at another daughter, no, never, only tears of joy at a whole curled-up life ready to spring. The exhilaration of cheating death, the immortality of it, the thumbing the nose at the Creator — I made this one, this new life is my doing. And it is me and not me, so I am the greater by a whole personage.

Oh the tears of his life! So few tears shed for sorrow — when Nanny was gone. Gone. When Salomé lost the baby after Abigail, he cried then for Salomé's grief not his own. Once after the war, when a man told him a story about being a Japanese prisoner. So few tears spread over forty years, and now tears in such abundance.

'I think I understand why you're here, Palliser, what your motives are.'

Jesus Christ! That's all I need. I'm defenceless. Kick me when I'm down, why don't you?

Hubert persisted.

'I think we understand your grief, that you wish to bury yourself as far away from the tragedy as you can. Your children remind you of things you wish to forget. Here you can be anonymous, here you are not forced to relive terrible scenes each day. But at the same time you are consumed with worry about them, and to blot out the pain you throw yourself into distractions – for example, planning a wonderful party allows you to forget that you will be parted from your dear ones at Christmas.'

Palliser could think of nothing to say that would not dig him deeper into the mire. He was too weak to frame a lie and he could not tell the truth.

'We feel privileged to be able to help. So many people have suffered this century – the Great War, the Depression, the last war – but all the misery has passed us by, and we haven't been able to help. Apart from having evacuees for a bit. It's a small thing, I know, but we do want to help you.'

Palliser felt like an old ram being chivvied into the slaughterhouse. *Follow the easy path downwards, old boy, and then lie down and die. Why don't you? What's left to live for, Pally, when all you made has been taken away.*

But the old ram has grown old by following his instinct for survival in the least promising situations.

'No, no, it's not so bad. Mrs Butterworth is very wealthy.' He hoped that the indirection of this remark would confuse Hubert while he recovered enough to gather his wits.

'I'd like to do more in a pastoral way, but it doesn't seem to come up.'

To mesmerise Blanche was one thing, but to fool Hubert into thinking that he dispensed charity was too much. Palliser decided that grief could act as a cover for straight speaking. He took out his handkerchief, and wiped vigorously at his eyes.

'Father,' he said, 'you are a kind man, but if you want to do God's work, don't waste your time on me. I'm past redemption. Spend your energies where there's crying need, not on an old renegade like me. Go and help your friend Jocelyn out in his slum parish improving some drains and drying out some drunks. Palliser Wentwood's a lost cause.'

Hubert was visibly taken aback, but his natural courtesy did not falter.

'I can't agree that anyone is a lost cause, especially not yourself. But I do take your point, I do take your point.'

It was only later, when he regained the safety of his bedroom, that the awful truth dawned on Palliser.

He sat on the side of his iron bed and unfolded the cutting on the bedspread. He read the article several times, as if it were a coded message, but there was not a great deal of information to be derived. There was comment on the state of the rural economy and the country's wine trade, and a certain amount of indulgent detail about the Wentwood women and their enthusiasm for trying something new while adhering to traditional recipes and methods. Mrs Wentwood, one felt, was probably a brave war widow turning around the family farm.

It was their happiness that accused and offended him. How could they smile like that when Philip Butterworth stood where Palliser Wentwood should stand. It was *his* name they proclaimed on their banner, on their wine labels, even on their clothes. They were his clan, and he was the chieftain. How dare they? The whole country was being sold Wentwood's Wines without the mighty Wentwood himself. It was a deception. They had taken over his tower, built with his own hands. Philip Butterworth had taken his tower. And what else?

The notion of anyone else touching his precious Salomé did not in itself appal him; he found her so desirable that he could not imagine any red-blooded man not warming to her. He was not a mean-spirited man, wheeling free while expecting his women to stay cloistered at home. He thought it only natural that Salomé should love and be loved by other men – within limits. What cut him to the heart was the thought that his place had been taken, the special space that Palliser and only Palliser inhabited, the essence of his being. Whatever he was, he was that thing in oneness with Salomé – and this perhaps explains, although it does not excuse, why he was able to be away from her so long. He was as secure in her love as he was in his own existence. Two people, one flesh; more importantly, two people, one person.

Or so he had thought. He had not thought enough, he had not seen enough. He had not looked ahead or looked around. He had not thought that if he were not present to renew his image as pressed into Salomé others would be busy rubbing it out for him – malignant and self-seeking others.

Mrs Butterworth. What was that poisonous old toad doing in his children's lives? Only one explanation was possible: she had taken them over because they were effectively hers. The train set in Philip's attic – what familiarity that betokened. Why had the termagant Butterworth prevailed upon Naomi to write? And enclose the carefully snipped-out cutting? Because she wanted to triumph in the fact that she and her soft-soap of a son had defeated him, smoothed him out of his own place. Mrs

Butterworth had his children, and Philip Butterworth, his wife.

Her face, the dearest thing in the world, was a series of black dots on a piece of newsprint.

And mine, goddammit, mine!

> *Something, something, valour, fire;*
> *A love that life could never tire,*
> *Death quench or evil stir,*
> *The mighty master gave to her.*
> *Something, something, something, wife,*
> *A fellow-traveller true through life*
> *Heart whole and soul-free*
> *The august father*
> *Gave to* **me!**

How could she love Philip Butterworth when she was loved by Palliser? Had she forgotten? How could she forget?

> *My desire and thy desire*
> *Twining to a tongue of fire*
> *Leaping live, and laughing higher . . .*

Poetry to Palliser was life – not a heightened version of it, but a melodious way of expressing what was real. As far as he understood, his love for Salomé and her love for him had been the very stuff of verse. It was never necessary for him to translate from poetry to real life. He lived inside a love poem.

Palliser James Wentwood – failed medical student, failed horse-doctor, failed farmer, disinherited, bankrupt, old-fashioned romantic chauvinist, washed up in the last corner of a world turned practical, a world in which women are picking up the skins of men and shaking their heads.

Is it not time we felt sorry for this old gryphon, prancing his outdated magic in a rational world, magic that has served him so well for so long? Can I prevail upon you, just and merciful reader, to look at him now, a handsome man past his prime, a thing of shreds and tatters, thin, silver-haired, barely a possession to his name, hunched on a narrow bed in a servant's bedroom, living in the scaffold of a lie that is threatening to collapse around him; can I prevail upon you to feel, if not pity, perhaps a little understanding?

Yes, he is one of those who profited from the old romantic world, in which to love a woman was to own her; yes, he is one who has made his way by exercising privilege not his own, by leeching on the resources of woman, yes, he is one who accepted that his family was his property, and yes, I, as a modern woman, despise such men.

And yet, poor creature, his heart is breaking.

A slow deadening realisation comes to him, alone in his narrow room, that love grows cold, and hearts harden against poetry. It comes to him, a grey wave breaking into his mind, that well-being is now more powerful than love.

Never, in all the months of his absence, had he imagined that he might be turned away from his doorstep. Welcome home has been the ground of his being, the one stable point in his tergiversation.

After all his planning and dreaming, all his indulgence in dreams and wallowing in guilt, he has come to this. He stares at the death of his heart, at the onset of nothingness, at the possibility that even Salomé cannot forgive him, and he is no longer welcome home.

VIII

ABIGAIL FOUND IT a relief to cast anchor on the rock of Vergil. She had worked her way steadily through the texts for the first term of Latin I: Catullus and Propertius, love poems, every one. Abigail despised love poems, even cynical, lecherous Latin poems. She had discarded her belief in romantic love and her belief in God at the same time and about the same matter – her father's desertion. She had been young enough when he left to accept without question that the love between her parents was the thing that all the soppy poems and love stories were about: it had to be, because her father was always quoting poetry to her mother when he wasn't kissing, embracing and pulling her on to his knee. It was a datum in the household, and indeed in the community, that Palliser and Salomé, whatever their vicissitudes, personified married love.

When he left, everyone thought it was just a temporary blip, a quick trip down south to earn a few pounds. He'd done it before, sometimes he went off and got rather drunk and came home with inappropriate friends or shares in an unlikely racehorse. But he came back, always with presents, sometimes nothing more expensive than flowers he'd picked by the riverside or a particularly lovely paua shell, or a comic he'd picked up on the train. Always returned, always with a token of apology, always to open arms and Salomé's smiling.

Then the days of his absence turned into weeks and the weeks into months. Naomi stopped asking for him, and Abigail stopped counting. Birthdays came and went unmarked. Salomé's face grew drawn and grey, and her fingers pinched. She did not rail, but she did not laugh any more.

After a while Abigail started to pray about it. She made a deal with God: if he brought Father home before Christmas, she would never ask for anything ever again in her whole life. Not ever, not if she was dying of cancer or even if her children were dying. She'd take whatever He threw at her without a whimper. But, on the other hand, if He did not bring Father back by Christmas, she would be reluctantly forced to terminate their relationship, and stop believing in Him. And so it fell out.

Sometimes she'd hear Salomé singing around the bottom of the tower.

I dreamt that I dwelt in marble halls
with vassels and serfs at my side,
and of all who assembled within those walls
that I was the hope and the pride.
I had riches all too great to count
and a high ancestral name.

But I also dreamt which pleased me most
that you loved me still the same.

I dreamt that suitors sought my hand,
that knights upon bended knee
and with vows no maiden's heart could withstand,
they pledged their faith to me.
And I dreamt that one of that noble host
came forth my hand to claim.

But I also dreamt which charmed me most
that you loved me still the same.

This song, no matter how beautiful, irritated Abigail. To her it implied, though she might have been wrong in this, that her mother's belief in love had not been shaken by her father's abandonment. She supposed that Salomé had not seen how, in leaving her, he had turned his back not only on the woman herself, but on the ideal that their life together supposedly represented. Abigail's rejection of the concept of romantic love was now complete, so much so that she did not bother to debate it, either with her mother or in the sanctuary of her own head. She held that it would hardly matter what her mother *said* she felt, since Salomé would naturally be inclined to hang on to the worthless paper scrip of her love, having invested so much.

So it was that Abigail, determinedly loveless, sat on the top floor of the tower, at the desk she had constructed out of apple boxes and tea-chests, rubbing her hands with cold. She frowned over Vergil, but was happy to be dealing with someone so eminently sensible as Aeneas, who left Dido, with her lamentations of love, and went off with the chaps to found Rome. Admittedly, he did it because it was his Duty and a Goddess told him to, but that was a lot better than going because he'd got tired of Dido and wanted a bit of Sabine woman. The best bits of Vergil were about the countryside and the wonders of bees, and, reading that verse, one felt that life could, after all, be elevated and rational, beautiful, well ordered and passionless.

Thaddeus had given her all the textbooks for first-year Greek and Latin, and she had decided that only A pluses would suffice to confirm Philip in his kindness. Naturally, Philip's kindness could only be motivated by what Philip perceived as his love for Salomé, but Abigail took a pragmatic view of that emotion. In Abigail's view, Philip's feelings for Salomé were mostly about creature comforts.

'Well at least,' she would say to Jemima, if Jemima would listen, 'if she married him, there won't be any pretence that it's for love. I think mutual comfort is a very good basis for marriage, don't you?'

It never crossed her mind that her mother might feel some species of love for Philip Butterworth, because her father, for all his faults, seemed an infinitely more attractive – and if one must love, then lovable – personage, than that nice, kind, dull man. If one had to propound a theory of romantic love, then it was plausible that Salomé might love Palliser, but not that she might love Philip Butterworth. Abigail feared that there was some contradiction in her position but she was too exasperated with them all to sort it out. Besides, she had a new world opening up to her, and she filled up her mind with it.

Next year she was to go to university. She had enrolled, paid the fees, secured a place in a women's hostel, everything. She was deliriously happy, but not a soul was going to find that out. She would never come back to the valley, except for holidays and visits to Mother. She'd strike out into the wide world, just like Palliser did, but unlike Palliser she wouldn't leave any wreckage behind her. She would never let something idly called love hold her back or strap her down. She wanted never to be answerable to another person, except, of course, for the natural affection she owed her family, for she was not hard-hearted.

She understood the demon that had driven Palliser away, the feeling of entrapment and the grinding tiresomeness of poverty. She knew how she would feel if she were stuck here for life, with the responsibility always of earning the family's income on diminishing resources. She understood that for someone who, if even half the stories were true, had lived a whirlwind life in the great world, to be trapped and helpless in this valley might be intolerable. She could forgive his leaving, but she could not forgive his silence.

Forsan et haec olim meminisse juvabit, she read and, consulting the literal translation on the opposite page and the construed text in another book, she discovered that this, coming from the mouth of the hero in adversity, showed him projecting a future time when he might look back on his present troubles and rejoice; rejoice, the tenses apparently implied, because he was looking back on trouble well and truly in the past.

How delicious to have life tidily arranged in compact phrases. One could imagine the Vergil-loving patrician of any age, in the midst of his woes, crying out *forsan et haec olim meminisse juvabit*, and making all hearts blithe. Abigail wanted this world, the ambit of men with clear world views and satisfactory incomes, the civilised world in which schemes worked out. Her valley did not mean stasis; it meant constant change and flurry, and an unclear future from which one could not guarantee that one might rejoice to have remembered the trials of the past.

But she had her future now. Palliser could not shake her from it, nor any other force. If the Butterworth empire collapsed, approximately as likely as the fall of the Bank of England, she would slave her way through university as a waitress in a coffee bar, but never, never give it up. She'd get a good degree, and then she'd teach Latin somewhere, any university in the civilised world would do, and there were plenty of them. South Africa, British Guiana, even Scotland, she wasn't fussy. She would not end her days like Palliser, roaming the world pathetically in search of a fortune, too ashamed to come home.

There was a price to pay. Earning the family's bread at fifteen had given Abigail precocious wisdom. She could see that her chosen course cut her off from the glorious madness of her parents' relationship and the sweet warmth that radiated from Jemima and Thaddeus. That was just fine by Abigail.

She glanced at the old alarm clock on the window-ledge and saw that she had been at her books for an hour, so got up to pace around the tower. It never failed to irritate her that the floor sloped and was inadequately braced, so that towards the middle one felt the structure sway a little, as the timbers bent. Why build such a thing if you didn't have the skill? Who needed a tower in the middle of this raw valley, where the mountains went up sheer to heaven and the sea rocks plummeted down to the abyss? And who needed a tower so absurd, with stones all higgledy-piggledy, and uneven floors, and doors that wouldn't shut because the frames weren't square? Only a fool built a folly, and then, ashamed by the sight of it, fled the country. Perversely, though, she loved the tower. Or more precisely, she loved the view from the tower, the feeling of a secret place, peering out through the telescope at the world going about its business, and then out to the remote seas beyond. She could see further than anyone else in the valley, she and the cockies up on the mountain slopes; between them, they could see to Chile and Antarctica, to Hawaiki and the seaboard of Gondwanaland.

If she had been of a romantic nature she might have whiled away her idle hours in this tower, with its endless vista and her treasury of books. For, as well as her desk and the alarm clock and the classical texts, she had in the tower her collection of books — such as it was — scraped up over ten years from every jumble sale and church fair in the county. Enid Blyton, Rider Haggard, Wordsworth, John Buchan, Agatha Christie, *The Poems of John Greenleaf Whittier*, Arthur Ransome, *Lyra Elegantiarum*, *The Decline and Fall of the Roman Empire*, Dorothy L. Sayers, Essie Summers, D.H. Lawrence, P.C. Wren, Aldous Huxley, *The Weekend Book*, Rumer Godden, Ngaio Marsh, Evelyn Waugh, Swinburne, *Gardiner's History of England in Three Volumes*, Thomas Hardy, Georgette Heyer, *Paradise Lost* with Illustrations by Gustave Doré (a snip at five shillings). And of course, *Palgrave's Golden Treasury*.

Yes, she might have spent her time here, reading verse, and falling in love, and growing melancholy.

> *Come to the window, sweet is the night-air!*
> *Only, from the long line of spray*
> *Where the sea meets the moon-blanch'd land,*
> *Listen! you hear the grating roar*
> *Of pebbles which the waves draw back, and fling,*
> *At their return, up the high strand,*
> *Begin, and cease, and then again begin,*
> *With tremulous cadence slow, and bring*
> *The eternal note of sadness in.*

The middle-aged misery of Arnold was too far from the world of Vergil, stern in duty, clear of purpose. Nor, a post-Darwinian, racked with existential doubt, had he any place in the brave new world of now. God was in His place, and it was not in heaven, but in history. Humans were wondrous machines, magnificent automata, self-determining, masters of the universe, as confident about their control of the created order as the Augustan Romans were of the Empire. Abigail was one of them, and she had already proved it.

She turned the telescope to the south-west and watched Philip's car, a great big black Humber Super Snipe, gliding towards them. The light was behind him, long shadows flung out over the plain towards the sea, enduing him with a mighty significance. A little man to cast such a shadow, but how could you tell from far away? How could you tell the truth of anything unless you were right inside it? But how long did it take to understand whether a Philip was large or small, petty or gracious? If it took years to be sure of one plain person, how long to be sure about Palliser, and how much longer to understand the world?

And yet to make any headway in the world, it was necessary to make assumptions. Simplifications. Generalisations. Neat phrases to sum up the world and manage it. *Meminisse juvabit. Nil nisi bonum. Varium et semper mutabile femina. Nihil utile quod non honestum.*

Philip slowed as he passed the big yellow grader forming the road to the farm. She watched him wind down the car window in spite of the dust, and shout some benign greeting to the driver, a large Maori, who sat in the cab like a jolly hermit. The driver waved back a response of unmixed cheerfulness. No more potholes, thanks to Philip. No more squeaking chalk on the blackboard, thanks to Philip. No more embarrassing rejections at Stoke's Drapery, thanks to Philip. Should she be uncomfortable because her start in life was due to the co-incidence that Philip Butterworth was well-off and sentimentally attached to her mother?

Not at all! She was doing no more than Philip did, nor more than all the confident men in the civilised world did — making use of convenient situations. Philip had been at school with the right chaps, and they happened to like him. That was not Philip's fault, and he was right to take advantage of it. Philip could not help the fact that he had been enrolled in the Club by his father and had kept up the membership ever since, because the parking was so convenient and the bar was such excellent value. To succeed it was only natural to make sensible use of good fortune. And to save oneself from penury, it was even more imperative to grasp and manipulate whatever luck came one's way.

She wondered why, therefore, she found it necessary to be acerbic to Philip. He had done her nothing but good. He was her ladder to the world. He had played into her hands by making her mother financially secure, and thereby ensuring Abigail's future. He had created enough diversion by his attentions and his business to allow Abigail to flee.

He was unfailingly pleasant, never expected gratitude, and was liked by all.

Was it possible, she wondered, tracking Philip's progress as he got out of his car, shut the door lovingly, tapped a cigarette lightly on his silver case, lit it from his silver lighter, resettled his hat on his head, and walked across the stone bridge to his place of business and seat of pleasure, was it possible that, in spite of everything, she resented him simply because he was not Palliser?

It was time for her to go down and see to things below.

Downstairs in the room once called the Barbican, and now more prosaically the Shop, Salomé was constructing wine racks. She and Naomi had taught themselves the rudiments of carpentry, since it was clearly inconvenient to call in a man every time a new shelf was needed. The results of their work were not always elegant but they were robust, and once smoothed, sanded and varnished, looked better than they had any right to. The major difficulty was that nothing in Palliser's tower was at right angles to anything else; hardly surprising in a tower, he had claimed. The unevenness of the floor meant that Salomé's meticulously measured shelves needed little slivers of wood under their feet to make them stand solid.

At present she was putting together a new set of unpainted racks, and Bathsheba was helping with the screws. The racks were to hold the latest batch of broom flower wine, something of an experiment, but so far delicate to the taste and an exquisite colour. Like maiden's pee, said Abigail. Everyone pretended not to hear, except Philip who grinned and went a little bit red. Salomé was more preoccupied with the maturing qualities of the new wine, put together in a rush to fill the thinning shelves. Stock was now becoming her problem, for although the Shop was crowded with racks, the rate at which it sold was faster than the rate at which it had, heretofore, been produced.

Until the fruit season started in earnest she was limited to rhubarb wine, orange wines and such cordials as could be made out of summer flowers and early fruits. She experimented with the funny furry fat little Chinese gooseberry, with its bright green flesh and eager taste. Managing the acid in that wine was a challenge; it would not be suitable for sale yet awhile. The English gooseberry, tiny tetchy version, was more reliable, simply because there were useful hints to be found in old English recipe books. Salomé had the Country Library Service scouring Australasia for suitable books. The librarian loved it; it made her borrowing figures look magnificent.

But the broom flower was promising, and would fill the gap. At least when the visitors came there would be something on the shelves for them to take away; they might also sample blackcurrant, elderberry, apricot and apple, and place an order for a case to be delivered when available.

'We cannot hurry the processes of nature,' she would say to the customers who wanted to know when. 'I am sure you would prefer this wine to be good than to be instant.'

Philip loved to talk about three-colour printing and contracts with wine merchants for supply. Salomé stood still and counted racks and recalculated maturity dates, and made careful samples. But she was no longer anxious; she fell asleep every night exhausted by her double workload of the business and the remnants of the farm. She slept perfectly.

'Here you are, busy as always. You have such energy,' Philip said, knocking and entering all at once. 'Hello, Bathsheba.'

'I saved it all up when I was young, by doing absolutely nothing,' she said and kissed him on the cheek. But in her heart she knew that her calm and energy was the delayed reaction to the emotional roller-coaster of her married life.

Philip put his hat on the coat-stand, where once Palliser's many canes and single greatcoat had competed for territory.

'I have good news!' he said, taking an envelope out of his inner breast pocket. 'I think you'll like this – well, I do hope so!' Then he stopped short. 'Why, Salomé!'

She was wearing black sateen trousers, stopping at mid-calf with a little slit, as was the fashion. Over this, one of Palliser's collarless white shirts, with the sleeves rolled up.

'Aren't they smart? Abigail whipped them up from American *Vogue*.'

'I haven't seen you in slacks before. I suppose they're comfortable?'

'Wonderfully. I feel like a new woman. What's your good news?'

'This letter's from my cousin Simon, the wine and spirits chap. We're stocking a bit of wine in our foods section next year, so I roped him in to advise: ". . . regarding your query as to the best wine to promote as the Butterworth's Special Christmas Offer, might I suggest Wentwood's fruit wine, on the following grounds: (a) novelty value and high local interest (b) modest price coupled with excellent taste quality (c) public perception of fruit wines as low alcohol, and therefore suitable for infrequent (Christmas) drinkers. The reasonableness of the original case price allows the offer to stand out as a considerable bargain in the minds of the frugal shopper, while the high standard of the base product enhances the Butterworth's image of traditional high quality."'

'Good heavens,' said Salomé. 'It rather sounds as if we have arrived.'

She sat down on a pile of crates.

'They're going to run with it, but the question is, can we supply? At this sort of notice?'

'I shall have to think very carefully. If we sell wines before they are ready, we risk losing customers almost before we've secured them. And if we can't supply enough decent wine for your store, we lose their goodwill.'

'It will be a Limited Offer. One festive bottle at a special price when you spend over ten pounds in our store between 5 and 15 December. It's designed to get them into the shops early. Limited to one bottle per customer. "While stocks last" – that's the critical phrase from our point of view. You tell me how many doz. you can supply, I'll put it to the board. With a back-up product from cousin Simon, in the event of Due to Unprecedented Demand, We Regret . . .'

'There *is* last year's cider. It's a risk.'

'Business is all about risk. This is the best possible publicity, Salomé. It gets the name into every household of the target buying group.'

She went between the shelves, to and fro, running her hand over her darlings, and brought out a golden brown bottle with Wentwood's Olde Englishe Cyder in squiggly black letters on a parchment background. It fizzed acceptably when she levered off the top and fizzed a little more as she poured them each a glass.

'I do like this job,' she said.

They sipped it silently.

'So do I.'

Another half-glass.

'What proof?'

'Eleven or something. Terrible. No, Sheba, you can't, darling. Only a wee taste.'

Just another drop.

'Wonderful for Christmas. Get great-aunts tipsy in no time. Lovely taste. We'll take the risk, shall we?'

Abigail's footfall could be heard on the stair; not so much a stair as a ladder between floors – Palliser's carpentry definitely stopped short of staircases. She came down backwards, but even an undignified descent did not ruffle Abigail.

'Good afternoon, Philip. Mother, what on earth are you doing?'

'Sampling the stock. Quality control, it's called these days. What's for tea today, dear?'

'Jemima's getting tea today. But I believe we are having the cod Naomi caught this morning *on her way to school*. And potatoes and the usual veg. And what's left of that cider.'

'*My* vegetables out of *my* garden, that *I* planted.'

'My word, Bathsheba, you are a little worker. Just like Mum.'

'Tomorrow I'll take the truck and pick up the sale or returns from Cheviot. And I'll drop by at Parnassus and see if they'll part with a few doz. They're pretty good sports.'

'Your mother has so much energy.'

'Nonsense, it's fun.'

Abigail pondered aloud what it was that Palliser actually did when he was present, since Mother seemed able to manage so well.

'Now, Abigail, be fair! We had a great deal more stock, and much more land, and the vegetable garden was enormous, not like Naomi's little strips.'

'And mine!' said Bathsheba.

'Bathsheba's garden is pretty good, isn't it?' said Philip.

'Yes, and we had farm workers. I don't remember seeing Father digging the garden.'

'You don't remember everything, Abigail.'

Abigail looked as if she did. She poured herself a finger of the cider.

'You will need help, next year,' said Philip, 'with Abigail away. You are wearing yourself out already.'

'I never felt better in my life.' Salomé leaned back in her chair, to show how relaxed she was in her new slacks. 'I don't believe we shall be able to afford help, without Abigail's salary.'

'On this matter of labour, I have been doing some serious thinking and have come up with an idea.'

'New territory, Philip?'

'Abigail! Manners!' said her mother.

'We'll talk about it some other time,' said Philip in a tone which quite closed the topic. He took out the cigarette case engraved with his name. It had been a twenty-first birthday present from his uncle. 'Perhaps, rather, we should discuss Christmas Arrangements.'

'Christmas Arrangements' – words that struck fear into the heart of every New Zealand woman. The inescapable requirement to provide a huge roast dinner for fourteen at midday on a stinking hot day.

'I had rather hoped to ignore Christmas this year,' said Salomé, 'but the little girls will insist on something.'

'And Jemima will insist,' said Abigail. 'Anyway, Mother, last Christmas was so grim, we need to lay its ghost.'

Perhaps the ghost of last Christmas skulked in the corner. It was hard to believe, in the sunlight and practicality of their new world, that it had ever harmed them.

'Well, you see, the thing is,' said Philip, looking rather studiedly at his cigarette case, 'Mother has suggested we gather at our house on the day, as it were.'

'Good Lord!'

'I knew you'd be a bit surprised.'

'Please, Mum! Please, Mum!' said Bathsheba. 'Mrs Butterworth is going to get the biggest tree and we're going to decorate it with stars and tinsel. And little lights with tiny bulbs in them, and electric. She said Father Christmas might visit her house, too.'

'You don't believe in Father Christmas,' said Abigail sternly.

'Yes I do when it's Mrs Butterworth.'

Philip said, 'It could be a bit uncomfortable for you, Salomé.'

'Compared to the last two Christmases, a prison cell would be cheery.'

And at the time they had been so resolutely cheerful, expecting a phone call at any moment.

'I shall have to think about it a bit,' Salomé said. 'It would be pleasant to celebrate Christmas without the past hanging over us, as it has done. A different setting will help us all forget. What kind of cook is your mother?'

'Naturally Betty does most of it, and she's an excellent plain cook. I expect Mother will order a ham and a Christmas pudding from the store.'

'Absolutely not. If we go, we shall make the Christmas pudding. Shan't we, Abi? And supply potatoes and peas.' Salomé laughed. 'You can buy a ham by all means, and some French champagne.'

'I thought Mother would enjoy a little Wentwood's.'

Philip lit his cigarette after all.

'She is most welcome to have our very best, but we deserve a change. Actually, I rather think the best apricot, which is the '57, would go well with the pudding.'

'Does it matter if we will enjoy it?' asked Abigail.

'Yes, and no. As one gets older, Christmas celebrations are more about making other people happy rather than oneself.'

'How pious.'

'Possibly, but you see, for an adult much of the pleasure of Christmas, or any other festivity, derives from arranging an event that as many people as possible can enjoy.'

'Then we should invite all the tramps of the neighbourhood and be done with it.'

'Let's be reasonable — look at it like this: suppose we have Christmas dinner here, the five of us? We work hard beforehand, we get into a flap, and on the day we sit here miserably, as we did last year and the year before, feeling lonely, because there aren't quite enough of us. Philip and his mother have dinner for two, which someone has worked quite hard to prepare, in a big house, and they feel a little bit lonely too. If we combine forces we do half the amount of work each, and because we are jumbled up we don't have the chance to feel lonely, any of us.'

'But Jemima and I don't want to sit up all stiff and starchy at Mrs Butterworth's. We want to relax at home and pull crackers.'

'I see no reason why we can't have crackers, do you, Philip? I expect Mrs Butterworth will buy fancy ones, and save us having to make them out of toilet rolls again.'

'Well I suppose if you put it to the vote, I shall lose,' said Abigail, 'assuming this family were a democracy, which it isn't. Jemima is even prepared to go to Thaddeus's in the evening to keep the peace, and that's much worse.'

'Why?' Philip asked, refusing to be offended by anything Abigail said. His question was followed by a small pause.

'Because,' said Salomé, 'they *disapprove*.'

'Of Jemima and Thaddeus?'

'No. Of you and me.'

After tea was finished and all the dishes washed and put away, and the traces of blackboy peach washed from Bathsheba's face, Salomé said she wanted to try out the new road in Philip's car. With him driving, of course, she added hastily.

Philip drove slowly on the new surface, as if he couldn't quite believe in it.

Salomé laughed.

'Palliser would say it has lost character,' she said.

'You haven't mentioned him for a long time.'

'I am trying to train myself out of it.'

He stopped the car at the end of the new stretch, by the gate on to the main road, wound down the window, and offered her a cigarette.

'Why not?' she said, though she had hardly ever smoked.

'Salomé,' he said after a quiet interval of smoking, 'do many people disapprove?'

Salomé mouthed her cigarette as people do when unused to smoking.

'I'm conscious of disapproval in the village, but since your mother mellowed a little I give it no thought.'

'You see, I thought, next year, since things are going rather well, I might hire a young chap for the practice and spend a bit of time up here, with you.'

'You already do, my dear.'

'I thought most days – as a routine.'

'Do you think the business can bear it?'

'I won't draw a salary. I want to spend more time on the store – retail is changing very fast, and we must move or die. But my usual place of work – I'd like it to be Wentwood's.'

Salomé was silent, looking across the valley to the sea, smoking.

'We'd need to put in a telephone, of course,' Philip continued. 'And I wondered, perhaps, in view of everything, I wondered, perhaps we should get engaged?'

Salomé slowly turned to him and a great big smile spread over her face.

'Let's go to the beach.'

The beach was completely deserted, as if declared ritually unclean. She kicked off her shoes and he took off his jacket and folded it over his right arm. Then he put his left arm around her waist as they walked along the seashore.

'There's so much to explain,' she said. 'Lately I've

started to think about my life, and a few things begin to make sense. You see, I always believed what I was told. I swallowed the bait when I was young, and it's taken all these years to get free. It's so hard to think for oneself . . .'

They walked along the low-water line, where the wet sand met the dry, his shoes leaving a firm impression, hers an uncertain one.

'Up till now, I've been a cipher – I've been what others made me. When I was a girl, I did what society expected me to do. Essentially, I did nothing and thought nothing. I knew that something was wrong, that my life was meaningless and empty, but I hadn't been taught or discovered how to think for myself. Then Palliser burst into my life, and I thought that was what I had been waiting for, and that all my emptiness was designed to be filled by his love and his life. But that too was a sham.'

She loosed Philip's arm to bend down for a tangle of fishing-gut buried in the sand, pulled it up complete with two lead sinkers and three hooks.

'Put that in your pocket for Naomi, would you, dear?'

Philip obliged; then he took out and lit a cigarette, and put his arm back around Salomé's waist.

'You have always seemed like a real person to me. More than real, larger than life.'

'But that was mimicry. I remade myself in the image of Palliser's dream Salomé – and it was such fun to be her. I saw myself reflected in him, and so when I saw myself, I saw him, who was my ideal of love and my ideal of life itself. I knew I was distinct from him, in that I was critical of his faults – but only as far as you criticise yourself – I was his conscience, I was his good angel, but I wasn't a separate entity.

'I remember once thinking about my silly name, and whether I should change it. I had become a little tired of Palliser's fantasy about the Dance of Seven Veils and him casting himself sometimes as John the Baptist and sometimes as Herod. I suddenly had a picture of myself performing the dance for him, taking off the veils one by one, slowly, ceremonially. But at the end of it, after the seventh veil had fallen, there was no Salomé there at all. Nobody was inside the drapery.'

They were now meeting the advance guard of small stones, preparatory to the take-over by the stony beach ahead of them.

The sea dashed up and ran towards their feet, but grew half-hearted and ran back. They stepped over the whitened body of a tree, far from its ancestral home, and the submerged remnants of a deep-sea fishing net, bedecked with solid corks and exotic seaweed.

'So while I have been tussling with book-keeping, I have also been trying to grow a personality. Doesn't that sound absurd?'

'Nothing you say ever sounds absurd to me.'

'Sycophant!'

She turned inland from the sea towards a tall tumble of rocks, and found them a broad driftwood log to sit on. Their backs against the rocks were pricked by a thousand tiny mussels trying to assert their right to living space.

They sat quietly together, watching the pull and push of the tide, the same sea that on a thousand shores was taunting lovers with its indifference.

'But does that mean . . .' he began, but his question tailed away.

Salomé wriggled her toes in the sand, and watched them as if they were the feet of another person.

'Yes, I am taking a long time to get to the point.' She patted his knee gently, as if he were a Labrador impatient for a walk. 'Part of my thinking has been about love. It all seemed so easy once. But I'm beginning to think that the poets are wrong about love. We grow up believing in a single, simple emotion, something you either have or don't have – like the Joker in whist. How many stories have you read where the heroine can't marry one man because she loves another, as if there was a single item of love and she couldn't give to *him*, because she'd already given it to *him*? Love is treated as a thing – and always has the same composition and the same value. A man has to prove his love by doing certain set things, and a woman has to show hers by doing a different set. But the thing we're supposed to be proving or showing is the same.

'I don't think I believe that any more. I think that love between people might be as different as people themselves. And each two people who care about each other define what their own love is. If I say I love you, Philip, I mean that I am always happy to see you, that I am happy to share my time and my house and my family and my meals with you, that I bathe in your kindness as in warm water, that I think of you as a truly good person, that I want you to be happy in your own terms. But that is not what I meant when I said that I loved Palliser.'

'But will you marry me?'

'Not for the wrong reasons. Not to stop gossips, or to make other people comfortable. I won't live with make-believe and deception, not any longer. I have to be myself now, whoever that person is. And I want to tell you the truth, even though I love you and don't want to hurt your feelings.'

'Please tell me. I hope I can bear it.'

'If I married you now, there would still be a ghost. I shan't pretend. You would feel his presence, and I would feel his presence. I could marry you for comfort, for security, out of gratitude, out of loneliness. I won't say

I don't want to make love to you, because I do. I'd love to wake up beside you in the morning. But to marry you now would be dishonest. And I'm through with that.'

'You only succeed in making me love you the more,' he said sadly.

'I am sorry. I wish I was kinder.'

Philip traced a pattern in the sand with his finger. It might have been a heart pierced with an arrow.

'Is it because you think he might come back?'

'I don't know. I don't know what I shall do or say if he does. I really don't know, Philip.'

An evening breeze sprang up, an easterly wind, narrow and mean-spirited, all the way from Antarctica, having shed all its grandeur on the journey. Salomé shivered a little and moved closer.

'But if he doesn't, or if you decide against him – in the future, perhaps?'

'Oh Philip, why is it so hard to get things right? I used to believe that Right was always Right, and there was always a Good Thing to do, that if only you looked and thought hard enough, you would see what was Right, and one had one's Duty, and none of that ever changed. Now I wonder if goodness isn't like love – every bit as complicated as living.'

'So you may change your mind about this?'

'Yes, I may change my mind. I will change my mind about all sorts of things. Our lives change every day, and we change with them, and I rather suspect that what is right and good changes too. Some things will stay – the love we all feel for each other, I don't think that alters very much, even though circumstances alter around us. But how we act on our love may change. Surely the best we can hope for is to do the right thing, every time we are asked to choose?'

He nodded his head, several times, as if shaking the ideas down firm inside. Then he squeezed her waist more tightly, and putting his lips quite close to her ear, said, 'You know what you just said about making love . . .'

IX

PROGRAMME OF EVENTS

3.00. p.m.   Guests arrive. The Lovelaces will receive their guests in the drawing room. Refreshments will be served. Children may be escorted to Library, where games, suitable for all ages, will be in progress.

4.15 p.m.   Children's tea served in the Library

4.30 p.m.   Christmas Concert (Great Hall)

Greensleeves — Thule Early Music Group

Pastime with Good Company — Thule Early Music Group

Bonny Sweet Robin — Fr Hubert Lovelace

Variations on Bonny Sweet Robin for treble recorder — Fr Jocelyn Startup

Two Eliz Love songs — Mr Palliser Wentwood & Fr Hubert Lovelace

The Boar's Head Carol — Thule EMG & St Cyriac's parish choir

The Holly & the Ivy — Thule EMG & St Cyriac's parish choir

5.00 — 8.00 p.m.   Continuous buffet is served in the Dining Room.

6.00 p.m.   Arrival of Father Christmas (front terrace) and distribution of presents (Great Hall)

6.45 p.m.   Christmas Carols (Music Room) – St Cyriac's Parish Choir with Comic Interludes by Mr George Burnaby
7.30 p.m.   Dancing (Great Hall) – The Watford Palm Court String Players
10.00 p.m.   Supper is served in the Dining Room
11.00 p.m.   Guests depart

'You must dance every dance, and not one of them with me.'

Blanche looked as if a new puppy had suddenly been taken away from her. 'But why? I want to dance with you.'

'When all the guests are gone, we shall put on the gramophone and dance till dawn. I am merely your butler. No one shall say of you, it was a wonderful party, but I wonder why she danced so much with her butler.'

Blanche blushed mightily. 'I don't mind if they do.'

Palliser was on the top of a high ladder, in the middle of the Great Hall, cutting wax candles to fit the chandelier. A light shower of wax flakes fell down on to an outspread newspaper, and a little on to Blanche.

'I am sure you do not, my dear, because you are not a snob. But one of the aims of this party is to launch you on county society, and many of them are. We cannot have any murmurs.'

'They're already speculating away like anything,' said Clarissa from inside the large fir tree.

'But they shall have no evidence. Now don't argue with Uncle Palliser.'

Blanche looked up beseechingly, miserable at this new social hurdle.

'I thought George might lead Blanche out for the first couple of dances,' said Clarissa, emerging from the tree with a coronet of green needles. 'My big brother George.

236

Such a lovely fellow, though I say it myself. Very droll. He's agreed to do some of his impressions during the evening – I dare say Hubert told you? He does the Prime Minister and Donald Wolfit and Lord Reith, what's his name Montgomery. He was much in demand during the war for his Hitler, but he doesn't do that any more of course. He's a tiny bit of a recluse these days, the war hit him hard. I told you, Blanche, didn't I? I'm sure I did – he lost his wife quite early on, poor chap. Lovely girl, Lettice.'

'It's so sad.'

'He doesn't seem to care for company. I think it's because he's rather deaf.'

'Such an undignified disability, deafness,' said Palliser.

Clarissa looked at him sharply.

'He spent quite a spell in a Jap prisoner-of-war camp, towards the end, and he's deaf because of what those people did to him. I shan't tell you, Blanche, it's too horrid. He never mentions it, of course.'

Palliser concentrated on the candles.

'But he *is* coming right,' Clarissa continued. 'That's why I was so pleased he agreed to come to the party. And he's staying for Christmas and New Year. Blanche, you will be nice to him, won't you?'

'And I take it he's a competent dancer, and a gentlemen through and through?'

'Oh yes! George was very popular at parties before the war. He used to do two, three balls in an evening.'

'There you are, Blanche my dear, your future is assured. And after George, perhaps Roland, then Hubert. Then Clarissa will have a word in the Bishop's ear, and Sir James.'

'You stick with me, Blanche darling, and I'll make sure you dance every dance. You *will* like George enormously.'

Perched on the ladder above the young women, Palliser felt a tide of panic threaten his composure. He had kept his grip so far, though he felt his heart was breaking. He had thrown himself into the preparations to drown his sorrows, just as Hubert predicted. By this means he fell into bed exhausted at night and willed himself not to think on his wife, his family and his home. He did not think of picking up a pen and writing to Salomé. It did not occur to him that he might telephone New Zealand. He did not think about New Zealand at all; he thought about the Lovelaces' Christmas party and about his seduction of Blanche.

The completion of his task at Thule became of overriding importance. In his mind it seemed that for this end only had he thrown away a jewel, richer than all his tribe. He could not bear to be cheated of his prize at the dreary end of his travail. Thus the mention of Clarissa's widowed brother, George, struck fear into him.

Heretofore, there had been no rival. The lover in the parkland, about whom he speculated in the early days, had never materialised. But it seemed to Palliser that Clarissa was determined that he should have some competition. Clarissa watched him as he fed Blanche's infatuation with tidbits of romantic sweetness and masculine panache, and she did not care for it. Palliser felt Clarissa rather fancied him herself; all things being equal, he guessed he might have indulged in a nice romp with Clarissa. But all things were not equal.

George posed a problem. He was the real thing. No one could pretend to deafness in order to elicit sympathy, and his wife really must have died and Clarissa must have walked behind the coffin in black. There was a moment, only a moment, when Palliser wished his wife had been swept away by the floods as he pretended. So much better a way to lose her than this – but the moment passed and he pushed the hideous thought away.

Certain women loved to comfort, and Blanche was one of those, although she herself was only in the process of discovering it. He did not know why she had this urge, given her barren upbringing, but Palliser had never bothered with psychology, merely with applying his experience and observation. Blanche loved to comfort, and one of his own great attractions was his sorrow. His present misery was real enough to him, but he doubted that Blanche would class rejection after desertion as tragedy on the scale of bereavement and ruin. George's tragedy was affecting and, worst of all, genuine.

Palliser acknowledged that Clarissa was as sharp a social engineer in the making as himself, but without the desperation. Unless George was absolutely graceless, Clarissa would probably succeed in making a match between Blanche and her brother, even in this liberated age. Assuming Palliser were removed, of course. Were he a disinterested observer, Palliser would have applauded her for this, but he was anything but disinterested.

He was in fact obsessed. Now he was cast out of his own country, more than ever he felt he must succeed here – he must secure his position, he must have some of Blanche's money, but most of all he must have Blanche.

The night of the party was his moment. He must strike before George made inroads into his territory, before any truth trickled out. He who hesitates is lost.

The night before the party he was visited by a delicious dream in which he was a small boy standing in the courtyard of the National Gallery of Ireland staring up at a naked woman with a fountain in her lap, and as he reached up to stroke the peerless marble foot – the only part he could reach – the foot started to turn from white to pink before his marvelling schoolboy eyes, from cold to wicked warm, and the great woman shook herself alive and sprayed water all over the courtyard.

The day of the party was as bright a day as could be pictured – whites and blacks and shades of bright grey and brown, like a fairy-tale illustration by Arthur Rackham, with a few dots of colour from some grimly determined roses. By three o'clock the rural peace of Thule was invaded by more motor cars than the lane had seen in its entire history. They were parked on every patch of mud and gravel, and right down the front drive, more than thirty cars – Rover, Armstrong-Siddeley, Austin-Healey, Anglia, Land Rover, Jaguar, and Morris Countryman. The snow started to fall, as if on cue, half an hour before Father Christmas was due to appear on the rooftops of Thule. By the time the guests crowded on to the front terrace to observe his arrival, the chimneypots and roof ridges were ribbed with exactly the right amount of snow. Roland did the honours with a portable spotlight, and to the strains of 'Jingle Bells' from the local handbell group, there appeared Clarissa's youngest's miniature pony bedecked in white feathers, tinsels, bells, red velvet trimmings and the contents of the nursery toy chest. Palliser, who had manoeuvred the creature up the stairs and stabled it in the larger attic, let out a long-pent-up sigh: it had all been worthwhile. The pony was pulling a cardboard and plywood sleigh, painted with bright red poster paint which was starting to streak in the snow. Santa himself materialised out of the darkness, a massive figure in crimson towering over the little horse, fit to terrify children, had he not waved in a stately but encouraging way. As he made his way across the front of the house, waving and beckoning the children inside, Palliser slid in the shadows towards Blanche, and positioned himself at her ear.

He watched the snowflakes nestle into her hair, and the streamlets of her hair curling out towards him, washed and brushed and scented and newly released from captivity. He watched crystals glide on to her bare shoulder, melt and slip down into the warmth. He breathed in the rustle of the fabric and its richness, and the glory of scarlet, of white warm flesh in scarlet. He saw her face turned ecstatically upwards to the magic, all her childhood years tumbling out into one complete moment of grown-up happiness.

It has all been worthwhile. I could go home now.

For a moment in his imaginings, Palliser brushed her shoulder with his lips, picked up his suitcase, turned up the collar of his coat, and slipped away into the darkness for ever.

Of course, he did no such thing, but as the idea passed through his mind he was pleased to know that he had honourable impulses remaining.

'Are you happy?' he murmured to Blanche as the adults started to follow the cheering surge of children into the hall, to wait by the great staircase for the creak of Father Christmas's descent, burdened by his heavy sack.

'Oh Palliser!' she said. He wished he could stop the film right now, take the frame of her smile and seal it in his heart for ever. If only this was the end and nothing more was necessary.

But there was nothing for it but to give her his not-quite-fatherly smile, before dashing away and up the back stairs to take the remains of the sleigh off the pony.

He had made himself busy, deliberately, to avoid any temptation to talk to Blanche, linger near Blanche or dance with her. The only endurable way to make it to midnight was frantic activity. Besides, it ensured that the party went swimmingly and that he was seen by the whole county as knowing his place and being damned good in it.

At nine o'clock he took a glass of champagne cocktail and made a circuit of his stage-set. In the library, now emptied of children, Helene, the Eltons' nanny, was pain-stakingly removing all trace of the spree. Palliser patted her kindly and told her to desist, as a troupe of cleaners were to descend on the morrow. In the kitchen, the Manor's cook and a gaggle of helpers in white aprons hovered in fear of their life, awaiting Mrs Nagy's instructions. Mrs Nagy was in the dining room laying fresh white cloths on the tables, with the precise assistance of the organist and choirmaster of St Cyriac's parish choir. Peter stood by watching them, resplendent in a hired dinner jacket which fitted as if he had been born in it.

In the music room, Fathers Jocelyn, Francis and Hubert, with the Bishop and Canon Perkins from St Cyriac's, were formed into a clerical huddle from which arose a rich aura of brandy and cigar.

In the front drawing room, the Bishop's wife, Mrs Canon Perkins, Mrs Elton Sen., and other worthies of the parish were dissecting the Thule domestic arrangements over whist and sherry.

In the Little Hall the tenor from St Cyriac's parish choir, Roland Elton and the husbands of the worthies of the parish, in blazers, were leaning against the wall nearest the bar and reeling off the vital statistics of motor cars they possibly might purchase, or had purchased, or had thought about purchasing, or knew someone who had purchased.

In the cavern of the Great Hall fourteen couples were dancing. They might have looked forlorn, had it not been for the Christmas tree, well lit up in one corner, and the Watford Palm Court String Players similarly in another. Between these corners hung a network of candles, tinsel, fairy lights, paper chains so exuberant that the shadowy Lovelaces had been obliged to recede further into the safety of their past. In the fireplace the first fire for half a century roared its approval. The dancers gave it a wide berth.

Palliser cast his eye over the dancers. The precentor and his wife, the schoolteacher and the other schoolteacher's husband, the young couple from Thule Farm, Clarissa and

Sir James, the chap from the bank and the glamorous widow from Turnstile Cottage, yes all in order, all in order. Except that Blanche was still dancing with George.

George Burnaby had turned out to be both more and less of a challenge than Palliser expected. Palliser couldn't read him, but suspected that he might himself be read. Luckily he was possessed of most memorable ugliness: khaki skin, bushy eyebrows, overly large dark brown eyes. He was long and lugubrious; his face and person hung down around him, like a bloodhound on a hunger strike. His hands stuck out of the cuffs of his borrowed dinner jacket as if he were an adolescent unsure what to do with them, which was absolutely not the case. For George, Palliser discovered within five minutes of encountering him, had a penetrating eye and a wiltingly dry wit, and a complete armoury of devices for avoiding tedium. He wore two jumbo-sized hearing aids with the air of one who had been given prized ornaments by members of a stone age tribe. With the aid of these devices, if he did not wish to hear, he did not hear. On the other hand, if he wished to comment, he did so, in a perfectly modulated cross between a groan and a whisper, designed only for the ear of the chosen recipient. Any other receiver picking up his signal felt immediately unwelcome.

'A butler from New Zealand?' he said on being introduced to Palliser. 'Sounds rather like a contradiction in terms. I thought every Kiwi was his own master – certainly seemed that way trying to command you buggers.'

His comic impressions had been delivered without a smile. Every time the audience laughed over his pause, he would fix one hapless person with his stare and then slowly pan around the helplessly laughing group until silence was achieved. Sometimes he let the silence ride for a few seconds while gathering himself painfully together. During which pause the laughter would bubble up again and require George to silence it once more. One felt that this performance had been given over and over again, until it had the fluency and timing of a circus act — false falls included.

He danced with unimpeachable gravity around the Great Hall, like a dowager gracing a prize-giving. Palliser was pleased to note that he held Blanche firmly at arm's length. On the other hand, given the expansive cut of her gown, it was possible that George did this to enjoy the view that it gave him of her attributes. And more worringly, he was making her laugh.

Palliser shook these ideas off, and allowed himself to admire his handiwork.

She was at home, at last, in her own setting, for the scale of the Great Hall suited her, as the Arena di Verona suits a properly proportioned diva. The magnificence of the dress, its extroverted colour, made her stature less, rather than more, obvious. A miracle of the corset-maker's craft had given her a defined figure, culminating in a display of bosom no one could possibly overlook. Its lasciviousness was belied by the sweet fatness of her neck and face, her little mouth disappearing among the cheeks, her young eyes peering out of their lardy casing in wonder.

He had always known she would come to this state of perfection, and it had taken frighteningly little effort. If he had not worked his Palliser magic, would George or some other have done the same? Or could he be proud, and a little bit justified — take my record into account, Your Honour! — in changing this young woman's life? Did incidental, accidental good palliate intentional wickedness? Fr Hubert might have an answer, but Palliser wasn't going to ask him. What's done is done. Another might have done it, but I am the man who did. But the next deed? The one which he alone would commit; it could not be done by accident. A deed for which he alone must take responsibility, before God or his peers.

Inside he was awash with the feeling he hated – the feeling which he had no name for with regard to Blanche, but which otherwise he would have called love. A passionate desire to protect, to make happy, to ward off evildoers, and to wrap close; to see the dear thing flourish like a green tree and need no netting to keep off predators. The terrible love of a parent which causes the belly to seize at the very thought of threat to the child, even years after the child has grown.

How could he do this thing? How could he tear her body, tear her heart, then get up and walk away?

And how can I not? Am I going to wade into the mud of decency, in some kind of dreary no man's land without woman or money? So you took away my family. You're not going to cheat me of my inheritance. Not while there is blood in me. I am Palliser Wentwood yet, and what I am I must be, and if I fry for it, I'll fry.

Besides, I may never walk away. What is to prevent me making here my dwelling place, in the land flowing with milk and honey and good brandy?

At eleven, the guests obediently took their leave. Palliser, in charge of the coats, made their exit easy. Caressingly he smoothed the furs and cashmeres over the ladies' shoulders, and murmured sweet goodnights as if he was reluctant to let them go. Nothing could have been further from the case.

At eleven twenty-three, only Clarissa, Roland and George remained, and a polite tussle ensued over the clearing-up.

'We have some people coming in to help tomorrow,' said Blanche. 'Palliser's arranged it all.'

245

'But there's so much to do!' cried Clarissa. 'You don't want to get up to this in the morning. It won't take long if we all get stuck in!'

George observed that Roland was unlikely to get stuck into anything more tonight except the brandy.

'It might be as well to take him home,' said Palliser to George.

'Another hour and it'll be just shipshape,' said Clarissa, 'then we can all go to bed exhausted but happy.'

'And don't forget to say your prayers.'

'Oh do shut up, George, you are frisky tonight!'

'I am sure Blanche is tired, and wants to go to bed.'

'No, I'm not actually. I —'

'Well, even so, I have agreed a price with the girls for the whole job. I shall be obliged to pay them the same whether they do half an hour or three.'

Happily this argument from economy prevailed where no other could, and the Elton party departed into the snow, full of thanks and kisses. Palliser shut the front door. He and Blanche were left alone in the Little Hall. They looked at one another; an elephantine awkwardness descended upon them.

Palliser started to turn off the lights in the hall.

'Are they all gone to bed?'

They stood in the darkness to listen. Bangings and crashings came from the kitchen quarters.

'I bought a long-playing record,' said Blanche. 'To dance to.'

Did you indeed?

'We'll need a gramophone — do you have one?'

'I asked Peter if I might borrow his portable. But he didn't bring it down.'

'I'll go and fetch it.'

Palliser sprang up the stairs two at a time.

I am swept along! I am driftwood, I am spindle, I am

tumbleweed. Over I go, over and over again. Who am I to —
Events are taking their course now.

Events were indeed taking their course.

Peter's room was, like Palliser's and Mrs Nagy's, on the
top floor in a mean row of servants' quarters. Palliser was
not leaping by the time he reached it. The light was on in
the corridor, one low-wattage bulb in all its narrow length,
which implied that Peter was already upstairs. Palliser idly
wondered whether he should disturb the boy so late, but
knew him to keep late hours, for his rock 'n' roll was dimly
audible if not around the clock, at least after a respectable
butler's bedtime. Besides, if Blanche had braved a shop to
buy a record, the least Palliser could contribute was the
borrowing of the machine on which to play it.

Arriving at Peter's room, he noted that the gramophone
was silent, but a light showed under the door. He knocked,
called Peter's name, announced his errand and walked in
without waiting for a response. He figured if the boy
was asleep he would simply take the gramophone and
glide away.

He wasn't sure what repelled him most. The act of
sodomy itself, which by some accident he had never
witnessed before, the gross discrepancy in the monstrous
fatness of Hubert and the slim beauty of the boy, the
dislocation caused by the boy's being mother naked and
Hubert fully clothed, or simply the difference in their ages
and conditions.

'Sweet Jesus.'

Crumpled on the ground lay the black trousers and
white shirt of Peter's dress. The made-up black tie had
been discarded close to the door, his shoes pulled off
without undoing the laces. A pair of underpants, patterned
with racing cars, lay by themselves near the bed.

Palliser had terrified them, and they had shocked him.
His first impulse was to flee, to pretend he had seen

nothing, to wipe it out of his mind. His second was to break up this unnatural coupling, to shake the boy and shout at him. Other courses of action came crowding in; his mind started to send out possibilities like fireworks. But uppermost in his mind was the need to protect everyone from discovery – himself, Blanche, the boy's mother, Peter, Hubert – nobody must know what he had seen. Above all he must protect himself from violence, and protect his investment, until he had time to work out how he might react.

Palliser was not easily shocked; he had been party to a great many sexual acts, and their occurrence rarely surprised him. But there remained the innate dislike of disturbing others at the most private of games, of being where one was not wanted, and in this case seeing what no one should ever see. Palliser framed no words to describe it. He wished to banish the sight and the thought immediately, but knew that he would never wipe out the disgust of that vision, what was to him the grossness, the abomination of what he had seen.

Hubert moved faster than one might imagine he could, but there was no possible way he could conceal his shame. But the boy looked up at Palliser with a mighty sneer, daring him to accuse, waiting for a chance to strike back. He had ammunition enough, but Palliser was not about to declare war. They were in this together, he and the little whore of a boy.

Palliser declined the contest. He drew himself up.

'Blanche wants to borrow your gramophone. I'll take it downstairs, if I may.'

With which he turned his back on Hubert and, without a word, removed Peter's current record of Buddy Holly, put it in its sleeve, closed the lid of the gramophone, unplugged the machine and picked it up.

He was just attempting to close the door behind him

without having to put down the gramophone when he heard someone coming up the stairs. It was clearly Mrs Nagy, and not Blanche, by the tread. Even before she came within earshot of her son, she starting shouting for him in furious Hungarian.

Palliser did not have time to think what he should do. He merely did what seemed right. He barricaded the gramophone solidly across his chest and stood his ground in the doorway. When she caught sight of Palliser, Mrs Nagy switched to English, although otherwise the recitative did not change.

'What have you done with him? Where is that useless boy from the devil? All of you have dressed him up like a lazy useless film star and when I need him to help me, he is gone.' She shouted at Peter in Hungarian. 'All this work I do, all this party, and everyone having a good party except me slaving in the kitchen and that boy nowhere to help me when I need him. Is he in there, listening to his records, smoking a cigarette? Did you give the drinks? Was it you? It was you, isn't it? You, Wentwood, only wanting the one thing, the poor Miss Blanche, and wanting to make my boy like you, a drinking lazy useless man.'

Palliser spoke out in a voice designed to carry into the bedroom behind him.

'Peter is changing out of his film star apparel, Doris, and slipping into somethin' more comfortable, the better to help you.' He called over his shoulder through the slightly ajar doorway: 'Peter, your mother requires your assistance in the kitchen.'

'Let me in, you thin man. Let me past. I want to teach that boy how to leave his mother and go for drinking with the men.'

Palliser and the gramophone stood their ground, blocking the doorway. Behind them were vague indications of someone getting dressed.

'Doris, Doris, don't be so harsh on the boy,' cried Palliser expansively, like one who has drunk quantities of champagne. 'He worked hard tonight. You should be proud of him; he was behind the bar the whole evening, gracing it for sure, but what's wrong with a boy with his looks taking advantage of them? If you didn't want him to grow up good-lookin' you should have smothered him at birth. He can't help lookin' good, now can he? And he didn't ask to be dressed up s' handsome, that was Mrs Elton's doing. Did you not see how long he was barman? And hardly a drop to drink, did you, Peter? Barely a drop. You should be proud of him – what's a cigarette or two, a drink or two, when a boy works so hard? Perhaps you were working too hard yourself, Doris, something he's inherited? And now when you accuse him of laziness, what's he doing? Just changing his clothes so as to help you better, and not endanger the fine feathers we put him in.'

'Let me in to him, you Wentwood. You are only saying this, you want to protect a lazy boy from hard work and take him from his mother so he can be like you. And all your kind.'

'On the contrary, Doris, I have little interest in Peter,' said Palliser, lowering his voice, 'but I care for the orderliness of this house. Now lower your voice, please, or we will have Miss Blanche alarmed, and coming to join in the fray, and I don't want anything to spoil *her* evening. Hurry up in there, will you, boy, your mother needs your assistance! Though I must say, Doris, I would prefer it if you called it a day, and retired yourself. No one in this house is expected to slave. You need your rest. See, you're quite upset, now aren't you? Over-tired.'

Mrs Nagy tried to beat on Palliser's chest but became embroiled in the gramophone, so contented herself with kicking his shins with the violent need to see her son.

Palliser registered considerable pain from this, but held his ground, as he felt he must at all costs.

'Let me in, let me in!' she cried.

'Shhh now, quiet please. You are making a scene.'

Behind Palliser the door was pulled further open and Peter pushed through, wearing black jeans and a huge sweater down to his knees, in the fashion of the young. His hair was wildly disarranged, but this might also have been attributable to fashion. He pushed Palliser and his mother out of his path.

'I need to go to the loo,' he said and stalked down the corridor.

His mother flapped in his wake, in a stream of French and Hungarian, leaving Palliser in front of the door. He waited until the corridor was empty.

'The coast's clear,' he said in a carrying voice. 'And I'm going downstairs to waylay Blanche.'

It was completely dark in the grand reception rooms at the front of the house, which all afternoon and evening had blazed with lights and chatter. The old house settled and groaned back into its comfortable discomfort, and all the stags' heads on the wall decided it was safe to come out again. The shadows thickened up in the corners of the Great Hall again, lapping over the old Lovelaces and their lives of tedium, sickness, luxury, exile, dissipation, loneliness, duty and frivolity. Their elegant hands, which had whipped the flanks of horses and counted the gold of mastery and stroked the buttocks of servants, lay folded before them, as if incapable of anything more demanding than displaying a handkerchief. They stood embalmed in oil, awaiting the judgment day, with calm unconcern at the outcome. *Lord, how could we possibly have missed You? Perhaps You were not introduced?*

Palliser put the gramophone down on the floor near

an electrical outlet, of which there were very few in the Great Hall. He fumbled about in the dark to plug it in, speculating from his ineptitude whether he had drunk more than he remembered. Then he realised that his hands were shaking, as if he himself had been discovered *in flagrante*. He succeeded in inserting the pins into the socket, but could not think what to do next. He sat back on his heels to absorb the new information. He was not surprised by what he had witnessed, his receptors being very finely tuned to pick up deviousness of any kind, but he had never sought or expected to have such evidence planted in his lap, so to speak. What to do? Was his position endangered or strengthened? Yet another twist had been added to his tale, before he had straightened out the other ones.

He sat back against the wall, linenfold panelling ribbed into his back.

I'm getting too old for this. I'm tired and I want to go to bed . . .

He heard Blanche's step in the Little Hall. She was looking for him, too timid to call out. He closed his eyes.

If I don't move, it will all be over. I can apologise in the morning and there will be an end on't. I can take a cheque from Hubert and pack my bags tomorrow and be home for New Year.

How lovely the shadows are, and the moonlight falling on these old boards. You forget the beauty of old things, living in a country where everything is new and made for use. Linoleum, that's what I remember, and carpets with hideous patterns. Never a decent floorboard. Except in my house, the floorboards I laid. In what was my house. Do they creak when someone walks across them? Salomé's bare foot, Philip Butterworth's well-shod members.

Blanche walked through the Great Hall, flick, flick, flick, as she passed between the moonlight and the shadows cast by the window frames, clutching to her bosom a long-playing record. What was it called? *Waltzes for Lovers*, Palliser rather feared.

She almost tripped over his legs.

'Palliser! Are you all right?'

To his amazement she was on her knees beside him, feeling for his hand.

'I'm perfectly well,' he said, allowing his hand to be located. 'I am sittin' here admiring the effect of the moonlight on the floor and recharging my battery, so as to give you my best shot. Now what have we here? *Waltzes for Lovers*, is it?'

And, not wanting to give her a moment of discouragement by appearing old, tired or unwilling, he put it on the gramophone and scrambled to his feet. He offered her his hand as she rose to join him.

'Miss Lovelace, may I have the pleasure?'

Afterwards, when he thought about that evening, he sometimes claimed to himself that it was kindness almost as much as baser motivations that pushed him on. And he was telling himself the truth, for it would have been very unkind to have denied her the late-night dancing she had so longed for. But if he had been determined to avoid a moral quagmire, he should have known better than to have danced alone with her in the darkness. He knew what must follow, as the night the day, or was it the day the night? His only defence, apart from that of gallantry, remained that she must have known, even in her simplicity, what was to follow.

The needle on the record is bumping against its terminus, *sccr-thump, sccr-thump* it goes, over and over, without ever getting bored with itself, at the same time begging for dispatch. It has faithfully trotted through six tracks of waltzes, only two of which were danced, and four of which have been as wallpaper to the dancers, as is the rhythmic banging for release. Or at the least it begs to be returned to the uncertain shores of the outer edge and to be allowed to slide into its first track again. But no, the waltzes have done their work too well. The lovers are no longer waltzing but lost, kissing, in a far shadow, such kisses as words turn trivial and debase.

I could describe what Palliser feels as the activities of his tongue and hands cause his whole person to become obsessed by one end and one end only, or what Blanche feels as she suffers the electrification of the senses, as the body is turned inside out at its own compulsion. But such experiences are common enough, and are not different in different persons. Just because Blanche is an unusual person, in whom we take a narrative interest, does not make her Pauline experience of lust any different from that experienced by any young woman erotically kissed in the dark after a party and groped without possibility of misunderstanding.

And as for the processes in Palliser's head, they are at this moment entirely absorbed by needs as common as life itself, and, one would imagine, and perhaps hope, experienced by most men on a fairly regular basis.

Those things that make this embrace and incipient coition particularly interesting are simply the contrasted physical build of the participants, her lack of experience and his vaunted over-supply of it, matters in which interest is surely nothing more than prurience?

But there is one matter of importance. All this time, while Palliser and Blanche are clamped together in the darkness of the Great Hall, and the needle of the gramophone is trudging its weary way around the centre of the record, a voice in Palliser's head is trying to make itself heard. It struggles against a tide of thoughts that are not thoughts at all, but wavelets of lust slowly taking over his conscious mind. But at last, in a final outburst before drowning, the voice is heard.

'She must ask *you*. She *must* ask you. *She* must ask you.'

He thinks if he can keep those four words in his head, he will have nothing to reproach himself with afterwards.

'Palliser,' she says. 'Oh Palliser.'

Ask me. You have to ask me. Please ask me. I shall die if you don't.

'I am so happy.'

Come on, it's not so difficult. Five tiny words will do it. All monosyllables. *Come to bed with me.* or *Please make love to me.* O Jesus, say it, woman.

A door in the depths of the house slams. The lovers freeze, as if they were in any particular visible. A brief scurry of voices. Then what passes for silence in an old house. But the interruption has reduced them to some kind of sanity.

'Let's release the poor old gramophone from its misery,' says Palliser and, holding her by the hand, goes back across the room to take the needle off the record. With one movement, as if practised, he switches the thing off without letting go of the woman.

Now.

He can see her, over here in the moonlight, and distressingly, she looks both lovely, as most people do in the romantic surroundings, and very young. But the straightening effect of romantic young loveliness is out-weighed by the effect of her bosom, which chooses this moment to rise and fall before his eyes.

'O Jesus,' he says, though he tries not to swear in front of her.

Thank God she is so fleshy or I'd have raped her by now. But it's because she is so fleshy that I can't contain myself. And so hot and innocent and vulnerable and desperate for me to love her and all the other reasons why *I must wait for her to ask me.*

'Blanche.'

'Dear, dear Palliser.'

'Do one thing for me.'

'Anything, I would do anything for you.'

Don't cry.

'Ask me.'

She doesn't fucking well understand.

'I don't understand. Ask you what?'

He puts her hand over his erect penis.

'Do you know what this is?'

'Yes.'

'Do you know what it means?'

'I think so.'

Sweet Jesus, help me out here, and I won't ask for anything.

'I can't – I can't – please help me out here.'

'I think I understand. I think I do. You are still in mourning. I don't expect anything of you. I love you too much for that. But let me comfort you. Let me hold you in my arms and comfort you.'

O God that will have to do.

'That will make me very happy,' he says, and escorts her to her bed, and into it, even though that was not precisely what she had meant.

A northern winter morning, and black as night. The only indication that day had begun was the worm in the belly that talked of urination and coffee. Palliser declined to open his eyes, struggling with unfamiliarity. He was so comfortable he wondered if he had died and gone to heaven. Unlikely, since even he could think of no reason why he should not be classed with the goats. Or was it the sheep? Then he opened one eye and saw in the dimness a small but monstrous face peering at him from a close distance. He closed the eye again, plumping for hell. If this was hell then he was well out of the pursuit of goodness, assuming he had ever pursued it. Had he not run in the exact opposite direction all his life, and now was he not reaping his reward?

He groaned and rolled over in the largest, softest bed he had ever dived into, and found himself naked and engulfed by the largest and softest body ditto. He almost immediately snapped erect, but his common sense, awakening rather more slowly than its master, suggested that he not follow the course of action the erection vociferously suggested. Instead he disposed himself upon and around the warm and bountiful flesh and discharged the erection in a straightforward and non-intrusive manner.

A version of dawn was breaking. He padded into the adjoining bathroom to relieve himself, weaving through discarded clothes, mostly his own. Her silk dress, however, was safe in the dressing room where he himself had hung it, after ceremoniously unzipping and unhooking it to reveal the wonderful corset and even more wonderful body beneath.

She was lying on her back, symmetrically arranged, an empress lying in state, her hands on top of the coverlet, her head full on the pillow. The coverlet should have been embossed velvet and the pillow fringed with Honiton lace. Thousands would file through the door, bow their heads by the icon and the candle, mouth a prayer for her soul, kiss her bejewelled hands and, weeping, pass on.

Except of course that she was breathing, her features smooth and promising as a child's. Not dead but sleeping, Snow White in her glass coffin awaiting the prince who would kiss her and cause the deadly obstruction to fly out of her throat.

But I am not your prince, dear child. I am nobody's prince. And we do not live in a fairy tale, with happy-ever-after. There is no end to this story except death, and perhaps not even then. There was a time when I thought I was building my castle to live in with my princess beloved.

But a gnome has taken over my tower and my bride, and I am here with you, the Wicked Step-Uncle disguised as a servant.

How she had talked, this sweet sleeping girl, in the night. When she should have slipped into deep exhausted slumbers, she found instead in the darkness and the arms of a lover the voice that shyness had so far denied her. And Palliser, longing for sleep, had to call on all his reserves of good behaviour to stay awake.

Her happiness was complete and triumphant. No matter what caution Palliser suggested, she would trumpet her achievement from the roofs of Thule, by her smiling. In the darkness he could hear her smile. She had never dreamed that such a thing would happen to her, in the bleak days of her childhood and adolescence, when the other girls giggled and whispered and only included her in the circle of secrets to contrast her ignorance with their new knowledge. She had long ago concluded that a woman of her build was cast as one of nature's nuns, or opera singers but, having neither piety nor voice, that she was a nothing person, for whom nothing could be expected. She had felt like a ghost in her own body – it so demanding and substantial a thing, she so mild and indeterminate. People reacted to her presence in all kinds of ways; she was always known and noticed, but nobody had ever been aware of Blanche herself – not even Hubert, though he was faithful and kind – as if there was no person inside the frame. Or rather that, because she was not a loud and bossy person, as big as her body, she did not exist at all.

Then Palliser came. And then Palliser made love to her. And now she was a real person.

'You were always a real person,' he had said, 'and I am a real man in need of real sleep.'

But she had all the energy of youth and the whole-heartedness of a child, and as he drifted off to sleep with his cheek against her left breast, he felt her talking still.

Now what was he do to? Having triumphed in Acts One and Two of his drama, what was he going to devise for Act Three? Always the tricky part of a Palliser production; you build the tower, then what do you do with it? Never thinking far enough ahead, always expecting the plot to sort itself out as the end approaches. Except that, as aforesaid, there was no end, just another series of complications.

He decided to get back into Blanche's bed. That at least made the first decision easy – he wasn't going to fly by night, had he the slightest inclination in that direction. Which he had not. This bed was large and warm, and had a woman in it. No contest. By staying put until she woke he was staking a claim, without appearing to do so. Of course, he remembered, as he readjusted himself to comfort he had begun to think was but a dream; of course, leaving a woman's bed early has the advantage of avoiding *those* conversations.

Half asleep he tried to enumerate what his choices were, but gradually it all seemed far too hard. Why not drift along on the back of events . . . Hard work had delivered Blanche into his lap (or perhaps the reverse), but Fortune had delivered Hubert into his hands. Unlooked for, and possibly never to be exploited. Blackmail was not Palliser's line. Not often. Not for very much or very explicitly. He felt that he lacked the requisite nastiness. Milking Hubert would curdle the good feeling he had laboured so hard to create. And while he was here at Thule he must have a pleasant atmosphere. And why should it be necessary to stoop so low? But if he were to go, or be dismissed, or the atmosphere somehow to chill, then perhaps a contribution from Hubert might be acceptable. Hubert might attempt a deal – a quid pro quo – silence for silence – but Hubert would be taught that their cases were not equal. Seducing a virgin, however innocent and rich, was not a criminal offence, nor likely to debar Palliser from any occupation; Hubert, on the other hand . . .

It occurred to Palliser that he might simply stay on exactly where he was, sleeping in Blanche's bed, eating at the table, drinking the brandy, smoking cigars, taking the car when he fancied, loading the fire with wood and disposing the domestics to his liking; acting, in effect, as the lord of the household. He might do this, and if Hubert was inclined to shift him out, or demand duties from him, a little hint might quickly slay him. How to have one's cake . . .

He slipped into a sleep of perfect happiness.

It is ten-thirty in the morning. In the Little Hall the telephone rings and rings. Blanche moves to answer it with unhurried tread, for she is like a woman in a dream of paradise.

'Hello, dear Blanche,' trills Clarissa. 'Where are you all today? No one has been answering your phone!'

'It all seems very odd. No one is about. Mrs Nagy is practically on strike, if you know what I mean, Palliser's in the bath still, and Hubert's gone up to London. I feel so naughty – I rather slept in and when I got up I found that all the tidying up was done. Mrs Nagy had organised the girls Palliser found, and it was all done. She must have terrified them.'

'Never mind, if it's done that's all that matters in the end, dear. Isn't she a treasure? Do give her the day off, won't you? But, Blanche dear, what a spiffing party! Wasn't it splendid? It's just got to become a tradition. I've had Mrs Perkins gushing to me already. And the children are full of it!'

'I'm so happy you enjoyed it. I had the best night of my life.'

Blanche always tells the truth.

'And Hubert's gone to London? Whatever for, so early in the day?'

'I don't know. I found a note in the breakfast room just now. He didn't say anything about it yesterday. I would have remembered. But I expect Palliser will know.'

'What a peculiar way to behave! You're not upset are you, dear? You don't sound upset. He is the tiniest bit unusual, your brother! But don't worry darling, not all men are like dear Hubert. But Mrs Perkins tells me the Bishop was very taken with him so that's super. I'm sure if he mixed a bit in the county it would do nothing but good! I'm not sure about those London clergymen. But you're the one who made a hit, darling! You know how little George has to say — well he's practically garrulous on the subject. I can't get a word in edgeways. He keeps asking me all sorts of questions about you.'

'What sort of questions?'

'Oh, the usual kind — background, school, beaux, how long have we been friends, that sort of thing. And a few about Palliser.'

'Why does George want to know about Palliser?'

'Oh you know what men are like! He's really quite smitten, darling, isn't that sweet? He is a lovely fellow, we all think so in the family, and families are far the hardest to please, aren't they? I thought while he was here I'd have a little dinner party. Can you come on Saturday?'

'Yes, I'd love to. I don't think Hubert will be back from London, but I'm sure Palliser will come.'

'That wasn't quite what I had in mind, dear. Four's company and five is — complicated.'

'But with Hubert it would have been five . . .'

'Never mind, dear. Shall George collect you about six? Wear the new black wool, and your pearls. Now, can you make the afternoon tea at the Deanery on Wednesday . . .'

Palliser descends the main stairs washed, brushed and shaven, wearing his day-off clothes — black roll-neck sweater and cream cavalry twill trousers. He heads for the kitchens, but she puts out her hand to detain him. For the first time ever, she cuts Clarissa off before she has quite finished talking.

'I must go now, Clarissa. I need to talk to Palliser. Thank you for everything. I'll see you on Wednesday. Bye-bye.'

'Palliser — don't bother Mrs Nagy, will you? She's worked so hard and she's upset. I think we should give her the day off. I thought we might go out. Let's go up to London! There are so many places I'd like to visit — St Paul's Cathedral, the National Gallery, the Victoria and Albert Museum.'

'I say,' says Palliser, with something less than his usual enthusiasm, 'what a splendid idea!'

He persuades her into a quiet domestic day, ending with dinner for two in a sedate hotel overlooking the river. In the taxi on the way home he falls asleep on her shoulder and she has to shake him to pay the driver.

The house is in darkness. They stand in its moon-shadow, as the taxi reverses on the drive and trundles away into the lane.

Palliser pulls up the collar of his coat against the cold, adjusts his scarf and thrusts his gloved hands into his pockets. She makes no alteration to her clothes, as if mere details like cold cannot touch her.

They watch the lights of the taxi flaring up against the trees as it vanishes into the long dark tunnel leading from the house. The sound slowly dwindles away, until there is absolute silence.

'I'm sorry you are tired,' she says. 'I expect you want to go to bed.'

'Not at all,' he says, revived by his nap in the taxi. 'I

will show you exactly how tired I am not. Let's not go in just yet.'

He takes his right hand out of his pocket and offers her his arm. She takes it, pressing close to his side as he leads her into the garden.

Under snow and moonlight the garden is transformed into a mysterious wilderness. A magical silence creeps through it, strange and wild. The slight sound of their feet on the grass is absorbed into the silence. All around them features look unlike themselves, as if a garden-wide metamorphosis had taken place as soon as the humans turned away. Here is the rose bower, its encircling wall topped by a perfect circle of snow; it has shaken off the warm welcome of daytime, and glowers at those who walk in. Under the wall are deep shadows cast by the moon. Rose bushes crouch under snow looking for an opportunity to spring and smite. Here and there a late bloom, drained of all colour and scent, hangs under a coating of snow, as a reminder of more polite behaviour.

He remembers a poem of Tennyson's.

> *Now sleeps the crimson petal, now the white;*
> *Now folds the lily all her sweetness up,*
> *Now lies the Earth all Danaë to the stars,*
> *And all thy heart lies open unto me.*

'Do you remember the first time you led me through the garden?' he says. 'The sun was shinin', the air was warm as a bath, and the bees were goin' mad. The roses smelt like heaven on earth. You took my arm, and I felt we were walking into – *enchantment*.'

'I remember I was scared. I felt like the girl in that painting in Hubert's study – the one called *The Wizard's Garden*. Where she's just stepping inside the garden and it looks so well-kept and peaceful, but she's afraid.'

263

'There was nothing to be afraid of, dear girl, after all, was there?'

'I don't know. I shan't know until afterwards.'

'Afterwards?'

'After the spell wears off, and I'm back to being ordinary me again.'

It seems impossible that Blanche or Palliser should be their ordinary selves, or that they should have ordinary selves to reclaim. Tonight everything about them is transfigured, as if some monumental piece of irreversible wizardry has taken place, some old incantation has been sung, and the natural world will never be the same again. Palliser loves such occasions, all too rare in his roistering life; he feels that there is a chance, albeit slim, for him to become a new creature.

He stops and reaches into the bushes, braving the snow and the thorns to break off one last rose. He holds it up to his face to see if there is any hint of scent remaining, but the petals fall off into his gloved hand as he does so, leaving his face wet with their legacy of snow.

He scatters the handful of petals on to the snow.

'Souvenir de la Malmaison,' she says. 'Bourbon. Amazing to find one so late. They don't like the rain. Faded pink, crammed with petals, like a pink cabbage. Lovely scent. Lovely name.'

'The Empress Josephine remembering the happy times she spent in an enchanted château,' says Palliser, hoping that he's got his history mildly right.

They leave the rose garden and walk arm in arm towards the sunken garden. It seems that they can walk together without the need for the niceties. No need for *Shall we go this way – After you – Sorry*. It is as if they have been lovers strolling through these gardens all their lives, not two strangers, disparate in age and condition, thrown together by the most material of causes.

They stand together at the edge of the sunken garden and look down on the pollarded trees and contorted statues, crowned with snow. Nothing looks like itself. Each object, living or dead, is warped into another by the snow and moonlight. The bright tempera of the wizard's garden is now the grisaille of a Fuseli nightmare, where creatures without proper names peer from underneath the twisted shadows.

'But I am not afraid now,' she says, inclining her head on to his shoulder. 'I suppose all my life I have been afraid of what was going to happen to me, of being left alone, of being laughed at and pointed at. Of what might happen, rather than what did happen. But now I am not afraid of anything.'

They walk down into the garden. They must go single file because the paths are narrow and tricky in the darkness. Blanche lets go of his arm and leads the way, sure of foot. From endless childhood games, she knows each step of the way. He is delayed by unfamiliarity and a strangely exaggerated fear of tripping in the darkness.

At the bottom of the garden, she stands perfectly still. She is waiting in the ring of gods and goddesses, heroes and demigods, beside a statue of Aphrodite; the statue coyly covers her nakedness with her hands, a wasted effort now that she is daubed in snow. Her stone beauty is caricatured by a crooked hat of snow, so that she looks absurd tonight rather than her usual teasing self. Beside her, Blanche, tall and still, seems more appropriately cast as the goddess of love.

Palliser wishes for a golden apple to give to his newborn goddess, but he has only the hip of a late rose, which he throws away. He makes it safely to the bottom of the sunken garden and finds he must remove his gloves and take her face between his hands and kiss her, because she is lovely.

The nameless creatures in the shadows slink away, become nothings. All the evil or tiresome things in the world are revealed as figments, the bailiffs and executioners, the violent and the parasitic, the avaricious and the self-seeking: they are the dark shadows that have been dreamed up by a deathly imagination. In this harsh, different world they shrivel up and cease to be. Only a bare stripped beauty exists, without the complicated minutiae of evil.

Palliser and Blanche stand facing each other in silence. Palliser says nothing because he refuses to sully this place with a shallow lie, and he can think of nothing truthful that is not pompous. He sees something here, which his facile mind cannot fix on. He wants to demonstrate to Blanche the nature of his vision, but he can think of nothing to say. He wishes for an action to express the difference he feels, the notion that there is a parallel universe, a world where lies and complexities are shorn away, where it is possible not to be that person one is, but another, a simple, naked innocent soul. It is a place, he wants to tell her, where he might be like her.

He feels that she has led him into that world, and he wants to convey his happiness, but because she cannot know the burden of being Palliser, he cannot describe the freedom of sloughing him off.

He takes a handful of snow from Aphrodite's hands, cupped over her pudenda, and he smooths it over Blanche's hair.

'Now you look like her, only more lovely.'

She laughs at him. She walks around the circle of gods, looking up at each one, her head thrown back. She starts to run, seizes a handful of snow from Hercules' podium and throws it at him. He dodges, goes for his own ammunition, throws, misses.

'Pax!' he cries, not sure if he'd win a snowball fight. 'Let's go and look at the terrace in the moonlight.'

They climb back out of the garden and make their way around the side of the house towards the terrace. The snow crunches under their feet. Behind them is a pattern of footprints, black against the white, like the diagrams for a dance.

No lights shine from the house; it almost seems not to exist. The terrace lies perfect before them, a swath of unadulterated whiteness. Beyond it the park, untouched white as far as the eye can see, tapering into the black woods.

'It's all ours,' he says.

'It seems a pity to walk on it, it's so perfect.'

'And tomorrow it will be gone,' he says, 'melted away into memory like all perfect things. "Where are the snows of yesteryear?"'

'But that doesn't make any difference *now*. And it is now we are standing on.'

'You're right,' he says. 'Of course, you're absolutely right. There is only now.' He laughs. 'All my life I have been scroungin' for tomorrow, lookin' out for some kind of bright golden future. Mortgaging m'self for it. But *now* is in the bank. We've got it, and it's the only damn' thing worth having.'

He wants to express to her the enormity of this idea, so self-evident, so banal. He wants to convey the exhilaration of the new world she has led him into, the world of innocence and simplicity, where it is enough to be, a place where everything is recreated and yet everything is itself.

The emptiness of the white field before him seems to say it perfectly, lying clear in the moonlight, the outline of trees etched against the sky, the prospect of the glittering distance, beauty of complete ordinariness, a temporary magic, a profound transformation which alters nothing. He can't find words. Words are too slippery. Then he finds something to do.

'Yes,' cries Palliser, 'now is all we've got. And it is bloody *wonderful!*'

He lets go her waist, throws off his coat, struggling to get out of the shoulders quick enough, as if passion has invaded him and he will die if he does not seize the moment. She watches in confusion, but accepts the coat he thrusts into her arms. He takes off across the untouched surface, in a trot, then breaks into a run, going faster and faster, until he is turning a perfect cartwheel on the long snow-covered lawn outside the south face of Thule.

He sees the world turned upside down, the stars rushing past him, the topsy-turvy glory of creation, that here is Palliser Wentwood, middle-aged rake, wrong side up on the wrong side of the world, in the garden in the winter, in the middle of a huge lie and huge happiness, with snow weighing down the roses, and a great white child, sweet monstrosity of nature, his dear bedfellow.

Let us draw breath for a moment. As Palliser had to do when he had completed his circumrotation, but for different reasons. He was short of breath because he was no longer the Till Eulenspiegel of his imagination. We are in need of respite because events have moved quickly, and Palliser's mind changes even more rapidly. He is like a youth in the grip of his earliest adult emotions. He wants this, and that; he longs for one thing, but seizes on another. He will act irrationally while being able, at any given time, to state his goals with passion and clarity. He is a man of feeling, and consequently is blown about by every wind of emotion. An exhausting person to love; equally an exhausting person to treat with understanding.

Poor Blanche – but why poor Blanche? Because she is intrinsically pitiable? She is as happy at this moment as it is possible for a human to be, so why pity her? Because she was previously so miserable? Because it is more than likely her happiness cannot last? Using those arguments to pity her, no one would ever be happy, since all lives start perforce in pain, and end in shadow and death. Every moment in our fairy tale is tinged with blood and haunted by agony, but should that deny us the enjoyment of that lovely moment when the prince rides out of the forest into the clearing, and finds the girl he has sought so long singing in her cottage doorway? No, I think not – for the happiest moment is also the moment of blood and terror, and the moments are the same. There is no concept of joy if there has been no understanding of agony. No birth without excruciating pangs, no resurrection without tormented death. Blanche's extremity of happiness springs directly from her years of sadness. If she were an ordinary girl, always befriended and courted and more or less loved, the attentions of one engaging fortune-hunter from the south would be a pastime. But for her, Palliser is the prince-deliverer, and will be so to the end of time.

Nothing, neither age nor infirmity, nor tedium nor loss, neither disappointment, nor years of long ordinary contentment, neither the onset of cynicism nor the realisation of sordid truths, nothing will take away her moment of ecstasy, as Palliser turns cartwheels in the snow.

X

ON THE SATURDAY following the Christmas party, Palliser insisted Blanche go to dinner at the Eltons', explaining that neglecting one's friends for a mere lover was bad form. He kept out of sight when George arrived to pick Blanche up. Then he went to the pub.

He had a fine time with his cronies at the Fortune of War, even to the extent of a recitation of 'Eskimo Nell', which he didn't often trot out. He completely forgot his concerns about what Blanche might say at dinner, whether she could get through a single exchange without mentioning his name. He forgot to worry about what plans the Elton household might hatch to unseat him from his unseemly place, and shelved the problem of his future, which, for the past week, had occupied what time his duties left him.

Palliser was intending, at some convenient moment, to open up discussion on the future, and discover delicately what Blanche had in her mind, or in her dreams, for him. There was such a magic lantern show of scenarios in his mind that he grew tired of viewing them, but he very much wanted to know her favourite scene, since sooner or later, if she proved serious in loving him, he would need to tell her the truth. Or some of the truth. Choosing the least damaging moment for confession would call for all his skill.

So far their talk of consequences had gone only as far as his vasectomy, which he had expounded on day two, with a lively account of how he had persuaded his GP to recommend to the surgeon this daringly novel procedure. He told her this in order to prevent her worrying in the small hours, for he knew how even the most innocent of girls understood the natural quid prod quo of sex and procreation. He had even shown her the scars, just in case she was disinclined to believe him, an event that proved rather fun. It had occurred to Palliser that he might use his impairment as a sound reason why he was unsuitable as a husband, should she propose marriage. By this device he might avoid the mention of his living wife altogether. But this would work for only so long; if he stayed at Thule, sooner or later the truth would come out, and the later it came out, the worse the damage.

Mostly he was far too comfortable, and far too tired, to pursue any talk of the future. Blanche was completely without guile or guilt, and seemed so delighted with the present that no thought of the future could penetrate. She was not troubled about anything except physical absence from Palliser and seemed unaware that she should consider the meaning of Mrs Nagy's black looks or Clarissa's peculiar questions. She was blissfully unconcerned about Hubert's likely reaction on his return. But Palliser worried about such things quite often, having been severely mauled in the past by relatives and friends; nonetheless he allowed himself to be carried along on a tide of satisfied, re-ignited and re-satisfied desire; also of good food, wine, warmth and a comfortable bed.

And, therefore, in the Fortune of War, fusty and masculine, after a mere two pints, he could forget about Blanche altogether. He forgot about Salomé, Jemima, Abigail, Naomi and Bathsheba. He did not forget the words of 'Eskimo Nell', and he boasted that he remembered the tenor part of every hymn in the English Hymnal, and was proving this to Jacob, down the village street with his arm around Jacob's shoulders, tenor to Jacob's bass. They had got to Ton-Y-Botel:

> *Once to every man and nation*
> *Comes the moment to decide*
> *In the strife of truth with falsehood*
> *For the good or evil side*
> *etc.*

'Now this is the good bit!'

> *By the light of burning martyrs,*
> *Christ thy bleeding feet we track*
> *Toiling up new calvaries ever*
> *With the cross that turns not back –*

when the passing of a dark car, which might have been George, alerted him to his domestic duties.

'Better get home to the little woman,' he said, causing Jacob to laugh uproariously. They parted the best of friends, brothers in hymnody till the end of time, at the point where the footpath to Jacob's cottage diverged from the lane to the Hall.

Palliser, toiling up the lane to Thule, saw Blanche through the drawing-room curtains (of happy memory). She was pacing to and fro, trying not to look as if she was listening to every twig crack.

Take the high ground, old boy. Take the immoral high ground. The 'boys will be boys and you just gotta love them for it' line. Works every time. A good drunken hymn should set the tone.

He went back down the lane a bit and came up again singing.

> *I, that of the dreadful heathen*
> *Trod the winepress all alone*

Right tune, wrong hymn, goddammit, wonderful hymn, how does it go?

> *Then it is the brave man chooses*
> *Offering each the bloom or blight*
> *Ere the choice goes by for ever*
> *Twixt that darkness and that light*

Crash bang goes the front door – yes, use the front door, why not? – dance into the house, dance and sing, a little jig, a few false steps. Hello my darling, how are we? Whirl her round a bit and be silly. O dammit, why are fucking women always waiting for one? Up, with all their clothes on, their damned armour on, rather than in bed where they should be, without any of it.

'I was worried.'

A big sloppy kiss. Hope that woman's not lurking. Make it clear that one is agreeably pissed.

'Never worry about me. Never. Not even when I don't come home. I'll be in a ditch singing hymns.'

'I shall go to bed, then.'

'What a splendid idea.' Don't give her the choice, not that we're up to much tonight, but there's always the morning.

'I think you should sleep in your own bed tonight.' And up the stairs.

Fuck, not to put too fine a point on it, fuck fuck fuck. Or rather no fuck.

'Must I? Are you cross with me?' On the knees, on the staircase, very theatrical. Can she resist me?

Laughs. Thank God.

'No, I'm not cross. I just think it would be a good idea.'

Look soulfully at front door, like dog who has been shut in.

'I should've stayed at the party. I hurried home especially.' Bad choice of consonants.

'I was looking forward to seein' you. Did you have fun?'

Follow her up the stairs, light on the feet, remind her of one's dexterity, don't get too pathetic.

'George is very amusing, though he doesn't say much. You and Roland make a good pair.'

'Now I resent that!' Keep on up the stairs, not too close behind, not too downtrodden, crestfallen, but not really repentant. 'Roland is a whisky and dirty jokes drunk. I'm a beer and hymns drunk. He gets amorous and wants to punch your nose, I just grow loving and lovable, like a teddy bear.'

'You are nothing like a teddy bear, Palliser.'

'But I think of myself as one, one great big pussycat.'

Laughing, but she's standing in the door as if she means to bar it. Can't use force on this one.

'Goodnight kiss then.' That should do the trick. And it does.

It is Saturday, night fourteen. Nothing has been resolved. Hubert has returned from London, full of talk of ecclesiastical doings and avoiding Palliser's eye, and gives a sterling performance as a man who is perfectly satisfied with the conduct of his household. Each night Palliser comes circumspectly into Blanche's bedroom to kiss her goodnight, and ends by staying there the night. Always, he claims, at her invitation. Hubert can hardly fail to hear their voices rising and falling as he creeps to bed, or to have noticed how late Palliser appears for his breakfast, but he is as a man under an oath of silence. His eyes follow Palliser, Blanche, Mrs Nagy and Peter about the house and gardens, but he says nothing.

Blanche loves to talk and to hear Palliser talk more than anything else. She bathes in the warm stream of lovers' chat and Palliser's intimate anecdotes.

He is in her bed, wearing nothing but his shirt, and that unbuttoned all the way down. She is naked, because, she says, she doesn't feel the cold and needs the practice. She sits upright while he kneels behind her brushing her hair.

'Tell me something more about your life,' she says. 'It's so exciting, like the Red or the Green True Story Book. Nothing has ever happened to me.'

'But the difficulty is,' he says, 'I'm not sure which bits of which stories are true any more. And I don't think you would like me to tell you fictions.'

'No. I like to know the difference. I think stories that pretend to be fact when they are made up are no better than lies. If I know a story is made up, then I can see the truth in it. Like the parables – the Good Samaritan, and the others – they are true stories in a different way from the ones is Foxe's *Book of Martyrs*, which are obviously made up, but pretend to be true.'

'Can't say I've read Foxe's *Book of Martyrs*.'

'But how can you *not* know the difference between what happened and what you made up?'

'It's like this,' he replies, somewhat muffled, because he has stopped brushing to bury his nose in the back of her neck. 'Something happens in your life – a wild pig eats your tent, or you see a footprint in the forest which might *just* be the extinct moa – and there's a story to tell. So you're sitting in the pub or round the kitchen table, and because human beings love a proper story, with a beginning, a middle and an end, you tell the tale with a bit more colour, and bit more drama than maybe it had. Then when you remember it the next time, what you remember is the story version along with the original, and with each retelling the story blots out more and more of the original in your memory, so at the end you can't remember what happened, only the story you tell. Now is that story truth or lying?'

Blanche furrows her brow as if this matter is of great importance.

'I think,' she says, 'I think it depends on the reason for telling the story. If you are telling people about the extinct bird to get them excited and interested in the forest and to make them wonder what things are out there, and make them think that maybe they hadn't got everything sorted out, then it's a good story. But if you were telling the story to city people to fool them into travelling into the forest so you could be their guide and make some money, then it would be a lie.'

Palliser leans forward and kisses her shoulder.

'Don't think so much, it's not good for lovely girls to think.'

Blanche accepts this, for she is too young yet to understand the insidious tyranny of the patronising, and she loves the compliment. She, Blanche, is classed with all lovely girls.

'Well, tell me a story, then. Tell me a true story about your girls. How tall are they, what colour is their hair?'

She has manoeuvred him without intention into a minefield. To avoid hating himself, he would tell the truth, but he must first remember it, and then select from it pieces that are consistent with the version she knows.

'I love their names,' she says. 'Jemima, Abigail, Naomi, Bathsheba. All from the Old Testament. Whose idea was that? Do you think names are important? What was your wife's name?'

'Salomé.' At least he can get that right. 'She hated her name. One couldn't resist making jokes about it.'

'Was she that sort of person – a Salomé sort of person?'

Palliser wants to laugh with pleasure at the visions of Salomé in his head, but stops himself just in time.

'It's hard to tell. I only think of the name as hers. One forgets about Oscar Wilde and John the Baptist. She used to dance for me, though . . . As a kind of joke . . .

'When I first saw her, I saw this lovely creature drifting about the dance floor, in one of those silk numbers that they wore before the war, with long scarves. All I knew about her was her name,' and the fact that she was wealthy and unattached, 'and I was absolutely fascinated.

'I couldn't speak to her because one had to be introduced,' – a situation made doubly awkward by the fact that Palliser was not, as he pretended, a guest at the hotel where Salomé and her mother and sister were staying. 'I was beside myself. I'd watch her over the roulette wheel and walking in the park, and on the hotel terrace, and across the tables at dinner, and from the other side of the ballroom. And I knew that she knew that I was watching her. And she wanted to break away and talk to me, but her mother was a harridan of the old school. Then one day, as luck would have it,' luck had nothing whatsoever to do with it, 'I met her in the Tiergarten, and raised my hat, and introduced myself.'

'But how could you introduce yourself if you hadn't been introduced?'

'I think I took the opportunity of saying I thought I had been at varsity with her brother. Something like that. That's what she told her mama at any rate.'

'Was it true?'

'I honestly can't remember. It scarcely seemed important, once we *had* been introduced. Thank God we don't have to resort to those ruses nowadays.'

'Well I'm very glad you decided to bring my curtain

material in person. That was the most wonderful luck for me.'

Palliser remembers that he was briefly the downtrodden manager of Hampton's department store; he reflects with ironic pleasure that his other impersonation, Miss Lovelace's beau, has turned into truth. *For my next trick* . . . He feels a certain boldness coming on.

'Has Hubert spoken to you at all?' he asks.

'Hubert and I speak all the time, what do you mean?'

'Has he talked about me at all – taken the big brother line?'

'No, all he ever talks about is how he's been asked to do the Orthodox Christmas service in Stoke Newington, and how the Bishop has asked him to represent the East at an ecumenical Eucharist, and to say a few words.'

'And Peter's scooter.'

'And Peter's scooter,' she says and laughs.

Peter's scooter. When Hubert returned from London he was followed by a wake of expensive presents, which washed into the house one after another by differing means of transport.

First to arrive was a huge television set with a real mahogany case. This was installed with due ceremony in the kitchen within perfect range of Mrs Nagy's chair by the Aga. Palliser had spent two hours running an aerial up to and on to the roof, a death-defying feat which no one took any heed of. Blanche and Mrs Nagy had their heads bowed over the *Radio Times*, savouring every possibility and exclaiming to each other in wonder – *I wonder what that's about? I wonder what that's like?* Hubert had walked in and out of the kitchen evaluating the picture quality and shouting up inaudible instructions to Palliser in the snow.

No sooner had the household recovered from this novelty than Peter went out one morning on his rusty old bone-shaker and returned with a brand new white

Vespa motor scooter. He proceeded to ride round and round the grounds, taking little heed of the appointed paths, and then out into the park where as a small black and white insect he made black lines all over the white field. Palliser said nothing about this. Mrs Nagy had a great deal to say about it, but was torn between delight at Hubert's generosity and Peter's happiness, terror at what Peter would now do, and suspicion of Hubert's motives.

'He wants to make him a man like himself, to join the club of men. Out at the pub drinking and not coming home.'

Palliser found no answer to this.

Blanche's present from Hubert was a dressing case the size of an imperial treasury, with three hairbrushes and a glittering array of cosmetics. He had thoroughly enjoyed having them chosen, and wanted her to get them all out then and there, so he could explain what they did, but she insisted that he wrap it up and put it under the Christmas tree.

Hubert gave Palliser a Christmas card containing a cheque.

'No,' Blanche says, 'he hasn't said a word about you. Except about the car.'

'And what has he said about the car?'

'Just that Roland says am I sure it's the right car to buy, and are the seats big enough. Things like that.'

The car – cause of one of Palliser's more memorable embarrassments. Blanche had decided it would be nice to have the Eltons and George to dinner, and could not be dissuaded. While dinner was in progress, and Palliser was making his way pussy-footed around the table, wearing white gloves and filling glasses, the subject of Hubert's Christmas largesse had arisen.

'Father Father Christmas,' murmured George.

'And you're joining in too, Blanche, aren't you?' cried

Clarissa. 'It's such fun buying presents for everyone, isn't it – 'specially children, but you know that from your grand trans-Siberian expedition to Hamley's – adults are rather harder. I don't have trouble with Roland, one just gets the latest book on "How to Grow the Perfect Lawn" and a bottle of Glenfiddich. George, I never know what to do for George. Yet another tie and the new St Trinian's I suppose. And what does one buy the perfect man who wants nothing? What do you give someone like Palliser for Christmas?'

'Oh that's easy,' Blanche had said. 'I'm buying him a car.'

An awful silence had followed, during which Palliser slunk out of the room. As he made for the kitchen he heard her describing the Sunbeam Alpine, much admired by Palliser, that she was proposing to buy.

On gaining the kitchen he had stood up against the wall, behind the door, and breathed deep. Mrs Nagy had glanced briefly away from the gâteau she was decorating, and sniffed.

'I am not sure you should be doing this,' Palliser says to Blanche that evening.

'But Palliser,' she says, half turning towards him, 'I love you so much I have to buy you something special.'

His heart sinks as he hears those words.

'Dear, dear Blanche,' he says.

He jumps off the bed, goes into the adjoining dressing room, brings out the full-length looking-glass and stands it in the middle of the room.

'Come here.'

He places her so the light from the lamp falls on her from behind, and carefully, so that when she looks in the mirror she sees herself with a halo of light and a backdrop of flowers. She stands obediently and looks in the glass.

She joins her hands loosely across her stomach, one

above the other, standing without posing. He presses himself behind her, his hands across her waist, his chin in her shoulder, his head peering over her shoulder into the mirror.

'Look in the mirror. What do you see?'

He wonders if it is ever possible for two people to see that same thing. What he sees is conditioned by images and symbols layered from his past. He sees a Veronese Venus without even a wisp of veil, unaffected as a washerwoman by Rembrandt. He sees chiaroscuro and Caravaggio and flesh that Rowlandson would have drooled to draw, and innocence incarnate. And he sees his own hobgoblin's face peering into the glass, and behind it, winking from the woodwork, the tiny faces like his own, sneering at him. But what does she see?

'I can see a naked body, rather a large one. And you peering over my shoulder like an imp.'

'Correction, you can see a large beautiful naked body. But look again.'

'I can see part of my bedroom, two, no, three of the faces of the carved people. The fish-woman, the man-tiger and the wild man. My arrangement of holly, bulrushes, bracken, sloe and dried roses. Um. Your shirt cuffs with cufflinks in them, silver ones. Your fingernails, which are quite long for a man, and really clean.'

'Look again.'

'Well I can see quite a lot of myself, but I don't really want to describe all of that.'

'Look here,' he says, and raises his hand to the place where his head nestles against hers.

He runs his hand through his hair and into hers, so that the fibres mingle.

'Do you see? This is white hair, and this is black. I am old enough to be your father. Other people see that, even if you do not.'

'I think we look beautiful together.'

'Yes,' he says, and sighs. 'I think we do. But no amount of beauty can take away that fact of age and unsuitability. I could dye my hair and pretend to be thirty, but to no avail. You have your whole life ahead of you, and mine is mostly over. It means nothing to you, but it means a great deal to others. I am nobody and have nothing. I am not a worthy recipient of your generosity or your love.'

'Oh Palliser, how can you say such things?'

She meets his eyes in the mirror. She puts her hands over his and hugs them in to her stomach.

'I only tell you because you care so much for the truth.'

'But not everything you just said was necessarily true. Some of it is only your opinion. It *is* true that you are old enough to be my father, and it's true that your hair is going grey and mine is dark. But it's not true to say that you are not worthy of love. I don't believe that is true of anyone, so how can it be true of you?'

As he returns the glass to its proper place, he wonders why it is once again his fate to be loved without condition and quite beyond his deserving.

The period between the Christmas party and the day itself was filled with social activity of a kind the Lovelace siblings had never known before. They were invited to three drinks parties, two afternoon Christmas parties, and a function at the Bishop's palace.

Whatever advice Clarissa gave to Blanche, veiled or unveiled, on the subject of buying suitable presents for the servants, the purchase of the car proceeded. Hubert seemed in favour; or rather he seemed not to be against it, but then Hubert treated every matter in which Palliser was involved with extreme delicacy. Roland Elton rang up several times to give Hubert advice on buying cars, a matter for which members of the cloth are constitutionally underqualified; George Burnaby came twice to call on Blanche, and took polite tea in the front drawing room. Palliser, loitering with intent, did not hear cars spoken of explicitly, but did pick up mention of the rigours of driving lessons. Clarissa rang every day and Blanche went to tea at the Manor. But the purchase of the car proceeded.

Palliser was uncertain about the car, as about many things in the days before Christmas. All his life he had lusted after a fast car, a sports car, never seriously expecting to own a brand new one. But the method of this acquisition was all wrong; there were invisible strings attached. He was beginning to feel mildly humiliated, though fortunately Palliser's ego could take quite a bit of punishment in the interests of pleasure. There was no deviousness in Blanche's actions, but that did not help Palliser to rest easy. Nor did her complete lack of discretion add to his comfort. It is very charming to watch a child with a new toy; it is not so charming to be the new toy.

Christmas Days make for dull retelling, whether the sun smiles fixedly out of a blue sky, or sulks behind a grey blanket. Families gather and eat, open a catalogue of presents, so promising in their paper, so ordinary when stripped. Children invariably display their worst characteristics while adults struggle vainly to display their best. Fresh causes for disagreement are discovered in the flush of food and wine, old antagonisms have their annual airing. Conversely, alas, new friendships and bonds of love are rarely forged, unless by the discovery, as in the case of the Wentwood-Butterworth Christmas dinner, that perhaps families can meet in harmony without the prerequisite of thorough liking. Or put more crudely, can rub along together amicably without needing to agree on detail.

At Thule a parody of the family Christmas was enacted,

with parent-and-child pairings all switched about. Of all present, in a remarkable reversal of standard practice, the one who most deserved to be happy was indeed the happiest. To Blanche any present under the tree, indeed the tree itself, was a precious object. Equally she was charmed by the intimacy that an invitation to the Eltons for a g&t after morning service on Christmas Day implied. It allowed her to give presents to everyone in the Elton household, including Helene, the wondrous nanny, and to experience the ultimate bliss of seeing presents with *her name* on them under someone else's Christmas tree. The festive table at Thule laid, at her insistence, for five, with holly and crackers and champagne glasses, was an altar of rejoicing.

Now it is the evening of Christmas Day.

Here is Blanche in her happiness, sitting in a comfy chair in the kitchen, warm as toast by the Aga, watching, with round eyes, the Christmas edition of *Face to Face*. Around her neck is the Victorian silver necklace, with a tiny chased locket, that slipped into Palliser's pocket in an antique shop one day. On her lap is the black kitten Mrs Nagy has acquired for her from Gerald the gamekeeper. Palliser sits on the arm of the chair, as close as he decorously can. Jacob the verger, on his way back from crib devotions, has popped in with a tray of mince pies from his sister, and has been inveigled into a nightcap before he braves the snow. Peter and Hubert are playing chess by the light of the television. Hubert is smoking a pipe. He and Palliser, and Gerald, who is perched on a stool in the corner, have glasses of port. Mrs Nagy has given up knitting and is sitting quite still concentrating on the English flowing out of the television.

It is tempting to feel sorry for Blanche because her happiness is based on foundations of deceit, because we know it cannot possibly last, because her love for Palliser is a chimera. Tempting, but misleading. For Blanche's happiness wells not so much out of her love for Palliser, although that is as pure an example of love as one could find in any fairy tale, but rather out of the transformation of her life and person, the resurrection of her body. She is happy because her life has changed, and she will never be the caterpillar she was before. She is happy, even though she already knows that this sweetest of all episodes is almost over.

How does she know this? In a sense, she has always known. But now she knows for sure, and yet she is happy.

This is the manner of Palliser's unmasking.

Three days before Christmas Palliser went to pick up the new car. He had long admired a particular model in the local car sales, but when it came to the sticking point of purchase, he was required to go up to the London depot and collect a different absolutely brand-new vehicle, without cigarette burns on the upholstery. He had no objections whatever to doing this, and was secretly pleased that the delivery day coincided with one of the drinks parties to which Blanche and Hubert were bidden. He would not let Blanche decline the invitation, and went off bright and early by train and Underground to collect his reward.

It was a bright breezy day, the sun glinting off puddles in the derelict railway yards and ribbons of smoke scudding out of ten thousand identical chimneys. Palliser smoked and read the *Mail* and the *Times* as cheerful as the day is long. He arrived without mishap at the Chesterfield Rootes agency in Vauxhall, and drove off in a brand new sports car without having to give any account of himself. This struck him as a useful ruse to add to the collection; probably the risk factor was too high, but it was a jolly idea.

Palliser thought he knew London, and so had not come provided with a map. In fact he had not driven through the city very much at all, even in his free-wheeling youth, for he had never owned a car. South of the river, that great sprawling ill-kempt mass of the city, had never existed when he was a young man about Soho, and he had only the vaguest notion of which suburb lay in which direction.

He drove in the direction approximately west, hoping somewhere to find a bridge across the Thames that would take him out of this motoring calamity and into broad carriageways of which he recognised the names.

So it came to pass that he found himself in Putney, in Putney High Street, to be precise, and while he was idling at the traffic lights he saw a street name that struck a chord in his memory. Budapest Road. He remembered it clearly because he had been amused that Mrs Nagy's boxes of Hungarian food should come from a delicatessen located in Budapest Road. He had wondered at the time if this indicated the existence of a Hungarian area in Putney, but Mrs Nagy had thought not. So finding himself practically in Budapest Road, an expansive frame of mind, and no hurry to return home, he turned down the street and went to look for Levi & Son, Purveyors of Fine Food.

Who knows the secret springs of action? Palliser did not plan to do what he did; he did not set out with a kind intention in his mind. It could be said that he acted on the spur of the moment. Perhaps he acted out of an excess of good fortune; perhaps out of fundamental good nature, finally allowed to surface after years of struggling with the need to survive; perhaps he acted out of guilt – one kind deed to assuage his conscience. He had had it in his mind for months to investigate and perhaps stem the source of Mrs Nagy's unwanted largesse, for what reason he was not sure. Whatever the motivation, it remains true that he did turn into Budapest Road, he did drive down it and stop outside the shop. He could easily have thought about doing so, and driven on.

Tucked in the middle of a row of benign semi-detached houses with tiled roofs were four compressed shops, set back from the road: baker, newsagent, off-licence and Levi & Sons. Palliser parked and locked the car ostentatiously. He pulled up the collar of his sheepskin coat and sauntered into the shop.

The mean frontage belied the interior, which was as long and tall as it was narrow. A wooden counter ran the length of the shop, terminating in a grotto of hanging meats. Shelves rose up the walls behind and opposite the counter, packed to the ceiling with every kind of tinned or dried food a discerning consumer might desire. Tea of every leaf, brands of coffee beyond imagination, biscuits, olives, gherkins, pickled walnuts, artichoke hearts, peppers, baby corn, mushrooms, truffles, caviare, pâté, salmon, locusts, snails, mussels, prawns, dried fruit, pickled fruit, fruit in rum, fruit in brandy, chocolates with hard centres, chocolates with soft centres, chocolates with liquid centres, fifteen marmalades, honey from Thyateira and honey from Skye. A long ladder was propped against each wall to reach the goods on the higher shelves. The front of the shop, the spaces by and in the window, was taken up by a marble slab on which rested a ziggurat of whole cheeses, teetering towers of Double Gloucester, Stilton, Matured Wigmore, Harmans' Truckle Cheddar, Red Leicester, Waterloo and Brie, some the size of cartwheels, some the size of mill-stones, and some as big as the round tower. From them had been cut portions of various sizes, threatening the stability of the tower and adding an element of Dada to the artistic whole. On the counter itself were baskets of bread, wafting the scents of heaven, and on the floor were stacks of items sporting triangles of white paper, inscribed in a continental hand: *Special Import – Smyrna Figs 2s 6d. Anchovies – very nice tasting 8d. try this Bombay Duck – only 4s 3d per tin. Fancy Biscuits – broken but still good 6s 9d.*

Palliser breathed it all in, and thought perhaps *now* might be a good moment to expire, crumple gently to the floor and rest for ever on a bed of clean sawdust.

A figure came out of the depths, a tall slim woman in a white apron, carrying a glass before her. Palliser's stomach turned over with a memory that short-circuited the brain and went from the eye straight to the gut. He looked around him in confusion, saw the car between the towers of cheeses, and remembered where he was. But some confidence had trickled out of him.

She was a tall dark Jewish woman, gaunt, inclining towards him graciously.

'How may I be of assistance, sir?' Her accent was indeterminate, as if its owner was unwilling to acknowledge its origins.

'I would very much like to speak to the proprietor. A Mr Levi, I presume?'

She put down the glass, smiled and held out her hand, crooked downwards.

'I am Mr Levi. Or rather, and Son. It was Mr Levi and Daughter always, but he lacked the necessary courage. How can I help you, sir?'

'It's a trifle delicate. Tricky matter really.'

'An account customer, sir?'

'In a manner of speaking.'

'I have a special coffee for account customers. Please to step this way.'

He followed her down the length of the shop, beyond the sanctum of the preserved meats, wondering how a person so evidently Jewish reconciled herself to such plenitude of bacon and salami, but not quite ready to ask. She took him into a tiny room that smelt of heaven, stacked, if anything, more densely than the shop, with plain tins and barrels and sacks of dry and loose goods. In one corner was the smallest and tidiest desk he had ever seen. He watched in mesmerised silence as she took a scoop of coffee beans out of a sack, poured them into a little green grinder affixed to her desk, reduced them to powder with a few powerful rotations, put the coffee into an espresso machine and set it to heat on a little gas ring. Palliser had never seen an espresso machine before.

Salomé would be like this; calm, in control, doing new things. Mistress of her kingdom. Not deferring to him, treating him like an equal. Wentwood and Daughters.

'Now while we are waiting, Mr –?'

'Wentwood, Palliser Wentwood.'

She was trying to recall his account details.

'Thule Hall, Hertfordshire.'

'Thule Hall, Hertfordshire. Mrs Nagy.'

'Absolutely, absolutely.'

'Do sit down, Mr Wentwood.'

He perched on the other chair, which was cane bottomed, carefully mended. She took out two tiny china cups and saucers, green and gold flowers.

'Is there some difficulty? Is the delivery imperfect?'

'Not at all, not at all.'

'I put in a jar of Stilton, for Christmas. I thought perhaps it might crack. There is always that risk.'

'No, no, it was perfect. We enjoyed it very much.'

'Excellent.' She smiled as one whose handiwork has been praised. 'I am happy.'

The coffee started to spit and gurgle. Palliser was entranced.

'Perhaps Mrs Nagy would prefer some other goods – it is hard to know. I try for Hungarian, what I can get of it, but we have excellent German goods now – torte, and sauerkraut, and sausages. Also some Danish biscuits just arrived – so wonderful. We must try one with our coffee.'

She found a tin among many tins and put a good quantity of the biscuits before Palliser on a matching green and gold flowered plate. He looked at them lovingly and almost hesitated before taking one. Then she poured the coffee, sat down opposite him, and smiled.

'Now, Mr Wentwood, what is the exact nature of your difficulty?'

Palliser wondered how many of her customers were in love with her. Such an ugly woman, so adorable. A postal romance. A courtship by courier. *Snap out of it, Pally.*

'I shall be frank at the risk of bein' indiscreet. Mrs Nagy is our housekeeper at Thule, and a very fine woman in every respect. But every month she receives a delivery from your establishment – and very much enjoyed by the whole household, I assure you – a delivery which causes her great distress. I don't understand these things m'self, but my wife is a tender-hearted soul, and she would much prefer Mrs Nagy not to be put to so much pain.'

'I am sorry to hear this.'

'Mrs Wentwood – Miss Lovelace as she was – persuaded me to come down here and find out who is sendin' the damn things – no offence meant, ma'am, your food is excellent – and see if we can stop the fellow doing it.'

'I am sending the "damn" things, Mr Wentwood.' She smiled to show she had taken no offence.

'Oh I am frightfully sorry. Yes, yes, one understands that. But you see, this Nagy, this estranged husband of hers. It's harassment, in effect. She's afraid of him, thinks he'll come and get her, take away her boy. So you see, every time a box arrives, it's a kind of threat. We were rather hoping perhaps we could persuade him not to send them, or perhaps I could collect them from you, in a more surreptitious manner –'

Her eyes were fixed on his face in amazement.

'Mr Wentwood, Mr Wentwood.' She poured him another cup of coffee. 'Please do have another biscuit. What you have said – it puts me in a complicated situation. There are facts which according to the ethics of business I should not divulge.'

'Ethics, eh? Almost as tricky as morals.'

'Almost, but not quite. Explain to me once again how it is Mrs Nagy receives the boxes I send.'

'She is most unhappy, not to put too fine a point on it. Terrified. She expects Nagy to appear at any moment. She is very much afraid of Nagy. Now I'm not asking for his address, I realise you can't divulge that, but –'

'Mr Wentwood, does Mrs Nagy read the notes and cards which are included with the food?'

'No, not to my knowledge. As far as I can tell, she consigns all letters unopened to the flames, every piece of correspondence she gets. She thinks they're either from Nagy, or from some official body interfering in her life. She holds the theory that if she pretends she did not receive the letters nothing will happen to her. And so far, I have to say, the device works.'

'Mr Wentwood, if I were an English person I would not tell you this, because it would be unethical. But I am going to trust in you. Mr Nagy is dead.'

'Good God!'

Palliser felt the world reeling round him, as if all the walls of his set were falling down at once.

'The solicitors surely wrote to her?' said the woman.

'She would not have opened the letter.'

The woman rose and went to a filing cabinet tucked into an impossible corner. She extracted a green file labelled NAGY in stencilled black capitals. She did not offer to show Palliser the contents, but sat and examined them.

'I will tell you the whole sad story, which I should not

do, but I feel I should trust you with this at least. When Grigor Nagy came to London he found lodgings not far from here; he sought out my shop, perhaps attracted by the name of the street, who knows? But also because I sold the food that reminded him of home. He would come in every week, and we would speak. He told me when his wife ran away with the little boy. He sat where you sit now and wept bitter, bitter tears. Slowly he began to understand why she had run away. Of course, a man does not change suddenly, but the loneliness he felt was terrible, and it did make some change in him. He did start to drink less, I believe; certainly he changed himself in appearance. He was a very handsome man, Mr Wentwood, in the dashing Hungarian style. He cut his hair and practised his English, and very soon he had a job selling automobiles. He was very good at this, being so handsome and charming to the ladies. But he did not forget his wife. One day he came to visit me, driving a very fine car, not unlike the car you have, Mr Wentwood, and full of joy because he had found where his wife was living. He asked me to send her a present, of all the food she loved best and would be missing, and he wrote her a letter to go inside. Then because he was so successful in his job, he began to do this every month. But she never replied.'

A customer came into the shop. The woman excused herself. Palliser eyed the folder of papers but something prevented him from riffling through them.

'Let me make some more coffee, Mr Wentwood,' she said on her return. 'Perhaps a little something with it? As the years passed, Grigor Nagy grew quite rich and bought his own car sales business. Almost every day he would come to buy bread and other food, and talk. And every month he would have me send a box to his wife, and give me a letter or a card to go with it. He was sure she would relent. He was sure he would see his son again.

'I am not a sentimental person, Mr Wentwood, I do not think he was now a saint, but he was perhaps a little less of a sinner. It was sad how over the years he never stopped hoping for some word from his wife. He was a romantic fool, I told him. He would not go to see her; he said that he was too ashamed, and she must forgive him first. I would say, let me telephone the household, and make sure she is there. But he was sure she was at Thule Hall. Perhaps he drove down to the village sometimes to look for her. He sometimes spoke of his son as if he had seen him. He would weep; then he would drink and weep, though I never saw this. Then one day I did not see him again. Instead a policeman came to visit me, and then the solicitor rang me on the telephone. Grigor Nagy was killed in his car, driven very fast when he was drunk. The car was found smashed against a tree.

'The police came to visit me because he left a note behind him, asking that I send a message to his wife telling her he had always loved her, and had died because she would not relent. In his will he had asked that I send the same present every month, with a letter or card. The police asked for the address, but I did not give it to them. I do not care for the police. Instead the solicitors wrote a letter. He left all his money to his son, except the money he put aside for me to use.

'So you see, I am the person who sends to Mrs Nagy each month. At first I wrote a short letter, but now I enclose a simple card, as there is nothing more to say. Poor Grigor Nagy is dead.'

Palliser felt tears rising in his eyes. He looked down at his hands and saw the tears drop on to them, two, three, five, a dozen salt drops, some for Grigor Nagy crumpled against a tree in the trappings of his success, some for Doris Nagy trapped in a prison of her own devising, some for Peter Nagy, denied his father, and a few for himself, who was neither faithful nor persistent, and who, also, could not be forgiven.

The woman went into her shop to serve a customer. Voices in German rose and fell, laughter and friendship. Palliser saw that a minuscule glass of Tokay was before him. He took out his handkerchief.

'Mrs Nagy will not believe me unless I have some written proof,' he said when the shopkeeper returned.

The woman sifted carefully through her papers.

'I have letters from the solicitors, but they are necessary for my records. But I can give you this.' She extracted from the file a newspaper clipping. 'It is the report of the inquest. I have no need of it.'

She rose and put it in a clean white envelope and handed it to Palliser.

'Now, the monthly order – how shall I proceed?'

'Oh, good God, how indeed? Much as before, I think, until Doris decides otherwise. And why don't you send us some of those Danish biscuits as well? Three tins. My wife will enjoy them. Charge them to us, of course.'

Then he thought of the consequences of a delivery addressed to Mrs Wentwood. It was too late now to retract.

'Certainly, Mr Wentwood, it is a pleasure to do business with you.'

She shook him by the hand, and escorted him out into the shop. Passing the array of cooked meats, the ham poised under a damp gauze waiting to be carved, the army of sausages, he plucked up the courage to ask.

'Impertinent of me, but the bacon – the salami – don't they pose you one or two problems? Food laws, and all that?'

She smiled.

'My father would not have them in the shop. I did think very hard before I began to sell them, very hard.

But I think, Mr Wentwood, there are rules and there are judgements. Religion can make the rules but it cannot make the judgements. That is our own business. I treat the rules of my religion as I treat a cookery book. It gives good guidance to cook well, and many hints and excellent instructions to follow. But following the recipe will not prevent me from producing a dry salami, any more than abstaining from pig meat will make me a good person. I make the choices myself, each time, based on the books I have read and the teaching I have received and the experience I have gathered.'

Palliser tipped his hat, raised her hand to his lips and prepared to take his leave.

'I'll never look at a salami in the same light again,' he said.

The lovely bright day fulfilled its earlier promise, so that as Palliser drove back to Thule in his new car he witnessed the countryside in all its barren beauty. Outlines of trees ink-sketched against the low sweep of low hills, low stone walls curving up and over in line with the contours of the land – mellow shapes, worn by centuries of rain and cultivation. Nothing to challenge the eye or disturb the mind; how different the massive desolate valleys without tree or house or human form that bided their time back home. Here in this ordered, handsome landscape it was impossible to feel lost. And yet Palliser felt lost, not geographically, but existentially. He was far from home – but no longer knew where home was. Surely not this dullingly familiar, man-sized, safe and comfortable place? Surely not that godforsaken barren shore where sea-birds and sheep outnumbered humans, and the floods came out of the mountains and washed civilisation into the sea? Not the long-forgotten soft wet green of Ireland?

Perhaps there was no home for a man who would not keep house.

There is no rest, saith my God, for the wicked.

Now he had what he wanted; years of struggle and mud and lying, and skirting round the law, doing deals and gabbing out of situations. All over. Comfort and love and an easy life; he could do what he pleased now. Tailored clothes, and nights at the opera, foreign travel and nights on the town, shooting, horses – why, he could even ride to hounds – *now there's a delicious thought.* Handsome French furniture, Italian statuary, a showpiece garden open to public, with Mr Wentwood glimpsed taking his ease. Havana cigars. Girls. Hand-made shoes.

It was possible then, and is still just possible now, to drive very fast on a country road in England, if you disregard opposing traffic. Palliser swooped around back-road bends between hedgerows that aimed to meet in the middle, slowing down and speeding up purely for the pleasure of it. He would not think about Grigor Nagy, handsome, successful and desolate; he would think only of Palliser Wentwood, who had made it, after all.

Made, old boy! You're home and hosed now. Dreams come true after all. Money in the bank; lovely rich woman; brand new sports car. And not a promise made or a bond signed.

What desiccated old maid taught us that crime doesn't pay? Of course it bloody does. Who persuaded us that you have to be good to be happy? Some anally retentive puritan who'd never had fun in his life. Who the fuck decided that having money made us miserable? St Paul? He never had any money to know differently. Of course the rich and the naughty have more fun; they can afford to.

Fast cars, although possibly the supreme solitary pleasure, are also designed to be shown off in – especially for one fond of cutting a dash. A woman in the other seat would make perfection perfect. Just under six foot tall – say five-eleven, five-ten and a half. Long brown hair, very thick, caught up, but with strands trailing, blowing in the wind. Slim and elegant, but not too slim, a good woman's body, bright flashing eyes, lovely teeth, smiling and exclaiming and not taking him at face value, but laughing at his jokes with her head thrown back, and enjoying, enjoying.

She'll wish she hadn't replaced me with that smooth dullard. Shall I send her a photograph in return? *Self on holiday in Scotland. Like the car? Wish you were here.* How she'd love it; how she loved speed. Loves speed. An old army truck indeed. Top speed of thirty miles per hour. Zero to fifteen in three minutes.

An old army truck. It would be wonderful up country, bouncing into the hills; you wouldn't care about scratching the paintwork. Straight through river beds, up into the gorse, just keep chugging along, what a laugh, ricocheting off the rocks, not giving a damn. How much room in the back? Room for a mattress. It gets damned hot in these old cabs, stop by a river, strip off, pure cold river water straight out of Eden, I think I'll wash my hair in it, she says, it's so soft.

Time to get back to Thule, fast, fast, fast, faster than the thoughts fly to other far-off places. *This* is lovely. *This* is what you wanted. Fun, sex, money and comfort. What more could you possibly want, you great fucking idiot?

While Palliser was fetching the car, Blanche fulfilled her social duty at the Vicarage. Hubert had accompanied her, but soon disappeared to a smoky room full of men in black. Far from standing around awkwardly, she found that, resplendent in a new dress, she was courted. George Burnaby never left her side, and people constantly came up to her to make conversation, talking about things she understood, and listening to her answers.

Nonetheless, she found it tiring, and was longing to get home and wait for Palliser's arrival. She could hardly wait to see him sweep up the drive in the new car, his arm casually over the side, his hair ruffled, like the man in the advertisement. As there was plenty to do in the house, with Christmas only three days away, she was allowed to escape the party. In fact George drove her home in his nice old Rover, telling her about a Christmas party he had been to in India once with a maharaja dressed as Santa and many of his proud sons as elves. She laughed quite a lot.

Back home, she visited the kitchens where Mrs Nagy was sitting knitting while Gerald the gamekeeper read items aloud from the newspaper. Peter was keen to show Blanche the accounts he had prepared for the party; she sat down with him and he went through pages of squared paper, every expenditure carefully itemised in beautiful neat black ink. On the last page, which he produced with a flourish, he had had some fun; he had worked out the number of guest minutes, child and adult, and divvied them into the costs, child and adult, of the party, and come out with what he called an enjoyment metric.

'You can use that to measure next year's party,' he said.

'That looks very reasonable to me,' she said, 'especially as you don't add in all the fun we had ourselves.'

'It's hard to put a figure on that.'

Then she started work on some flowers. The trouble with winter arrangements was that they needed so little attention. After she had arranged some hellebores from the vicarage garden in a blue jug, and wondered about and rejected Mrs Perkins's suggestion of cones painted silver, she was at something of a loose end. She had finished her library books some time back, and had not had much inclination to visit the library recently. She looked at her sewing machine and shook her head at it, forever converted to the tailored dress. She thought of reading a little poetry and wandered into the library and searched amid the ranks of classics for a copy of Palliser's favourite book, *Palgrave's Golden Treasury*. Not finding it, she went upstairs to look in his room.

Blanche's moral upbringing had been haphazard. Her reading of Christian classics and attendance through long sermons had convinced her of the unbending importance of truth and righteous doing. Good was a simple thing – one must tell the truth and strive to help and heal. For Blanche, finding ways to put this moral truth into action was harder than understanding it.

On the other hand, she had never been taught about the evils of sex and the sacredness of virginity. No one had ever thought it necessary to fill her mind with images of the depravity and ruin which await girls who deviate from respectability. She had no notion of respectability; to her Madame Bovary and Anna Karenina were unhappy but otherwise ordinary women. She had read *Lady Chatterley's Lover*, and felt sorry for the husband because he was crippled; what Lady C. did seemed perfectly reasonable to her. Nobody had preached the perils of sex to Blanche because they had not thought her prey to them.

Nor had she been lectured on the sacredness of privacy. Having nothing to hide herself, she could not conceive of a moral universe in which one might refrain from reading someone's letters. At school – her only experience of life with others – diaries and letters were fair game. If one wrote a secret in one's Secret Diary with the lock, it was only in order to have the secret spread right through the dorm. Letters from boys were given the same treatment, and passed around like the scribblings of the master, pored over and quoted. *Does that mean he loves you? Does that mean he wants to do it?* Hubert had locked drawers in his study, but in her innocence she assumed this was to protect legal documents and chequebooks.

So when she went to Palliser's room to fetch his *Golden Treasury* she had no sense of trespassing on his private space. She did not think that she should ask for leave to borrow his book; she knew of nothing that was private between them any more. She did not invest his room with any special qualities, because his head did not rest on the pillow there, nor his body warm the bed.

But when she entered the room, she had a sense of something wrong; not something she was doing, but something being wrong. Unused to analysing feelings or situations, she took some time to work out what it was. Then she noticed how empty the room was.

Palliser's bed was neatly made, but that was hardly surprising since he had not slept in it for some time. Under the bed was a single brown suitcase and one pair of polished shoes. On the chest of drawers were his hairbrush, razor and shaving brush; in the corner by the window the two Indian clubs he sometimes used for exercise. In the wardrobe hung his overcoat, black suit, a pair of moleskins and two white shirts. In the chest of drawers were underpants, vests, black socks, two silk ties, a scarf, his cufflinks, a pile of handkerchiefs, blinding white, ironed and folded, boot polish and polishing cloths, nail-scissors, an extensive sewing kit, screwdrivers, writing paper from the White Hart Hotel and an expensive fountain pen.

There was nothing to make the room personal: no photographs on the mantelshelf, no postcards stuck in the frame of Our Lady of Perpetual Succour, no personal trinkets, no scribbled notes. All that spoke of Palliser's life was in the suitcase under the bed – two race books, betting slips, a sheaf of orders of service from cathedrals, a postcard view of Naples and another of Hong Kong, a membership card for the Wrest Park Angling Club. Nothing. No pictures of his wife, no pictures of his daughters, no mementoes of his home, no books, no pressed flowers or faded ribbons, no letters, no notebooks, no bank records. Nothing.

It became clear to Blanche that he had never intended to stay. She felt she had always known this, but the extremity of his transience surprised her. He could walk into this room, pack his case in ten minutes, collect his silk dressing gown from her bedroom, and be gone without a trace. And yet whenever he was in a room everyone was aware of him, and remembered him. His presence was so strong everywhere in the house you could practically smell it, everywhere except here, where he didn't seem to be at all.

She sat down on his bed, wanting to find something of him in the empty room to hold on to and love. Yes, his Palgrave was there after all, on the floor beside the bed, the one object that spoke of him. An India paper edition, with soft brown cover, gold-tooled edges and marbled ends. It had *Palgrave's Golden Treasury* embossed in gold Gothic letters on the cover, and P.J.W. at the bottom. What did the J. stand for, she wondered? Where had he come from, where had he been all these years to acquire so little? A suitcase of anonymous clothes and a single book of poems.

Blanche did not have enough knowledge of the world to know about tricksters; she had read the wrong books to associate a gentleman with fraud. But she knew instinctively that there was something wrong about a man of Palliser's years having so little. Just as she knew by instinct that there was something wrong with his grief, and something wrong about his absence from home. In the book of poems was a card. She let the book fall open at the place, a poem by Robert Louis Stevenson entitled 'Romance'.

I will make you brooches and toys for your delight
Of bird-song at morning and star-shine at night.
I will make a palace fit for you and me
Of green days in forest and blue days at sea.

I will make my kitchen and you shall keep your room,
Where white flows the river, and bright blows the broom,
And you shall wash your linen and keep your body white
In rainfall at morning and dewfall at night.

And this shall be for music when no one else is near,
The fine song for singing, the rare song to hear!
That only I remember, that only you admire,
Of the broad road that stretches and the roadside fire.

Blanche read the poem slowly, twice over, seeking to understand the heart of the man she loved beyond sense or understanding. She knew that he did not love her as she loved him. She knew that he had never once said *I love you*, never, not even in the extremity of love-making. Many endearments, many sweet words, but he had never said those words, or any that implied them, nor had she ever asked him to. She felt it was right that his love still belonged to his wife; she thought it mean-spirited to grudge the dead. She loved him all the more because his heart was faithful; after all, she had his kindness, his attention and his dear, dear person.

But reading the poem cut her to the heart. She could hear his honey tones reciting it, see him lying in bed gazing at his wife, fanning her hair with his fingers and the lines rolling off his tongue. It was so clearly a poem addressed to Salomé and not to Blanche.

She tried to imagine how it felt to be loved, to rest assured in another person. To be able to take love for granted, be surrounded constantly by its presence, like golden sunlight, like warm water. Having Palliser at her side had given her some idea of how it might be, and more than a little hope that she might herself one day be loved. She had dreamed that one day Palliser himself might find himself in love with her, his *dear sweet girl*, his *dearest Blanche* taking wing into *my beloved, my love*.

But when she read the poem she saw that the transformation would never happen. The woman in the poem, the woman in his heart, was not so much a real woman as an image of a woman, an image that was Salomé and not Blanche. Salomé's image was enshrined in his heart as Blanche's would never be. She understood all this from reading one simple poem, not because of the words in the poem, but because she had known it from the beginning, from the first moment he kissed her and she spread her arms to comfort him.

Loving him was an action she would not regret. She had not been fooled with words; he had not asked for her heart and broken it. He had asked only for comfort and in return he had given her her own body. She did not consider her love for him to be the grand passion of Guinevere which demands an answering passion in Lancelot. Palliser lacked the necessary qualifications for a Tristan, as much as she fell short of Isolde. She knew she loved him impulsively because he had saved her, that being pulled from her depths she had no possible reaction but to fall in love with him. But she also felt that somewhere, in the core of her heart, in the Blancheness of her person, was a steadfast love for him which would survive unshaken when the passion had cooled and the infatuation dissipated, when the truth was told, and when Palliser was gone, as inevitably he would be gone.

She wondered if at least in the endurance of her love she had something in common with Guinevere and Isolde. She loved him for the very Palliser of his person, whoever and whatever he was, and she longed to see him naked, without the shifty trappings of his charm.

She opened the Christmas card. Inside it was a newspaper cutting, folded four times flat. Perhaps if there had been other personalia these items would have taken on less fascination. But as the only objects of Palliser in the room, she, who loved him, could not resist.

you have been away to long and we miss you . . . Mum is very well.

What simple words to end an idyll.

She unfolded the cutting. The date was plain at the top. This year. Last month. The caption was plain beneath. MRS SALOMÉ WENTWOOD.

Mrs Salomé Wentwood.

Salomé Wentwood smiled. She was more than alive, she was smiling. She was busy. She had two men beside her and two beautiful grown-up daughters. Blanche's age. And she was Mrs Wentwood. She had possession of his name. She had first call on his person. She had first and only call on his heart.

She was alive, and she was pictured in the bright sunlight of a new land full of hope, the land that flowed with milk and honey, bringing her new enterprise to birth, and smiling. No floods had washed her and her farm away and left a broken-hearted widower. *You have been away to long and we miss you.*

He had left them behind. He had lied. He had continued to lie. Palliser, right down to his core, was a liar and a cheat.

Jan 12th

    Dearest Palliser,

    I know this letter will reach New Zealand long before you do, but I am sure you will not have forgotten what you said when we parted. I hope you have had a comfortable journey. Hubert tells me that your cabin looked very spacious and comfortable and that the steward he spoke to was very civil. I am sorry I did not come on board before you left.

    I was so miserable when I watched your ship sail away. Right up to the moment when the ropes were let go, I expected you to run back down the gangplank and explain that it was all a mistake.

    I love you as much as I ever did, and I expect I shall love you for ever. It seems a funny thing to write, like something in a novel, but I have started writing this letter so many times that it will just have to stay written.

    I hope your home-coming is happy. I do so much want you to be happy. I hope your family are all well. Please don't feel you have to write to me. I don't expect letters from you, but I hope you don't mind if I write to you from time to time. It helps me to remember that you were (are) a real person and not just a dream I had.

    I hope you will forgive me if I have done you any wrong. I hope I have not acted out of anger or jealousy. I hope I asked you to go home only because it was the only right thing to do, and because I love you.

    The house is very quiet without you, and the evenings are very long. We sit quietly quite often, in the kitchen with Baby Yaga (kitten) and watch TV. People have been very kind, but at the moment I prefer to be quiet and by myself.

But the days are getting lighter already, and George has started to teach me to drive, in your car. I shall always think of it as your car, and I shall never ever part with it, no matter what happens. It is a funny thing to remember someone by, but it seems right. George has come over every day and we drive to a different village each time and go to a different pub. George says that he is conducting a survey of Hertfordshire pubs, but I think this is a joke. At Easter we are all (the Eltons, George and myself) going to the Lake District where one of the family has a house, so that is something to look forward to.

Hubert has been in London a great deal recently, helping Jocelyn in his parish, also been very busy with the Orthodox Christmas. He tells me he has preached three times since Advent Sunday – twice for Jocelyn and once for the Syrians, and spoken at a Diocesan event. I heard him at the latter and he was very good!

Peter is going to try for a place in a commercial college in London. Now he has the money from his father he has grown quite bold! But Doris (as I am supposed to call her now) does not seem to mind.

Dearest Palliser, please take care of yourself. I cannot bear to think that I shall never see you again, or hear your voice, but what I have done, I have done myself. I hope you will be happy. Please don't forget me altogether, because I shall never stop loving you.

Yours for ever and ever,
    Blanche

2nd of February

Feast of the Purification of Our Lady & the Presentation of Our Lord in the Temple, commonly called Candlemass.

Dear Wentwood,

I hope this finds you well, and that your passage has been pleasant and home-coming harmonious!

Thule is a much less lively place without you, but Blanche is bearing up well. She reads and walks a great deal and has filled the place with floral arrangements, but does not suffer excessively from melancholia. We are rather inured to the solitary life, I suppose. George Burnaby is very attentive; I have no quarrel with this, as I find him a most agreeable chap, if a trifle taciturn. Clarissa has been a brick, as one might expect.

I have to confess to being out and about rather more than perhaps I ought, but Blanche encourages me in my work. Fr Jocelyn and I are planning some extensions to his mission, which will require quite an outlay of energy and money. We are going to put in a kitchen and ablutions area so that the crypt can be used as a sanctuary during the night for the street-denizens of his parish. These are, as you can imagine, a colourful collection of people! Nonetheless their needs are great.

I have been in discussion with the Bishop quite frequently of late, having quite hit it off with him over Christmas! He is proposing that I enrol for a special-entry theological degree at King's, and he is proposing to put in a good word for me with the Selection Committee, in view of my current orders (valid) and the work I am engaged upon. So it looks as if God is working in His mysterious way once again!

I hope you find the enclosed useful in re-establishing

your farm. If you will be so kind as to send me details of your bank account in New Zealand, I shall in future wire your bank rather than sending a cheque. You can expect to receive the same amount three times a year. I hope you will regard this money as a loan to help you in your work in New Zealand, a loan which will not be repayable unless you find it necessary to return to England. I appreciate the decency and gentlemanly behaviour you have exhibited in all your dealings with myself and my sister.

I sincerely hope that God will bless you, and that all your doings in future may be begun, continued and ended in Him. I thank God for the gifts of friendship and encouragement you gave me, and shall pray for you and your family continually.

Yours sincerely,
    Hubert Lovelace

Time to go. Time to pack up the books and throw away the scraps of paper, and start a new life. A melancholy emancipation.

Farewell – to a world built of paper and ink, traced in a darkened room from the mirrors cunningly angled in the dome, a camera obscura in the mind, with all the little creatures, dots and smudges of ink, all of whom one loves piteously, as the creator is doomed to do.

It is St Valentine's Day – of course – balmy, shiny and green, and everybody is bursting with happiness. The house is full of summer flowers, picked by Thaddeus from all over the valley, and by Philip from the best florist in town. The tower is full of fruit, cases and cases of it, smelling of sunlight and plenitude, betokening back-breaking work. The household has been working since six, grateful for the coolness of the tower against the ripe summer sun. After tea they are all going down to the beach for a swim, and never has a swim been more richly deserved. Abigail has a swimsuit on ready under the slacks and T-shirt.

The sea beckons her from the top of the tower. She is packing her books for the morning's carrier, and tidying away her things for the term. She hardly needs to take the texts, so well does she know them, but no fellow student ever will find this out. Abigail will smile and laugh and never claim precedence; she will translate with fluent charm, as if surprised by her luck in understanding so much. She will notch up A grades in everything, and never seem to swot. But she will not be a good-time girl either, drinking and smoking, and taking Café Honours. She will steer a course right down the middle to her goal.

No more time for the sea, no more family meals and games of Five Hundred to milk shillings out of Philip. Sad to be packing up, leaving the tower for its next inhabitant. Who will take it over? Naomi for target practice, Philip for book-keeping? In four days' time she will not care a jot.

At this moment it is still hers and she bids farewell to the scape of the sea and mountains and the skies which will haunt her memory for ever, and never let her see another place as perfectly beautiful, no matter where she goes.

In the distance she sees the Railways Bus coming along the valley as it does every day at this time. Quite often it slows and drops a parcel in the wooden hutch at the end of the road. But today it stops outright by the gate and a man gets off.

In the middle of nowhere. The bus stops and a man gets off. Here by the Wentwood Farm road. There is nothing but the farmhouse for miles and miles and miles. She stands ice-rigid by the window. She can't watch. She can't turn the telescope and look. In case. In case not.

But she must, for her mother's sake, if nothing else. Her heart beats like a seagull, and she can't focus the damned thing.

He is wearing a thick coat, far too thick for the middle of summer, and carrying a single suitcase. He puts down the suitcase and takes off the coat. It's clumsy to carry under his arm; made more difficult by the bunch of flowers in green paper clutched in his other hand. He has to put down the coat and the suitcase to open the farm gate.

Abigail's breathing has become unreliable. For the first time in her life she doesn't know what to do. She doesn't know whether to scream or laugh or jump around the room, whether to stay frozen at the telescope or run for cover. She can't be quite sure, but she can't be mistaken. His hair is almost silver; surely it never used to be that colour.

She is shaking, and cold, but her hands are sweating. She is still holding Vergil in her left hand; the red dye on the cover is staining her palm. She must run, she must tell them all, tell the world, dance and sing – but what if she is wrong? What if it's not him – if he's a figment of mind, a trick of the light?

He opens the gate very gingerly, examines the catch, pushes it back and forth several times to try its hinges. He picks up his case and coat and the flowers and passes through the gate, puts them down again and finally shuts the gate behind him. Then he bends down to pick up his belongings as if he is very tired, and starts to walk up the new road.

Abigail lets go of the telescope and watches the little figure in the distance. A dot, a smudge, a concentration of emotion in one tiny point. He is walking towards them. There is no mistaking his manner.

She throws down the book. She runs down the stairs, sandals flapping, two, three at a time. She runs through the shop, dodging through the racks and cases and barrels, runs out of the tower, along the stone path, flying, panting, into the house, through the front door, along the passage, pounding, clumsy, dashing, flinging into the kitchen.

She leans against the door frame, reaching for breath. Everyone is in the kitchen. It is full to bursting. Philip and Thaddeus, Salomé, Jemima, Naomi and Bathsheba, everyone mucking in getting ready for tea, the kitchen table laid for seven, flowers in bowls and vases, potatoes bubbling in a big black saucepan. Everyone stops dead as she flies in, frozen in a moment of action. Philip in his shirt-sleeves, sharpening the carving knife on the steel, Thaddeus with green fingers chopping mint into tiny fragments for the sauce, Salomé wiping her hands on her apron, Naomi licking her finger from the cream she is whipping, Jemima with a handful of cutlery, poised in mid-air above the table, Bathsheba lining up her plastic menagerie on the table top.

Everybody is looking at her, Abigail who never runs, Abigail who is never harried, Abigail, who now stands speechless and shaking by the door.

'Abi, what is it? What's the matter?'

A great racking breath.

'There's a man. A man coming down the road. Walking.
I think – I'm pretty sure. No, I'm quite sure it's *him*.'

'Who?' cries Philip, gripping the carving knife.

'Who?' Salomé asks.

'It's Father. I know it is. It couldn't be anyone else.'
Abigail breaks into tears.

No one else moves or speaks. They all look at Salomé
to see what she will do.

And she is frozen, years of waiting for and wondering
about this moment come juddering to this point in time,
and stop in their tracks.

She is frozen for no more than a second. It takes her
only a second to know how she will react. She does not
need to consider. So often she has said *I don't know, I don't
know*. But she does know after all.

'Quick Naomi stop that and put on another pot of
potatoes a small one small potatoes there's some by the
door Jemima darling go into the safe and get the ham
down the honey-cured one quick now Thaddeus be a
darling and get another chair there's one in my bedroom
Philip darling it's all right it will be all right don't worry
please don't be unhappy it will be all right can you go in
the cellar and get the best two bottles no three hurry girls
Philip the best there is you choose and bring the crystal
out of the morning room eight glasses one for everyone
even Sheba yes she's got to join in too quick Abigail stop
that and help Bathy lay the table – another place darling
for your daddy and the linen napkins Abigail and put some
of those flowers on the table make it look lavish –'

And she pulls undone her apron and discards it, doesn't
stop to look for her shoes, and runs barefoot out of
the house.

The girls will race through their tasks and follow her out

and meet him on the bridge, but Salomé has a head start. She's alone as she runs down the front path between the marjoram and thyme thrumming with bees, scattering hens as she flies across the stone bridge and on to the road.

There he is in the far distance. It can only be him, there is only one Palliser in the wide wide world.

She runs across the bridge and down the road towards him. He sees her coming and drops his belongings there and then on the road and runs too.

As she runs she spreads her arms out wide towards him as if to embrace the world, and he, the very Palliser, runs faster and faster and turns a perfect cartwheel along the new road home.